SHORT
SEASON

SHORT SEASON

A NOVEL BY DJ SCOTT

SEXTANT PRESS
Suite 278
2531 Jackson Av
Ann Arbor, MI 48103

Published 2018 by SEXTANT PRESS
Printed in the United States of America

20 19 18   1 2 3 4

ISBN 978-1-943290-69-7
Library of Congress Control Number: 2018905783

For Detachment 11
Surgical Company A

A NOTE ABOUT TIME: Each chapter shows the time in both Universal Coordinated Time, or Z time, as well as the local time. The following time zones appear:

IOT India Chagos Time (Z +6)

MST Moscow Standard Time (Z +4)

AST Arabia Standard Time (Z +3)

CEST Central European Summer Time (Z +2)

BST British Summer Time (Z +1)

EST Eastern Standard Time (Z -5)

EDT Eastern Daylight Time (Z -4)

CDT Central Daylight Time (Z -5)

PDT Pacific Daylight Time (Z -7)

PROLOGUE

FEBRUARY 1, 1991, 1745Z (2345 IOT)
Diego García, Indian Ocean

MAJOR KERRY SIMPSON had just completed the pre-flight inspection of his B-52G Stratofortress, which meant examining every control surface, every tire, all of the external ordnance, and each of the eight aging Pratt and Whitney TF-33 engines, all the while working in the tropical humidity of remote Diego Garcia. Drenched with sweat, but satisfied that everything they could check had been checked; Simpson, his co-pilot Jumbo Loewe, and his crew climbed aboard the big bomber and began their pre engine-start check list.

By time they were strapped in, five hours had passed since the mission briefing. As operations officer for the 233rd Bomb Squadron, 2nd Bomb Wing, Simpson had given the briefing himself. The squadron's other mission, a three air-craft strike on Iraqi Republican Guard positions deployed north of Kuwait City was more interesting. His was to target a new collection of vehicles, some armored, parked around a group of concrete block buildings just north of the Iraqi border and dispersed over several acres where no military activity had been previously observed. During the rest of pre-flight and engine run up, Simpson, Jumbo, and their EW officer, a sharp young Lieutenant named Ethan Brandt, reviewed everything they knew about the target, which wasn't much. He and his crew were basically blowing up a parking lot.

The preflight complete, all engines running perfectly, the vast array of instruments all nominal, and electronic systems showing no faults, Simpson called the tower and requested permission to taxi. The controller held them for just a minute while a huge C-5 Galaxy cleared the taxiway, and then let Simpson taxi and hold at the southwest end of to the island's single runway. They swung into position and the tower cleared them for takeoff.

"Air Force 6058, rolling." Simpson and Loewe both grabbed the eight throttles and pushed them to the stops. Burdened by almost twenty tons of ordnance the bird crept forward at first, but then gained speed. With 12,000 feet of runway in front of him, Simpson wasn't worried about finding flying speed, even though he was now racing straight towards the Indian Ocean. Long before he ran out of runway, he pulled back on the yoke and the big bomber climbed gently into the night.

At eight thousand feet they passed through low clouds and into a clear, star-filled sky. Simpson engaged the autopilot and relaxed for the long mission.

About two hours and a thousand miles out, Lieutenant Randy Carlson, the navigator, got his attention. "Sir, getting a weather update. Looks like that storm cell south of the Strait of Hormuz is developing a lot faster than predicted. Recommend we divert eight degrees left. We can get back on course after we clear the weather."

"Roger. Diverting now. Recalculate our tanker rendezvous and set it up. They'll be happy to have quieter air to pass the gas."

"On it."

Simpson received the new tanker rendezvous and exact course and speed from his navigator. He selected the tanker frequency, "Junction, this is Kestrel." In less than a minute, the crew of the KC-10 tanker had the details and confirmed time and location.

The storm continued to develop. In half an hour, lightning flashes were visible to the northeast. Simpson wasn't worried; thunderstorms were not much of a threat to the B-52, especially at this distance. Nonetheless, he asked Lewis to keep him updated with changes from the satellite weather center.

He was thinking about a cup of coffee when the cockpit was flooded with a tremendous flash of light.

"Holy shit!" Jumbo yelled. "What was that?"

Simpson's first thought was there had been a nuclear explosion. Then his training kicked in, and he knew that what he had just experienced was not nuclear. Lightning then, but if it was, it was the most intense he had ever encountered. As the afterglow faded, he could see red and yellow warning lights flashing across the instrument panel. They confirmed what the seat of his pants was already telling him. His bird was hurt. "Crew, report status," Simpson ordered.

"Navigator okay," said Carlson, though he sounded anything but.

"We're both good down here sir," Garcia said from the bombardier's station, "but we've got two Christmas trees worth of warning lights on our panels. Give us a minute to sort it out."

"Roger that."

The co-pilot, EW officer, and their lone enlisted man, Staff Sergeant Andy Lewis—the gunner—all reported okay but, except for Lewis whose system seemed unaffected, all needed a minute to sort out just how bad things were.

The bombardier was first to report. "Sir, we got trouble. I have arming lights on the external stores. Can't tell if it's some kind of electrical malfunction or if that mega-lightning strike somehow overloaded the system and actually armed those weapons."

"Internal stores are okay though?" Simpson asked.

"Looks like it, assuming the system's giving me good data."

Simpson was not happy. With their recently upgraded wing pylons, the B-52G could now carry twenty-four Mark-82 500 pound bombs on each wing. He was sitting just forward of twelve tons of bombs. Armed bombs. The B-52G had been hardened against the intense electromagnetic pulse released by a high altitude nuclear blast, so whatever hit them must have delivered an enormous amount of energy. He had to assume those bombs really were armed.

"Comm trouble, sir," Carlson said. "Satellite receiver seems fried. Radar is down and my compass bearings don't match. You have comm up there?"

"I've got nothing on satellite either," replied Simpson, "but my HF looks good."

"Yes, I can hear one Navy ship on the HF. Cannot hear Eagle, and he was clear just a minute ago."

So they'd lost touch with the AWACS bird. "Not a problem. We can manage fine with local HF. Anything else?"

"I'm going to reset the breakers on the radar and see what happens. Back in five."

"Roger. EW?"

"Got a lot of warning lights and several breakers that won't reset." Brandt sounded rock solid. "Right now I wouldn't count on anything."

Simpson and Jumbo went over their own warning lights, concentrating first on their most critical systems. Again, what he saw confirmed how the bird felt. He got on with the rest of the crew. "Looks like our other problem is fuel flow. We are slowly losing altitude, but only about a hundred to a hundred-fifty feet per minute and starting at 32,000 we have a lot of room to work with. Best guess is that if we lose the bombs we should be able to make Jeddah. Bombardier, what's your take on that?"

"Hard to say. I can't confirm any information the system is giving me. If we can do a drop we better lose the internal stores as well since I can't really be sure of their arming status and Jeddah sure won't want us dropping in with those weapons on board."

Simpson considered that for a moment. "Risk of pre-detonation?"

"The mechanical safeties should still be working."

"Cut 'em loose."

"Bomb doors open."

Simpson took a firm hold of the controls waiting for the uplift as the B-52 suddenly shed 36,000 pounds. It didn't come.

"Negative release, sir. Internal and external. Three tries."

"Not your fault, Garcia. Time for Plan B."

Great. And here he had been looking forward to a boring mission.

"Got the nav radar back up," Carlson said. "Low power setting only so figure a hundred kilometers range at this altitude, and less as we descend. Looks like we just passed the western tip of a little island called Adb al Kuri, south of Yemen. That puts us on a good course for Jeddah."

"With those bombs aboard we're not making Jeddah. Looks like Yemen." Simpson said this with more confidence than he was feeling. The crew was dealing with a type of emergency that nobody had experienced before, or at least nobody who survived to write a report.

"Uh Major," Jumbo said, "aren't there CENTCOM orders about Yemen?"

"Least of our worries, Jumbo." There were indeed orders forbidding over flight of Yemen. Landing was not even mentioned. But their options were limited, very limited.

Major Kerry Simpson had never lost an aircraft, never even come close. In the twelve years since he graduated from the Air Force Academy he had experienced some engine problems, communications glitches and one complete hydraulic failure—the kind of problems he'd been trained for. This was new, and it might cost him his aircraft.

But he would be damned if it would cost him his crew. Time to talk with the Navy.

FEBRUARY 1, 1991 2030Z (2330 AST)
USS *Alvin L Bowman*
Gulf of Aden, 170 kilometers east-
southeast of al-Mukalla, Yemen

THE USS *BOWMAN*, a Perry Class frigate FFG-62, was making a comfortable fifteen knots in the six foot swells that were just starting to calm as the storm system receded to the southeast. They had just left the Red Sea after transiting the Suez Canal, and were proceeding to the Persian Gulf to join the *Saratoga* battle group.

Lt Dan Sherman, officer of the deck, was standing out on the port bridge wing enjoying a mug of coffee. A Miami native, Sherman preferred the warm, humid air to the artificially cooled, dry air on the bridge. He had just taken his first sip when Petty Officer Derrick Morales stuck his head out. "Comm sir, got a call from a B-52 in trouble."

Sherman stepped onto the bridge and grabbed the handset. "What's up?" he asked.

"Kestrel, a B-52 out of Diego Garcia," said Morales. "Took some kind of high intensity lightning strike and they're having trouble maintaining altitude. Their SATCOM is out. Good comm with us on HF, but they can't raise Eagle so they must be having receiver trouble or low power output."

"Put them on with ops. Advise the alert helo crew. And notify the skipper."

"Aye aye, sir."

Within a few minutes, operations had relayed Kestrel's situation to the AWACS commander and had assessed the situation. When CDR Vince Piotrowski, Bowman's CO, arrived, they would have most of the information he needed.

Piotrowski, a tall, rail-thin Chicago native, was in his quarters reviewing information on Persian Gulf ops. When the messenger told him he was wanted, he changed quickly into freshly pressed wash khakis. That, and a thirty second shave, let him seem alert, rested, and totally on top of the situation. From what the messenger had told him he knew he needed to be in the Combat Information Center, but he chose to climb the ladder from his small stateroom to the bridge in order to consult with Sherman, the officer of the deck. This was a courtesy, a formality really, but Piotrowski had learned years ago as a junior officer that maintaining respect and courtesy at midnight when rushed and weary was just as important as when doing routine ship's business at noon. Probably more so.

Piotrowski confirmed with Sherman what had happened so far, checked Bowman's course and speed, and then climbed back down to operations. He opened the door to the darkened space, lit mainly by the radar and electronic status boards and took a quick look around. The watch standers were all at their stations, all systems appeared to be functioning, and there was nothing unusual in their demeanor. They were on top of it, and there was no immediate crisis. Relaxing, he walked over to several officers talking near the search radar and asked for a report.

Lt Pete Hull, who had the watch in the combat information center, distilled what information they had down to thirty seconds and waited for questions.

Piotrowski turned to LCDR Ken Zimmerman, the Officer in Charge of his aviation detachment, which consisted of two UH-60F LAMPS III helicopters. "What's your take from a SAR standpoint, Ken?"

"As Pete said, they were on course for Jeddah. We got them corrected east to close on us, and based on current course and speed we can reach them anywhere between their current location and the coast of Yemen. Keep in mind, though, that bird has a six-man crew and there's a world of difference between a one or two man search and rescue over open ocean and a six man mission. The alert helo is good to go right now, but we have number two down for engine maintenance with a good four to six hours before we could launch. There's no other SAR assets between here and the Strait of Hormuz, so unless they punch out feet dry there is a real risk we'll lose one or more."

"Are you suggesting Yemen?"

"Well sir, we have to trust their pilot when he says their original goal of Jeddah isn't going to work, and that he can't reach any other coalition airfield. Besides, his external ordnance may be armed so nobody would let them land anyway. Eagle just relayed orders from AIRCENT forbidding them to land in Yemen, so getting them out on the coast and letting the aircraft go down in those mountains just north of there looks like the best bet. There is a flat area about eight by eight kilometers just east of the little town of Qishn. Should be easy to spot on their nav radar and big enough for their entire crew to hit if they don't punch out too high."

Piotrowski realized Zimmerman had put together a workable plan in just a few minutes. Well, aviation was his specialty. On the other hand, Yemen was not part of the coalition against Saddam, had recently developed tense relations with Saudi Arabia, and had a history of instability. Besides, Piotrowski had seen orders listing Yemeni waters and airspace as no go for coalition ships and aircraft.

"Ken, Yemen's off limits." He said this more as a question than a statement of fact.

"Well, skipper, Eagle seemed okay with them landing at Jeddah, and from their current position the only way to do that would be by overflying Yemen. I think we can take that as authorization for an exception to that policy."

That . . . was a stretch, especially if he considered that the Yemeni government would probably disagree. On the other hand, the survival of six men was at stake. The Skipper considered for a moment the man for whom his ship was named. During the Meuse-Argonne Offensive in WW1 Pharmacist's Mate 2nd Class Alvin L. Bowman had advanced under heavy fire to carry three wounded men from the 5th Marines back across the Meuse River. He was awarded the Navy Cross—the first corpsman from the 5th Marine Regiment so honored.

So, yeah, the six men were worth the risk of an international incident. After all, what were the Yemenis going to do?

"Ken, if their pilot agrees, set up a rescue plan for the Yemen coast. Coordinate with ops. Ops, I'll need course and speed recommendations in the next two minutes. I'll be on the bridge."

"Aye, sir." Zimmerman turned immediately to Pete Hull and began an animated conversation.

Piotrowski stepped out of the CIC and climbed the ladder back to the bridge. There he found his watch standers alert and eager to know what was happening next. "This is the Captain, I have the deck and the conn." He realized there actually were some things the Yemenis might do. Best to be prepared. "Sound general quarters."

The petty officer of the watch, a blond California surfer type, replied instantly, "Sound general quarters, aye." The alarm was sounded and the Bowman sprang to life. In the enlisted quarters, feet hit the deck and uniforms were hastily pulled on as men rushed to their battle stations. Weapons systems were manned, watertight doors were dogged down, and the aviation detachment stood to flight quarters. As stations reported in, Piotrowski had the satisfaction of knowing that whatever happened, his crew would be ready.

FEBRUARY 1, 1991 2045Z (2345 AST)
22,000 Feet over the Gulf of Aden

SIMPSON DIDN'T LIKE what he was hearing. Jumbo had been working on the fuel problem and reported little progress. Shutting down the outboard engine on each wing seemed at first to improve flow to the remaining six TF-33s, but the B-52G continued to lose altitude at a slowly increasing rate. Frank Garcia had been working with gunner Andy Lewis on the bomb release problem, but the bombs remained firmly attached to the aircraft. Now Simpson was hearing from the SAR coordinator and the ops officer aboard a frigate that their best plan was for him and his crew to eject over the beach in Yemen. He had to admit, though, he had nothing better to offer. "Carlson, you been getting what the Navy is suggesting?"

"Got it, sir. Recommend course 318. I'll have an update when I get the coast on radar. What altitude are you looking at for us to uh, eject?"

Simpson considered this for a moment, "Since this thing will probably be going boom, I'm thinking we punch out at 5000 feet to give us separation from the impact."

"Roger that. Recommend 400 knots with 750 feet per minute rate of descent; that will put us over the coast six clicks east of Qishin at 5000 feet in twenty-two minutes. Coast is just appearing on my radar. That course looks good."

"Excellent. Okay crew, checklist for ejection. Report when ready."

As each station reported ready, Simpson concentrated on his instruments. The autopilot was still working so he didn't have to match course, speed, and rate of descent by hand. Relieved of the burden of fighting for altitude while starved for fuel, the remaining six engines sounded normal and instrument readings looked good. His panel still glowed with more than a dozen warning lights, but mostly for systems he wouldn't be needing. Like the nose gear.

FEBRUARY 1, 1991 2205Z (FEB. 2, 0105 AST)
USS *Alvin L. Bowman*
120 kilometers southwest of Qishn, Yemen

BOWMAN **WAS NOW** making twenty knots with only one of her two General Electric LM 2500 gas turbines turning. She could easily have done over thirty, but Piotrowski was concerned about fuel. They had an underway refueling from a fleet tanker scheduled in thirty-six hours and he didn't know how long he would have to remain south of Yemen to effect their mission. He reasoned that with the SAR helo already launched, a few extra knots wouldn't mean much, but once that second turbine was brought online, *Bowman* would suck fuel. Kestrel was due over the coast in seven minutes, and there the crew would eject. Ten minutes after that, Rabbit, Bowman's SH-60B LAMPS III helicopter, would arrive on scene, and he would know a lot more about the situation. If a high speed sprint was needed, the second turbine could be brought online in a few minutes.

Bowman's XO, LCDR Randy Chen, stepped onto the bridge and came directly to Piotrowski. "The flight deck is clear and ready for recovery. Chief Johnson reports medical ready for casualties." Chief Petty Officer Eugene Johnson was their independent duty corpsman, a specialty unique to the Navy. Small ships like *Bowman* didn't rate a full-time medical officer, so a few of the most qualified enlisted corpsmen were given extra training to allow them to function autonomously, but with backup from the larger ships.

"Randy, as soon as we recover Rabbit, have it refueled in case we need a medevac. Also, talk with ops about our medevac options."

"Been thinking about that already, skipper. The closest friendly airfield is at Salalah, just inside Oman. It isn't a military field, but we can probably get permission for a medevac."

"Good work, XO. Keep on top of all our options as we know more."

At 0115 Piortowski picked up the handset. "Radar shows Kestrel just went feet dry," ops reported. "They should be ejecting right now."

Instinctively, Piotrowski looked out towards the distant coast.

FEBRUARY 1, 1991 2215Z (FEB. 2, 0115 AST)
5 kilometers east of Qishn, Yemen

JUST SOUTH OF the coast, Simpson had cut the throttles and deployed his flaps. Careful not to stall the heavily loaded bomber, he got the airspeed down to a reasonable two-hundred knots for ejection.

"Eject, eject, eject!" Simpson activated the ejection system and after that it was all up to the aircraft. Simpson could have used the escape hatches, but he wanted everyone out together so they wouldn't get too separated on the ground. Besides, the ejection system showed no faults and being largely mechanical and powered by compressed gas it would probably work just fine. Probably.

Kerry Simpson's last thought before he hit the two-hundred knot slipstream was that ejection system seemed to be working. After being slapped away from the plane by the slipstream, there was a moment of freefall, then his chute yanked him around yet again. He was a little surprised that not only had the system worked, but that he had so far survived the event.

He looked around quickly. To the north, the huge B-52G had turned somewhat east and was gracefully descending her last few miles, God bless her. To the south and east he could see three other chutes. He prayed he just hadn't spotted the other two.

The light from the stars and the quarter moon allowed Simpson to see the ground only a few seconds before impact, and he had the sensation that rather than falling, the ground was rapidly rising to meet him. The impact rattled his teeth, but he'd had worse during training, and he found himself lying on a fairly flat plain sloping gently up to the north. The ground was covered with coarse, gritty sand and small rocks. At the edge of his vision to the north he saw another parachute descending, and after releasing his own chute and harness, he headed that way, homing in on the glow of a small flashlight.

It was Lieutenant Brandt. "You okay?"

"Twisted my knee, but otherwise fine."

He hardly paused to enjoy the relief before looking for more chutes. At that moment he saw a flash on the horizon to the north followed by an enlarging orange glow. He felt compelled to keep looking at it. He knew exactly what it was; thirty-six thousand pounds of high explosives and nine tons of JP-5 jet fuel made one hell of a signal flare. There was a tremor in the ground that was stronger than he expected, and after more than a minute, the rumble arrived. It was like thunder and lasted four or five seconds.

"That's going to leave a mark," he said.

"Timed it, sir" said Brandt. "Ninety-five seconds from the flash to the sound, puts the crash site about thirty kilometers north of us."

"Good thinking Ethan," replied Simpson. "Should have thought of that myself. But enough of this, we need to find the rest of our crew." Just then he thought he heard something, cocked his head and asked, "Do you hear a helicopter?"

Less than a minute later, an MH-60 loomed out of the dark and settled on the sand fifty meters away. He got a shoulder under Brandt's arm and helped him over.

A crewman jumped lightly to the ground and met them halfway. "Evening, gentlemen. I'm Petty Officer Dave Wells. Let's get you aboard."

As soon as he strapped in, Simpson grabbed an unused headset. "Thanks for getting here so quickly. We still have four men still out there."

"On top of it, Major," Zimmerman assured him. "There are two on the beach. Spoke with them on the SAR frequency and they're both okay. Plan is to pick them up on the retrograde. There's an IR strobe about a click north of here, so only one unaccounted for right now."

Simpson did not care for the sound of one man unaccounted for, but he knew that, so far, the rescue mission was going amazingly well. He told Zimmerman, "The guys on the beach must be my navigator and bombardier; they eject downward and get a head start to the ground. My EW officer is with me so we're looking for the co-pilot and gunner."

"Roger that," the pilot said. "We're heading north right now for the next man. Maybe he saw something that will help us find number six."

Within minutes, Jumbo Loewe was aboard the Navy helicopter, uninjured except for a dislocated pinkie finger. To the co-pilot's great relief, the corpsman popped it back into place with a snap just audible over the engine sound. "Jumbo," Simpson said, "have you seen Lewis?"

"Doesn't make sense that he would be north of me, the gunner is the first one out of the topside crew stations."

"He's right," added the pilot. "We should be looking south."

Zimmerman was trained mainly in anti-submarine warfare, but had a fair amount of SAR experience. Nonetheless there were always going to be small details, like the ejection sequence of the B-52G, he just didn't know. Funny things happened in ejections—updrafts, parachute malfunctions, and changes in wind direction during descent that could put crewmembers down where they weren't supposed to be—but these guys were right. That gunner should be down somewhere between their current location and the two men on the beach. "Okay then, we'll lay out a search pattern one click wide between here and the beach."

Lieutenant (jg) Neill Washington, his co-pilot, was already laying out a pattern on his map board.

The helo began its search from where it had picked up the co-pilot, making east-west sweeps a kilometer wide, each one a half-kilometer further south. On the next to last leg before reaching the beach Zimmerman saw one quick flash in his IR goggles while making a steep turn. Flying level over the same spot, he saw nothing.

He was about to move to the final leg, when it occurred to him that if the strobe were in some kind of hole or deep depression, he might see it only when looking almost straight down—like in a steep turn. He went into a tight circle to the left, and there it was again, this time two flashes.

Washington was wearing night vision. "Neill, you see any kind of hole or depression that would make the strobe visible only from directly overhead?"

"There's a cluster of rocks. If the strobe was between them, it would act like a hole."

"I'm putting down," said Zimmerman. "Wells, check out the rocks just to out east."

"On it." In a matter of seconds, they had settled onto the coarse sand, about thirty meters from the rocks. Wells, his rescue swimmer, and HM3 Tony Angelo, the corpsman, leapt out of the helo and headed for the rocks. In less than a minute came the report, "He's here sir. Looks like a broken leg and probably a concussion. Angelo's putting on an air splint and I'm coming back for the Stokes."

Welles jogged up to the helo, grabbed the Stokes stretcher, and less than ten minutes later, the two petty officers had the injured man aboard and strapped down.

Zimmerman was now faced with a decision. Between his crew and the flyboys he'd already picked up, there were eight aboard the aircraft. The UH-60 was more than capable of handling the weight of ten men, but being configured for anti-submarine warfare, they were tight on space. He could be out to the ship and back in about forty minutes, but he couldn't help thinking about what CDR Steve Watkins, a legend in the SAR community, had told them in SAR school again and again, *In SAR there is no later, there is only NOW!*"

"Wells," said the pilot, "get those guys stowed as best you can; we have two more to pick up."

In minutes the bombardier and navigator were running towards the helicopter, smiling broadly when they saw the rest of their crewmates aboard. They shoehorned into whatever space the crew could find as Zimmerman took them up to five-hundred feet and headed back to *Bowman*.

FEBRUARY 2, 1991 0015Z (0315 AST)
USS Alvin L Bowman
88 kilometers southwest of Qishin

"SKIPPER," HULL ANNOUNCED on the sound-powered telephone to the bridge. "Rabbit inbound with six, one serious injury. Recommend course 105 for recovery in ten minutes."

Piotrowski smiled. They got 'em all. "Good news, Pete. Course acknowledged. Give Chief Johnson a heads up."

In ten minutes Piotrowski ordered the course change and felt a moderate pitch and roll as Bowman stopped taking the wind against her superstructure and was now heading directly into it. As the wind made small shifts in direction, it would nudge *Bowman* back and forth creating a slight roll. Piotrowski had expected this, and as soon as he got the feel of the wind, he began making small course changes that dampened the effect.

Zimmerman smiled when he saw Bowman's lights, and his smile broadened as they approached and he could see that, despite the gusting winds pushing him around, the skipper had the ship amazingly stable with only a modest pitch from the wave action.

Zimmerman completed a tight 60 degree turn to align his course with the ship's. He steadied up directly behind the ship and, while talking with a sailor in the tiny control tower just above the hanger, he brought the aircraft over the small flight deck. The stern pitched up and kissed the landing gear just as Zimmerman reduced power. A small jolt, and they were down.

As the pilots went through the shutdown sequence and the aviation detachment prepared to secure the helicopter, the door was opened and Chief Johnson looked at the man strapped in the Stokes.

"Broken leg, Chief," said Angelo. "We need to get him below."

On the bridge, Piotrowski had just confirmed from operations that there was no radio chatter from the Yemeni military and no airborne or military surface radars within two-hundred kilometers. He had just ordered secure from general quarters when Chief Johnson climbed up to the bridge.

"Everybody's home, skipper."

"The injured?"

"The broken leg needs a hospital, but he's stable until we can get him there."

"What about the other injury?"

"Cartilage tear in the knee. I've seen worse on a basketball court. I'm going to give him an ice pack and elevate. He'll need to see an Ortho doc at some point, but it isn't urgent."

"Thanks, Chief."

When the Chief had gone, Piotrowski went back out on the bridge wing and stared north towards Yemen. Still radio silence from the Yemeni government, such as it was. He shook his head. A fully-laden B-52 had plowed into the ground, and apparently no one had noticed.

SHORT SEASON

SOMEONE HAD.

Senior cartographer Drew Simpson had found what he was looking for. After dinner with his younger brother, in DC to brief Air Force officials on the unusual lightning strike that had downed his B-52G, the older Simpson had a pretty clear picture of where to look for the remains. The satellite images from both high and low angles showed the tail—oddly intact—about two hundred meters from a knife-edge ridge that ran east to west thirty kilometers north of the Yemeni coast. Most of the remaining wreckage had been reduced to pieces too small to identify on the satellite image.

The really interesting thing, though, was how the explosion of twenty tons of bombs propelled into the ridge at over 200 knots had gouged out a semicircle of rock almost forty meters wide and twenty meters deep in the top of the ridgeline. Below lay boulders ranging from basketball size to pieces bigger than Volkswagens. Quite a notch.

Then it hit him. For years he had been looking for an opportunity to attach his family name to a terrain feature and to insert it into the map database. This was it—Simpson's Notch.

Within an hour, the topographic mapping programs had updated the change in the ridgeline along with the small notation: 'Simpson's Notch.' Over time he would see that the name was distributed to civilian map databases. It didn't matter if no one ever noticed it. They were on the map. For a cartographer, that was everything.

CHAPTER 1

JUNE 8, 2005 2230Z (JUNE 9 0030 AST)
76 kilometers North-Northeast of Al Bukamal, Syria
(5 kilometers west of the Syria-Iraq border)

THE MISSION WAS proceeding exactly as briefed; not bad considering the entire plan had been slapped together in Baghdad only eight hours before. The four man team had been lifted by an aging 'Huey' helicopter an hour and a half earlier to a remote stretch of the Syrian border north of the heavily populated Euphrates River region. They had walked into Syria and, carefully avoiding the occasional small farm, had approached their target from the north. From a distance of about a hundred-fifty meters they could see a compound consisting of a small house and two out buildings. On closer inspection, through the eerie green and white of their night vision, the team could see no goats, or other animals, nor any evidence of cultivation. The random desert brush had been cleared to a distance of about one-hundred meters from the buildings. The hum of a generator carried easily to the observers and explained the lights burning in the house, and in one of the smaller buildings. The night sky was clear and there was a half-moon which allowed an excellent view of two vehicles, a pickup truck and a Range Rover, parked under camouflage netting on the north side of the house. Two men were visible, both carrying AK-47 assault rifles, one on the north, and one on the east side of the house. No doubt there were similar guards on the other sides. Despite everything visible from their observation post, only one man, the team leader and mission specialist, knew exactly what they were looking for.

Lieutenant Commander Joe Castelli smiled. He knew what they were looking for, and there it was. There had never been guards visible on the satellite images. Something was happening tonight.

A short, but powerfully-built man in his early thirties, with close-cropped dense black hair, a large Roman nose, and huge eyebrows, Castelli was an up-and-coming Academy grad from an old Navy family. Four generations back, when Antonio Castelli, newly arrived from Italy, was unable to save even a few pennies from his job in a New York ice house, he looked for something that would either pay better or provide a place to live so he might save enough to get married and start a family. That's how he came to be a stoker in the U.S. Navy.

He was aboard the cruiser USS *Baltimore* when Commodore Dewey defeated the Spanish fleet at the Battle of Manila Bay in 1898. He left the Navy after five years, but the tradition stayed with the Castelli family. His son, Antonio Jr., served on destroyers in WW1 and ultimately retired with the rank of Chief Petty Officer. His grandson Bill, Joe's grandfather, was the first commissioned officer in the family. Like his father, he served on destroyers and, as a Lieutenant, was executive officer on the USS *Terry* (DD-513) during her service in the Marianas and at Iwo Jima. Joe's father, Vince, was the first Castelli to attend Annapolis. He defied the family tradition of serving in the surface Navy, and opted instead for aviation. Flying the F-4 Phantom off the USS *Enterprise*, he destroyed three Mig-21's and was awarded the Navy Cross for repeated aggressive low-level attacks on entrenched North Vietnamese positions. He was instrumental in the development of the F-14 Tomcat, and retired with the rank of Captain.

Young Joe was determined to surpass them all.

As a second generation Academy man, Castelli was well prepared for the rigors of life as a midshipman. He knew how to put a blinding shine on his shoes and a razor sharp crease in his trousers. He excelled in the classroom, where he wrote an honors thesis on the Battle of the Philippine Sea which was later published in the journal *Naval History*. It was as a wrestler, though, that he became best known to his classmates. He lost a few matches on points, but 'Tiger Joe' was never pinned.

Only three hours ago, he'd flown unannounced into Camp Butler, a small Marine Corps FOB in the parched desert of western Anbar Province carrying orders directing the battalion based there and Marine Air Group 39 to provide any and all support requested for a top-secret operation.

The battalion commanding officer, Lieutenant Colonel Henry Ahrens, had been a little trouble. He'd refused to take

Castelli seriously until he'd called up the chain of command and confirmed his orders. Then he sighed.

"Okay, Commander, what do you need?"

"One NCO, a rifleman, and a corpsman. I need people with dismounted patrol experience."

"Ordinary infantry? You're sure you don't want SEALs or Force Recon?"

"If I wanted Recon, I'd have said so."

Ahrens gave him a long, and not too friendly, look. "Wait here and I'll bring your people."

But Castelli recognized the scent of white mutiny—screwing with someone while technically obeying orders—when he smelled it. "I think I'll just stick with you, Colonel."

"And I told you to wait here." Ahrens stuck his head out the tent flap and spoke to someone briefly. A large Marine with dark, penetrating eyes and an utterly humorless expression entered and stood at parade rest. "Sergeant Major Cruz will take care of you until I get back."

"Right." Castelli leaned back in his chair and avoided the gaze of the Sergeant Major.

Ahrens returned in fifteen minutes with a huge Marine who looked like a lumberjack—or a linebacker. "Lieutenant Commander Castelli, this is Staff Sergeant Al Johanssen. He'll select the rest of your team. If you give him a bit more information about your mission, he can find the best people for the job."

"Staff Sergeant, all you need to know is what I told your CO. I need a rifleman and a corpsman with experience in dismounted patrols. Period. I'll brief you all when the team is together. Have your people ready in thirty minutes."

Johanssen glanced at Ahrens, who gave an almost imperceptible nod, before responding, "Aye aye, sir," and left the tent.

Pointedly ignoring Ahrens, Castelli turned to the Sergeant Major. "Take me to the airfield. I need to talk with the CO of MAG 39."

"My pleasure Commander. Please come with me." Castelli brushed sand off his pants and followed the Sergeant Major.

At the airfield Castelli ordered the first Marine he met to take him to the Commanding Officer. A quick display of his orders got the MAG-39 CO into motion, and this time without the fuss. An operations order was written, and the alert crew notified. He told the CO the approximate distance of the required flight, but that further details were only for the actual flight crew. The Commanding Officer seemed to accept this without hesitation.

Returning to the 5th Marines area, Castelli found Johanssen and the men he had selected in a small, well-guarded tent. He introduced himself to his team and began the briefing.

"My cell," he began, "has developed strong evidence that the principle producer of improvised explosive devices, IEDs, killing Marines in Anbar Province is working out of a farm just across the border in Syria. We've been trying for days to get authorization for an airstrike. Cross border strikes are touchy, as you're probably aware, but we finally got the go ahead earlier this evening. The weapons, GPS guided GBU-31 two thousand pound bombs, will have to be released inside Iraq to avoid violation of Syrian airspace. That's not a problem, but the second condition is a bit more complicated." He said this in the casual way British officers in movies always described difficult missions, something he'd practiced in front of a mirror. "We need to enter Syria and put eyes on the target." For emphasis, he poked at the air with two fingers. "We confirm it is what we think it is, and then call in the strike.

"Naturally, there can't be evidence of American presence in Syria. So we're going to helo up to the border, walk in, confirm the target, call in the strike, and walk back to the border for pick-up. Simple enough?"

Johanssen and the other two enlisted—Lance Corporal Luis Delgado, and Petty Officer Second Class Mike McGregor—listened in silence and asked no questions. When Castelli was finished, he distributed maps, copies of reconnaissance photos, and communications protocols. "Staff Sergeant, what do you recommend for ammunition load and gear?"

"Well, sir, you didn't mention what we might encounter as far as opposition, but normally I would go with 210 rounds per man, four grenades—two smoke and two frag—six liters of water, night vision, two MREs, and a radio for each member of the team. I see you're carrying a Beretta. You should probably have an M4 as well."

"Good. I have the radios. Each has crypto already loaded as well as the comm frequencies for the air assets. Unfortunately, I was provided with only two." This brought a scowl from Johanssen, and raised eyebrows from the corpsman, but neither said anything. "Round up the rest of my gear while I go back to the airfield and brief the helo crew. As for opposition, our mission is to avoid contact. If we have to shoot our way out, we're doing it wrong"

Johanssen said, "We'll just have to hope the opposition has the same mission. Sir."

Castelli gave the big Marine a sharp look. "Just get my gear, staff sergeant."

The team drew seven thirty-round magazines each of 5.56 mm., rations, and a rifle for Castelli. Except for the corpsman—in theory a non-combatant—they drew the smoke and fragmentation grenades. McGregor took only the two smoke grenades plus a pop-up flare and a star cluster, useful for signaling medical evacuation helicopters from the ground. The rest of their gear—body armor, pack, canteens, knives, and all the other items required for even the briefest mission—they each retrieved from their tents. Each man carried three two-liter canteens, one on their load-bearing vest and two in their rucksacks. In the desert heat, six liters was enough for a day, but not much more than that.

While they were waiting for the arrogant Castelli to return from the airfield, Petty Officer McGregor sidled up to Staff Sergeant Johanssen. "Joe, this mission has a funny smell to it. What's really going on?"

"What's on your mind, Doc?"

"For starters, this guy Castelli is clearly no field operator. He puts together a cross border mission on the fly with orders that keep the Colonel out of the loop. This is about more than some bomb maker."

"I always thought you were too damn smart for your own good," replied Johanssen. "Sure this guy clearly hasn't a clue about field ops—did you see the creases in those cammies? And he's definitely not sharing everything. What you're forgetting, though, is that we are just three grunts—or considering you're a corpsman—maybe two and a half. We follow orders. You know what they say about orders—you have to go out, you just don't have to come back."

McGregor was considering the wisdom of a response when Castelli pulled up in a Humvee and said, "Okay men, let's saddle up," as if they were going to a church picnic.

On the short drive to the airfield, he handed Johanssen a handheld radio. "It's the new PRC-148; most units won't get them for a year or two. Crypto is controlled here and frequencies here." McGregor and Delgado both leaned in for this explanation, too. They might have to use the unit someday.

"What's the range?" asked Johanssen.

"About twenty clicks line of sight. Not a problem, the F-15's will be just inside Iraqi airspace and the AWACS bird has been pulled westward. Their comm gear will have no problem receiving us."

The Staff Sergeant raised his eyebrows. "This mission has enough priority to reposition an AWACS?"

"It does."

Johanssen scowled at McGregor, who couldn't resist a slight smirk.

Arriving at the airfield, the team saw the crew of a Huey, the venerable Viet Nam era helicopter, completing their pre-flight checks. True to their motto, "Any Time—Any Where," the Marines of Light Attack Helicopter Squadron 267 had prepared the alert helicopter to launch within minutes of Castelli's arrival. In two minutes the crew and Castelli's team were aboard, and the engines were turning.

Once away from the ground lighting, they were enveloped by darkness with only the half-moon illuminating the desert below. After about half an hour in the air, during which time Castelli, the only team member with headphones, maintained a steady conversation with the pilots, the helicopter circled for a minute then landed just west of a packed-sand road. The team quickly disembarked and walked away from the helicopter, which roared off to the southeast, kicking up clouds of grit and sand.

Castelli produced his map and a GPS unit, but when he pulled out a small flashlight, Staff Sergeant Johanssen pulled out his own and handed it over. "Sir? It's got a red lens. Lets us keep our night vision and can't be seen beyond about ten meters."

Castelli took the flashlight without a word. After reviewing their position and destination, they headed west, into Syria. Johanssen put Delgado at point, followed by himself, Castelli, and McGregor at the rear.

It was just before midnight, but the temperature had barely begun to drop from the day's high of 122 degrees. The ground was fairly flat, just small ridges and a few shallow wadis—dry stream beds, but the sand was soft, and walking took a lot more energy than on hard ground. Half an hour out, McGregor suggested a break for water and a brief rest. He knew Johanssen and Delgado wouldn't need it, they'd acclimated to the desert and were hard from months of foot patrols. But he was concerned that the Lieutenant Commander, living in air-conditioned comfort in Baghdad, probably did. And he would be too proud to ask for it himself.

Castelli smiled when the arrogant little corpsman suggested a break. He probably figured Castelli was soft. But he'd figured out long ago that a high level of fitness and a recruiting poster look went a long way in the Navy. Every day he went for an hour run in the Green Zone just as the sun was rising, and every evening he worked out in the gym. He liked showing up the younger enlisted men. His lean, hard appearance had also gotten him selected for press and flag officer briefings, while the dumpy reserve Commander with the PhD and the fluent Arabic was kept behind the scenes. He'd enjoy showing McGregor what he was really made of.

As they walked, he moved over to Johanssen and asked quietly, "Why them?"

"Sir?"

"Why did you choose Delgado and McGregor? I know Lieutenant Colonel Ahrens picked you, but you picked them."

"Nothing complicated. Delgado is one of our best Marines in a fight. He's an excellent shot, very cool under fire, and he grew up in the desert south of Tucson, so he's comfortable out here where a lot of guys are not. Doc is probably the best all-around corpsmen in the battalion. He has been through paramedic training and worked the streets in Detroit before joining the Navy. He knows his land nav, communications, and is a pretty fair shot, for a sailor."

"What are their weaknesses?"

"Weaknesses?"

"I think you heard me, Staff Sergeant."

"Well sir, Delgado is a follower. He knows how to take orders and if he's still breathing you can rely on him to carry them out. But don't count on him to make decisions. The Doc, well he is just the opposite. Thinks too much. Wants to understand his orders. He will definitely take charge if you need him to. Problem is, I think he probably wants to be in charge right now."

"That's useful, thanks. One other question, why are we moving in column? The manuals recommend a diamond formation for a unit this size."

Johanssen carefully considered his response before saying, "That would be true in daylight, but for night movement, especially with only two radios, the risk of losing contact with a man in the dark is too great."

"Why not use the night vision?"

"Are you experienced in overland movement using NVGs Commander?" responded Johanssen.

"No, I'm not."

"Then it isn't a good idea. Anything else, sir?"

Castelli considered reprimanding Johanssen for his attitude, but realized the Staff Sergeant did know more than he did about foot patrols. "No."

With the half-moon providing reasonable light and with the sand getting firmer, progress was good. Just after midnight Castelli checked his GPS, changed their course slightly, and after five minutes signaled the team to get low. According to the recon photos, their target was just ahead. He instructed everyone to approach a low rise in a crawl.

And there was the target, exactly as Castelli had expected it to be.

He keyed his radio and said very softly, "Crossbow, this is Lancer. Eyes on target."

"Roger Lancer. Be advised Archer is now on station." Archer was a flight of two F-15E Strike Eagles that had launched out of nearby al-Assad Air Base, and was now flying in a racetrack pattern just east of the border.

"Delgado," Johanssen ordered, "work your way far enough west to see beyond those buildings, report in, then maintain your position." He handed the young Marine his radio and tiny combined microphone-earpiece. "Doc, find a good spot about a hundred meters north and use your NVGs to look for any sign these guys have put out security patrols. If you see anything, come on back and report. If nothing shows up in ten minutes, report back anyway."

The two men moved off to their assigned positions, and in less than ten minutes Delgado reported, "Two guys on the west side of the house about twenty meters out. One has an AK and the other an RPG. With the NVGs I can see two more about three or four-hundred meters further west doing a foot patrol."

Castelli told Johanssen of this development, but before he could respond McGregor returned, much sooner than expected.

"Doc, what's up?" Johanssen asked.

"There's a little rise about fifty meters straight north of us. I was low crawling over it with my NVGs on when I saw the flare of a match about five-hundred meters further north. It was a guy lighting a cigarette. I watched them for a couple of minutes, and they seem to be on a foot patrol working their way south by doing east-west legs."

"With any luck we'll be out of here before they get too close," Castelli said.

"Luck sir? Those guys are out on patrol looking for people like us. Aside from luck, what exactly is the plan?"

Castelli had to keep a lid on his temper. He keyed the mike on his radio. "Come on back Delgado, you've seen all you need to." He shut off the radio and gave Johanssen an even glare. "We're going to maintain this position. It's the best place to observe the compound."

Delgado crouch-walked back into the wadi and made his way over to Johanssen. "Staff Sergeant Joe, what's the plan?"

"I think the Lieutenant Commander will have to answer that. There are things going on here you and I don't know about."

Castelli's hands clenched into fists. "Look Staff Sergeant, I'm getting damn sick of you second guessing me. There is one person in command here, and that's me!" He took a deep breath. A good commander didn't need to pull rank.

"Look, the decision to withhold some information from the briefing was made above my pay grade. But now that we're on site and seeing more than expected opposition, I should probably fill you in."

"Thank you, sir," said Johanssen, with just a hint of sarcasm.

Castelli let it go. "That second building"—he pointed at the building closest to the house, an adobe structure about the size of a one-car garage—"really is a bomb factory. We could have blown it awhile back and without sending anyone on site. We left it standing because of intel that a meeting was planned for this location. Tonight. A meeting of several important bomb makers, one of the senior Sunni insurgents, and most important, a major Saudi financial backer. He is bringing funds, and negotiating for further funding if he likes what he hears. We have to confirm the principals are on sight before committing to the strike. Do I have your attention now?"

"Yes sir," from each of the enlisted men. Castelli had made his point. Some officers might think that the mission would be more likely to succeed if he'd by been straight with his people from the start. But the intel business didn't run that way.

Thirty minutes passed. They heard only the soft conversation of the guards, the hum of the generator, and the occasional whine of a sand fly. To the north, the foot patrol had closed to within two hundred meters, and their next pass was going to take them dangerously close to the teams' observation post.

Then, on the road from the south, two vehicles pulled around an rock outcropping and into view. A Toyota Land Cruiser and a large, black Mercedes, both running without headlights. "Contact," Castelli said. "The guests are here. Let's start the party."

They pulled into the open space east of the house, and two men, each armed with AK-47s, jumped out of each vehicle. They conferred briefly with the guards, one of whom went to the house and knocked on the door. In a moment two bearded men wearing the traditional long disha dasha and knit kufi skullcaps walked out of the house.

One of the armed men from each vehicle spoke with the drivers and, after a moment, one man stepped out of each. From the Land Cruiser, a short man with a prominent beard emerged. He wore long white robes and a colored head scarf.

"Shiek Abdul al-Tikriti," Castelli said softly. "Related to Saddam and a major player in the insurgency. Reported to pay a thousand dollars for every American killed."

"I can take him out right now," replied Delgado. "An easy shot."

"Tempting," Castelli whispered, "but in a few minutes they'll all be road kill."

From the Mercedes stepped a tall man in flowing white robes and a long headscarf. He wore gold wire rimmed glasses over a prominent nose and a short pointed beard.

"Abdullah Nazer. The money man." Castelli adjusted his radio. "Crossbow, this is Lancer. Fast Arrow, I say again Fast Arrow."

"Roger Lancer, Fast Arrow confirmed. Suggest you clear the area."

"Roger, weapons free in two minutes," came the terse reply.

Captain Jeremy Rogers, weapons officer of the lead F-15E, made a quick calculation as to course and speed to place them in position for weapons release in two minutes. He passed this on to his pilot, Major Denise "Scooter" Callahan, who then ordered her wing man to take the same course.

The GPS in the GBU-31 2000 pound JDAM (Joint Direct Attack Munition) was already tracking its location, and the target coordinates were pre-programmed into its onboard memory. A combination of the reliable Mark 84 2000 pound bomb with a bolt-on tail incorporating navigational and guidance capability, the GBU-31 would typically land within thirteen meters of its intended target. The arming sequence completed, instrument displays were quickly scanned for signs of problems or malfunctions. There were none—in less than two minutes, two tons of death would be on its way.

At 0147 and eight seconds both weapons released and Major Callahan reported, "Weapons away," to the AWACS and simultaneously to the Crossbow team on the ground. Mission completed, both F-15 crews completed a broad turn to the southeast and headed back to al-Assad for a debrief, a shower, and a few hours of sleep.

"Time to go. East." They moved quickly in a low crouch and in just under two minutes had moved an additional hundred-fifty meters, and were face down in a shallow wadi. Castelli knew how much punch a GBU-31 2,000 pound bomb could pack. If they were standing, they would still be within the kill radius of the weapons, but down in the wadi three hundred meters away, they should be relatively safe.

Less than a minute later, the sky in front of them lit up brighter than daylight.

At that point everything changed.

CHAPTER 2

AUGUST 18, 2017 0635Z (1035 MST)
Gadzhiyevo Russia (30 kilometers northwest of Murmansk)

DESPITE ITS SIZE and industrial trappings, the missile assembly facility of the 3rd Nuclear Submarine Flotilla of the Russian Northern Fleet was a quiet place to work, with only the whine of the crane and the occasional metal on metal clink of tools disrupting the silence. Perhaps working with nuclear weapons inspired silent respect.

Captain Second Rank Anatoly Grishkov, senior weapons officer of the Second Division, was personally supervising the mating of six thermonuclear warheads to a recently delivered R-29RMU2 submarine launched ballistic missile, NATO codename Liner. The three stage liquid fuel missile was an upgrade of the older Sineva missile and was designed to carry up to twelve small warheads with special capability to evade anti-ballistic missile systems. The project was years behind schedule, however, and—unknown to the West—Russia was fitting half its Liner production with refurbished warheads from the decommissioned Sinevas, both to speed their deployment and as a cost-cutting measure. Because of their larger size, only six of the older warheads could be mounted on each missile.

Shipped in specially-designed stainless steel containers weighing five-thousand kilograms, the conical warheads were about two meters long and just over half a meter in diameter at the base. The massive steel boxes, which also incorporated a thin lead liner, were designed to provide radiation shielding, to protect the warheads, and to make theft nearly impossible. The sheer mass of these steel coffins was itself a deterrent, but there was also a unique digital locking mechanism, produced at the same facility that overhauled the warheads, that would deactivate the weapon and render it useless if even a single incorrect code were entered into its keypad.

Anatoly had traveled to nearby Severomorsk, site of the First Light Machinery Maintenance Factory—the typically cryptic Russian name for the warhead reconditioning facility—to personally code the containers for the six warheads now being mounted.

His predecessor had made the mistake of forgetting one of the codes, thus damaging a warhead to the extent that it required complete rebuilding. That error had set back arming and loading a missile submarine by more than two weeks and had ended that particular officer's career. Anatoly Grishkov, son of a submarine skipper and nephew of his flotilla's commanding officer, was determined not to repeat the error.

In addition to the technical side of nuclear warheads, Anatoly understood the geopolitical significance of these awesome weapons as well. One had only to look at North Korea or Pakistan, insignificant nations made large by their possession of these devices. The significance of a robust fleet of missile submarines was the reason the aging Delta IV boats were still in service. Originally destined for the scrap yard after introduction of the new Borei Class boats, the Deltas' life had been extended several times due to production delays, shipyard accidents, and costly redesign of the Boreis.

The shipping container for the sixth and last warhead, for the sixteenth and final missile destined for the submarine *Karelia* —K-18—was opened without incident. A small crane lifted the massive lid, then removed the warhead and placed it onto a custom dolly for movement by elevator up to the assembly level, twelve meters above the floor.

At this point Grishkov attached a small cable from an instrument the size of an ordinary voltmeter to a connector inside the mating ring at the base of the warhead. The unit ran a quick check of the weapon's small nuclear battery and electronic systems. When the indicator LED turned green, he disconnected the cable.

He then attached a different cable for the permissive action link encoder to a connection nearer the center of the base. The PAL encoder programmed the warhead for the conditions under which it could be armed. First, of course, was the arming code to be entered by the crew of the submarine. There were also conditions such as acceleration, altitude, and time which would ensure that the weapon had actually been launched as intended. These security measures were not as complex or elaborate as those used by the Americans, but to Grishkov's mind they were entirely adequate. The PAL parameters were programmed into the encoder by the Defense Ministry, and Grishkov had only a vague idea what they were. The encoder was delivered from Moscow under heavy guard and was stored and guarded entirely separately from the missiles and the warheads.

Despite the complexity of what it did, the encoder was actually quite simple to operate. He had only to switch it on and press 'PROGRAM' after which small green LEDs would light in sequence. When all six were lit, he was done and simply had to disconnect the device. There had never been a problem.

Until today. One light lit, then flickered and went out. The next two lit but did the same, then all stayed dark. He tried 'PROGRAM' several times without result.

God damn it. The last warhead of the last missile for this boat, and there was a malfunction! These warheads were freshly reconditioned, and he had never encountered the slightest problem. He knew the commanding officer of the submarine was expecting this missile to be transported to the boat and loaded today. Feeling desperate, he then did something he had never even considered before.

Grishkov found a torx wrench and removed the small access plate next to the encoder socket.

He had no idea why he did it. It wasn't like he could repair the warhead. But ever since he was a boy, he had been fascinated by nuclear weapons—their ingenious design and meticulous construction stood out so clearly amidst a world of makeshift design and shoddy workmanship. And now he simply wanted to know what was wrong.

The plate was about the size of the palm of his hand and came off easily. To the astonishment of his crew, Grishkov then peered into the interior of the warhead with a small flashlight. He had seen the interior of many warheads and was familiar with the basic design of every nuclear warhead in the inventory of the Russian Navy.

This did not look at all like any of them. In fact ...
Oh shit.

There was a bare circuit board mounted on a bracket just inside the base which was attached by wire bundles to both the test and PAL sockets. There was also what appeared to be about a dozen large disc-type batteries wired together and attached to the circuit board. One of the leads to the PAL socket had a loose solder joint which probably accounted for the malfunction. Looking farther up into the warhead, he saw pieces of steel reinforcing rods and a large blob of what looked like concrete.

The warhead was a fake! But that was impossible. He had seen it loaded into the case, had programmed the lock himself. Each warhead was shipped under the tightest security in separate trucks. Every truck and every case was accounted for; he had accounted for them personally. Despite the chill of the Arctic morning, Anatoly Grishkov was suddenly drenched with sweat.

Procedure called for him to notify the Division Commander immediately, followed by notification of the Flotilla senior weapons officer. The Division commander, however, was out on one of the boats, and the weapons officer was nothing more than a political sycophant. He made a quick decision. He replaced the inspection plate and ordered his crew off the assembly platform. He then told the senior security officer that, pending further orders, no one could leave or enter the building.

He went to his small office and dialed a number he knew well. The phone was answered after one ring, "Sergei Grishkov."

"Sir, Uncle, it's Anatoly. It is imperative you come at once to the assembly building."

His uncle, a long time survivor of both the Soviet and Russian military systems asked no questions. "On my way."

In fifteen minutes, Vice Admiral Sergei Antonovich Grishkov, Commanding Officer of the Third Submarine Flotilla, arrived in a dark green staff car, his personal Mercedes having been left at his office. A large bear of a man—actually too big for submarines—especially now that advancing years had begun to expand his middle—the elder Grishkov wore a broad moustache which, before it began to grey, was sometimes compared to Stalin's. He had publically bristled at the comparison, but was privately amused by it. His rank of Vice Admiral qualified him for a comfortable senior post in the Defense Ministry, but his health was failing, and he requested his last assignment be back with the Northern Fleet. He had friends in the Arctic, and in this post he could keep watch over the career of his nephew. Such nepotism was frowned upon in the American Navy, but was tolerated—even expected—in the Russian.

He was quickly shown into his nephew's office, his aide Captain First Rank Piotr Kulakov, in his wake. His nephew snapped to attention.

"So Anatoly Ivanovich, what exactly requires my attention. I expected to see the building on fire, but am gratified to see it is not."

"When you see what I have discovered, you might prefer a fire."

Sergei Grishkov raised his eyebrows. "What then?"

"Come with me." The younger Grishkov threw a glance at Piotr Kulakov.

"Piotr is my aide and trusted friend. Whatever this is, he will have to know."

They rode in silence up the elevator where the access plate was again removed. Holding his nephew's flashlight, the Admiral peered inside and then motioned for his aide to look as well. Both men understood immediately what they were seeing.

Sergei stood aside while Piotr replace the plate. "Who else knows about this?"

"The four men working with me and the senior security officer know something is wrong, but not what. No one else."

"Good, good. Let's keep it that way. Dismiss your crew. Tell them there is a problem with the warhead that must be addressed. They are not to return until notified. Security will seal the building and no one permitted to enter unless accompanied by you, Piotr, or myself." The Admiral took a deep breath and looked up, as if for inspiration. "Clearly, the fake must have been substituted at the reconditioning facility. I will order a helicopter, and we can be there in thirty minutes. I will arrange for Northern Fleet security to detain the facility director and hold him until we arrive. I'll have to notify Admiral Sokolov as well, but that should be done by secure telephone from my office."

"The Commander of the Northern Fleet?"

"Don't you think he would want to know? He will find out something is happening anyway as soon as I contact his security people. He is an old Communist, but a good officer, a submariner, and I don't want him hearing anything second hand. I also want to suggest we keep this within the Defense Ministry and use their GRU intelligence people to investigate."

"You mean you're going to hide this from the FSB?" asked his nephew with alarm.

Piotr cleared his throat. "I believe the Admiral wishes to direct the problem where he feels it will receive the most . . . efficient response."

"Yes, Piotr, very tactful. You might add that I also wish to avoid dealing with the knuckle-breaking incompetents of our esteemed President's former employer."

Within minutes the three officers had been driven, at breakneck speed, to the admiral's office where he and his aide both made a number of urgent calls. They then embarked on a Kamov Ka-29TB helicopter for the brief flight to the First Light Machinery Maintenance Factory. When they landed in a lot normally used to load and unload trucks, they were approached by a security officer who told them that the factory manager, Alexi Kovolenko, was away on vacation. He had departed one week ago, the same day the latest group of warheads had been shipped out to the 3rd Flotilla.

Sergei looked at Anatoly and Piotr. None of them needed to say it. This was where the warheads had gone missing.

There was no point in remaining, so Sergei Grishkov ordered his helicopter to return to Gadzhiyevo. Enroute he told his nephew, "Bring enough trusted men back to the Assembly Building to remove each of the remaining warheads from that missile. Inspect them, and reload them into their transport boxes. I think we all know what you will find, but we must be sure."

Anatoly nodded, unable to speak.

CHAPTER 3

AUGUST 18, 2017 0805Z (1005 CEST)
Aboard the Frecciarossa
High Speed Train South of Rome

ALEXEI KOVOLENKO, ACCOMPANIED by his fiancée, Anna Voronina, was traveling in comfort towards Salerno. Not that they were going by those names. At the moment, they were Arvid and Ilse Hämäläinen, Finnish school teachers on holiday. They could not speak a word of Finnish, but neither could anyone else outside of Finland so they were getting by in heavily-accented German. They smiled knowingly at each other as they enjoyed their business class breakfast of fruit, cheese, and smoked meats. Aided by a second glass of local wine, the couple was beginning to relax for the first time in more than a week.

They were an incongruous pair. Alexei was a large man in his early forties—broad shoulders, big hands, and a large, slightly-crooked nose. His long dark hair comb over periodically dropped down over his forehead, landing on the top of steel-rimmed glasses. The typically-Russian eyewear was an

oversight which he would have to fix at the earliest opportunity—and they did make nice eyewear in Italy. Anna, by
contrast, was a petite blond with short hair, sparkling blue
eyes and infectious laugh. The latter, plus her spectacular
figure, was what had attracted Alexei in the first place. He
still didn't know what had attracted her to him, and he had
long ago decided not to ask.

He had degrees in both Physics and Mechanical
Engineering, while she had a high-school diploma, but
her worldliness was immensely appealing. You don't see
much of the world when you're running a secret warhead
maintenance facility. They had met at a small coffee bar in
Severomorsk where she was what the Americans would call
a barista.

Alexei was fascinated by the fact that she had once lived
in Chechnya, to him a place both exotic and dangerous.

Indeed, her father, a minor bureaucrat, had moved Anna,
her mother, and her little brother, Boris, to Grozny in 2000
as part of a program to prove that Moscow had the rebel-
lious province firmly under their control. They did not, of
course.

Anna's mother was killed in 2005 by a car bomb while
shopping at a vegetable market. Both teens by this time,
Anna and Boris learned to navigate the streets and to
instinctively recognize danger. Anna finished her schooling,
and her father arranged a job for her with the Ministry
of Economic Development, North Caucasus Region. Boris,
small but cunning and quick, became a runner for Chechen
criminals, who more than once steered the two Russians
away from ambushes and suicide bombers.

In 2009 their father suffered a fatal heart attack, brought on by years of chain smoking, heavy drinking, and mediocre health care. With no reason to stay in Chechnya, the brother and sister moved, along with most of the Russian troops, back to Russia and an uncertain future. Like the American veterans of Viet Nam and the French civilians fleeing Algeria, Russia had little interest in the plight of its citizens returning from the ill-fated mission in Chechnya. They lived in Moscow for a few years, Boris working off and on for his contacts in Chechen organized crime and Anna as a bartender in a club frequented by the spoiled children of the new class of Russian plutocrats. On the same night in 2012, Boris was badly beaten by members of a rival mob, and Anna barely avoided a full-blown sexual assault while serving, and being groped, in one of the private rooms at her club. They both realized there was no future in Moscow.

Exploiting her charm and good looks, Anna convinced an old friend of their father, a senior official in the Defense Ministry, to arrange a low-level job for Boris at a new, and very secret, facility being built in Severomorsk. He had no work for Anna, but convinced her that the closed military city would also need a young woman with her 'talents.' They arrived in the high Arctic a month later where Boris began work at the First Light Machinery Maintenance Factory, and Anna began serving espresso.

At first, Alexei was content simply to chat with the vivacious young woman, but in time he wanted to know her better. Three years ago he had asked her to join him at a performance of a balalaika band. To his astonishment and relief, she had agreed to the date. Following an evening of

Korobienki and Zaporozhian, they retired to a small bar where they sipped vodka and exchanged the stories of their lives. Anna had been mesmerized by Alexei's intellectual achievements and awed by his rapid progress in the highly-secret and prestigious Russian nuclear weapons program. Alexei found himself speaking of highly-classified matters to this woman without the slightest regard for security.

Over the following months, as they spent increasing amounts of time together, he went into some detail about his engineering work at Lesnoy, in central Russia, where bombs and warheads were actually produced. For the first time, he was able to share his pride in mastering the awesome complexity of these devices. He went into even greater detail about his plan to perform warhead maintenance for the Northern Fleet in the Arctic and to run the facility himself. This, he thought, would be his ticket to a senior post in the Defense Ministry.

As he courted Anna Voronina, however, his world view began to change in unexpected ways. The first time they had sex, for example, Alexei was utterly stunned by her beauty and her passion, and even more by the passion she aroused in him, feelings of which he had never imagined himself capable. During their long evenings of lovemaking, he found himself utterly uninterested in his work or in the Defense Ministry. If, at the end of the day, he had given Anna pleasure, he felt he had accomplished all he ever wanted.

As Anna shared her small apartment with her brother, Boris, it was inevitable the two men would meet socially. Alexi found that he liked the younger man. His disregard for authority should have outraged the plant manager, but it did not. Alexei found him something of a rogue, and when he learned about his connections to the Chechen mafia, he was thrilled at knowing someone who had lived so well outside the system. If his superiors in Moscow had known about his relationship with these two marginal citizens, they would almost certainly have disapproved. Fortunately, they did not know.

Alexei began to talk with Boris about his desire to provide for his sister a much better life than they had in this isolated Arctic outpost. At first they talked about small plans, pilfering of scrap metal and instruments, which Boris could sell through his underworld connections, the kind of thing that was common, almost expected, of management all over Russia. Then, one bitterly-cold evening, Boris and Alexei were talking over glasses of mediocre vodka when the older man said, "You know, Boris, so far what we have been talking about is what the Americans would call peanuts."

"Peanuts?"

'Yes. Small change. Sure we can sell bits of scrap metal, but what's that worth? A little vacation to Prague? So what? What do we have that could allow us all to live in style, away from this freezing rat hole, for the rest of our lives? You, Anna, and me."

Boris looked at him blankly for a moment, then his eyes opened wide. "A warhead? Are you talking about selling a nuclear weapon?"

"Six, actually." Alexei poured more vodka into his glass. "And the first thing I'm going to do after that is to stop drinking this shit!" He drained the glass and slammed it onto the table top.

"Alexei, you're drunk. They will kill us."

"No, no, no. We will be long gone before they even suspect the warheads are missing. It's actually very simple. We will build six fake warheads using extra re-entry vehicles. I can get them easily."

Boris leaned forward, his elbows on the small table. "You really can make the Northern Fleet missile officers believe they're real warheads?"

"Sure, the testing they do at the time of assembly is quite basic. I have already constructed a small circuit board that will respond correctly to their tests. Only when the missile is loaded aboard the submarine, and they try to integrate it with the onboard weapon system will they have problems. By that time, they will be at sea and to discover the fakes they will have to return to port, off-load the missile, and remove the warheads. If you, Anna, and I all leave as soon as the fakes are shipped, it will take weeks before they're discovered."

"Yes, I see. And the real warheads will be out of the country and already delivered to the buyer. We can send them out in shipping containers."

"Exactly. But we will need to do a lot of work. I will need your help in fabricating the extra shipping boxes—I'll assign you to that work group next week—and I will also need your contacts to help with financial arrangements. We will need accounts impossible to trace back to us. We are going to move a large amount of money, a very large amount."

"How much?"

"About a hundred-fifty million euros, twenty-five million a unit. Hard to say though. As far as I know—or should I say as far as the SVR knows—no one has actually sold an intact nuclear weapon before. We will be the first. We will set the price, so to say."

The younger man inhaled sharply "Who are you going to sell these weapons to, Alexei?"

"High bidder, I suppose. I would prefer not to deal with Muslim terrorists, but we probably can't be too selective. I do have a contact in Prague who has some useful connections. He believes this to be a realistic number."

"Who is this contact?'

"He is known simply as Janos now. He was once quite high up in the procurement section of the Defense Ministry. I worked with him when I was at the old Arzamas-16 laboratory. He acts as a go between on weapons deals, big deals. He has a lot of contacts." The two men sipped vodka, and they planned.

The project ran into problems almost immediately. First, Boris allowed his enthusiasm to get the better of him, and he revealed the entire plan to Anna. She was horrified, not so much at the idea of stealing nuclear weapons, but of getting caught. The sense of constantly being watched is deep in the Russian genes, and the transition from the old Soviet system to the new Russia under Putin had done nothing to change that reality. It took some time, but her confidence in Alexei, plus the inevitable blindness of love, calmed her nerves. She began studying Portuguese at a local language school, as did Boris and Alexei, though they had no intention of going to Portugal. She dyed her normally blond hair very dark and grew it long. After a few months, she applied for a new identity card, claiming to have lost her old one. As she smiled for her new photograph she recalled how Boris had discovered the system did not retain the old images, but simply replaced them with the new ones in its digital memory. A few days before their departure she would have her hair cut and dyed back to its original straw blond.

Boris did something similar by growing a full beard and reporting his identity card stolen. He had hit himself in the face with a piece of pipe and filed a police report to give credence to the ruse, and to further hide his identity with the new picture. Only Alexi Kovolenko needed no disguise. Already wearing an enormous beard worthy of a Patriarch, he would need only a close shave after they departed to entirely change his appearance.

The second problem was potentially more serious. In order to build the massive transport boxes, Alexei had to order twenty-five thousand kilograms of specialty stainless steel from a mill in Sweden. The steel was delivered in three standard twenty-foot shipping containers which Alexei failed to return. The large purchase raised questions in Moscow, and it took several telephone calls for Alexei to explain he was preparing both for increased production demands, and to ship several containers to other facilities to copy. Both were blatant lies of course, but he was fortunate, and none of the bureaucrats ever followed up. They could not imagine what else he could do with that much stainless steel and were ultimately convinced the purchase was legitimate.

It took almost a year, during which Alexei procured a small workroom in the plant for his private use. He had a cipher lock installed, and he then gradually accumulated spare re-entry vehicles, test instruments, and a basic set of electronic tools. Such was the authority of managers that not a single person questioned what he was doing. Likewise, the lucrative overtime work given to his girlfriend's brother was nothing more than would be expected. Authority was suspicious only when not abused.

Boris was also busy arranging documents and untraceable bank accounts through his Chechen contacts. Alexi wanted genuine identities, not forgeries. To do this, however, required money—a lot of it—and to get the money, Alexei had to involve Janos. This gap in their security worried Boris and Alexi, but they had no choice. In the international arms business, cash was king, and Janos seemed to have plenty of it.

At last, the fake warheads were ready. They had been loaded into transport boxes with identical serial numbers—etched onto them by Boris—and security locks—also identical to those with the real warheads. On the night of August 10, Alexei and Boris stayed late. They waited until most of the security staff was eating a late dinner and there was no security in the area of his workroom. Using special heavy-duty forklifts, Boris and Alexei moved the fakes into the secured holding area where the real warheads were awaiting shipment the following day. They then loaded the real weapons into the three twenty-foot shipping containers, still sitting at the plant's loading dock. A few quick spot welds secured them to the floors of the containers. They then covered each with crates which they quickly labeled, 'machine tools', in three languages.

Alexei knew the crates would, at best, stand up to only a superficial inspection. But he also knew that only a miniscule number of shipping containers, out of millions crossing the globe on a daily basis, were ever inspected, and that most of those were in America or Western Europe. He also felt the risk of being found by a radiation detector was low; the massive steel shipping boxes would conceal the weapons from gamma ray detectors. Neutron detectors were another matter, but these were rare.

In the morning, trucks would pick up the shipping containers and begin a long journey back to Sweden via Tallinn, Estonia. A port official in Tallinn would, for the modest sum of ten-thousand euros, replace the container numbers and reroute them to a new destination. Anna, Boris, and Alexei would travel the next morning by air to St. Petersburg, and from there by train to Tallinn where they had reserved flights to Warsaw, and then on to Prague. They would miss their flights. And that would be the last trace of Alexei Kovolenko, Anna Voronina, or her brother Boris Voronin.

At the same time the trio of thieves departed St. Petersburg, Anatoly Grishkov, having programmed the cipher locks with his personal code, was supervising the loading of six warhead containers onto six trucks of the Northern Fleet for the short trip to the missile assembly facility.

CHAPTER 4

LT (JG) ZACH Miller was well into his fifth cup of coffee for the day. As action officer for the newly activated Project Bearpaw, his job was to sit in a cubicle at the sprawling National Security Agency complex at Ft. Meade and listen to intercepts from telephone conversations at the Northern Fleet Submarine Base at Gadzhievo. He would translate them, and write summaries for his commanding officer at the Submarine Warfare Operations Research Division, or SWORD, of the Nimitz Operational Intelligence Center. A Russian Studies major at Georgetown, he had received a direct commission as a Reserve Intelligence Officer. During a brief mobilization the previous year, his work had been so exceptional that his request for transfer to fulltime active duty was readily approved.

Bearpaw was not a typical Navy operation—normally it would have been run by the CIA. It was the CO of the Nimitz Center, however, who had been the only person in the vast American intelligence apparatus who saw enough potential in the proposal from British MI-6 to fund the required hardware.

The concept was simple enough. The British had an asset, Stella, well placed within the Russian base, who said he could tap into their secure landlines by placing a special receiver directly over the trunkline as it ran under a small warehouse. The instrument would be placed in an unobtrusive box screwed to the inside of a wall. It would then send a millisecond burst transmission of stored conversations once an hour to an NSA satellite in low earth orbit. All they needed was funding for the receiver/transmitter. The British, having cut their intelligence budgets to the bone and beyond, could simply not afford the costly gadget.

Both the CIA and the NSA were interested in receiving the product, but only Captain Jean Kraus, CO of the Nimitz Center, was willing to put up the funding. The Navy bought it so the Navy ran it.

As Miller listened to officers complain about their wives and praise their girlfriends in between calls about delays in delivery of provisions, he understood why other agencies had passed on Bearpaw. Nonetheless, this little project was good practice for the Russian linguist, and he worked diligently typing out summaries at dictation speed. As a new call began, Miller started a fresh paragraph.

Two sentences into the call, he gave up on the summary, loaded the entire conversation plus all other data not yet translated onto a secure portable drive, made the appropriate log entries, and called his commanding officer for an urgent meeting.

CHAPTER 5

LOCATED IN A huge federal campus of undistin-
guished office buildings just southeast of the nation's
capital, the National Maritime Intelligence Center is home
to the ONI and its major subordinate commands, including
the Nimitz Center. Miller had made near record time driving
down from Ft. Meade, and was now sitting with the director
of SWORD, CDR Denise Nguyen, in the Nimitz Center's
SCIF. Both officers snapped to attention when Captain
Kraus entered. She was accompanied by a civilian whom
Miller recognized as the center's senior Russian Navy specialist, though he couldn't think of his name at the moment.

Kraus, a cadaverous woman with pale pasty skin, salt
and pepper hair, and absolutely no patience for social pleas-
antries, nodded at Miller and even before she was seated
asked, "Okay, what have you got?"

"Briefly, Captain, we have multiple Bearpaw intercepts
within the base at Gadzhiyevo and from Gadzhiyevo to

Northern Fleet Headquarters at Severomorsk. Someone apparently stole six nuclear warheads from a reconditioning facility in Severomorsk. Fake warheads were shipped up to Gadzhievo for loading onto their new Liner missiles. There was one call to the head of the GRU office at Northern Fleet Headquarters asking for a Colonel Kepinsky to meet with Admiral Grishkov at the First Light Machinery Maintenance Factory, that's the warhead reconditioning facility. So far no calls to the FSB or the SVR. I brought the original product with me for review."

Captain Kraus tented her fingers and thought for a moment. "Interesting that they seem to be bypassing the FSB. Give the originals to Mr. Fletcher," she jerked a thumb towards the civilian. "Jack, I'll need translated transcripts and your analysis by the end of the day."

Jack Fletcher, a retired naval intelligence officer, knew the day would be ending late, very late. "I'll get right on it, Captain. How do you want to follow up on this?"

"Lt Miller, get back up to Ft. Meade. I want you to monitor what comes in overnight and be back here at 0800 tomorrow. I'll arrange a helo to bring you there and back; I don't want you wasting your time in rush hour traffic. She turned back to Fletcher and pointed at him with a long bony finger. "Jack, prepare a briefing, a page—two max—for me and the director on whatever we have regarding Gadzhiyevo and this facility in Severomorsk."

"Can I talk with the Russian Navy people at Farragut? They have a lot of data on the Russian ballistic missile submarine program."

Kraus shook her head. "Better keep this close hold for now, at least until we brief the director. Besides, we're interested more in where those warheads are going, not where they have been." She then turned her attention to CDR Nguyen. "Denise, let's see what else NSA can come up with. Track down someone who can tell us about communications out of Northern Fleet and in particular to the GRU. And see if there is anything out of the regional FSB offices. Just because we didn't hear them called doesn't mean they weren't."

"Captain, as far as I know, most of those communications are heavily encrypted with protocols we haven't broken. We get the unencrypted traffic from Bearpaw only because the Russians encrypt and decrypt beyond our intercept point. We can't decrypt conversations from the GRU."

"I just need to know if there's more chatter. We need to know who's getting involved in this. It's in their interest—and ours—to keep this off the radar. If there is a lot of traffic with Moscow the chance of a leak goes way up."

"I'm on it, Captain." The diminutive Commander scribbled rapidly on a yellow legal pad, paranoia about electronic intercepts having led to resurgence in the use of pen and paper.

Jean Kraus stood, and before her subordinates were out of their chairs, had left the SCIF. Miller could hear her shouting orders to her assistants as she hurried to her next meeting.

CHAPTER 6

AUGUST 19, 2017 1200Z (0800 EDT)
Office of Naval Intelligence, Suitland, MD

ADMIRAL JUSTIN COSTELLO, sharp-eyed, lean, and wearing perfectly-tailored summer whites, strode into the SCIF accompanied by a uniformed aide, and a civilian no one recognized. As he motioned everyone to be seated, he introduced Rick Suarez from the Nuclear Emergency Support Team—NEST, a division of the National Nuclear Security Administration.

"I hope nobody minds that I invited Rick. He's an old friend so when Jean let me in on the subject of the briefing I thought he might provide some useful insight. He studies the technical characteristics of foreign nukes." Of course, as a Rear Admiral and Director of the ONI, Costello could invite anyone he wanted to any meeting, but unlike many Washington insiders, he also understood that respect began at the top.

"Jean, can you get us started?"

Kraus nodded towards her subordinate. Costello listened intently as Lieutenant Miller, eyes red from lack of sleep, but clean shaven and wearing a fresh uniform, began by recapping what he'd discovered the day before. He added, "Overnight we learned they suspect the director of the reconditioning facility along with his girlfriend and her brother to be responsible for the theft. All three have disappeared. Most of the communication on this subject has been handled through Northern Fleet headquarters and we can only intercept calls to and from Gadzhiyevo. We do know there are orders to do complete systems tests on all warheads of the Third Submarine Flotilla, no matter what their origin."

"Did we know they were using reconditioned warheads on those Liners?" the admiral asked.

"I looked into that without letting on why I was asking," Kraus said. "Farragut has known about production problems with their new miniaturized warhead, but apparently this is the first confirmation as to the purpose of the plant in Severomorsk, or that they're actually mounting old warheads on their new missiles."

"Not really relevant to our current problem." Costello looked at his aide. "But make a note to look into their warhead production problems in more detail. There might be something more to it."

His aide nodded and scribbled a note.

CDR Denise Nguyen followed with a summary of new NSA communication data. "Sir," Nguyen said, "there's been a dramatic increase in message traffic between Northern Fleet and the GRU, but not the FSB or Moscow. All heavily encrypted. We were able to decrypt some traffic between

GRU and the border police at St. Petersburg asking about that factory manager. Apparently this Alexi Kovolenko, his girlfriend Anna Voronina, and her brother Boris all arrived in St. Petersburg on a commercial flight from Murmansk on August 11. They stayed the night and the following day took a train to Tallinn where immigration notes their arrival. As of last night, there is no further information on their whereabouts."

"They're gone now, probably under new names," Costello said. "Monitor their search as best you can. And work with our friends from Langley. They're good at finding people who don't want to be found. It would be in our interest to find these people before the Russians do. Any word on movement of the warheads?"

"The theory in Gadzhiyevo is that they were sent out in three twenty-foot shipping containers. They apparently had the container numbers on file so we were able to track them. They arrived by truck at the port in Tallinn on August 15. Records show they were then loaded on a small container ship bound for Sweden on the 17th, cargo listed as machine parts."

"And what are the chances that the containers with the weapons still carry their original identifiers?" growled Costello.

"Pretty small, sir," replied Nguyen. "That would require people who have been very smart up to now getting very stupid."

"Exactly. But we better check it out. When is that ship due to arrive?"

CDR Nguyen consulted her notes. "Tomorrow, Admiral."

"I know Nils Jensen, the Swedish Naval Intelligence Chief, pretty well. I'll get him to check out those containers." Costello looked down at his notes. "I'm going to arrange a meeting this afternoon with the National Security Advisor, and I'm sure he will want both CIA and Homeland Security represented. The Director of National Intelligence, as you know, is up at Walter Reed with a bad gall bladder, so we better take this directly to the top."

"Sir," Miller said. "Forgive me, but...if the containers do turn out empty, what do we do next?"

Costello closed his notebook. "That, Lieutenant, is what we're trying to figure out. Good morning."

CHAPTER 7

NATIONAL SECURITY ADVISOR Richardson 'Sonny' Baker was not a happy man. Only one month on the job and already beset by multiple crises. But hell, maybe constant crises were the job. He was now about to meet with the Directors of ONI, CIA and Homeland Security about the latest threat.

And yet the media acted as if he'd taken this plum job away from the disgraced Samuel Morten. They knew damn well that Morten had earned his dismissal. A year and a half ago when Iran detonated its first small nuclear bomb, Morten, a think-tank academic, had called for an immediate and massive U.S. attack to eliminate the Iranian threat once and for all. He became a senior strategist for the then virtually unknown presidential candidate Brendan Wallace, who rode fear of Iranian nukes all the way to the White House. When Wallace tapped Morten to be his National Security Advisor, the new administration had to deliver.

In late February, the United States launched the largest air campaign since the 2003 attack on Saddam Hussein. Cruise missiles followed by B-2 stealth bombers wreaked havoc with the Iranian air defense system. This was followed by bombing of the nuclear installations, and anything even remotely connected to them, by B-1B Lancers. These strikes included the 30,000 pound massive ordnance penetrator which, after multiple hits, destroyed even the deepest facilities. The air campaign also included destruction of as much of the large Iranian stockpile of ballistic missiles as the strike planners could find.

Morten and Wallace confidently predicted the Iranian government would fall, and be replaced by one eager to restore normal relations with the outside world. But that was before dissidents in the majority Shia island nation of Bahrain staged a coup against their Sunni rulers. Aided by Iranian agents already in place, they then 'invited' Iran to help secure their revolution. The Iranians obliged by landing more than a thousand of their Quds Force special operations troops—who were conveniently waiting on a ship in the harbor. It took three months for the Bahraini National Guard, assisted by Saudi troops, and a regiment of U.S Marines, to dislodge all the Quds operators and to get the government back under control. More than two thousand Bahraini citizens were killed, and an American destroyer in port at the time of the coup was heavily damaged by hits from multiple RPGs. The Marine regiment remained in place to protect the U.S. 5th Fleet Headquarters and anchorage.

Even worse for American prestige, on the third day of the air campaign, the Iranian Kilo class submarine *Tareq* penetrated the protective screen around the three American carriers operating in the Gulf of Oman, and put two torpedoes into the USS *Ronald Reagan* before being sunk. Though not at risk of sinking, the huge carrier was put out of action, spent three months in Singapore undergoing temporary repairs, and was now in San Diego where estimates were that it would take at least a year to put her back at sea. The Iranians crowed over their victory; "Allah has blessed our holy warriors" read the signs—in English—held aloft for the TV cameras in Teheran. The press had, of course, dwelled on the subject with story after story asking whether the age of the carrier was over and whether they were 'sitting ducks.'

Winston Churchill, when Prime Minister, reacted with some equanimity to the loss of the HMS *Repulse* and HMS *Prince of Wales* off Singapore. Not so Brendan Wallace. The CNO was a holdover from the previous administration and was forced to resign. His replacement, an old friend of the President, understood that destroying Iran's remaining submarines was his top priority, and that each such destruction was to be accompanied by maximum publicity.

Both Bahrain and the *Reagan* were bad, but were ultimately tolerable prices to pay for the successful elimination of the Iranian nuclear threat. But it was what happened a few weeks after the bombings that changed everything.

On March 27, a Liberian-flagged, Dutch-owned tanker was seriously damaged by a mine in the Strait of Hormuz. A second incident the following day involving an American-owned vessel resulted in a large spill of crude oil. Three days after that, small boats operated by the Iranian Revolutionary

Guard boarded a small Greek general cargo vessel bound for Oman. They killed the crew and sank the ship with explosives. Teheran announced that the Gulf was now closed to all shipping.

Almost immediately, the U.S began round-the-clock bombing of Iranian Naval facilities; if it could float, it was sunk. There were raids by Special Forces on Revolutionary Guard facilities along the Gulf and at this point even reluctant European allies began to send a few ships, mine sweepers in particular. Saudi Arabia, in a vote of no confidence, accelerated construction of an oil pipeline across the desert, through western Yemen and down to the Gulf of Aden where it could move its oil far away from the troublesome Iranians.

On April 16, in an operation put together with phenomenal speed, a brigade combat team from the 82nd Airborne Division was flown non-stop from Ft. Bragg using most of the available C-5 and C-17 transport aircraft, and then parachuted onto the western end of Qeshm Island which controlled the northern side of the Strait of Hormuz. At the same time, an amphibious assault—the first since the Korean War—landed the Fifth Marine Regiment on the middle of the island. The island's garrison was overwhelmed, the secret underground submarine facility was seized, and three *Ghadir-Nahang* class submarines destroyed.

Secretary of Defense William Jackson, another holdover from the previous administration, had been largely cut out of the planning for this operation after he voiced opposition directly to the President. When his counsel was ignored, he resigned. There was now no SECDEF, Wallace's choice for a replacement being mired in a confirmation battle. Morten, and now Sonny Baker, essentially served the strategic functions of the SECDEF pending Senate approval of Jackson's replacement.

On Qeshm, engineers quickly constructed an expeditionary airfield and a floating pier to unload ships. Within a week, almost sixteen thousand troops, with artillery, attack helicopters, and two battalions of Stryker armored vehicles were in place within sight of the Iranian coast.

The Iranians were not happy. Thousands of troops poured into the nearby port city of Bandar Abbas, and many were infiltrated onto the island in small boats. The result was that American forces were engaged in persistent daily combat. Continuous artillery fire was rained onto U.S positions, dozens of Iran's remaining ballistic missiles targeted the airfield and port, and Iran sent scores of civilians living on the island towards the invaders as suicide bombers. The mullahs also targeted the Sunni states in the Gulf with occasional longer-range missiles landing in Dubai, Oman, and the Saudi oil terminals. Newly-upgraded American Patriot and ship-based Aegis anti-ballistic missiles stopped the majority of these weapons, but at a cost of millions of dollars per shot.

U.S. casualties were already mounting even before the so-called 'Qeshm Massacre'. Unable to make any headway against the U.S. conventional forces, the Iranians infiltrated increasing numbers of their Quds force with the goal not of taking back the island, but of simply killing as many Americans as possible. A force of eighty Quds fighters infiltrated deep into the rear area, and attacked an Army field hospital. Due to scrupulous adherence to the laws of war, the American commanders had only provided a platoon of light infantry for security, and the medical personnel were minimally armed. Attacking with grenades and automatic weapons, the Iranians focused on the wounded and the medical personnel. When finally cornered by Marines who arrived after twenty minutes to join the battle, the Quds men then became suicide bombers. When it was over, one-hundred-eighty Americans, including eighty-nine wounded and fifty-one medical personnel, were dead, along with all the Iranians.

The fury of Brendan Wallace and the American people was unlike anything seen since 9/11 or possibly Pearl Harbor. A congressional resolution to withdraw from the Geneva Accords was passed on a near unanimous voice vote, and the President signed it within the hour. He then announced that the U.S. would not attack the medical personnel of other nations, but from then on our personnel would be fully armed like regular soldiers and be regarded as regular combatants. Unlimited combat troops could be attached to medical, supply, or engineering units. Hospital ships would be armed and henceforth travel with the fleet. By Presidential order the distinction between line and staff officers was erased.

A twenty-mile exclusion zone around the island was declared, an area which included well over a hundred thousand civilians, most of them on the mainland. When Iran refused to evacuate civilians, and indeed began to move their forces into civilian areas, American aircraft began to bomb Iranian artillery positions and vehicles, without restriction.

Over the succeeding six weeks Bandar Abbas and most of the civilian areas on Qeshm itself were reduced to rubble with an unknown, but huge, number of casualties. Intelligence intercepts revealed total Iranian military losses at more than sixteen thousand killed and about three times that number wounded. Civilian losses were even larger. At the same time U.S. losses of twenty-six hundred killed and almost nine thousand wounded were horrifying the public.

By early summer Qeshm was relatively secure. Almost all the surviving civilians had finally been driven off the island, which was now held by the entire First Marine Division and the Army 4th Infantry Division. Marine air and logistic requirements meant that the remainder of the First Marine Expeditionary Force, the 1 MEF, was spread between Qeshm, Bahrain, and ships underway in the Gulf. There were also substantial troop commitments to the nervous Gulf States. Virtually the entire Iranian port infrastructure had been destroyed, and American air power was now starting to focus on Iran's oil production. Though embargoed by sea, both their Shia neighbors in Iraq and their Russian neighbors to the north were providing food, fuel, and most important—weapons. The American President was demanding removal of the Islamic Government, a demand to which Iran would not even respond.

With Iranian oil exports reduced to near zero and production from the other Gulf States also down, oil prices—despite increased US fracking production—soared to well over a hundred dollars a barrel. U.S relations with China had also fallen apart. China, which imported almost 10% of its oil from Iran, had stated publically that they regarded the bombing of Iran's ports and oil infrastructure as 'an attack on China's vital interests.' India was also hostile, but its criticism was muted by oil production from her new oil platforms in the Andaman Sea, a joint project with Burma, and by recent Iranian support for Pakistani acts of terrorism.

By July, public concern over cost and casualties, plus international outrage over civilian deaths and environmental damage, was putting tremendous pressure on the President. On July 3, North Korea's mercurial Kim Jong-un launched several artillery bombardments along the DMZ, one of which killed a dozen civilians near Seoul. He announced that resumption of hostilities was imminent. Though most observers felt this was just more North Korean bluster, President Wallace was forced to dispatch a regiment of Marines, two Army armored brigades, and an Air Force fighter wing of the new F-35s to South Korea, both as a show of support and to make clear to other potential trouble-makers that America could still respond when necessary.

Stories with titles like "America Under Siege" became staples on the evening news. To placate his critics and in hopes of putting a floor under his plummeting approval numbers, the President asked National Security Advisor Samuel Morten, architect of the Qeshm Island operation, to resign. In his place, he appointed his old friend and classmate at The Citadel, Sonny Baker, to try to clean up the mess.

So, here they were. Baker was sensible enough to realize

the Iranians could not be bombed into cooperation. He recommended scaling back on the air campaign. That helped with both the allies and with the public. Though not formally acknowledging the connection, Iran responded by stopping their missile attacks on Qeshm and their Gulf neighbors. This was probably because they were running out of missiles and didn't want to throw any more at the increasingly effective missile defense network, but Baker understood it to be a vital first step.

And, now what?

Richardson Baker along with his own Chief of Staff and a couple of specialists from the NSC entered the secure West Wing conference room where the Directors of ONI, CIA and Homeland Security, along with a small group of subordinates, stood to give him news that certainly would not be good. Aware that the Director of National Intelligence was hospitalized, Baker had decided to take the lead on this new problem rather than letting the gathered intelligence chiefs jockey for position.

Baker laid his well-manicured hands flat on the table. "Okay Justin, lay it out for me."

Admiral Costello began by describing the telephone intercepts from Gadzhiyevo and increased message traffic between Northern Fleet headquarters and the GRU.

Baker interrupted, "You're convinced this is real, not some Russian deception?"

"They would have to know about Bearpaw, and there is no suggestion that they do. Agent Stella has confirmed that the intercept instrument is well concealed and that, aside from himself, nobody has even been into the building in weeks. Besides what do they gain by convincing us they've got loose nukes?"

"Off the top of my head?" Baker replied. "The Russians have shipped those warheads to the Iranians and are using this deception as cover. Alex, what's your take?"

Alexander Clarkson, Director of the CIA, turned in his chair to look directly at Baker. Another holdover from the previous administration, Clarkson was the intensely ambitious, Princeton-educated scion of a New York banking family, all qualities Baker normally despised, but Clarkson had cleaned out a lot of deadwood at Langley and put energetic young officers into key positions. Clarkson got results, and that Baker could live with.

"I have to agree with ONI," Clarkson said. We have nothing to suggest Bearpaw's been compromised. Also, voice stress analysis shows that the officers involved, particularly Admiral Grishkov and his nephew Captain Grishkov, are manifesting high levels of genuine stress—too high to fake. I think those nukes really are on the lam."

"Right then. We consider this a real theft of nuclear weapons unless there's some kind of new evidence that suggests it isn't. How easy will it be for anyone to use these things?"

The ONI Director introduced Rick Suarez from NEST who pulled a page of notes from a thin folder. "We know the Russians have an advanced PAL—permissive action link—that controls arming of the weapon. Typically, sensors in the warhead must detect acceleration appropriate to launch, temperature consistent with re-entry, and the internal clock will require timing of these events to be as expected in order to arm and to detonate. Also, the warhead must receive the authorized launch code before it can respond to the sensor inputs. The Russians enter the launch codes into the warheads at the same time they enter the other PAL parameters. Worst case, the buyers have a PAL encoder and can set these parameters to whatever they want. Zero altitude and zero acceleration, for example. We know from other sources that the encoders are not located at the weapon maintenance facilities, but we have to assume that this Kovolenko guy got hold of one."

Baker doodled on a yellow legal pad and nodded slightly as he took in the worst case. "Could these warheads be mounted on a different missile than the one they were designed for?"

"Easily. The Russians are actually doing that in mounting them on the Liner. You'd need some modifications to the docking ring, but nothing a decent machine shop couldn't handle. The warhead is less than two meters long so it would fit under the fairing of most intermediate and long range missile systems. At about three hundred kilos it's also well within the lift capacity of any ballistic missile. I'm no expert, but I recall that the Iranians have been using an electrical system very similar to the Russians' on their ballistic weapons so that would be no problem. All they would need then is a PAL encoder. I assume you're thinking of the Iranians?"

"That's exactly what I'm thinking." Baker paused for a moment and added, "What about the North Koreans?"

"I don't think we have much by way of technical data about their missile systems, but we do know they have purchased missile technology from Iran. CIA probably has information I'm not aware of."

"We don't know shit," the CIA man said. Everyone waited for him to say more, but apparently, that was it.

"If they don't have a PAL encoder," Suarez continued, "they'll have to disassemble the warhead. Our weapons have safeguards that disable all the electronic components and release the tritium gas if there is even the slightest attempt to breach the system. The tritium gives a significant yield boost to the fission primary. We think the Russians have a similar system in this particular warhead. That's one of the reasons they have to replace all the electronic parts; even they can't open their own warhead without deactivating it. They probably have a way to preserve the tritium, but everything else is fried. We know this warhead uses a hollow ovoid, or egg shaped, pit—the plutonium core—surrounded by explosives that are detonated at each end. This gives a low yield, but is extremely simple and reliable compared to the old multi-point detonation with a dozen or more detonators that must be activated within a few microseconds of each other. This simple design relies on tritium to boost the yield. Even without tritium, though, it would be fairly easy to detonate with low yield, maybe a few kilotons."

"What I'm hearing then," Baker said, "is that with this PAL gadget they could have a fully-functional ballistic missile warhead, but even without it they can still put together a low yield atomic bomb. Am I getting this right?"

"That's about it."

"Well shit!" The National Security Advisor sat back in his chair and looked down at the conference table for a moment. He then looked at a tall blond in the uniform of an Air Force Major. Above her right pocket was a nametag which read National Security Staff, Major Sherman, Nuclear Policy Group. "Jennifer, what's your take on this? Can they activate those weapons?"

Though one of the most junior people in the room the young major seemed perfectly comfortable addressing the National Security Advisor. "Sir, the Russians have been very secretive about the upgrades to this warhead. For sure, anyone with a PAL encoder can utilize the weapon, but I'm not so sure about the second scenario. We got one report that hinted at changes in their latest upgrade. They can probably deactivate the security features with a PAL encoder when the warhead is removed from the missile. This makes sense; some of those components are durable and don't need replacement, but are expensive to manufacture. We also suspect a feature that causes a single point detonation if the security system detects tampering. This would completely destroy the weapon and scatter the plutonium in a way making it unrecoverable. We looked at a similar system, but computer simulations showed that twenty percent of the time there would be a fission reaction yielding up to a few hundred pounds of TNT equivalent."

"So maybe they can make it work and maybe they would blow themselves up trying. I like the sounds of that."

"No way to know. It is possible. I'll investigate this further and send any follow-up information," added the Major.

"Okay, fine." Baker, nodded at the Major to be seated. "What about finding these things?"

Rick Suarez answered first. "Depends on how well shielded they are. Admiral," he turned to Justin Costello, "do we have any information on the transport boxes?"

The ONI director turned around and looked at Captain Jean Kraus, who was standing behind him along the wall. She pulled a small stack of notes from a portfolio, found what she was looking for and replied, "Stella reports they're stainless steel, about five centimeters thick, with an additional centimeter of lead as a liner. The warhead sits in molded high density foam."

Suarez thought for a moment. "We know these are plutonium warheads which are much easier to detect than highly enriched uranium. Each warhead should put out just over half a billion fairly hard gamma rays, and about half a million neutrons a second. The cases you describe would provide good gamma shielding, but not so much for neutrons."

Baker didn't need to get lost in thickets of technical jargon. "Meaning?"

"Meaning to detect these things from any distance we would need neutron detectors, and hope they didn't add neutron shielding outside the cases. Neutron detectors are common in America and Western Europe, but not so many in Eastern Europe. Most of the screening detectors at ports and other points of entry are gamma based, even in the U.S. To find them we need to know fairly specifically where to look and to concentrate neutron detectors in a few locations."

"Major?" Baker looked at the young Air Force officer.

"I think Mr. Suarez is right. Not likely that routine screening procedures will turn up the warheads. We need to know where to look."

Sonny Baker took a deep breath and looked over his notes. The picture was filling in, and it was grim. "Jim, assuming

CIA is correct that the warheads last known location was Tallinn, could they reach Iran from there?"

Colonel Jim Galloway was one Baker's Iran experts. With a background in both special operations and intelligence, he had been tracking movement of arms into Iran. "We've pretty well shut down sea transport into Iran. A few smugglers get across the gulf, but that's small stuff. They'd never move something this valuable that way. Best bet would be ship to Karachi in Pakistan and then by truck to Iran. I doubt the Pakistani government, such as it is, would participate, but there are plenty of terrorist, dissident, and just plain old criminal groups who would. Another possibility is movement across Turkey—we know the Kurds have cooperated in small-time arms smuggling. The Iranians might be desperate enough to cut a deal with the Kurds for more autonomy if it meant getting hold of half a dozen nuclear warheads."

Baker nodded and scribbled more notes. "Alex, set up whatever radiation detectors you need to monitor shipping through the Bosporus and at Karachi. I know you have assets in both places. Take whoever and whatever you need from whatever agency has them. The first person who gives any pushback is on the street. Period. Any further problem and their next stop is Guantanamo. We cannot fuck around with this."

"Mr. Suarez, I want you to survey the port at Tallinn to be sure those warheads aren't still there. My office will arrange a direct flight from Andrews. How soon can you leave?"

"I can get the equipment I need from our D.C. office and be ready in an hour."

"Do it. Admiral, contact your opposite number in Sweden. See if they can check out those containers when they arrive or find them if they already have. Tell them as little as possible."

"I've already been in touch with their Chief of Naval Intelligence. The Swedes take this kind of thing very seriously. They'll be all over it, and will do it quietly."

"Good work, Justin. Other thoughts?"

"Two, actually," added Clarkson from CIA. "First, it's probable these weapons are not destined for the U.S. as their first stop. They need some kind of work to activate them. Also, if we are the target they would likely separate them. Right now it sounds like they are traveling in three sets of two. We naturally want Homeland Security to ramp up surveillance at East coast ports, but our main focus should still be Europe and the Middle East."

"And your second thought?"

"We should try to get detectors on or near the Suez Canal. That's an even more likely a transit point than the Bosporus. Justin, what can the Navy do? Our Egyptian assets have been seriously degraded since Sisi."

Justin Costello thought for a moment. "I'll get back to you later this afternoon."

"All right, then." Richardson Baker rose. "I'll brief the President in an hour. We'll meet at 1300 tomorrow in the Situation Room. I'll expect answers and you can expect the President to be in attendance."

CHAPTER 8

AUGUST 19, 2017 2100Z (1700 EDT)
The White House

PRESIDENT BRENDAN WALLACE was sitting behind his desk in the Oval Office, enjoying a few moments of privacy after meeting with a senate delegation about overhauling Social Security, a subject fairly low on Wallace's priority list. As a former Army intelligence officer and senior policy analyst at Homeland Security, he had made security his signature issue during the two terms he served in the House of Representatives. By sidestepping the domestic wars over economic policy, Wallace had become of the very few Washington insiders who was respected by both parties. Viewed as a benign, non-controversial policy wonk, Wallace had been persuaded by several like-minded and well-heeled backers to enter the Presidential race, not so much to win, but to get security issues back onto the front page.

The Iranian bomb, something he'd been warning about, had electrified the world. Suddenly the young Congressman from South Carolina was being compared to Churchill and his warnings about Nazi Germany. The addition of Samuel Morten—shrewd, articulate and aggressive—to his campaign staff had provided the academic polish and prestige Wallace himself had lacked.

Then the press revealed the frontrunner had paid for college on a Navy ROTC scholarship, and later faked a knee injury to avoid service. This scandal, coming within weeks of a nuclear Iran, had ended his campaign almost overnight. Even Wallace had to admit this was pure luck.

Finally, the economy had several quarters of unexpected growth and reduced unemployment. The resulting increase in tax revenues had cut into both the federal deficit and the purely economic campaigns of his remaining opponents. In the end, Wallace gained the White House by a comfortable margin of just over a hundred electoral votes.

Then came the *Reagan* and Qeshm Island.

Wallace had studied American involvement in Viet Nam, Somalia, Iraq, and Afghanistan and thought he had learned all their lessons. Like other men who had occupied the Oval Office though, he understood too late that he had not. There was still time to mitigate the damage, to get American troops out while keeping the Strait of Hormuz open. And to do it without the threat of a nuclear Iran—that at least, he had accomplished.

He was interrupted by a sharp rap on the door. "Good time Mr. President?"

"Not particularly, but come on in."

Karen Hiller, his Chief of Staff, came through from her adjacent office. A former South Carolina basketball player, Hiller stood a full six feet tall, but she never avoided heels.

She had been intimidating Washington power brokers with more than her height ever since she graduated from Georgetown Law and began working for the Senate Select Committee on Intelligence. Later, as Counsel for the Minority Leader she had evolved into one of Washington's premier deal makers. She was ruthless, ambitious, dedicated, and in love with Brendan Wallace.

"Sonny Baker wants a few minutes, Mr. President."

"About?"

"He called it national security immediate, but didn't elaborate. You know how he loves his jargon."

Brendan Wallace chuckled. He knew that Hiller's nickname among the staff of the West Wing was 'Flak Jacket' for the way she aggressively protected the President from bad news. "I better see him, jargon or not he rarely exaggerates. Show him in. And you better sit in too."

"Yes, sir." With a swish of her shoulder length black hair she turned, opened the door, and motioned towards Baker who was waiting in the Presidential secretary's office.

The President took a seat in a wing-back chair while Baker and Hiller shared a large sofa across the low coffee table. Wallace noticed his old friend looked tired, eyes a bit red, shoulders down. Even his signature bowtie was starting to droop. "How bad is it, Sonny?"

"Pretty bad, sir." Over the next ten minutes, Baker summarized the new crisis.

"Jesus Christ, Sonny. Am I hearing that the Iranians have just bought six top-of-the-line Russian nuclear warheads?"

"We don't know that, Mr. President. Iran is, of course, a likely suspect, but for now we're spreading a broad net."

"Add North Korea to that net. I want the Navy to monitor shipping headed for North Korean ports. If there is strong reason to believe those warheads are aboard, I'll authorize an intercept in international waters."

"Yes, sir. I'll talk with Admiral Greene at PACFLEET. We're setting up monitoring around the Suez Canal so that would give us a heads up."

"Sure, unless they go around the Horn."

"Right. ONI can monitor the movement of all ships out of Europe going that route. Fortunately there aren't too many. Anything else Mr. President? We have a full briefing laid on for tomorrow. I'll get Karen the details."

Before Wallace could reply, Karen Hiller looked sharply at Sonny Baker. "Sonny, in future I'd appreciate it if anything of this magnitude was brought to my attention immediately."

The President looked directly at his Chief of Staff. "Karen, I appreciate your desire to stay in front of every issue, but this is national security immediate and Sonny was right to come straight to me."

"Of course, Mr. President."

Karen Hiller and Richardson Baker left the oval office together, trading icy stares. Hiller said a few words to the National Security Advisor, but they were lost in the hum of the air conditioning.

The President walked back around the Resolute Desk, an 1880 gift from Queen Victoria, and resumed reviewing his notes. His mind, however, was not on Social Security, but rather on the whereabouts of six thermonuclear warheads.

And more specifically, what to do when he found them.

CHAPTER 9

THE MV *MILOS Tethys*, 4200 tons and owned by Theologides Shipping of Piraeus, was tied up alongside the wharf and going nowhere. Scheduled to leave the day before with a load of parts for agricultural equipment, five tons of canned olives, fifty pallets of bottled mineral water, and six shipping containers, she was now waiting for a replacement oil pump for her aging diesel engine.

Nikos Antoniou, master of the *Milos Tethys*, and son-in-law of Theologides, was sitting in the small harbormaster's office. Like all such offices worldwide, the room smelled of cigarettes, stale coffee, and a hint of diesel fuel and lubricating oil. The harbormaster, an Albanian known to Nikos only as 'Fish', was an obese man with a huge drooping moustache and breath that reeked of sardines and tobacco. He was asking for an additional daily dockage fee for the time the *Milos Tethys* would use its berth awaiting repairs.

"That is not possible," Nikos said. "Mr. Theologides' contract calls for a single fixed cost regardless of stay."

"So I am to lose money while your worthless ship just sits there?"

"I did not write the contract. And I doubt Mr. Theologides would agree to pay more. He is not a charitable man."

"Can I at least load your cargo and free space on the wharf?"

"Sadly, no," replied Nikos. "Mr. Theologides contract also calls for delivery within a certain period after loading. If we load now, before repairs are completed, it could expose Mr. Theologides to penalties. Again, to this he cannot agree."

"Perhaps I will contact your Mr. Theologides directly."

"Be my guest. I'm sure you will be referred to his maritime attorneys."

"The Port of Zadar has attorneys too," replied Fish. "They even have an office in Piraeus."

"Theologides Shipping employs a firm in London."

At this, the harbor master spat out the open window. It was a particularly expressive gesture.

"Again," Nikos said, "I am sorry for your additional costs, and for bringing you out here on a Sunday. But perhaps I can relieve you of at least some of your burden."

The older man raised his eyebrows slightly and smiled. "I am listening."

Nikos laid five fifty-euro notes on the desk. It was where the conversation had been heading from the beginning.

The harbormaster scooped them up. "Yes, that would be a great help. Indeed, I will personally guarantee that the best local diesel mechanic will be immediately available when the part arrives."

They shook hands, and the skipper of the MV *Milos Tethys* left the grimy office and walked back along the wharf towards his ship. As he did so, he passed six twenty-foot standard shipping containers, three of which had originated in Tallinn, but due to an error enroute had been relabeled as originating in Lodz, Poland. Indeed, no record—paper or computer—now existed which showed their whereabouts prior to being loaded onto a railroad flatcar in Lodz. Their destination, he knew, would require a transit of the Suez Canal, something Theologides' ships did infrequently in the era of Somali piracy. Most of those trips involved shipping containers which came to Theologides via freight forwarding agents with no address, only satellite telephone numbers, and whose payments were usually delivered to Piraeus by anonymous couriers bearing cash. It would not be unusual for Theologides Shipping, notorious for careless record keeping, to misplace all records involving those containers.

CHAPTER 10

THE DIRECTORS OF ONI, CIA, and Homeland Security were seated on one side of the long conference table, chatting amiably. Sonny Baker sat less amiably across from them next to Karen Hiller, with whom he traded short, clipped sentences. At the far end of the table was the Chairman of the Joint Chiefs, General Theodore Roosevelt Lennox, accompanied by several very senior officers. Politically astute, but operationally inexperienced, Lennox succeeded to his job at the same time Sonny Baker had succeeded to his. Standing behind each of the principals, along the wall, aides huddled to review updates and possible questions.

Hiller would normally have come in with the President, but he'd sent her ahead largely as a way of putting her and Baker on an equal footing, at least for the duration of this crisis. As the President entered, everyone stood until he took his seat at the head of the table. After a few perfunctory remarks about the potential seriousness of this new situation, he asked Baker to begin.

Baker felt more confident and rested than he had the day before in the Oval Office. "Mr. President, let me have Admiral Costello start with an update from Sweden."

Costello stood, looked briefly at the President and began. "Yesterday, members of the Swedish Coast Guard inspected the suspect containers at the port facility in Gothenburg. Each was emitting a significant amount of gamma rays, so they were removed by truck to a secure military warehouse. They found each had a patch of new paint concealed inside one of the lower lift brackets. The paint contained a small amount of cesium 137, a highly radioactive substance with several industrial uses. The amount of radiation was fairly small, not really dangerous except to someone standing right next to it for hours, but more than enough to give a strong reading on radiation detectors. The containers themselves were, as the manifests stated, filled with machine parts, mostly old rusted junk."

"What would be the purpose of this?" Wallace asked.

"I was asking myself the same question, Mr. President, until I heard back from Rick Suarez, a nuclear threat expert from one of the NEST teams, who was sent to inspect the port at Tallinn. He found three more containers painted exactly the same way. Those containers were empty. I believe, sir, that the people responsible for the theft of the warheads have created a shell game. I wouldn't be surprised if more of these containers begin turning up throughout Northern Europe."

The President leaned back in his chair and shook his head slightly. "So we know where the warheads aren't. Any progress on where they are?"

"Not yet, sir. CIA has radiation detectors in place on the Bosporus, and we are flying units to multiple ships operating south of the Suez Canal and along the Eastern and Western approaches to North Korea. We've quietly contacted the security services of all nations with ports along the Atlantic or Mediterranean to be aware of a possible radiation threat. We have not mentioned the warheads specifically."

"Good. We don't need to get people too excited yet. General, what do we have in place to recover these weapons when we locate them?"

The Chairman rose to address the Commander in Chief. "Mr. President, there are SEAL teams on two amphibious ships in the Arabian Sea. They can be in position to assault any ship within a few hours. PACCOM is making similar arrangements for the Korean Peninsula. In that case, the plan is to keep them on alert at Osan Air Base. A possible movement via Turkey presents more of a problem. The Turks are a bit sensitive about foreign ground troops there and have been walking a very fine line between us and the Iranians. If we thought those weapons were in Turkey or their territorial waters, they'd probably allow us to act—with Turkish participation, of course. To cover that possibility, we've moved the amphibious ship *San Antonio*, with two-hundred-eighty Marines embarked, along with the destroyer *Bainbridge* from the Eastern Med up towards the Bosporus. They should be in the Black Sea in two days."

"Good, General, thank you. Sonny, how much of a shit storm will we face if we board a ship in international waters?"

"Not much, Mr. President, so long as the nukes really are aboard. If we're wrong, then we have to announce the reason for the boarding, and whoever really has the nukes will know that we know."

"Then we better be right." The President pointed back at the Chairman of the Joint Chiefs. "Ted, what if these things are going to a country other than Iran or North Korea—not some terrorist group, but someone with a real army to defend them?"

The Chairman stood again and looked directly at the President. "Sir, there are a huge number of possibilities. In some cases, we could do an amphibious raid, but in others it would require a full-scale invasion of a now nuclear-armed nation. Right now we don't have enough information to begin that kind of planning."

"Yeah, well start planning anyway. If these weapons can't be intercepted at sea and end up in say, North Korea, then we're screwed. We can't mount a major invasion, and we'll have to deal with it another way. If it isn't Iran, which is still my best bet, then it's probably some half-assed state like Somalia or even one of the Gulf States; they all seem mighty nervous these days. So put together a proposal for an amphibious operation somewhere between the Horn of Africa and the Persian Gulf."

"Yes, Mr. President."

The President peppered his intelligence chiefs with additional questions about locating the Russian fugitives and received frustratingly vague responses. He was likewise unhappy with Harvey Lyon from Homeland Security, who told him that screening every incoming shipping container was physically impossible. His best recommendation was putting neutron detectors at the exits to the ports, a location through which most containers would pass. It would, he admitted, take months to acquire and deploy enough advanced neutron detectors and doing so would at some point come to the attention of the press.

"We'll deal with that when it happens. Karen, work with the Press Secretary's office to prepare for any questions."

"On it, Mr. President," said Hiller who was tapping furiously on a small, super-secure tablet.

Without warning, Wallace rose and announced that the briefing was over. As he headed for the door, he motioned to Sonny Baker who stepped forward and walked out with the President.

"Call me twenty-four hours a day if anything develops," Wallace said, "and I mean anything. I know Karen's touchy about access, but Sonny, this is potentially the biggest crisis of my, or anyone's administration. We're not going to play politics with it."

CHAPTER 11

AUGUST 28, 2017 1145Z (1245 BST)
The Orange Public House, Pimlico Road, London

IT HAD BEEN a week of little news. Finally, the break, when it came, came in London.

Maxim Korshkin was seated at his usual table at his usual Pimlico Road restaurant and was enjoying his usual lunch of mussels steamed in Guinness, honey, and black pepper accompanied by a truly superb pinot grigio. Korshkin doubted there was another man in all of London enjoying life at that moment more than he.

Maxim Korshkin was, as they say, living the dream. A mid-level logistics officer in the old Soviet Army, Korshkin faced, in 1991, decades of downward spiral in the new Russia before he decided to leave the motherland and to take with him compact discs loaded with every technical manual, parts list, supplier, warehouse location, and design specification of every weapons system in the Russian inventory. He then set himself up in London, a city which offered every possible advantage to a man dealing in arms—or more specifically arms-related information.

His first, and most lucrative, sale was to Saddam Hussein's Iraq. His army decimated by the American-led Gulf War, Saddam needed to restore his military power at any cost. With his Soviet backers gone and the new Russia in chaos, Korshkin was able to offer technical information, arrange contacts for replacement parts, and even provide recently-unemployed Russian technical experts. The proceeds of that transaction went to the purchase of several flats in the Chelsea area of London, one of which he occupied and two he rented. Though income from his arms deals waned, Korshkin's real estate skills allowed him to accumulate holdings worth millions of pounds. Nonetheless, he still enjoyed the cachet of being an international arms dealer and maintained his contacts. If nothing else, arms dealers—even short pudgy ones—seemed to attract a more exciting class of attractive young women than landlords.

There was just one problem.

"Maxim, so good to see you."

Commander Neville Cathcart of the Counter Terrorism Command, formerly known as Special Branch, sat down across from him. He was the problem. Twenty years ago Cathcart had patiently explained that arms deals with Saddam simply wouldn't do. His choice was simple, cooperate or come to a very bad end. From that moment on Korshkin had become an unwilling employee of the Counter Terrorism Command. As the years passed and Korshkin moved more and more from arms to real estate, he saw the annoying Cathcart less and less. This suited Korshkin very well, for every time he betrayed the name or location of some new group of smugglers, he risked having his throat cut or his car blown up—with him in it! But now, here he was.

"Commander," Korshkin said, "I heard you've been promoted."

"Yes. So I have." Cathcart, looking very smart in an impeccably-tailored Saville Row suit, ironically from the same tailor Korshkin used, signaled the waiter and ordered tea. "Maxim, I really am terribly busy so let me get right to it."

"A situation involving Russian nuclear warheads has come to our attention. It goes without saying that this is all very—and I mean very—confidential. Have you heard anything?"

Korshkin always thought very carefully before answering Cathcart. Sharing information could be dangerous, but so could withholding information, so he had to find just the right balance. "Several months ago a very...specialized dealer known as Janos contacted me. Are you familiar with him?"

"Only by name; operates somewhere in Eastern Europe. That's about all we know."

"He is very specialized indeed. High class merchandise, very expensive, and with an appropriately small client base. I happen to know he brokered the sale of that stolen German Type 212 submarine to Iran. I believe the cost was eighty million euros of which he received ten percent."

Cathcart was surprised and angry. "And you didn't see fit to inform me of this at the time?"

"Commander, our arrangement was that you would ask me questions now and then. I never agreed to ring you up with every piece of gossip that comes my way. Besides, that's old news. The Americans destroyed that sub earlier this year."

"Very well then." Cathcart took a sip of tea. "What about Janos?"

"His first contact was rather vague—an encrypted email telling me to call a certain number. I purchased a throw-away mobile and called. Using very circumspect language, a man who identified himself as a close associate indicated Janos would soon have some very expensive special weapons. When he mentioned the sum of a hundred-fifty million euros, I knew they must be nuclear. I had no interest in getting involved in that kind of deal and told him so. I was also skeptical, to be honest, as these stories crop up now and then and later turn out to be, what do the Americans call them? Scams."

Cathcart was intrigued by this and nodded as he listened. "You said that was his first contact?"

"Yes," replied the Russian. "Two days ago a messenger delivered a small package to me while I was having a beer a few blocks from here. I was naturally surprised to have a package delivered to me at a pub. I opened it when I got home and found an encrypted satellite phone. A note said to call a number already programmed in its memory at eight that evening and then deposit the phone in the river."

"And?"

"I did. I walked across the Thames over to Battersea Park and called. The man on the other end answered, 'Janos.' I had not heard his voice in over ten years, but I'm sure it was him. He wanted to know if I could refer him to sources for

Russian military circuit boards. I gave him one name in Kiev whom I recalled, Nicolai Pelevin."

Cathcart wrote the name in a notebook.

"This seemed to be a secondary issue, though. The real reason for his call was to find an operating manual for a Russian permissive action link encoder. I knew then he actually had access to nuclear weapons. Why else would he need a PAL encoder?"

"Excellent, Maxim."

"There is one other thing. He asked that if I found one, to have it translated into Arabic. I told him again that I wanted no part of this deal and ended the call. I walked back to my flat and on the way dropped the phone from the Albert Bridge."

Cathcart stood and laid a business card on the table. He added, "Call me any time twenty-four hours a day if you hear from him again. Next time, if there is a next time, agree to provide whatever he wants." With that Commander Neville Cathcart hurried towards the door and out to his car, which was illegally parked.

As he drove away Maxim Korshkin said to himself, "Good to see you too Commander. Certainly, I'll be happy to pay for your tea."

CHAPTER 12

BRENDAN WALLACE HAD just finished a long meeting with his military advisors on the stagnating situation in Iran. The level of fighting had dropped, but there was no end in sight. Now his intelligence chiefs were telling him the only progress made on the missing warheads was that someone wanted a PAL manual in Arabic.

He wanted to crack their heads together, but that probably wouldn't help

"Arabic covers a hell of a lot of ground, Alex." He pointed an accusing finger at CIA Director Alexander Clarkson. "They speak Arabic from Morocco to the Turkish border, do they not?"

"Yes, Mr. President, that's true, but most of those North African countries are broke and could never afford to buy those warheads. Libya is generating some cash from its oil now, but their new government is pretty moderate by regional standards. Besides, their security services and military are riddled with agents—ours, the Brits', and the Israelis'. East Africa and the Arabian Peninsula are still the best bets."

"What about Syria?"

"We can't rule it out, but none of the factions still fighting has the funds to buy them, the means to deliver them, or for that matter a target worth using one."

"Dammit." Wallace brought his fist down on the table. "You're all stovepiped into you own little worlds. Look at the larger picture; who would benefit most? I cannot do all your jobs," though Wallace admitted to himself that he wished he could and was confident he could do each of them better.

"Sir," Karen Hiller said. "May I remind you of your meeting with the Senate Majority Leader? You know how he leaks to the press when you're late."

"Yes, yes. Don't want to keep the old geezer waiting. I do want to hear about the plans for that amphibious action, though. Someone was supposed to be here to brief me."

"That would be me, Mr. President." A trim, good-looking African-American Navy officer wearing aviator's wings stepped forward from the gaggle standing behind the principals. "Captain Neil Washington, sir. I'm representing NAVCENT and Fifth Fleet Operations. Admiral Dawkins directed us to prepare a contingency amphibious operation to recover special weapons in an arc from East Africa to the head of the Persian Gulf."

"Okay," said the President. "Let's hear it."

"Operation Ocean Reach," he began, "will consist of two amphibious task groups which, for security, will remain separate until it is time to execute the operation. Because 5th Fleet amphibious assets are currently engaged in operations in the Persian Gulf, two amphibious groups will be transferred as follows. " The officer then pointed to a graphic on the large flat screen display.

Task Force 58: Expeditionary Strike Group

Task Force 58.1 USS *Essex* (LHD 2)
group transferred from 7th Fleet (Pacific)

USS *Essex*, USS *Stockdale*
(DDG-106), USS *Lake Erie* (CG 70)

Task Force 58.2 USS *Iwo Jima* (LHD 7) group
transferred from 6th Fleet (Mediterranean)

USS Iwo Jima, USS Dewey (DDG-105), *USS Bowman* (FFG-62)

"IN ADDITION, THE auxiliary oiler *Yukon* will be forward deployed to Diego Garcia and tasked with supporting TF 58. Air support will be drawn from the embarked AV-8 Harriers. Depending on the location, additional air support may be possible from the three carrier strike groups currently operating south of the Strait, or we can move a squadron of Marine F-18's down from the Med to Djibouti. Finally, the USS *Jimmy Carter*, a Seawolf Class submarine, will be moved west to provide additional anti-submarine cover."

"Are the Marines already aboard?"

"No sir. The 22nd Marine Expeditionary Unit was disembarked from *Iwo Jima* to add to our forces in Korea.

The 11th MEU from *Essex* disembarked two weeks ago in Naples and was flown to Qatar and Bahrain. If Ocean Reach becomes operational, the plan is to mobilize the reserve alert regiment, the 28th Marines, and to augment them with several other units. They would be flown to Diego Garcia to board the ships."

"Reserve troops, is that what we've come to?"

The Captain did not flinch. "These are first class Marines, Mr. President. The vast majority are combat veterans."

"We are heavily committed in multiple theaters," Sonny Baker said. "This kind of contingency op is exactly what the reserve alert unit is for."

Wallace took a deep breath. It was a bitch working a bigger than expected war with a diminished military budget. "Very well, then. Captain, how long to get these ships and Marines in place?"

"Ten days from when you give the order, sir."

To everyone's surprise, Brendan Wallace did not solicit opinions or comments from the gathered intelligence chiefs or from his National Security Advisor. He looked at the display with the task force organization, then he looked down at the table.

"Make it happen," he said, then rose and headed for the door.

CHAPTER 13

DETECTIVE KELLI MOORE and her partner, Jerry Costanza, had been waiting for more than two hours in the back of a hot, cramped undercover van. Their target, a suspect in five campus sexual assaults, should have arrived at the house on Detroit Street more than an hour ago. That piece of information had come dearly—she had allowed a small time coke dealer to skate on a good arrest, though the man was so stupid he would certainly be busted again. The worst part was she hadn't expected the stakeout to last long, so when Costanza bought a hot pastrami on rye at nearby Zingerman's Deli; she'd decided to wait until later. The smell of pastrami was making her crazy.

"Here we go," said Costanza, with his mouth full.

The suspect was climbing out of a car right in front of the house.

She made a quick note of the license of his ride. "Looks like he got a lift." They had expected him to arrive on foot.

"No way we can get him before he goes in. We don't know how many are inside so let's take him on the way out. Our information is that he's buying a few smartphones so he should be in and out. One thing we do know about this guy; he likes to keep moving. I'll slip around to the back, you cover the front."

Moore got out, followed a minute later by her partner. She walked down the block, around the corner, and made her way through two back yards, until she was out of sight behind several trees with the back door of the house in view.

Just over twelve years ago, Kelli Moore would have been voted 'least likely to be a police officer' by her senior class at upscale Grosse Pointe North High School. The tall redhead excelled in school as well as cross country and lacrosse, the latter a sport she played mainly because her father had told her not to. He'd also expected her to join her brother in the family's private banking business. When she announced one day at dinner that she'd accepted an appointment to the Naval Academy, the reaction was...satisfying.

At the academy, she continued to perform at the top of her class, and also lettered in cross country. Then a member of the track team had pounced on her in a hotel at an away meet. Not the type to scream for help, Kelli Moore channeled her rage into her defense. She succeeded in fracturing her assailant's jaw and knocking out three teeth by a brutal blow with her elbow. The young man was allowed to drop out, after a number of surgeries, and was never charged. Moore did not object; the knowledge that he would never eat anything tougher than macaroni without pain was enough for her. The remainder of her time at Annapolis was marked by a cool wariness on the part of her male classmates, but a covert pride and admiration from the other women.

Graduation let her spring another surprise. Her mother—her father had cut her off entirely—had expected her to enter an appropriate field such as intelligence or—better still—supply. So she was more than a little surprised to see her at graduation in the dress uniform of a Marine Corps second lieutenant. She chose military police, which in the context of Iraq and Afghanistan, was as much a combat branch as infantry. At the Basic School, a grueling six-month course for new officers, Kelli Moore was in her element. During the five-day urban combat operations exercise, she achieved the highest score ever recorded. She was also second in her class in pistol marksmanship, being bested only by a former enlisted Marine who had previously served as a combat pistol instructor.

After the rigors of the Basic School, the Military Police course at the Army's Fort Leonard Wood presented no challenge. The challenges started with her first assignment as a platoon commander with the Marine security forces in Baghdad's Green Zone. There she learned that her responsibilities as a platoon commander had very little to do with herself, her needs, or her ambitions, and everything to do with her mission and the needs of the men and women under her command. The first time she came under fire on a security sweep she had to overcome her aggressive instinct to attack head on, and to work with her experienced platoon sergeant to develop a plan to pin the snipers down with direct fire while two squads enveloped them from the side; all the while staying alert for an ambush or IED. Finally, standing on the shoulders of her tallest Marine, she was able to throw a grenade through a second story window of the building with the snipers nest. One squad then rushed the front and after a brief fight found two snipers killed by her grenade, while two more in another room were killed by her troops.

That evening she was debriefed by her CO, a tough grizzled major from New Mexico. "Lieutenant, when you got here those bars on your collar gave you your Marines' obedience. Now you've got their trust and respect. Well done."

Kelli Moore had never valued anything in life, before or since, as much.

In 2013, as a newly-promoted captain, she deployed to Afghanistan where she was tasked with route security. During a mortar attack on an EOD unit, Moore received several small shrapnel wounds. Despite her injuries, and angry as hell, she took a squad of Marines up a rocky hillside and, under intense enemy fire, maneuvered into position to destroy the mortar while killing five Taliban. For this she received a Bronze Star, as well as the Purple Heart.

The next two years were spent doing investigative work after which her commitment from her academy education was over. Feeling she had nothing left to prove, Kelli Moore accepted a job with the Ann Arbor Police Department, but missing the Corps, she also joined the Marine Corps Reserve.

The creak of a door caught Moore's attention. She peeked around the tree and saw her suspect, lit by the back porch light, walking down the back steps and into the yard. "Game over," she whispered softly.

The suspect, a large blond man wearing a muscle shirt which displayed huge tattoo-covered arms, stopped. He glanced around, then took off across the adjoining yard.

"Shit." She took off after him, grabbing at her shoulder mike. "Jerry, he's moving north on Detroit Street."

In black jeans with ankle high boots and a short jacket, Moore was not exactly dressed for the chase, but she was having no trouble gaining on the muscular felon. Before they made the next cross street, she was able to reach out and grab the back of the suspect's shirt. A quick jerk, and the big man was on the ground with her heel on top of his hand and her weapon leveled at his face.

He was bleeding from a gash on his forehead. Damn, this meant a stop at the hospital. Costanza pulled up in the van while she was cuffing him. He applied a dressing to the wound. They read him his rights and were off.

As they drove by the deli, Moore still regretted her decision not to get dinner.

CHAPTER 14

Dr. Mike McGregor was placing the third of what would be twelve stitches in the manacled suspect's forehead. "So Officer Moore," he said with a grin, "strange how you keep getting the resisting arrest types. Didn't I put a cast on one of yours just a few weeks ago?"

"That's Detective Moore, and that idiot's arm had already been broken by the guy he was trying to rob. How long is this going to take, anyway?"

"I think we're going to need a CT scan. His lawyer will insist we rule out a brain injury."

Moore groaned. She had been working since noon and there was no end in sight. "Can't we do it tomorrow?"

"Nope. If there really is a problem, he could be dead by tomorrow. You are quite the hard ass Detective—I can see why you were such a good Marine."

Moore bristled. "And what gives you the right to insult Marines? Or hard asses for that matter?"

"Long and sad experience. I could tell you all about it over drinks some time."

"In your dreams, Doc." Her tone was sharp, but she could not help but smile. She had recently broken up with a junior faculty member and had no interest in dating another nerd, even if he did have an infectious smile. Besides, there was something more going on behind those pale grey eyes, and this was not really the time to find out. She took a chair to wait for her suspect to be taken for his CT scan. While waiting, she unconsciously fussed with her short red hair.

Just then Albert Johanssen, evening supervisor for hospital security, walked in. Moore knew him better as the First Sergeant with the Headquarters Company of the 1st Battalion 28th Marines, a unit that also served at the Ann Arbor reserve center. "Evening Detective. Looks like you have everything under control."

"First Sergeant, thanks for stopping by. Yes, we'll be out of here as soon as your overly cautious doctor gets a CT scan of this guy's head."

Johanssen gave her an understanding grin, "Give him a break. He does know what he's doing."

"I hope so; I'm tired and hungry and want nothing more than to get this moron booked and to get some dinner. By the way, your doctor says he knows Marines, what's with that."

"Oh, we were together back in Iraq with the 1/5." Kelli Moore was surprised, and it showed in her bright green eyes.

"What? He was a medical officer?"

"No, a corpsman, HM2. Now he's our battalion surgeon. I think that after his fiancé died—you knew about that didn't you?—he was sort of drifting. So when I got off active duty and took this job, I told him they were putting a new headquarters here. That's when he decided to get back in."

Moore was learning way more than she had bargained for. "Fiancé? Do tell."

"A few years ago. Danielle was Canadian, a grad student in architecture. Got killed in some kind of construction accident in Toronto doing an internship. I never met her, but everyone says she was perfect for him."

The detective, not wanting to probe into that sensitive area, but in fact intensely curious, changed the subject. "I thought that physician's assistant, Lieutenant Ellis, was your battalion surgeon."

"She's the assistant surgeon; they just started allowing PA's into the assistant surgeon job a few years ago. You probably see her more since Doc is on the road a lot visiting the companies, getting the physicals done, and keeping an eye on the corpsmen."

Just then the transport team arrived to move her suspect to radiology. "Good to see you First Sergeant," she said as she followed the gurney out of the ER.

God, that nerdy doc was a Corpsman. Probably pulling shrapnel in some nice, safe Green Zone hospital.

But . . . if so, what had he done to impress the First Sergeant?

CHAPTER 15

June 9, 2005 0045 Z (0115 AST)
76 kilometers North-Northeast of Al Bukamal, Syria
(5 kilometers west of the Syria-Iraq border)

A FEW SECONDS FOLLOWING the detonation of
the GBU-31s, LCDR Castelli stood up to assess the
damage.

"Commander," Delgado said, "that's not a good—"

Castelli screamed.

Castelli had stayed down long enough for the bomb
shrapnel to pass over, but he hadn't considered that some
of the debris would travel upward in a long slow arc. Not
until a piece of rock about the size of a baseball smashed
into his right thigh just above the knee.

McGregor was already fishing a battle dressing out of his
bag. Around him, he could hear the thuds as other pieces of
debris—metal, masonry, body parts—hit the ground around
him. As soon as they stopped, he was at the wounded officer's side. A quick assessment told him everything.

"This is bad Staff Sergeant, really bad," he said. "The bone's broken. I can mostly control the external bleeding, but not the bleeding inside the leg. In a few hours he can put a lot of blood into that thigh. And he sure isn't walking anywhere. Do we have medevac?"

"Don't know, Doc. Something else the Lieutenant Commander kept to himself."

Gunfire and muzzle flashes, far too close.

Lance Corporal Delgado crawled up the far side of the wadi to look for the enemy patrol. "Two of them, maybe twenty meters—"

A short burst of fire, and a spray of arterial blood from Delgado's neck. He was dead before McGregor could reach him. Luis Delgado would never again walk the sands of the Sonoran Desert.

McGregor stayed low and gave a quick, sad, nod to Johanssen who was by then crawling up the side of the wadi, weapon ready.

Johanssen popped up, took a quick look, and fired a short burst. He then dropped down and moved quickly to his right.

Fifteen meters along the rim, Johanssen rose just high enough to get his elbows down in a steady firing position. He saw the insurgent prone with an AK-47 aimed directly at his last position. He fired three quick shots. "That's one. They never expect you—"

There was another burst of fire, this time from the other direction.

Johanssen whirled to confront the new threat when the

insurgent, who had moved quickly away after Delgado was shot, fired again. Johanssen gave a grunt and dropped, gripping his ankle.

McGregor was actually closer to the shooter than Johanssen, but he was in the shadows while the big Marine was in full moonlight. Rather than exposing himself to grab his M-4, he drew his Beretta 9MM pistol from its thigh holster and took aim. The man was focused on Johanssen, giving him that precious extra second. He fired four shots.

The enemy was thrown back and spun around, falling on his side.

McGregor ran forward to disarm him. A glance told him there were two wounds, one in the right chest and one in the upper abdomen. This guy would bleed out before he could do anything. He took the man's weapon and threw it over the side of the wadi. A quick search of the wounded man's pockets yielded a satellite phone which he put in one of his cargo pockets.

McGregor returned quickly to Johanssen and could see the big man was in extreme pain. He wasn't groaning, but he was pale and sweating profusely. The bullet hole in his boot was the obvious problem and the absence of an exit wound made it clear the bullet was still in his ankle.

"Let's get this boot off so I can check you out."

"No time, Doc," responded the Marine. "There's another guy out there. He's the one who fired that long burst of cover fire for the one who got me."

"Dammit Joe. I should have been backing you up."

"Okay, apology accepted, Doc. Now pull it together."

Johanssen was wheezing through gritted teeth. "It's a simple problem, find that guy and kill him or we all die. Right here and right now."

"Sure Joe, I'll get this asshole. But we're probably going to die anyway."

"Here, take this, it might come in handy." Johanssen handed McGregor an M-67 fragmentation grenade which he clipped it to his body armor. "I'll cover the wadi. Hand me my rifle."

McGregor did so and turned without another word, walking along the dry stream bed to the south.

After about thirty meters, the wadi became shallower and provided very little cover. McGregor began to crawl to the west, using his night vision to search for the last insurgent. Nothing. If the guy was smart, he would have crossed the wadi and would now be approaching from the east. If so, McGregor would have to move quickly.

He crawled back down into the wadi where a curve shielded him from the two wounded men. He sat for a moment to consider his options.

There was a metallic click.

At first he thought it had come from his own men, but no, it was to the east and close, very close. The insurgent must be moving slowly towards the wadi and had probably grazed his rifle or magazine on a rock.

What now? Stand for a quick shot? No, this guy probably has his muzzle pointed right at the wadi with his finger on the trigger. Move north? No, moving over the rocks this close to the enemy would certainly give him away.

Then he felt for the grenade on his vest.

Knowing that he had only a few seconds, he worked the pin free as fast as he could and released the handle. The insurgent would certainly hear the sound of the firing pin and the handle flying free.

McGregor held the live weapon a second, a process known as cooking the grenade, which everyone who ever taught him anything said was a stupid, stupid thing to do because the burn time of fuses varied. Hearing nothing, he tossed the grenade over the side. He heard a quick movement and half expected to see the grenade flying back, but in less than two seconds there was a tremendous 'crack' and a flash. He waited the few seconds it took for his eyes to recover from the flash then stood quickly, finger on the trigger, and scanned the rim of the trench-like wadi.

There was no need for his rifle. The grenade had exploded only a meter from the Arab. McGregor recoiled from the smell of the man's bowels mingled with the remnants of composition B. The darkness allowed for limited detail, for which he was grateful.

Mike McGregor had never killed a man. He had seen plenty of corpses and had been in several firefights. Tonight he had killed two within fifteen minutes. As an infantry corpsman he had experienced the jitters and the bitter metallic taste that comes from the adrenalin of a combat high—but never like this. He was trembling so hard he could barely hold his rifle.

He had to get a grip. Things were probably getting worse before they got better. If they got better.

He moved quickly back down the wadi, no longer worried about being quiet. He found Johanssen next to Castelli.

The Staff Sergeant was now alert with his weapon ready, but Castelli was lying flat and moaning softly.

"I was worried that grenade was incoming Doc," said Johanssen with a slight smile. "Good work," he added.

"Yeah, dandy. Now that the shooting's over, how the hell do we get out of here? It's obvious neither of you are walking out."

Johanssen handed him one of the radios while putting on his own headset. "Let's see what Crossbow can do for us." He keyed his transmitter. "Crossbow, this is Lancer. Impact confirmed, but unable to avoid enemy contact. One KIA, two wounded. Request Medevac. Our corpsman will provide details on casualties."

"Roger, impact confirmed. One KIA, two wounded. Requesting Medevac. Wait one."

They waited, listening to the quiet of the desert.

After about thirty seconds of silence another voice came on. "Request damage assessment."

"What the fuck!" shouted McGregor. "We're shot to shit and they want us to evaluate the target?"

"Just take a quick look and tell them what you see," replied Johanssen, who was also annoyed, but trying not to show it.

McGregor stood and looked towards the house. A light wind had mostly cleared the smoke and dust and he could see a large crater, actually two overlapping craters, and pieces of debris. "Looks like a direct hit, just a big crater and scattered debris. The buildings and vehicles are gone. Wait, I see the Range Rover about fifty meters from where it was. Totally burned out."

Johanssen relayed the information.

"Roger," the second voice said. "Be advised that medevac from your location is impossible. Syrian Government has already communicated its strenuous objection to our strike, and Baghdad has ordered no incursions into Syria for any reason. Sorry."

"Sorry? You're sorry? Well, we're pretty fucking sorry too!"

"Calm down McGregor."

"Crossbow is returning to normal operational location," the voice said. "There will be no further communication on this frequency. Good luck. Crossbow out."

"Crossbow," Johanssen said quickly, "please advise our command of situation."

He received no reply.

Johanssen turned to McGregor. "You can bet there are more of these guys to the west of the house that survived the strike and called in the information. You know what that means?"

"That someone in the Syrian government knew about this meeting, that there are more bad guys around, and that at some point even more bad guys are going to show up."

"You really are too smart for your own good." Johanssen gave a weak smile and then turned serious. "Doc you need to get the hell out of here—you're the only one with any chance of making it. I want my family to know what happened to me. They deserve more than the 'missing on a classified mission' bullshit."

McGregor was on one knee, leaning on his rifle. He looked straight at Johanssen. "No Staff Sergeant," he said with slow intensity. "We are getting out together: you, me, and the Lieutenant Commander. I feel bad we can't take Delgado, but I think the skipper will find a way to bring him back. He isn't into this spook crap. He'll take care of him, and hopefully of us."

"Doc, I appreciate your spirit, I really do. But we both know that's not happening. Now get going."

McGregor began digging through one of his cargo pockets.

"HM2 McGregor," Johanssen said, "that was an order."

"Staff Sergeant Johanssen, I have officially determined that neither you nor LCDR Castelli are medically fit to command this mission. I am now in command."

"You little bastard . . . Only a medical officer can make that determination, you know that."

"Actually, under these circumstances, I believe the senior medical practitioner—that would be me—can make the determination. We can look it up when we get back." McGregor then sat down next to the wounded Johanssen. "Look Staff Sergeant, we can't waste any more time."

Johanssen reflected on this for a moment. "All right, Doc. What's your plan?"

McGregor found what he was looking for and pulled out the satellite phone "I borrowed this from one of the dead guys."

"McGregor . . ." Castelli, who had been semi-conscious, seemed to be more alert now. "That thing can't be secure. Besides, who are you going to call?"

"Sure as hell not your intel buddies back in the Green Zone. They're the ones who stranded us here after we did the heavy lifting for them."

Even weak from blood loss the officer bristled. "Look, McGregor, they were undoubtedly following orders, sensible orders. But you're right; calling Baghdad won't get us any help."

Johansen felt in his breast pocket then groaned. "I have a notebook with dozens of cell and satphone numbers. Because of the border crossing, I left it in camp. I do know the skipper's satphone number."

"That'll do." McGregor dialed as Johanssen rattled off the numbers. "Voicemail, I don't think we should use that. His phone is probably turned off. I'll try Commander Jenkins, the battalion surgeon." After punching in the number; "Same thing, and it looks like the battery is low. We can try later. Time for Plan B."

CHAPTER 16

IT WAS THE kind of day college football was meant for. Cool for early September, a light breeze and just a few scattered clouds to make the sky more interesting.

Michigan took the kickoff and returned it to the thirty yard line. With the offensive line opening huge holes, the highly touted new freshman running back had moved the ball to midfield.

Mike McGregor turned to Al Johanssen. "You see, I told you this kid was going to be great. He has that combination of speed and power we've been looking for. I don't think Michigan has had anyone like this since Tyrone Wheatley."

"Easy Doc." Johanssen grinned. "He's only run two plays. Let's at least wait until the second half before giving him the Heisman."

Another play unfolded.

"Look at that, twelve more yards. I'm telling you Joe, he's the real deal."

Before Johanssen, who was starting to think McGregor might be right, could reply, he felt his phone vibrate. This was not his regular phone, it was a secure phone issued to members of the Marine Corps Reserve alert regiment. As he reached for it, he noticed McGregor was doing the same. They both saw the same message.

1. *Fastball*

2. *Two*

3. *Delta*

THIS SIMPLE MESSAGE had worked its way from Captain Neill Washington through the Marine Corps Reserve chain of command to the duty officer at 28th Marines based in Chicago. He had the ability to notify every member of the regiment via secure cell and after contacting the commanding officer, Colonel Aaron Mark, he did so.

'*Fastball*' indicated that the entire alert regiment was being mobilized. '*Two*' was the second most urgent mobilization with each member required to report the following morning by 0730. And '*delta*' indicated members should pack desert uniforms.

Johanssen deleted the message. "Let's at least stay for the touchdown."

Two plays later, Michigan scored on a thirty-eight yard sprint draw by the same young back and both men began to make their way out of the stadium.

Just outside the entrance, they saw Kelli Moore leaning on an Ann Arbor police car, and talking to one of the uniformed officers. She pulled a cell phone from her jacket pocket and looked carefully at the screen. She looked up at the doctor and the big Marine and then noticed a few other people she immediately recognized as part of their battalion. She nodded and smiled.

"Detective Moore seems happy about something," Johanssen said. "Maybe the MPs will be joining us."

"Or maybe she was just watching a replay of the touchdown."

As they crossed the parking lot, Mike McGregor looked at his friend. "Looks like it's going to be a short season, Joe."

Al Johanssen smiled grimly.

CHAPTER 17

TODAY'S BRIEFING ON the Russian nukes was looking to be as brief as yesterday's. There just wasn't much new information coming in, mostly status reports on current operations. Still, Sonny Baker had to sit through them.

Rick Suarez, who had been following the quiet efforts of NATO countries to scan their ports, went first.

"There have been a total of six incidents involving containers painted with that cesium 137. In each case there was a major response with every container showing radiation being searched plus an extensive search of the entire port facility. Several shipments of improperly-shielded medical isotopes have also turned up, as well as one shipment of smoke detectors containing tiny amounts of Americium-241. The search activity has attracted some attention, so the Dutch put out a story about stolen medical waste. So far it hasn't created much excitement. The primary result of the cesium incidents has been to divert a lot of skilled people and technical gear away from looking for those nukes. We assume that was the intent."

"No doubt," replied Baker. "Looks like it worked. Anything on the people responsible?"

"Six-seconds on a security camera in Antwerp. It shows a small man in a hooded jacket leaning over a container later found to be painted with the cesium. He disappeared into a maze of containers and is not seen again. Nothing that would help with an ID."

"Obviously this was pretty well planned. Okay, ONI, anything for us?"

Jean Kraus, representing Admiral Costello, began. "A few things. Bearpaw captured several new conversations between Admiral Grishkov and his nephew. GRU is still running the operation from their end though apparently FSB has gotten wind that something is up. They're both concerned about the consequences of this getting outside the military."

"You mean Putin's still in the dark?"

"Apparently. They assume that if Putin knows the SVR and the FSB will know and vice versa. They're betting they can either retrieve the weapons or pretend they were never lost. At this point a leak would end very badly for both Grishkovs and the GRU."

Baker nodded at Kraus.

"GRU has information from their own sources that this Janos brokered the deal and that a hundred-fifty million euros flowed from accounts in Dubai into accounts owned by a business Janos controls, and then into several Eastern European stock markets. They were unable to trace a hundred-twenty-five million euros after they left the markets. Twenty-five million, retained by Janos went back to his business account, but then disappeared into a maze of banks in West Africa. We shared this information with NSA and CIA, but they can't trace it either."

"We did confirm that the one-fifty came from banks with major Saudi ownership," the CIA Director added, "and that it had been on deposit for years. We have a few contacts in the Gulf banking community that are helping us discretely track the owner, but it's likely this is Saudi financed."

"Good work, both of you," Baker said. "We'll have to be very careful about approaching the Saudis. If we get too direct, they'll feel compelled to stonewall. I'll talk to the President about working some back channels." As an afterthought he said, "Saudi financing makes an Iranian connection a lot less likely doesn't it?"

Nods of agreement.

"One more item," Kraus said. "We now have a frigate and a destroyer carrying helicopters with neutron detectors in the Red Sea, working the area south of the lower Suez Canal. They're doing fly-bys of exiting ships and the technical guys tell us there is a high probability they'll get a hit if those nukes pass through the canal. Nothing so far, though."

"I'll inform the President. Anything more?" Baker looked around the table. Everyone knew Baker disliked people who felt they had to speak at meetings even when they had nothing to say. There were a few shrugs so Baker headed for the door.

CHAPTER 18

THE NEW RESERVE center in Ann Arbor was just south of the city on Stone School Road. There was still a Stone School, though it hadn't been a school for many decades—at the moment it was a daycare center. Almost everyone who had been alerted arrived early.

In the women's locker room, Captain Kelli Moore was just lacing up her desert boots when Navy Lieutenant (jg) Nicole Ellis opened the locker next to hers. The petite blond had her hair done in a complex braid that was carefully pinned up to conform to regulations. Moore assumed Ellis had never done a deployment, otherwise she would have gotten her hair cut yesterday. "You're going to have a lot of trouble taking care of that mane," she remarked.

Ellis glared at her, but said nothing.

Changing the subject Moore said, "Nicole, I just learned you're not the battalion surgeon; I see you so much, I assumed you were."

"Oh no," Ellis said without looking at her. "I'm a physician's assistant. Lieutenant Commander McGregor's in charge."

"I just discovered that. Interesting guy, but kind of a nerd. I hope he's up to this deployment."

"You don't know? How do you think he got that scar on his face?"

"Whoa, Lieutenant. Don't get excited." It was starting to look like something was going on between the PA and the doctor. "If I recall, he said it was an accident."

"Yeah, he stumbled into a bullet. That's what he got his Purple Heart for."

Kelli Moore raised her eyebrows in surprise. "When did that happen?"

"Same time he got the Navy Cross."

"The what?" Moore's eye were now round and her expression one of complete shock.

The PA rummaged among a stack of envelopes on the top shelf of her locker and pulled out a photograph of a group of Navy enlisted, many of whom she recognized as corpsmen with the 1/28, as well as Lt (jg) Nicole Ellis and LCDR Mike McGregor. All were wearing dress blue uniforms. Above McGregor's left pocket she could clearly see the blue and white ribbon of the Navy Cross as well as the Purple Heart along with several rows of other decorations.

"Taken at last year's Marine Corps Ball." Ellis thrust it in her face. "Guess you missed it."

"She stared at the Navy Cross. And the scar on McGregor's face. Who the hell was this guy?

CHAPTER 19

June 9, 2005 0045 Z (0115 AST)
76 kilometers North-Northeast of Al Bukamal, Syria
(5 kilometers west of the Syria-Iraq border)

"**P**LAN B?" ASKED Castelli.

"Watch and learn."

McGregor climbed out of the wadi and jogged in the direction of the still smoking craters. After poking around for a few minutes, he found what he was looking for—the trunk lid from the Mercedes. It had apparently been blown clean off and was more or less intact. God bless German engineering.

He dragged it back to the Wadi and slid it down the slope before following it.

Johanssen stared at it for a moment, then gave a forced laugh. "Let me guess, you're going to find more parts and build us a car?"

"No, I'm building us a sled."

He pulled his Beretta and fired two quick shots into the metal.

"I see what you're up to," Castelli said. "Great idea. Do you really think you can pull us on that thing?"

"We're about to find out." From his pack McGregor pulled a ten meter piece of paracord, a strong but light nylon rope originally used on parachutes. He doubled it up then ran loops through the bullet holes in the trunk lid and attached the free ends to his body armor.

What about Delgado?" asked Johanssen.

"Yeah," said McGregor. This was no small thing, for every Marine expected that—dead or alive—he would never be abandoned.

Mike McGregor removed the entrenching tool from his pack and began to dig into the wall of the wadi near the bottom. After about five minutes he had a trench large enough to accommodate the small frame of Luis Delgado. He rolled him, along with his rifle and most of his gear, into the shallow grave and covered him with sand and then an assortment of rocks to mark the site. Then he took two compass bearings and a reading from his GPS, which he wrote in his notebook.

He came to attention and snapped a salute. "We'll be back," he whispered, taking with him only Delgado's dog tags, canteens and magazines.

Getting Johanssen out of the wadi proved fairly easy. Pushing with his good leg while McGregor pulled, he was out in a few minutes. Castelli was another matter. Still in severe pain and getting weaker from loss of blood, he wasn't able to help much. McGregor ended up throwing him over his shoulder and doing a fireman's carry up the side of the dry stream bed. Once both of the wounded men were laid out on the trunk lid, the corpsman donned his body armor and began to pull.

Nothing; they were too heavy to move more than a few meters.

Johanssen rolled off the improvised sled and told his Petty Officer, "Try one at a time, Doc. I think that might work."

Without a word McGregor began pulling again. After a moment the trunk lid began to slide across the coarse sand at a slow, but steady pace. McGregor turned, and told Johanssen he would go about a hundred meters then come back, which he did. Moving Johanssen was harder, but possible, and after a total of ten minutes, the team had progressed one hundred meters.

"Doc, the math is not on our side," Johanssen said. "At this rate it's going to take an hour and a half to go a kilometer, and that assumes you won't need any rest."

McGregor studied the situation. He pulled the ceramic plates out of his body armor and helped Castelli and Johanssen out of theirs. Between them, they shed more than thirty kilos.

"That should help. Let's see if I can pick up the pace."

He did. The ground sloped slightly downhill with no obstructions, and the heat finally abated. A GPS check after an hour showed the small band of Americans had moved a kilometer towards the Iraqi border. Only three and a half to go. McGregor was sweating profusely, however, and the two wounded men agreed he should have all the water.

After another kilometer's progress, this marred by a

fifteen minute delay crossing a wadi, McGregor pulled out the phone and hit speed dial. This time the battalion surgeon, Commander Ron Jenkins, answered.

"McGregor, where the hell are you? I heard you were out on some kind of special mission."

"That's right sir. We're in deep shit and I really need to talk with the CO. Like right now."

"Okay, HM2. Hold one." There was the sound of the tent flap being thrown open and feet on sand. In less than a minute, McGregor heard the soft baritone of Lieutenant Colonel Henry Ahrens' New York accent.

"Petty Officer McGregor, situation report."

"This phone is totally unsecure, Colonel. Retrieved from enemy KIA. We have one enlisted KIA, one officer and one enlisted wounded. Location is three-hundred twenty-four kilometers from your location on an azimuth of 022 degrees. Our heading 090." Johanssen had worked out the distance and direction from the camp on his GPS to avoid giving their exact location over the unsecure satphone. "Sir, what can you do for us?"

"Working on it. Out." Ahrens terminated the connection.

JUNE 9, 2005 0145Z (0445 AST)
Forward Operating Base Butler, Western Anbar Province

HENRY AHRENS HAD never wanted anything more from life than to command Marines. The father he idolized had been a Gunnery Sergeant in Viet Nam, and young Henry had absorbed a lifetime of Marine Corps lore. Unable to gain entry into the prestigious Naval Academy, he attended

Fordham on a Navy ROTC scholarship and entered the Marines as a second lieutenant. After graduating from the Basic School at Quantico, he progressed steadily from platoon to company, and then to battalion command with a few stops at various desks as personnel or recruiting officer. But he had no interest in desks. When he volunteered for a second tour as battalion commander, his mentors advised against it, but he took the job with relish, vowing to put everything he still had into the assignment and then to retire on his own terms. To command the 1/5, a legendary unit which had fought in every campaign from WW1 onward was, to Ahrens, the pinnacle of his career.

The secret mission thrust upon him was one of those unexpected complications. Obviously things had now gone sideways, and his men were stranded in Syria. But why? Had that smug Navy officer screwed up? Or was it just bad luck? Whatever the reason, Ahrens intended to do everything humanly possible to get his people out.

When he pushed open the flap to the operations tent, the small staff on duty all stood quickly to the call of "Attention on deck."

"As you were." Ahrens pulled up a chair next to the duty officer, an eager young Captain. "Message traffic?"

"Routine, except for this," he said while handing Ahrens a message form. "Something must have happened in Syria; message from Baghdad ordering no entry and no over flight under any circumstances."

"Well, that explains it. Whatever the hell happened, it involved three of our people who were on some kind of spook mission with a Navy intel officer. I just got a satphone call from HM2 McGregor. There's two wounded and a KIA. They are trying to make the border, but with wounded it's obviously going to be tough. Here, find this position on the map." He handed the Captain the information he had received from his corpsman.

After a minute with a large map and several old fashioned map tools, the officer placed a small mark on the map just west of the Syrian border. "About here, Colonel."

Ahrens pondered the map for a minute. "There's no way we can get up there by road. Look at this." He pointed to the circuitous route from Camp Butler up to the border area being traversed by McGregor and the wounded men. "It would take four or five hours, at least. Call ops at the airfield; tell them I'm on my way and that I'll need to see their CO. We have an emergency mission, here's what I'll need." He scribbled rapidly on a piece of paper. "I'll be in direct command."

Surprised by the last remark, the operations officer asked, "Departing when, sir?"

Ahrens looked at his watch, "Ten minutes. Make it happen." As he walked from the tent several enlisted Marines sprinted out behind him.

The CO was not surprised to see his driver and HUMVEE waiting outside operations. The young Lance Corporal seemed to have a sixth sense for action. In three minutes he was at the operations tent for MAG 39 where he ran into their commanding officer, Lieutenant Colonel 'Buddy' Gaston, a notoriously early riser. A short ruddy-faced Alabaman, Gaston was the opposite of Ahrens in everything but rank. Despite his good ol' boy affect, Gaston was an intensely ambitious Academy grad on the fast track. He had attended every school, taken every staff job, and had smoked cigars with every colonel who could help him on the climb to flag rank. His current combat command was a vital ticket to the top, and he was determined to complete this tour without any kind of screw-up.

"Buddy," said Ahrens. "We have some Marines out in the deep weeds and we need a couple of your helos to pull them out." He quickly briefed the aviator on the situation.

"Yeah, one of our Hueys flew those guys up to the border a few hours ago. What's with that Navy officer? He seemed mighty impressed with himself?"

"I suspect he's less impressed, now."

"Damned straight." Gaston took a quick sip of stale coffee from an old Academy mug, an affectation which annoyed Ahrens. "Henry, we just got very clear orders about Syria. I assume you got them as well. We have two alert Hueys and can fly you up to the border, but those guys will need to get out on their own. Sorry."

That was about what Ahrens expected. Orders were, after all, orders, and Gaston was not about to violate Syrian airspace and risk his career for a couple of Ahrens' people. "That's fine, Buddy, wind 'em up and get us up to the border. I'll have my people here and an exact location in a few minutes."

"Okay then. I'll have my ops officer notify the alert crews and you're on your way. Gaston stepped into the operations tent, strode over to the duty officer and spoke for just a minute. On his way out, he turned and said loudly enough for Ahrens to hear, "No Syria, absolutely no Syria."

JUNE 9, 2005 0425Z (0725 AST)
100 kilometers North-Northeast of Al Bukamal, Syria

MIKE MCGREGOR LAY face up on the hot sand of eastern Syria. The sun was up, and it was well over 100 degrees.

Every muscle screamed. His head ached, and he could feel blisters oozing blood into his boots. The GPS told him they were within five-hundred meters of the Iraqi border. But so what? He had been counting on help from his CO, but he could see nothing ahead. He tried the satphone, but the battery was dead.

At about 0600 he thought he heard helicopters, but he saw nothing, and the rotors quickly faded.

Lying on the improvised sled, Castelli was unconscious. His pulse was well over one-hundred, and his breathing rapid and shallow. He was bleeding out, and McGregor could only think about how much easier it would be to move without the extra weight.

Johanssen lay prone, looking south.

"Doc, some kind of vehicle approaching."

They both watched as a wispy trail of dust resolved itself into a black vehicle heading straight towards them.

"A Range Rover," Johanssen said. "They found us. Well, at least it's just one vehicle."

Both men took hold of their rifles and crawled a few meters to the minimal cover of a small outcropping of jagged grey rocks. Castelli was on the trunk lid in a small depression behind them, about as safe as he could get. They watched, mesmerized, as the big black SUV approached. At about three-hundred meters, they saw a small puff of smoke from the front of the vehicle followed immediately by a loud clunk and a second later, by the distant report of a rifle. The Range Rover coasted to a halt and four men leapt out, all carrying weapons. Three of the men had the ubiquitous AK-47, but the fourth had a long rifle with a scope—a Russian Dragunov sniper rifle.

Yeah, they were in trouble.

Within a second of exiting the front passenger door, however, one of the men was thrown violently against the fender and even at three hundred meters McGregor could see an explosion of blood from his chest.

"Well, I'll be damned," said Johanssen. "Somebody out there has a Barrett." The M107 Barrett Light Fifty was the premier sniper rifle in the Marine Corps inventory. Capable of hitting a man-sized target at more than a thousand meters—or disabling a vehicle—the Barrett fired the venerable .50 caliber machine gun round. "Let's give them a hand."

McGregor and Johanssen began returning fire. The Syrian sniper, lying next to the driver's side front wheel, was placing accurate rounds into the rocks on either side of them. It wouldn't be long before one of them was hit. Both men were having difficulty getting a good sight picture as their target was in the shade of the vehicle, while they were in direct sun.

McGregor took aim at the front tire and moved slightly right. Just as he was about to fire, he felt a sharp pain in his cheek and right arm. It took less than a second to realize what had happened—one of the sniper's bullets had fragmented and several of these fragments had hit him.

Not taking his finger off the trigger, McGregor regained his sight picture and squeezed off the shot. The sniper jerked.

He rolled to the left to avoid a second shot, but in doing so exposed himself to another Marine sniper who placed a .30 caliber round through his neck.

The fourth insurgent, after watching the rapid demise of his comrades, began running west and, after passing below a small rise, was soon out of sight.

Mike McGregor saw four men approaching from the east. Two were pushing litter carriers—metal frames on oversized bicycle wheels with an attached standard military stretcher. In a minute they were close enough for him to recognize the Old Man himself in the lead, followed by Commander Jenkins and HM3 Bell, the other paramedic. Bringing up the rear was Battalion Sergeant Major Cruz who carried an M-25 sniper rifle, a modified M-14. It was the Sergeant Major who had taken out the man with the Dragunov. The first three were heading straight for the men on the ground while Cruz scanned the horizon for threats.

McGregor rose and stood at attention, blood dripping down his face. Staff Sergeant Johanssen said, "Please pardon my lying down, sir. I'm having a little trouble with my leg."

"So I see Staff Sergeant. What say we get the hell out of Syria. Doc, you're a mess, get a dressing on that face." He turned to the Sergeant Major who spoke into his radio and in a few minutes the helicopters, which had withdrawn a few kilometers, were now visible, and the wounded men were being wheeled back towards the border. The medical personnel were busy with the seriously wounded men, so Mike McGregor held a battle dressing against his own face and found the strength to shuffle the last few hundred meters to safety.

In a little over an hour, they were back at Camp Butler where Castelli received blood, IV fluids, and antibiotics while Johanssen had his boot cut off and a temporary dressing applied. He also received antibiotics. During this time, Ahrens debriefed Johanssen and McGregor, then the battalion operations and intelligence officers debriefed them again. Castelli, now conscious, aggressively refused debriefing saying Ahrens had no need to know anything about his highly-classified mission. He did, however, report that despite his overall competent performance, he felt it necessary to point out that HM2 McGregor had been insubordinate, had assumed command under highly questionable circumstances, and had used an unauthorized and insecure form of communication.

Henry Ahrens considered this for a moment, said, "Noted," then turned and walked away.

JUNE 12, 2005 0010Z (0310 AST)
60 Miles North-Northeast of Al Bukamal, Syria

THE ROCKS WERE piled along the west side of the wadi, exactly as McGregor had reported in his debrief. Two Marines with entrenching tools quickly uncovered the body of Lance Corporal Luis Delgado and carefully placed him in a body bag. He was then loaded into the back of a Humvee while four other Marines, including Lt. Colonel Henry Ahrens and Sergeant Major Cruz, provided security. When Ahrens had quietly asked for volunteers to recover Delgado, the entire Battalion had stepped forward.

Mission completed, three Humvees headed for the border

and the five hour trip back to Camp Butler. From there Luis Delgado began the long journey to Baghdad, to Dover Air Force Base, and finally to the cemetery of a small rural church south of Tucson.

APRIL 7, 2006 2115Z (1715 EDT)
Red Hawk Bar and Grill, Ann Arbor MI

THE BAR AT the Red Hawk was already busy with the usual Friday mix of students, faculty, and locals. Sitting at the far end, in his usual seat, Mike McGregor sipped a local micro-brew while contemplating the FedEx envelope which had arrived at his rooming house a few hours earlier. The return address was, "Headquarters Marine Corps", which seemed odd. Since transferring to the Reserves McGregor rarely heard from the Navy and never from the Marines. He didn't perform monthly drills, and his only obligation was to keep his address current, maintain his medical readiness, and to appear at a reserve center for the occasional inspection. Finally he tore away the sealing strip and extracted several pages.

It was a set of orders. After the usual incomprehensible accounting data, the orders consisted of just a few lines. First, he was being recalled to active duty for a period of forty-eight hours starting 0600 April 14—a week from today. He was to report no later than 1100 to the Marine Corps Base at Quantico, VA. Uniform was service dress blues. Also enclosed was a brief letter in standard military jargon informing him that air travel had been arranged, with tickets for an 0630 flight enclosed, and that he would be met at the gate by...his old pal Gunnery Sergeant Johanssen. So Staff Sergeant Joe was now Gunny Joe. Well, orders were orders, and he would find out in a week.

APRIL 14, 2006 1430Z (1030 EDT)
Marine Corps Base Quantico, VA

IF THE ORDERS had been surprising, events after landing at Reagan National Airport had been surreal. Gunnery Sergeant Johanssen was indeed his old Staff Sergeant, and McGregor was surprised to learn he was now working on the Commandant's staff. Probably explained how he was able to bypass security meet McGregor at the gate. It also explained how they were able to enter a back gate at Quantico.

They proceeded to the base headquarters at Lejeune Hall. While changing into his dress blues in a small locker room, McGregor asked, "Don't you think it's time to tell me why I'm here?"

"There's going to be a little ceremony. Colonel Ahrens is going to be here."

"That's great, but for what?"

"I don't think the he wants me to spoil his surprise. I will say that he somehow got the Commandant's ear and he gave a nudge here and there to help it along. He has a soft spot for corpsmen. Did you know he was wounded twice in the first Gulf War?"

"I've seen the Purple Heart in his photographs."

"Okay Doc, time to go."

He was led onto the parade ground behind the building where a few dozen people in Navy dress blues or Marine alphas were standing in formation. He recognized Henry Ahrens, who had made full Colonel after all. There were also several senior medical officers and a Corpsman Master Chief. There was a tiny middle-aged Hispanic woman accompanied by a Marine Gunnery Sergeant and to McGregor's amazement there was LCDR Castelli accompanied by a Navy Captain wearing aviator's wings—and the Navy Cross.

Taking their position at the front of the small formation, McGregor took his cue from Johanssen who stood at parade rest. With the call of "Ten-Hut," everyone snapped to attention. Striding towards them was Colonel Henry Ahrens, tall and lean, ramrod straight, with sharp features and his signature closely-cropped grey hair. He was accompanied by a heavily-decorated Sergeant Major and a very young looking corporal.

The Sergeant Major barked, "Gunnery Sergeant Albert Johanssen front and center."

Johanssen took three steps forward and was presented with the Purple Heart. This was followed by the posthumous presentation of a Purple Heart to LCPL Luis Delgado. The medal was given to Maria Delgado, his mother, who accepted with great dignity. Castelli was then awarded both the Purple Heart and the Bronze Star for his leadership of a classified mission that seriously degraded the Iraqi insurgency at its highest level. When he stepped back into ranks, Castelli gave McGregor a long look. It was not a friendly look.

Then McGregor's name was read.

He stepped forward and saluted the Colonel whose return salute was quick and fluid. The Sergeant Major opened a folder and began to read: "The Secretary of the Navy is pleased to present the Navy Cross to Petty Officer Second Class Michael Graeme McGregor for services set forth in the following citation: For extraordinary heroism while serving as team corpsman on a highly classified mission....."

As he read through the carefully vague descriptions of McGregor's actions during the still-secret mission, the young sailor's scars began to sting. His mind was back in Syria reliving the loss of Delgado, the men he killed, the wounds he'd received, and his burning resentment at being left behind. As Ahrens pinned the Navy Cross with its blue and white ribbon and the Purple Heart above his other decorations, the older man smiled indulgently. He knew what McGregor had done to earn these awards and understood he was best left to his own thoughts.

Castelli walked away from the ceremony next to his father, Vincent Castelli, retired but wearing his uniform as was his right.

"You're not happy about that corpsman getting the Navy Cross are you?" his father asked.

"Not really. It was my mission—one that had a real impact on the insurgency. And that kid was an insubordinate smart-ass. I'd love to have him on my ship some time."

The older man smiled. "Joe, you're an ambitious young man, and I respect that. Remember, you were recognized for your leadership of that mission and the Marines were the ones who did it. That Bronze Star did not come out of Baghdad, I can tell you that."

Joe Castelli looked at his father with raised eyebrows. How did he know that?

"As for your corpsman, that Navy Cross had nothing to do with your mission. It was about bringing you and that Marine back. And if I recall from the report I read, killing two and wounding one insurgent while he was at it."

Again, Joe Castelli tried not to show how surprised he was at his father's connections.

"It's the Marines, Joe. For them 'no man left behind' isn't just eyewash. Frankly, when I was flying missions in Viet Nam I always felt better when the Marines were doing search and rescue—there was no quit in those guys. You'd do well to remember that."

Joe reflected for a moment. McGregor was an insubordinate bastard, but he did owe him his life.

The older man then put his arm around his son and said, "I have dinner reservations at the Army and Navy Club. I happen to know Admiral Yount, who just took command at PACFLEET, will be there, and I think he will be mighty impressed by that Bronze Star, even if you're not."

CHAPTER 20

SEPTEMBER 3, 2017 1000Z (0730 EDT)
Navy and Marine Corps Reserve Center, Ann Arbor

B Y 0730 THE battalion staff, A company 1/28, and B MP Company 4th Marine Division were all standing at attention behind the building. Lieutenant Colonel Jeremiah Walsh, the battalion commander, stood in front of the formation, and the two company commanders were with their Marines. Walsh, a very lean African American of average height ordered, "Stand at ease." As the assembled Marines and Sailors relaxed, but only slightly, Walsh held up a document and read from it.

"September 3, 2017
From: Commanding Officer 28th Marine Regiment
To: Commanding Officer 1st Battalion, 28th Marines
SUBJ: MOBILIZATION ORDERS

1.   As of 0730 this date the 28th Marine Regiment is mobilized under Presidential authority as the Marine

Forces Reserve alert regiment. Duration not to exceed 365 days without Congressional authorization.

2. First Battalion has been augmented by B MP Company 4th MARDIV. You are now reporting senior for Commanding Officer B MP Company.

3. First Battalion has been further augmented by two platoons from 6th Engineer Support Battalion. You will attach these Marines to your command and utilize them where appropriate and at your discretion.

4. New York Air National Guard will transport all Navy and Marine Corps personnel mobilized from or attached to Reserve Center Ann Arbor from Willow Run Airport at 1130 this date.

5. I am confident 1st Battalion will in every way display the courage, honor, commitment, and professionalism for which the Marine Corps is known. Semper Fi.

A Mark, Commanding"

He added, "I share the regimental commander's confidence. Individual orders will be distributed to the company commanders immediately after formation. Every individual will have his or her orders by 0900, no screw-ups. Busses will depart at 1000, exactly." He executed an about face and walked away.

First Sergeant Al Johanssen barked, "Dismissed," and the formation disintegrated into more than two hundred individuals, all seeming to move in different directions.

CHAPTER 21

SEPTEMBER 3, 2017 1845Z (1345 CDT)
34,000 feet over Kansas

MAJOR KIMBERLY GRANVILLE had her big C-17 Globemaster III transport on autopilot, just keeping half an eye on the instruments while she discussed navigation with her co-pilot. The senior pilot in the three-aircraft mission, Granville had just gotten her orders the previous evening. Less than twenty-four hour notice for a transport mission was unusual in itself, but these orders were unique. Three C-17s from the 105 Airlift Wing of the New York Air National Guard were to proceed from Stewart ANG base just north of New York City to Willow Run in Michigan where they would be met by a senior officer with further orders. Two aircraft were configured to transport personnel while hers was prepared to handle a half load of passengers and half palletized cargo. No explanation why they weren't using nearby Selfridge Air National Guard Base or why they started the mission with only enough fuel for the short hop to Michigan.

Granville, a Federal Express pilot in civilian life, was familiar with Willow Run, which served primarily cargo and general aviation while Detroit Metro, located not far to the east, served the major passenger airlines. After touchdown, the three aircraft were directed to park on the ramp, where a black SUV approached from a nearby hanger and an Air Force Colonel hopped out and signaled her to open her rear cargo door. A few minutes later, the Colonel appeared in the cockpit and without bothering with introductions simply handed Granville an air tasking order.

"We've arranged fuel to your next destination," he said, "which is the expeditionary airfield at Twentynine Palms California. Have you ever put down there?"

"No sir. Isn't that one of those interlocked metal runways?"

"Right. But it's 8,000 feet and you'll be coming in fairly light so you should have plenty of room. A bit bumpy maybe, but better than a lot of runways in Afghanistan. They can't refuel these monsters, so after unloading you'll head down to March Air Force Base for fuel and any maintenance. Hold there for orders."

Granville had indeed handled truly brutal runways in Afghanistan, so if they didn't run into blowing sand at the desert base, she should be fine. She was a bit concerned about Captain Jim King, her most junior pilot, who had just transitioned into the C-17 from the venerable KC-10 tanker. King had spent his entire active-duty career flying from the luxurious 11,000 foot runways of Travis AFB. She would need to spend some time briefing him and have him last in line when they landed so he could watch his fellow pilots. Her third pilot, Mitch Baxter had started his career in the

C-130 and had put down on dirt strips in Iraq, back roads in Africa, and even an ice runway in Antarctica. Twentynine Palms would be no problem for Baxter.

Behind Granville, in the cavernous cargo space, the Marine Corps—and two Navy—officers all sat facing backwards or sideways, one of the many differences with civilian air travel. Behind the officers, on pallets, were the crew-served weapons—mortars and machine guns, communications gear, and the duffel bags, seabags in Marine speak, for both the officers and enlisted.

LCDR Mike McGregor was trying to sleep, though without much success. What the hell was all this about? What kind of mission would require an infantry regiment plus the division MPs and combat engineers? His mind had been chewing on the question since their recall. Finally, he gave up and fell asleep over Colorado.

Kelli Moore was wide awake for a different reason. She was reviewing her platoon training records on a small tablet computer, noting deficiencies to be made up as soon as possible. Like most ambitious female military officers, Moore believed she had to perform better than her male counterparts just to break even. At least this was true with her current commanding officer.

James "Jimmy" Griggs was a former Georgia Bulldog linebacker and good 'ol boy with recruiting poster good looks and a ton of ambition of his own. He was an administrator in the Justice Department personnel division and flew out to Ann Arbor for his unit's monthly drills. He had made it clear from the beginning that he felt there was no place for women in the Marine Corps, but he was very careful not to openly violate any regulations. Careful, that is, with the exception of several affairs with enlisted women under his command. Moore knew he wasn't worried that he would ever suffer consequences from this 'perk of command'. She had also heard he was thinking of adding her to his list of conquests. Apparently he had never bedded a female officer. Something held him back though.

He had probably heard about that broken jaw from friends who had attended the academy. Moore was determined that such a move by Griggs would be the biggest, and possibly last, mistake of his life.

In any case, Griggs had decided the best way to deal with Moore was to marginalize her. Which is why all the enlisted women in the company—sixteen as of today—wound up in her platoon. That way, when requests came in for an MP platoon to augment a deploying unit, Griggs could simply pass over hers and shove all the women to the sidelines at once. Moore had several discrete discussions with the Headquarters Battalion commander who was sympathetic, but unwilling to take on the politically well-connected Griggs, especially since that would have meant challenging other senior officers who quietly agreed with Griggs. So for now she was running her platoon as sharply and as professionally as she could while waiting for Griggs to either screw up or get promoted out.

CHAPTER 22

THE CRANE WAS just loading the last of the shipping containers onto the deck of the MV *Milos Tethys*, where a group of crewmen in sweat soaked shirts was securing them with heavy chains. The oil pump was repaired and the ship would receive fresh provisions and depart the following morning.

The master was not entirely happy with his stay at Zadar, but what could he do? The harbor master had required an additional two-hundred-fifty euros for his ongoing cooperation, and the diesel mechanic was unsure if the replacement part would fit without expensive modifications. When he discovered a case of American Jack Daniels whisky in the back of his truck, however, the part seemed to fit perfectly. But Mr. Theologides understood how the game was played for small operators working out of small ports. He would be happy the *Milos Tethys* was getting underway and that the delay and the added expense were just part of doing business. The master was confident that the remainder of his voyage would be uneventful.

CHAPTER 23

ABDULLAH NAZER GAZED out his office window at the smooth turquoise of the Gulf of Aden, leaned back, and smiled. The message from his freight agent relieved the anxiety of the last few days. That the package would be delivered in three to five days was even better. Nazer was finding the delays less and less tolerable, but he forced himself to remain patient lest he do something that would betray his plans.

Now that the primary shipment was moving, he could concentrate on his other problem, the permissive action links. Janos had included the technical diagrams, but actually building one was much harder than he had expected. The obscure Russian parts were hard to find and the Iraqi 'expert' he hired to build it could not read Russian, so another technical expert had been brought in, creating yet another security risk. The only good news on that front was a message from Janos that he could acquire a PAL operating manual translated into Arabic. The price of two-hundred-fifty thousand British pounds was modest, considering what he had already invested.

Though 'the project', as he liked to think of it, was still uppermost in his mind, Abdullah Nazer had other responsibilities. Variously described as a warlord, transformational Arab leader, or a Saudi puppet, Nazer's official title was Military Governor of Hadramawt and Al Marah—the two eastern, sparsely populated, administrative divisions of Yemen. Son of an army officer, Nazer had risen through the ranks of the Yemeni military and had served throughout the country. The greatest day of his life, so far at least, was the day he succeeded to his father's old post as commander of the military district based in al-Mukalla, his home. It got him away from the capital, Saana, a filthy hole which teemed with corruption, violence, and intrigue. And it put distance between him and his country's political leaders, petty and self-serving thugs who had forgotten their distinguished history as home to the Arab peoples.

A small historic city on the southern coast, al-Mukalla was far from the ongoing fighting among the northern Zaidi Shia minority, with their Houthi militants, and the majority Sunnis. The relentless infiltration of foreign fighters from al Qaeda, the influence of the fanatical Islamic State, and the corruption of the central government were challenges, but ultimately manageable ones. Inspired by the relative peace of his small domain, two years ago the cunning and far-seeing Nazer had simply declared himself in full command of his region and expelled representatives of the national government. Supported by weapons and 'volunteers' arranged for by wealthy Saudi relatives, he had repulsed the half-hearted attempts of the central government to reassert control. Using a combination of local tribes and his own troops—and supported as needed by the Saudis—Nazer relentlessly killed or drove out the foreign militants. The presence of a stable ally on their southern border won Nazer great favor with the Saudis who then poured development funds into his small kingdom.

The central government, to the extent there really was a central government, settled upon a simple face-saving solution. They appointed Abdullah Nazer the Military Governor. They pretended they were still in control, and he let them pretend. So far, this charade had worked surprisingly well.

A relative calm had descended upon the eastern provinces and Nazer had not objected when the western press began to refer to his region by the name used by the Romans, 'Arabia Felix', Happy Arabia.

Understanding that Saudi cash could allow his small kingdom both independence and a degree of economic prosperity, Nazer worked with his cousin Muhammad Nazer, a senior official in the Oil Ministry, to buy out the local assets of Petro Masila, the Yemen-based oil company. The Saudi investment was not so much for the modest oil output of the Yemeni fields, but for access to the oil terminal. So long as the Iranians controlled the Strait of Hormuz, the Saudi's oil, and thus their entire economic base, was hostage to the whims of the mullahs in Teheran. The Saudis intended to revitalize the proposed pipeline from their own oil fields down to Ash-Shihr.

This realization was also the seed which grew into 'the project.'

Muhammed Nazer loathed the Iranians as much as he loathed the Americans, who had killed his beloved father—a man who bore the same name as his cousin, Abdullah. The two men convinced the King that security lay in an alternative option for oil shipment, a pipeline to the Gulf of Aden ending at Ash-Shihr. It would be a way to serve their customers in a crisis and would send Teheran—and Washington—a powerful message that the Kingdom was taking a more active role in its own future.

At this point only a road had been constructed, but that served as a direct link between eastern Yemen and Saudi Arabia.

So during a meeting between the cousins Nazer in Riyadh, both men had lamented the fact that, while their pipeline would enhance Saudi economic security, the cursed Persians still loomed as an oppressive reality to all the Arab nations of the Gulf. Despite entreaties from their King—and paradoxically from the Israelis as well—the Americans had refused to take the measures required to disarm the mullahs. And even if they did, doing so would only solidify American domination of the Arab Middle East for decades to come. How to rid themselves of both of these burdens?

Then Janos called.

Janos had worked with Muhammad Nazer's father on several small deals for arms destined for the Sunnis of Iraq's Anbar Province. The son maintained contact after his father was killed by an American bomb in 2005. In the last few years there had been some contacts related to arms for the Sunni insurgents in Syria, but Janos had apparently graduated to much bigger projects than a few cases of AK-47s or a thousand kilos of Semtex.

This was much bigger.

When an encrypted satellite phone was delivered to his home, Muhammad Nazer took the call and was intrigued to hear the aging arms dealer describe the possible delivery of 'unique and extraordinary weapons capable of changing world history.' When the sum of one-hundred-fifty million euros was mentioned, Nazer realized it had to be nuclear weapons. Negotiations went on for several months over a succession of encrypted phones. Once he understood that Janos was referring to six Russian thermonuclear warheads, it was his nephew Abdullah who suggested their target.

"Uncle," Abdullah began, "imagine if Teheran and Qom, home of the mullahs, as well as their largest military bases, all disappeared in a few seconds. Also imagine if half their oil infrastructure was also vaporized. Now imagine if the Americans were blamed."

He sat back in his chair and smiled. "The Persians would be critically weakened for a generation or more, and the Americans would be driven from the Gulf. During the period of chaos in Iran, the Arab states of the Gulf would enjoy a substantial increase in oil revenues. We could expand our militaries, oil infrastructure, and economic base. We, not the Persians, would be the regional hegemon. All for one-hundred and fifty million euros."

Nazer quickly grasped what his nephew was suggesting. "How could we deliver the weapons? And how could the Americans be blamed? We possess a small number of Chinese ballistic missiles, but the King would never consent to such an attack. Besides, satellites would pinpoint the launch site."

"Not missiles, Uncle. Trucks."

"The warheads could be shipped to al-Mukalla and then on to Saudi Arabia in shipping containers. A new set of container numbers would be arranged before going on to Kuwait City. The Kuwaitis have little trouble moving trucks into Iraq. Once in Iraq, in Basra perhaps, we again alter the containers so it looks like they originated in Iraq and drive them into Iran. Most of the contents will be legitimate goods."

"And we have many loyal Sunni brothers in Iraq who will gladly assist us in the holy project," his uncle added.

Thus 'the project' was born. Now the American attack on Iran had left the Iranians critically weakened with their nuclear capability erased. And the vicious combat on Qeshm made the possibility of an American nuclear attack credible to the people of the region. The timing was perfect!

Now Nazer dialed a number on his secure satellite phone. It was answered on the second ring. Ali, his nephew and a company commander in Nazer's small army, was sullen, as usual.

"Ali," said Nazer, "meet me in Mukalla in two days. I will have an important assignment for you." The phrase 'important assignment' was their code for delivery of the warheads.

"Yes Uncle, I will be there," replied the young man, now filled with enthusiasm.

"Travel safely."

CHAPTER 24

SONNY BAKER LOOKED around the table and did not like what he saw. The number of people attending the briefings was getting bigger every day. Karen Hiller, in a grey Armani suit and no jewelry save an American flag lapel pin, arrived last. She was now attending every meeting, and reminding him at every meeting that she represented the President. Hiller nodded at Baker, signaling he was now free to begin.

Baker sighed and returned his focus to the business at hand. On the upside there had been some buzz about significant new developments. "Let's get started. Alex, I'm told you have something."

The CIA Director had been handling the briefings personally, and to Baker's surprise had so far avoided the grandstanding typical of his predecessors.

"Several interesting developments, actually. First, a

British asset was contacted by Janos. He had acquired the Permissive Action Link operating manual and got it translated into Arabic. Unfortunately, he didn't inform the Brits until after he made the handoff."

"What the hell?" Karen Hiller rarely lost her composure, but she was obviously incensed by this gaffe. "How did they let that happen?"

"Their source was pretty open with them. Said if he had told them ahead of time they would have altered the document, the buyers would likely figure that out, and in the end the op would be blown and he would probably get himself killed. Reasonable, from his point of view at least."

Though not from theirs. But Baker had other things to worry about. "Where's the document now?"

"They tracked the courier to Dubai, where he was picked up at the airport by a vehicle registered to a Saudi rental agency. They've been heading southwest and are now on that new road the Saudis built into Yemen."

"Yemen? That's a new twist." Baker seemed puzzled.

Clarkson nodded. "Remember that the warlord, or whatever he calls himself, of eastern Yemen has close family ties in Saudi Arabia. In fact his cousin, Muhammad Nazer, is a major player in the Oil Ministry.

Jean Kraus from ONI added, "If I remember right, this guy's father was killed by an American air strike in Syria while doing business with the Sunni insurgents."

"Good memory, Captain," said Clarkson. "So the Saudi Nazer has both the resources to purchase nuclear weapons, and an axe to grind with us. And he has a cousin in control of an obscure port and a lot of really desolate territory to hide in."

"Alex," Baker added, "keep a close eye on that courier. Find out where he ends up."

"Both satellite and a long range Global Hawk surveillance drone are following the vehicle."

"Good, now we're making progress. Immediate update once this guy arrives at his destination."

Hiller said, "Keep me in the loop on this as well, Alex. The President will want to know immediately."

Clarkson nodded and went on. "There's been some trouble with the Russians. One of our teams was following up on the shipping containers that went out through Tallinn. They encountered two guys who turned out to be GRU. The details are sketchy, but apparently one of them spotted our team, got suspicious, and pulled a weapon. One of the GRU agents was killed and the other wounded. Our people got out clean, but just before the meeting I received a Bearpaw intercept that SVR got wind of the incident and is asking questions. It's likely SVR, and of course Putin, will become aware of the whole thing very soon. Probably less than a day. We don't know how they will react, though it's unlikely they'll go public."

"Pull your people back, Alex." Karen Hiller was emphatic. "The President absolutely wants to avoid any kind of confrontation with the Russians. We have our own leads now, and frankly the President doesn't care whether the thieves get caught or not. Leave them to the SVR or the FSB. Our focus has to be those warheads."

"I agree, Alex. We can't afford to have any more trouble with Putin than we already have."

Baker scribbled a note to himself. "We sure as hell don't want them to know just how much we know about their nukes."

"All right, but those fugitives will have answers we can't get anywhere else. I want the record to show my objection. "

"Oh don't worry. Your ass is covered," said Baker. "Captain Washington, what does NAVCENT have for us?"

Neill Washington stood. "The *Iwo Jima* and *Essex* groups have arrived at Diego Garcia and have been fueled and provisioned. Ammunition's been loaded to support a full regiment for ten days of combat operations. The Air Force has flown in the required vehicles that are now on the ships' landing craft. In addition, the USS *Ashland*, LSD-48, has joined the task group as well. The *Ashland* has two large cranes amidships that can easily load the steel transport boxes with the warheads. Some specialized equipment was loaded at Singapore which will allow the engineers to open the containers immediately and confirm the weapons are there."

"Very good," said Baker with a smile. "When will the Marines get aboard?"

"We start flying them out in three days."

"The President wants me to emphasize the need for absolute security," Hiller said. "We do not want this on Facebook, Twitter, or Instagram."

"Yes, ma'am. No cell phones or personal computers will be permitted. In fact the entire force has been restricted to the training area at Twentynine Palms with no communication in or out."

"Good, keep it that way. When this mission is over, the President will decide when to go public and with how much. Not some corporal. Are we clear on that Captain?"

"Very clear, ma'am."

Washington was about to take his seat when a young Navy Lieutenant stepped in and handed him a folder emblazoned "TOP SECRET" in bright red letters. The Captain opened it and smiled. "One of the helicopters patrolling the northern Gulf of Aden just reported a solid hit on a neutron detector. It's a small Greek registered freighter, the *Milos Tethys*."

"How reliable is that detector?" asked Baker. "How sure are we that we're picking up the warheads?"

"They're the latest stilbene-based neutron detectors," Rick Suarez said. "Very sensitive. And by overflying them at night we can get the detector relatively close to the ships. Captain, did they send any hard data?"

Washington showed him the report. "It's a pretty strong hit. I would say medium to high probability the nukes are aboard."

"I want that ship boarded and searched immediately," demanded Karen Hiller.

Everyone in the room looked first at Hiller and then at Baker.

"Karen," he said, "with all due respect, you represent the President, but you're not him. You're talking about boarding a ship which is probably in Yemeni territorial waters. For an act of war I need an order from the President himself."

Karen Hiller glared at Baker for a moment, stepped to the wall, and picked up a phone.

Two minutes later Brendan Wallace entered the room.

Everyone stood as he stepped to his chair at the head of the small conference table and took his seat. "So what's the problem?"

Hiller outlined the situation and her position—fairly accurately, Baker had to admit. The President looked to him. "How likely is it that those nukes are aboard this Greek freighter?"

Baker nodded to Rick Suarez. "Better than 50-50, sir. Some people might say as high as eighty percent."

"Not good enough," said Wallace. "Too risky. If we move without confirmation, and they aren't on board it will tip off the buyers that we know about the warheads. Also, the damn Yemenis will howl about our invading their territorial waters without cause. No, we need confirmation. Get it!"

With that the President stood and strode to the door, not even acknowledging the "Aye, aye sir" from Neill Washington, and not looking at either Karen Hiller or Sonny Baker who, as soon as the President turned his back, were again glaring at each other.

Baker glanced at Washington and Suarez who nodded. Both knew what needed to be done.

CHAPTER 25

SEAL TEAM LEADER Lt Jason Brown checked his gear while two of his men manhandled the rigid inflatable out of the Multi-Mission Platform amidships. The *Carter* had been specifically designed for this kind of classified SEAL mission and was, among other things, able to hover in a fixed location despite the tricky currents of the Gulf of Aden.

Since they'd arrived on station two days ago, *Carter* had already conducted an operation which no U.S. submarine had performed since World War 2. Approaching the Gulf from the east, *Carter* was advised on her daily satellite communications update that a Somali pirate mother ship deploying numerous armed skiffs was operating in the area of interest to NAVCENT. Concerned because they might harass American inflatables performing boarding operations—or worse might seize the vessel carrying the warheads—a decision had been made to eliminate it, but in a way in which the US Navy could not be implicated. This meant both boarding and air strikes were out. An attack by an American surface vessel was considered, but rejected.

That left *Carter*.

That night *Carter* had tracked the ship on her sonar for several hours and had a constant firing solution for her torpedoes. Her skipper, CDR Dave Krenz, wasn't comfortable destroying a minimally-armed vessel with all hands, but they were, after all, pirates—as Cicero said, *hostis humani generis*—enemies of all people, and had no protection under any law. They were also in a position to interfere with a vital mission. Still, he was about to fire the first live torpedo shot from an American submarine in decades, and he somehow wished for a target more distinguished than this floating pile of rust.

After taking care that American surface ships and aircraft were well away from the area and that no local shipping was within visual range, Krenz gave the order, and two Mark 48 torpedoes sped towards the target from a range of two thousand yards. Without sonar, the pirate had no warning of the torpedo attack, and when the two three-hundred kilogram warheads struck, the vessel was blown to pieces so small that only the sheen of diesel fuel, a few pieces of floating debris, and a cloud of smoke remained.

Carter raised her communications mast, reported the kill, turned north and proceeded on the next phase of her mission.

The SEAL team consisting of Brown, Petty Officer Jim Brewer—the boat driver—Petty Officer Hassan Ahmed—the area specialist—and Carlos Ventura—the

NEST specialist—were ready to go within minutes of surfacing, and as soon as they were away, the *Carter* slipped beneath the light chop of the Gulf of Aden.

SEALs never liked any mission involving outsiders, but Ventura was a former Army Ranger and possessed skills the SEALS did not have. Like the other team members, he had a beard and spoke Arabic, though only Ahmed could credibly manage the dialect unique to this part of Yemen. The plan was for Brewer to take them to within a few hundred meters of the beach and from there the landing team would swim to shore. The tide was inbound so the swim would be quick and easy. Once on the beach east of town, they would hide their swim gear and don the soiled white robes their logistics people had provided. An hour's walk would bring them to the harbor where, hopefully, Ventura's lightweight neutron detector would get the information the President demanded. Each man, the civilian technical expert included, was armed with only a suppressed .22 caliber pistol. Discovery, even if everyone survived, would be a critical mission failure. Stealth, not force, was the point.

The swim ashore went smoothly, and in a few minutes they were all off the beach, their gear hidden, and were walking towards town. At about 0140 they encountered a boy leading three goats. He enquired why they were on the road so late. Brown gripped his pistol tightly, but Ahmed explained they were on their way to the port to meet a boat arriving very late. The boy accepted this, and they proceeded into the largely deserted streets of al-Mukalla. Ahmed walked ahead while Brown and Ventura lagged behind.

The port area was quiet, but was not deserted. Ahmed, moving very naturally, aroused no suspicion, but the others were noticed by more than one local—most worrisome, a security guard. As the man walked towards them, Ahmed stumbled into him, angering the man. When he turned to strike out at the bumbler, he was felled by a vicious blow to the head. This attracted several other men, and while Ahmed glibly explained the family quarrel they had just witnessed, Brown and Ventura drifted toward the dock and nearby warehouses.

When they passed a stack of shipping containers, Ventura pressed his tiny earpiece to confirm the tone he was receiving, walked behind one of the containers, and nodded to Brown. The two strolled away to the east and were soon joined by Ahmed.

"I told them this guy had dishonored my sister. They actually encouraged me to kill him, but I told him our father had asked me to be merciful. I doubt he'll have much memory of anything that happened when he wakes up."

The trio moved at a pace that was brisk, but appeared leisurely. In just over an hour they were back aboard the *Carter*, and fifteen minutes after that the communications officer sent an encrypted report by satellite to the National Security Council with NAVCENT as an information addressee.

TOP SECRET
FLASH!

THREE TWENTY-FOOT SHIPPING CONTAINERS ON DOCK AT AL-MUKALLA ADJACENT TO MV MILOS

SHORT SEASON

TETHYS ARE EACH EMITTING NEUTRON SIGNATURE OF
TWO STANDARD RUSSIAN TYPE PLUTONIUM PITS.

PHOTOGRAPHS AND IDENTIFICATION DATA INCLUDED
IN ATTACHED FILE.

MESSAGE ENDS
TOP SECRET

CHAPTER 26

MIKE MCGREGOR HAD just finished his duty at
the aid station, the small clinic in the training area,
and was walking the perimeter to relax and clear his head.
Since arriving from Michigan, there had been long days of
weapons training, reviews of amphibious procedures, and
exercises with the engineers designed to cross obstacles, as
well as his work maintaining the health of his battalion,
and his shifts in the aid station. He had been concerned by
the constant coming and going of obviously senior people
from several agencies, but mostly he was concerned about
an encounter he had the day before.

A man in an old pattern desert uniform pulled open the
tent flap. "I heard you were here," he said.

McGregor looked up to see Rick Suarez, an old friend
from his undergraduate days at Michigan. He jumped
up and slapped his friend's shoulder. "Good to see you.

And why am I not surprised you're part of this spook show. I assume you're still doing the same job."

In a hushed voice Suarez replied, "I really can't say anything about what I'm doing here."

"Okay, now I'm really worried," said McGregor, only half joking. "Is this whole show something like the paper we wrote for that course in Public Policy? The one where we described the possible theft of–" Suarez raised a hand.

"Best not to discuss old times right now, Mike. Could you take a look at my ear, it's been hurting like a bitch for a couple of days and now it's even worse."

Switching quickly into doctor mode, McGregor picked up a small otoscope and examined the painful ear. "You've got an infection of the eardrum called myringitis. Hurts like hell, but responds quickly to the right antibiotic." He opened a green footlocker, took out a bottle of Zithromax, and poured some into an envelope. "Take two right now and one a day until they're gone. Don't worry; it won't keep you from going wherever we're going." He wrote a short note on a record form. "Here, you must have a medical record somewhere, be sure this gets to it. They're not letting us anywhere near computers, so from the Marine Corps perspective, you were never here."

"Thanks Mike. I'm really sorry I can't tell you more."

"You, your CIA pals, and a Marine infantry regiment all in the same place spells a big shit storm. That's pretty much all I need to know."

Suarez smiled, gave his friend a half salute. "Good luck to us all." He then tossed two capsules into his mouth, took a swallow of bottled water and walked out.

McGregor was still chewing on this when he spotted Kelli Moore walking from the direction of the women's showers. She wore boots, utility pants, and a T-shirt, with a towel draped around her neck. Her short hair was wet and the light breeze carried the scent of lavender.

"Captain," he said with a smile, "got plans for the evening? I heard you used to play lacrosse, maybe we could work on our stick handling?"

She stopped. "Geez, Doc, you don't give up, do you? I don't have much time, we're pulling out at 0430. You?"

"They told us 0300, then 0630, and now just 'stand by.' Hurry up ... "

"And wait."

"Did you get the same orders, bring gear for an amphibious op plus one seabag?"

"Yeah. I suppose we'll get a briefing when we get to the ships."

"This is all very strange," he said slowly. "A lot of things are happening I don't like."

"Such as?"

"Like all the spooks that have been coming and going. Not to mention the nuclear guys?"

"Nuclear, spooks—how do you know this?"

She seemed more curious than defensive. She really didn't know more than he did. "For one thing, a guy I went to college with was here yesterday. We took physics together and wrote a paper about theft of nuclear weapons for another course. Now he works for a NEST team. They do searches for nuclear weapons and dirty ... "

"I know what NEST is. What about the spooks? I haven't run into any agency types."

"They fly in during the night and talk only to the big guys—regimental command and a couple of senior ops officers they brought up from Pendleton. I heard they flew in some kind of equipment too. One of them had a skin infection, and they brought him over to see me. Black cammies, obviously brand new. I convinced him I couldn't see him without some kind of ID."

"That's crap."

"He didn't know that. Agency ID"

Kelli Moore wondered why the doctor was so concerned. She was good at reading people, but not this guy. Then she had an insight. Spooks, maybe he got that Navy Cross—and the scar—on some kind of classified mission. She knew more than one Marine whose trust in the system had gone out the window after a secret mission gone wrong.

He went on. "The way I see it, we're doing a regimental-sized amphibious op, which we will only find out about while on ship, to retrieve some missing nukes. This many Marines means serious opposition. Remember that the mission is everything to the people planning it, and we are just part of the equipment. Casualties are just the price you pay."

Then he did something that surprised her—and him—even more. He reached out, and for just a moment, put his hand on her cheek.

Then he quickly turned and hurried away.

CHAPTER 27

ABDULLAH NAZER SAT on the veranda behind his
office building, just a few blocks from the harbor. He
sipped a small cup of rich Yemen Matari coffee while he
waited for his nephew, Ali. Though Yemen was the world's
first commercial coffee market, a tradition dating back half
a millennium, between climate change and political fighting,
the legendary Yemen mocha had become almost rare.

His reverie was interrupted by some kind of commotion
outside the rear gate of the enclosed courtyard. The door
was opened by one of the guards—with a freshly a cut lip.
He admitted a short, but handsome, young man in an army
uniform—Ali al-Ahmar.

Ali smiled, revealing white teeth that gleamed above a
short, neatly-trimmed beard. He strode across the courtyard
towards his uncle, who rose to confront him. The only son
of his sister, Yasmin, young Ali's father had died in the 1994
civil war, a largely pointless conflict which left the ongoing

tensions between North and South still unresolved. With his sister a young widow caring for an infant son, Abdullah had taken both into his household and had raised Ali as his own.

"Captain al-Ahmar, what was going on out there?"

"Oh nothing, Uncle. One of your guards forgot himself and failed to salute when I approached."

Nazer was afraid it was something like that. Ali's father had been cruel and impatient, quick to anger at any insult—real or imagined. It was unfortunate to see these traits now manifesting in his nephew.

"When you strike one of my personal staff, he said, "you are striking me. Never, and I mean never, do it again."

"I...yes, Uncle."

Nazer knew he should have corrected the boy earlier in life, but the past could not be helped. Besides, the needs of the project must come first, and in important matters it was always best to trust family. Even when family was a young hothead.

"Uncle," exclaimed the young man as if nothing had happened, "You have good news?"

"The best."

Ali made a move to step into the building towards his uncle's office, but the older man placed a restraining hand on his shoulder. "Best we talk outdoors. I have my office swept daily for listening devices, but I am not so vain as to believe we are smarter than the Americans, at least not in this area."

They both took seats in carved wooden chairs tucked back in the shade, away from the rising desert sun.

"The items we've been waiting for have been moved to a warehouse in Arad," said Nazer. The translated PAL manual has been delivered by the courier. Our Iraqi friend..." Nazer scowled at the use of the word, "has begun to assemble the PAL encoder. We should be ready to ship in five or six days."

Ali stroked his short beard for a moment. "You are thinking you can use the new road to move the warheads into Saudi Arabia? Are they delivering them to their final destination?"

"No. They wish to remain in the background."

"Uncle, isn't it time you reveal to me the purpose of this project?"

His Uncle smiled and replied, "Today is the day. Circumstances have developed far better than anyone could have suspected. Put simply, we wish to eliminate the threat from the Persians. So long as Teheran dominates the Strait, pursues nuclear weapons, and controls an enormous military, none of the Arab states west of the Gulf can ever be safe. A truly dramatic act is required to change the status quo."

His nephew nodded. "And what could be more dramatic than six thermonuclear warheads?"

"We also need to drive the Americans from the region. It is true they have provided a measure of security, but their presence inflames the likes of ISIS and al-Qaeda, fosters dependency, and ultimately serves their interests instead of ours, the interests of the Arab peoples."

"But we don't have enough warheads to target both Iran and the Americans."

"Fortunately, we don't have to. The Americans, in the course of their foolish war with Iran, have seriously damaged the mullah's military forces for us. What remains is the heart of Persia, their cities and their oil production. As soon as the warheads are armed, we will move them by truck into Iran via Saudi Arabia, Kuwait, and then Iraq. They will move through a series of obscure intermediaries; my cousin now owns small trucking companies in each of these countries staffed by loyal men. In about ten days, we will vaporize their four largest cities. Destruction will be total. In a few seconds, they will be set back a thousand years. One container will be delivered by a small supply ship to their oil terminal at Kharg Island which will then be completely destroyed. There will be a lot of fallout, fortunately most of it will land on the accursed fanatics in Pakistan."

Abdullah Nazer, at heart a militant Sunni with a deep and lifelong hatred of non-Arabs in general, and the Persian Shia in particular, leaned back in his chair, took a small sip of coffee, and smiled at the image he was creating.

"What of the sixth warhead?" Ali asked.

"Even at a pivotal moment in history it may well be wise to prepare for what the Americans call a 'rainy day.' I propose we retain one weapon for unexpected contingencies. There is little that can be achieved with six of these magnificent devices that cannot be achieved with five."

"But how will this rid us of the Americans?"

"Who will the world blame for this new holocaust? These are sophisticated devices. Who possess such weapons? Who is engaged in a struggle to the death with Iran? While Iran is not popular with anyone, the use of thermonuclear weapons on a Muslim state, even a deviant state, will produce such a spasm of anger across the Middle East that the Americans will have no choice but to go home."

"It would be natural to assume it was the Americans," replied Ali. "But I have read that scientists can tell the origin of nuclear weapons by analyzing the fallout. Won't it be obvious they were Russian warheads?"

"It pleases me that you have read on this subject. The seller, this Janos, has provided information that shows such analysis is much less reliable than many believe. Besides, few citizens of the Gulf region are sophisticated in matters of science. The circumstances will dictate their response. Our family has connections with al-Jazeera which will broadcast the horrific details of an American nuclear attack on a Muslim nation. That will ensure the outcome we seek."

Ali smiled broadly. "Perhaps our final weapon will yet find its way to the doorstep of America?"

"All things are possible. For now, though, we must focus on the mission before us. Get up to Arad. We cannot be certain that the Americans, or even the Russians, have not somehow found out the destination of these weapons. Some kind of Special Forces attack is always possible. Major Ismail, one of my best men, has a company at our warehouse and dispersed throughout the town. I want you to be in a position to block removal of the weapons should they be seized by our enemies. The transport boxes are far too heavy to remove by helicopter and there is no landing field nearby. Any attempt to retrieve the weapons would require removing them by road to the coast or to an airfield." Nazer jabbed a finger into his nephew's chest. "Do not allow that to happen."

"Yes Uncle, I will defend our project to the death."

"When can you leave?"

Ali paused for a moment. "We have some men on leave and others are out patrolling the back country. Two days. It will take two days to prepare for movement."

"Very good, Captain. Nothing is going to happen in the next two days"

CHAPTER 28

KONSTANTIN DUROV HAD a photographic
memory for people. Much better than facial recognition software, since he could also identify individuals from
their minor mannerisms and habits. He had once recognized
a British agent by the way the man held a cigar.

His usual job was to scan covert video taken outside
various London offices of the British security services, MI-5
and MI-6, and then compare them to arrivals at Moscow's
Sheremetyevo International Airport, surveillance videos of
public transit, and of popular meeting spots near the western embassies. Once he identified a potential intelligence
agent they were followed until caught committing espionage,
or better still, compromised into working for the Russian
Federation.

Because their informant network included both the military and the GRU, Durov's employer, the FSB, had learned
fairly quickly about the missing warheads. They had decided

to withhold this information, at least for the moment, from their colleagues in the SVR to allow the GRU to conduct the search for the weapons. The thieves, that was another matter—finding people was their specialty. They also began an investigation of the Grishkovs to assess just how much they were involved in this act of treason. This, however, called for a degree of caution. The elder Grishkov had highly placed friends in the Defense Ministry, so the case officers decided to begin with some very discrete inquiries.

Durov was surprised when his unique skill was suddenly required outside Russia. He was given dossiers on three individuals from Severomorsk who were high value fugitives probably on the run somewhere in Europe. Finding and returning them was assigned highest possible priority, and Durov was to work on no other assignment until the fugitives were back in Russia. Or dead. He could travel anywhere, and expense was not a consideration.

Durov had heard rumors about the theft of nuclear weapons, so an urgent assignment to locate fugitives connected to a weapon reconditioning facility could not be a coincidence. This was a difficult problem, but one if concluded successfully would certainly push him even higher in the FSB hierarchy.

He began by scanning videos from St. Petersburg and Tallinn, the fugitives' last known locations. The older man and the young woman were easily located arriving in both cities. The younger man was seen only arriving at St. Petersburg. Durov's first break came when he recognized the couple—they were clearly acting like a couple—leaving from the Tallinn train station. The man, Kovolenko, who had left Russia with a huge beard, was now clean shaven, but his height and the shape of his face were unmistakable. The young woman, Anna Voronina, had cut her hair and dyed it blond, added very high heels, and a pair of fashionable Italian sunglasses. These two obviously had some skill at counter-surveillance. Nonetheless, her unusual earlobes gave her away despite only a second on camera.

He traveled to Poland, where he worked his way south and managed another quick look in Warsaw. He played a hunch and continued south. A combination of bribes, threats, and bravado gained him access to surveillance footage at train stations in the Czech Republic and Austria without result. He considered heading west into Switzerland, but stopped at Venice as much for his own amusement as for the mission.

He was rewarded by a quick glimpse of Kovolenko changing trains.

Two more days of harassing station managers, local police, and security personnel brought him to Salerno. There he saw the backs of a tall man and a blond woman boarding a small coastal freighter he identified as belonging to Theologides Shipping of Piraeus. It did not take long to discover the ship's next stop was Porto-Vecchio on the east coast of Corsica. He used his diplomatic passport and American Express Platinum card to charter a small plane, which landed in Corsica an hour and a half later.

The French immigration officials, masters of bureaucracy, referred him from one office to another. Finally, after the exchange of two five-hundred Euro notes, he discovered no one from the Theologides ship *Milos Oceanus* had passed through immigration. So by this point they had European Union passports and simply walked off the ship. What phenomenal laxity in security. No wonder Europe was such a mess!

An additional five-hundred Euros, however, allowed him a high-speed review of several security cameras in the dock area from the day *Milos Oceanus* had arrived. And there was Kovolenko, wearing a black sport jacket and driving cap, accompanied by Voronina, now sporting a punk look, with nose ring and pink hair. They were behaving more like father and daughter now, another sign of advanced tradecraft for a couple of amateurs, assuming they really were amateurs. He doubted anyone else in the FSB would have been able to trace them beyond Warsaw. Despite their efforts, though, they had chosen their current location poorly. Porto-Vecchio was a small town, and a skilled investigator would be able to find them in hours.

As he prepared to leave the docks for his next stop, Durov noticed a furtive movement to his right, near a collection of shipping containers. In that quick glance, he felt sure he had seen the so-far elusive Boris Voronin. His beard was also gone, but his rat-like nose and closely-set eyes gave him away. Durov quickly drew the small Makarov 9 mm pistol he carried in a holster in the small of his back. The weapon, the primary reason he carried a diplomatic passport, was largely obsolete, but Durov clung to it as a link to the old KGB.

He walked briskly towards the containers, confident his suspect had not seen him. Moving past the first container he looked quickly left, then right but saw nothing. He passed the second and third doing the same. Again Voronin was nowhere to be seen. At the end of the fourth container he paused briefly, then stepped forward and looked left, the muzzle of his weapon preceding him.

The blow was as forceful as it was unexpected. He instantly realized the error that would cost him his life. He had looked left three times, and Boris Voronin, hiding at the fourth intersection, had counted on him doing the same.

The last thing Konstantin Durov heard was, "Goodbye, Checkist bastard."

Alexi Kovolenko and Anna Voronina, once again blond and without the nose ring, were now aboard the car ferry to Nice. Just before sailing they had purchased a well-worn Volkswagen for cash. From Nice, they would drive north using Maltese passports as Adelina and Cezar Miklos. While not Maltese, these nondescript eastern European names would arouse no suspicion—Malta was well known for selling citizenship to those who could afford it. In Nice, Anna would acquire several Hermes scarves and a Fendi bag while Alexi looked forward to a new gold Rolex plus an Armani jacket to augment their cover. They could certainly afford it. Now that delivery had been completed, Alexi and Anna had access to accounts holding eighty million euros.

CHAPTER 29

BRENDAN WALLACE SIPPED coffee from a mug with the presidential logo while graphics were loaded onto the wall displays. He looked at each of the assembled officials.

So did Baker. But if the President was trying to take a read on their true feelings about Operation Ocean Reach, he was out of luck. The Situation Room was the ultimate high stakes poker game, and none of these players was revealing a thing.

Wallace broke into the soft background noise of quiet conversations. "Let's get started. Ted, are we ready to go?"

General Theodore Roosevelt Lennox was present for the first time in over a week, replacing Captain Washington, who was now deployed with the command group.

"Mr. President, the elements of Task Force 58 are in position. Nothing's occurred that makes us believe this Abdullah Nazer, or anyone else in Yemen, knows what's coming. The *Abraham Lincoln* strike group has been pulled east overnight and is now positioned to provide additional air support. They've been temporarily designated Task Force 58.3. Our Marines are on deck in helicopters or in vehicles on the landing craft and ready to go. We're just waiting for your go ahead." Lennox looked expectantly at the President.

"Thank you General." Wallace turned to Baker. "Sonny, just how sure are we that when we get there we'll find those nukes?"

Baker stifled a groan. Now that the operation was actually ready to go, Wallace was getting nervous and repeatedly asked for more and more assurance of success. "Sir, you've seen all the data I have. It's very strong. We have solid satellite surveillance showing those shipping containers being trucked east, then north, to the small town of Arad. Last night you felt quite confident after seeing the data obtained by the SEALS." Two days before a dozen men from SEAL Team 4 had been infiltrated north of Arad into a blocking position to prevent further movement of the warheads to the north. They had sent a small battery-powered drone fitted with a lightweight neutron detector on a single pass over the suspect warehouse.

"Sonny," said Karen Hiller, "the President knows what he saw last night. He wants to know what you think now...today...right this minute!"

Wallace seemed taken aback with his Chief of Staff's outburst, but agreed with her sentiment. He simply looked at Sonny Baker with raised eyebrows, as if to say, "Well?"

Baker cleared his throat then stood to give himself a bit more gravitas. "The nukes are there Mr. President. Every shred of evidence supports that conclusion and that's what I believe."

"So you think we should launch the operation?"

"Yes sir, I do." Baker knew this question was for the purpose of putting him the on record. But there was obviously no choice; so there was no point in being evasive.

"Are all six warheads in that warehouse?"

This was the question Baker was hoping to avoid. There was strong evidence that there was more than one and probably more than three. It was impossible to say, however, that all six nuclear weapons were there. But he had to be upfront with the President. This was just too important. "We hope so, but there is no way to be sure."

"We all hope so Sonny. One more question. I know it's the one nobody wants to ask, but as Commander-in-Chief, I have to. Can they use one of those nukes against our people?"

Sonny Baker glanced around the room. Although the question was not specifically directed at him, everyone was looking in his direction and nobody else seemed about to answer. Depending on how the operation went, Baker's entire career in public service might be judged on what he said in the next minute.

"Mr. President, that's really two questions. First, can they? We don't think so. Mr. Suarez and his NEST colleagues don't think there's been enough time to fabricate the PAL. Without that they can't arm the weapons. Second, would they even if they could? CIA analysis of Abdullah Nazer shows him to be shrewd and calculating, but not a psychopath. Such an act would certainly end in his death and the destruction of his little empire. No, sir. We don't think he's a nuclear suicide bomber."

Brendan Wallace took a deep breath and looked at the video screens, one of which was a live feed from the flight deck of the *Essex*. The huge helicopters and the men and women crammed aboard added to the sense that everyone was waiting for his decision.

"All right, do it," he said. "Remember, though, that the United States is not declaring war on Yemen or on this little rump state run by Nazer. Our mission is to get in, get the nukes, and get back out. Minimum casualties on both sides. After we have those nukes, I'll decide how to deal with Nazer."

"You know where to find me." With that Brendan Wallace stood, turned, and followed closely by Karen Hiller, left the Situation Room.

General Ted Lennox looked at Sonny Baker who nodded. The General picked up one of the secure lines, this one to the National Military Command Center. In a moment the duty officer came on the line. Lennox identified himself and said, "Send the following order to Task Force 58, all elements, info CENTCOM: "Execute Ocean Reach, repeat Execute Ocean Reach." He took his seat, turned to the National Security Advisor, and asked, "Sonny, can you get us some coffee?"

CHAPTER 30

REAR ADMIRAL NATHAN Tucker looked across the expansive flight deck of the USS *Essex*. Six massive CH-53E Sea Stallions, each loaded with forty-four Marines, communications gear, and ammunition were ready to go. Tucker was impressed that Colonel Mark, the regimental commander, was leaving with the first wave to establish his command post just south of the target at Arad. There was some risk in this, but in Tucker's experience, Marines were most effectively led from the front. He had not been able to spend much time with Mark, one of the many liabilities of an operation put together on the fly, but he seemed like an officer motivated more by duty than by ambition, the primary quality he sought in subordinates. The fact that in civilian life he was the senior operations manager for a major airline, who dealt every day with an operation consisting of thousands of moving parts, was also a plus.

Tucker, himself, was no stranger to complex amphibious operations. He was selected for this job specifically because he had put together the Qeshm Island landing. Although the operation had suffered serious and controversial setbacks, everyone involved felt Tucker had performed brilliantly. Feeling there wasn't much left for him to do, or to prove, he decided after Qeshm to apply for retirement. He was on terminal leave enjoying an afternoon of reef fishing at his home in Key West when General Ted Lennox called personally to ask if he would plan and command one final, very secret, operation. Knowing he could not really refuse, he was after all not actually retired; he did ask the Chairman for one concession. "No politicians, no trips to D.C., and I choose my own staff." Lennox decided to grant the Admiral's request. It was exactly what he wanted every day, he just couldn't have it.

Despite its wealth of material support, Ocean Reach was still a complex, fast-moving plan. It was technically not an assault; it was an amphibious raid. The plan was to deploy the 1st Battalion, the 1/28, just south of Arad where they would block movement to the south. They would then deploy two companies into the town to secure the nukes. Division MPs would maintain order and secure the streets around the warehouse. When the engineers, who would land on the beach with their heavy equipment, joined them, they would load the warheads and then transport them back to the *Ashland*. The third company would be held in reserve.

The 2/28 would deploy a company east and west of Arad both to prevent the Yemenis from moving the weapons and to prevent any hostile reinforcements from arriving. The

SEALS held a position just north of the town near a short bridge and were prepared to blow the bridge, if necessary, to block movement north. The only place known to have none of Nazer's forces was north of Arad so the SEALS would not be reinforced. They had the option of being retrieved by helicopter, taking their desert 'dune buggies' south to the landing craft, or if necessary they could exfiltrate across the desert into Oman. The 3/28 would similarly block the coast road east and west with a company held in reserve at the landing beach.

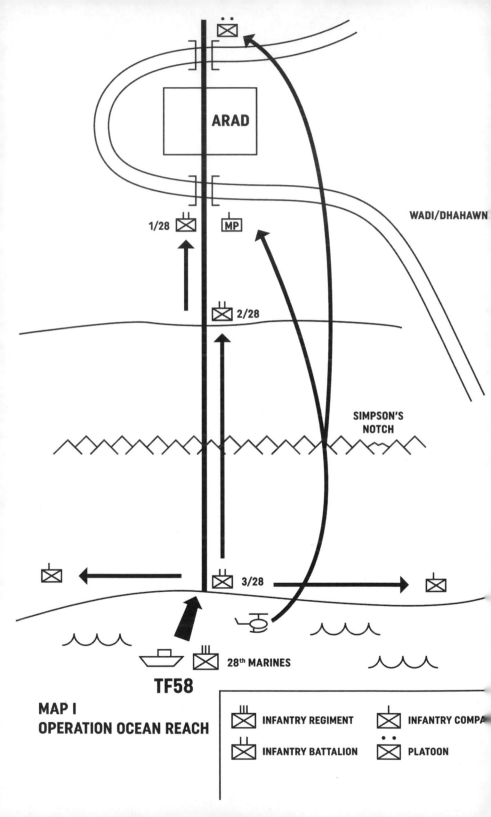

THE FACT THAT the plan called for all Marines to be in position within two hours of launching the mission worried him. In principle, though, he had everything required to make it work. Each of the big amphibious ships, the *Essex* and the *Iwo Jima*, had six huge CH-53E helicopters and three LCACs, high speed landing craft capable to cruising across the sea at over thirty knots. The *Ashland*, designated to receive the nukes, had two more assigned specifically to the engineers. That was a lot of lift capacity, and Ocean Reach would need all of it.

Just then he was handed a single message sheet with one line on it. "Execute Ocean Reach." It was dated September 13, two days after the infamous date in 2001 that had begun sixteen years of almost continuous warfare in this part of the world. He said a silent prayer that this September day would have a far better outcome for America than its predecessor.

Tucker scanned the tactical displays. Unconcerned that the Yemenis would detect their radar emissions, the task force sensors reached out in a relentless search for potential threats. Seeing none, he nodded to Captain Neill Washington, now designated his operations officer. "We're go."

Washington spoke quickly to several sailors manning their small operations center. Immediately, the order was passed to Air Operations, the well deck where the LCACs waited, and to the other ships of Task Force 58.

Just below him the Air Boss of the *Essex* picked up his radio handset and bellowed, "Okay, gents; let's start 'em up." Turbines whined and the massive rotor blades began to turn.

Showtime.

CHAPTER 31

HIP TO HIP and kneecap to kneecap Mike McGregor sat among the tightly packed Marines of the leading element of the 1/28. As he listened to the turbines of the forward CH-53E winding up, he pulled a pair of foam earplugs from a small plastic container clipped to his body armor and screwed them in. He looked at the Marines near him and pointed to their ears.

The two corpsmen accompanying him, HM2 Courtney Kales and HM2 Brad Greene, already had theirs in place. He gave them both a thumbs up. Greene, a streetwise firefighter/paramedic and adrenaline junkie who reminded McGregor of himself ten years ago, grinned broadly and returned the gesture. Kales, highly skilled, but with only hospital experience and no previous deployments, smiled weakly and nodded. Thanks to the new combatant status for medical personnel, each carried an M-4 rifle—an updated version of the venerable M-16—muzzle down, but were burdened with only three extra magazines compared to the twelve carried by each Marine. The battalion surgeons, at the direction of Colonel Mark, still carried the M-9 Beretta. This was all right with McGregor, who carried his in an old fashioned shoulder holster on the left side of his body armor. He knew that by time the doctors had to start shooting, there would be plenty of rifles available.

The Marines, who a few minutes ago were smiling and joking, now had their game faces on.

Two days before, they had finally been briefed on their mission. McGregor had the small satisfaction of knowing that the prediction he'd related to Kelli Moore had been amazingly accurate. He wished he could have seen her face when they brought up the nukes.

The briefing had taken place on the hanger deck of the *Essex*. Six Russian warheads. When the briefer said that, he had everyone's full attention—except McGregor's. He had rubbed the scar below his right eye. Another high priority, top secret mission.

Colonel Aaron Mark and Lieutenant Colonel Jeremiah Walsh, seated at the forward end of the same CH-53E, weren't thinking about anything but the business at hand. Each man was reviewing the operation order, which if printed, would have run over two-hundred pages. There were no printed pages, however. Each had a tablet computer which was built at a secure facility run by the NSA. Inside its Kevlar and titanium case was highly encrypted satellite communication, massive databases, and unique security feature—a single incorrect password entry would ignite a ten gram thermite charge that would destroy the entire unit in seconds.

Both officers knew that the next few hours would define their entire Marine Corps careers. Typically, the Marine Corps Reserve was deployed in company-sized units to augment active duty battalions. With the new system of alert regiments, though, they knew an assignment like Ocean Reach was possible, at least in principle. Now here it was, and the stakes were as high as for any mission ever. For both of them, failure was simply not an option.

The big Sea Stallion rose from the deck, hovered briefly, then made a broad turn around the stern before heading north. Colonel Mark got a quick glimpse of the ship through the pilot's windscreen. He saw the second helicopter in line just rising from the deck and then, as they passed the stern, saw a massive LCAC pulling out of the well deck and into the pale blue of the Arabian Sea.

As they began to head north towards Yemen, he returned to reviewing the available maps, satellite photos, and intelligence reports on Abdullah Nazer and his military forces. Mark normally liked brevity in his intelligence reports, but what he got from both CIA and Naval Intelligence for this operation was too damn brief. They reported only that Nazer controlled a small, but well-trained, army that was augmented by Saudi 'volunteers'. The estimates of its size, about ten thousand, came with a large margin of error. With just over a million people in an area of 88,000 square miles, Nazer's little empire consisted of mostly empty desert. Specific information about forces in Arad was maddeningly vague.

Reports showed that Nazer had a number of old Soviet era BTR-60 armored vehicles and one battalion of modern T-72 main battle tanks. The tanks, and the bulk of his troops, were fortunately located on the western side of his territory facing his old Yemeni comrades. There were a dozen attack helicopters of several types located at al-Mukalla, with estimates that about half were flyable at any time. The small navy, also at Mukalla, consisted of five old Osa Class missile boats and a single relatively modern Italian-built Maestrale class frigate. This was located more than two-hundred-fifty kilometers away south of Socotra Island and was reported to be on patrol against Somali pirates. If necessary, it could be dealt with by *Carter*, which remained on station halfway between Socotra and the landing beaches.

The original plan had been for drone surveillance to update the status of Nazer's forces, and in particular those in position to attack the beachhead or those around their target at Arad. This was vetoed by the White House for fear that evidence of intelligence gathering, especially near Arad, might lead to the weapons being moved prematurely. Satellite imaging was useful, but intermittent sandstorms had left a number of holes in what they knew.

The six helicopters from *Essex* had now formed up in two groups of three and crossed the coast east of the small town of Qishn about ten minutes later. They proceeded northeast to the road that led to Arad, and ten minutes after that they passed over the knife-edge east-west ridgeline, with its wide highway cut surrounded by boulders large and small. Several of the flight crews remarked on how many thousands of tons of rock had been blasted away to permit the passage of this remote road. One pilot noted the unusual width of the cut, far wider than the road required and was reminded that the road would be followed by an oil pipeline.

Most of the aviators also noted the unusual half-moon bite in the ridgeline to the east and one took the trouble to consult his map.

"Simpson's Notch," he said. "I wonder who Simpson was?" No one aboard had a clue.

It wasn't long before the sweeping curve of the Wadi Dhahawn and the town of Arad became visible. Their destination was a broad plateau on the south side of the Wadi Dhahawn where the road crossed a bridge, or more accurately a causeway, about a hundred-fifty meters long. The wadi was only six or seven meters deep at most, but the south side was too steep for vehicles and tough to ascend even on foot, so Arad was dependent on the bridge for its commercial life.

Each crew chief signaled one minute to their passengers and prepared to lower the rear ramp. Rifles were turned muzzle up, and rounds locked and loaded. The plateau was large enough to land all the CH-53s simultaneously so each slowed, flared, and touched down. Ramps were dropped and the lead element of the 1st Battalion, 28th Marine Regiment stormed out to establish a defensive perimeter. A second flight was due in less than an hour, and the Marines landing by LCAC were expected in two to three hours. Being Marines, however, meant they didn't expect things to go as expected, so they also unloaded ammunition, water, cases of rations, medical supplies, and four M224A1 60 mm mortars.

A platoon immediately ran across the bridge and secured the north side. They were quickly reinforced, and within ten minutes of landing both ends of the bridge were secure.

CHAPTER 32

CAPTAIN SECOND RANK Anatoly Grishkov picked up the phone in his office. "Grishkov."

"We have new orders."

He was too stunned to speak, but it didn't matter, since his uncle had already hung up.

The phrase, 'we have new orders' was a warning both men had agreed to shortly after the disappearance of the warheads. It meant that not only had the FSB learned of the missing warheads and the GRU investigation, but were also prepared to move against the Admiral and himself. The call required an immediate response any time of day.

He left the headquarters building of the Second Submarine Division, telling the two sailors in the outer office that he would return within an hour, and he walked up the street towards his uncle's office, where he was greeted at the door of the building by Captain First Class Piotr Kulakov.

As he followed the grim-faced Kulakov towards the Admiral's office, the elder Grishkov hurried around a corner carrying a small duffel. Kulakov took his bag without a word. "It is time to go," his uncle said. "Right now. We will take my official vehicle."

As they exited the rear of the building and walked to the Admiral's staff car, Grishkov noticed for the first time that Piotr Kulakov was carrying a sidearm. They drove quickly from the building, Kulakov at the wheel.

"Uncle, what is happening?"

"Nothing good Anatoly. But I believe we will have just enough time. My people called—" he looked at his watch—"about ten minutes ago. Four senior officers of the FSB landed at the airfield without warning and without a flight plan. They demanded transportation directly to my office. Fortunately, the vehicle they were provided stalled and could not be restarted." The Admiral gave a sly smile. "I am sorry I could not give you more warning."

At that moment the staff car skidded to a halt in front of one of the base helicopter hangers where a Kamov-27 anti-submarine warfare helicopter sat waiting. Located about twelve kilometers from the regular airfield, the fleet's ASW training unit was based there.

The Admiral approached the ground crew and told them the flight crew would arrive shortly, and that they would wait in the aircraft. They climbed through the access door, and Anatoly was surprised to see Kulakov strap into the pilot's seat while his uncle took the seat beside him. Both donned communication headsets and signaled him to do the same as he strapped into one of the crew stations behind them.

He was even more surprised to see Kulakov begin to work with the various cockpit switches which was quickly followed by the whine of the turbines.

The radio crackled. "Why are you starting the engines without the flight crew?" asked the ground controller.

The Admiral activated his radio. "I'm afraid we are in a hurry. Captain Kulakov has received basic flight instruction and is simply warming up the engines."

When Kulakov increased power, pulled back on the cyclic, and lifted the helicopter into the air, the radio crackled again. "Admiral, you must know this is very much against regulations."

"Yes, I do." His uncle then switched off the radio. Over the intercom he told his nephew, "Do not be alarmed. Piotr has completed basic helicopter training and has about one hundred hours in the Kamov. I authorized it. Fortunately, this helicopter practically flies itself."

"But won't the FSB send the Air Force after us?"

"Eventually. Remember, the control tower at that helicopter field is not about to report a Vice Admiral for taking a little ride. Only after those FSB thugs arrive at my office and begin to make inquiries will they ultimately discover what we have done. At that point they will have to call Moscow to find someone with enough authority to get our friends in the Air Force off their asses and into the cockpits. After that, aircraft will have to be fueled and armed. By then we will be in Finland."

Indeed, after an hour and a half of low level flight over the lakes and pine forests of Arctic Russia, Kulakov and the Admiral consulted the small handheld GPS unit the

Admiral had taken from his duffel, and both men pointed at a clearing in the dense trees.

They descended, and less than a minute after shutting down the engines their aircraft was approached by a dilapidated van. Three men wearing colorful outdoor clothing piled out to meet them. The three Russians were handed similar waterproof windbreakers and odd-looking hats which they donned in the back of the small van.

One of the men, a muscular young man with a British accent said to his uncle, "Good to meet you Agent Stella. The Americans passed along your signal, and we headed here straightaway. Don't worry about your helicopter. In a few minutes several of our Finnish friends will fly it up to a deserted bay on Lake Inari where it will disappear into the depths."

"Uncle," said Anatoly. "You're an American agent?"

"Of course not. I'm a British agent. The Americans supplied a piece of vital equipment, so they have become like the camel with its nose under the tent." One of the men, apparently an American, scowled at the comparison. "Think about it Anatoly, just where is our president leading us? He is trying to bring back the cold war, to impoverish the nation by rebuilding a military machine we cannot afford, to alienate our European neighbors and for what? To regain part of the Ukraine? Okay we have it—now what the hell are we going to do with it? A few years ago I decided I had to do something. This was it."

Anatoly Grishkov listened in silence as his uncle spouted what was both treason and . . . he had to admit, truth. In any event, he had known the day he discovered the fake warhead that his life would be changed. He just hadn't imagined he would end up fleeing Russia in a stolen helicopter with his treasonous uncle one step ahead of the FSB. What could he do? He was a wanted man in his own country. All he could do was trust his uncle, and put himself in the hands of these western agents, men who up until today had been his sworn enemies.

He leaned back in his seat and closed his eyes as the van bumped along the back roads of northern Finland.

After half an hour of driving along winding roads, they arrived at the airfield. The men running the operation hustled the Russians out of the van, and they all walked a short distance to a waiting Gulfstream G-650 which bore a UK tail number, but no other markings. They boarded quickly, and the door was closed. A man wearing a generic pilot's uniform stepped back to greet them. "We're cleared for takeoff. No traffic, we can go any time."

As they belted themselves into the Gulfstream's luxurious leather seats, they were approached by two cabin attendants, a male and a tall, very attractive female with short, very dark hair, who asked if they wanted something to drink. All three Russians asked for vodka which brought a smile to the woman's face—as if she had been expecting exactly that order.

The flight attendants, both sergeants in the RAF, actually were there to provide service, but as instructors in armed and unarmed combat, they also provided security for the aircraft.

As they taxied into position at the end of the runway, Grishkov's uncle explained that when he began to suspect trouble from the FSB, the aircraft had been staged from

Britain to a NATO airbase in Norway, and when he made the call telling him, "We have new orders," the message was intercepted by the American NSA and passed immediately to British MI-6, who then dispatched the plane to Finland. The engines increased from a low whine to a roar, they rapidly accelerated, took off, and climbed into the Arctic sky. Vodka glasses were refilled and the three agents, none of whom had introduced themselves, began making urgent calls on encrypted satellite phones.

CHAPTER 33

LIEUTENANT COLONEL JEREMIAH Walsh stood at the north end of the bridge with a pair of German Leica binoculars to his eyes. The terrain around Arad was flat and sandy, with only occasional small tufts of brush near the edge of the wadi. He knew most of the buildings had been constructed in the last twenty years, but they were of classic Middle East design, tan adobe, one or two story. The town looked as if it had been there for a hundred years. Or a thousand.

Arad was laid out in a rectangle four hundred meters wide and about six hundred long. The main road was wide enough to accommodate large trucks, but the side streets were narrower to keep out the blazing desert sun. The layout reminded Walsh of the claustrophobic streets in the towns of Anbar Province, where he had learned the basics of infantry command the hard way.

Binoculars back in their case, Walsh put out his hand, and his driver gave him the handset for the AN/PRC-150(C) tactical radio mounted in the command HUMVEE. "Eagle six, this is Eagle actual. Confirm position."

In the first deviation from his original plan, Walsh had dispatched a platoon from E company and four engineers to the bridge across the Wadi Dhahwan just north of Arad. Due to some oddity of geology, the wadi on the north side was only twenty meters across, but more than ten meters deep, with near vertical sides. He wanted to secure that bridge despite the SEALS having secured a position at another bridge further north. He did not want to chase the weapons north to the SEALS' location and then have to truck them back through the middle of Arad. He knew the SEALS, who were already unhappy about their participation in a Marine Reserve operation, would object to the redundancy, so he avoided the inevitable showdown by resolving the problem once the operation was underway.

"Six in position north of the bridge. We have one squad on the south side. Everything quiet. The Saudi Aramco gas station on the north end of town has a couple of pickup trucks at the pumps, but we don't see the drivers."

"Roger six. Report any changes. Eagle out."

His driver handed him the handset for a second radio, this one dedicated to the command net which was monitored by every commander in the 1/28 down to platoon level as well as Colonel Mark, the overall commander. It was time. "Okay people, let's move out."

The plan was simple—the best plans usually are. In Phase 1, A Company would advance on the west (left) side of the road and secure the town west of the main road. E company would do the same on the east side. B Company and the command element would advance directly to the target and secure the weapons. Phase 2 would have the MP Company, now holding just south of the bridge, secure the area around the target warehouse and the egress road and handle any prisoners. The engineers would bring up their heavy equipment and load the warheads. Finally, in Phase 3, the engineers would transport the warheads back to the beach and move them to the *Ashland*. The Marines would then follow the engineers to the beach where the troops deployed as blocking forces would also withdraw. One company would remain south of the bridge to prevent any pursuit, and when the beach was cleared they, along with the SEALS, would be extracted by helicopter. If all went well the operation would be completed no later than 1800.

If all went well.

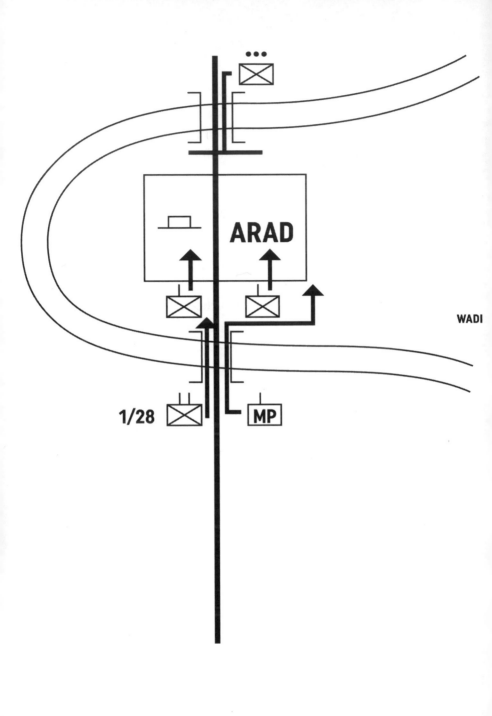

MAP 2
ATTACK ON ARAD

THE MARINES OF first battalion began to advance, moving in squad-sized groups abreast. At first the town remained completely quiet. Then came the crack of rifle shots, a dozen at least, and Marines began going down. Walsh heard his company commanders ordering their automatic weapons teams to put fire onto the nearest buildings. He looked quickly at the wounded through his binoculars and saw seven men being tended to by their platoon corpsmen.

Each appeared to have a leg wound. Odd.

The suppressive fire discouraged, but didn't eliminate, the sniper fire. As they approached to within a hundred meters, Walsh heard a small explosion, a sound quite different from a rifle shot. To his right, four men down. He knew immediately it had to be a mine. This particular mine bounced a foot into the air before exploding, its load of three-hundred steel balls intended to wound, not to kill.

Walsh pick up the command radio and spoke, "Get to that first row of buildings on the double. Look out for small mounds of sand; they conceal the mine detonators. Get moving!"

Junior officers and platoon sergeants shouted orders, and Marines attacked at the run, dividing their attention between the sand beneath their feet and the buildings ahead. In thirty seconds the first Marines reached the buildings and began to kick in doors. Only one more mine was heard.

CHAPTER 34

MIKE MCGREGOR DECIDED to stay with the battalion aid station that was set up just south of the bridge. The action would be close enough to allow immediate evacuation of wounded, and he was much better equipped to handle casualties where he was. By time the 1/28 reached the town, twenty-one Marines had been wounded, twelve gunshot wounds and nine shrapnel wounds. Each casualty had a leg wound, and several of the mine casualties had been hit in an arm as well. Fortunately, none of the mine shrapnel had penetrated anyone's body armor. Several injuries were minor enough to treat with just a dressing—they could worry about surgery later. Four, however, were very serious—major arteries hit or bones shattered. McGregor and Nicole Ellis were working hard to control bleeding and to limit nerve damage that could ultimately lead to amputation. Medevac helicopters from *Essex* and *Iwo Jima* were inbound.

The ambulance McGregor was using as the center of his battalion aid station had two radios, one for the command net and one for the medical evacuation net. His driver, Lance Corporal Keila Jordan, was monitoring both. "Got Colonel Mark for you, sir. Wants to talk on Tac-7."

Tac-7 was the commander's personal frequency.

McGregor hopped into the passenger seat and put on a pair of headphones. Jordan had already set it to the new frequency. "Eagle one-two here."

"Doc, give me a quick casualty report."

"Twenty-one so far, Colonel. Mix of gunshot and shrapnel from the anti-personnel mines. Mostly leg wounds. I think their idea is to create a lot of casualties which will require evacuation. We had to use quite a few Marines as litter bearers."

"Sounds about right, Doc. Hopefully once we have the perimeter secure, their snipers will have a tougher time. In the meantime, do you need any help?"

McGregor was not used to having someone so senior ask if he needed help. He didn't want to admit it, but he and Lt. Ellis were getting overwhelmed. Each of their wounded required pain management, control of bleeding, IV fluids, and dressings. His corpsmen were doing a great job, but...

"Sir, could you ask Commander Barnes to send Lt. Russell from the evac station at the beach up here with an additional ambulance?"

"Will do. Falcon out."

He turned to Ellis, "Help on the way."

"Russell had a lot of surgical training before he went into emergency medicine," she said. "We really could use him.

But won't Commander Barnes be unhappy you bypassed him and went directly to the CO?"

"Fuck him."

Ellis recoiled at this.

"I didn't go to the CO, he called me and asked if we needed help. We're up to our eyeballs in wounded, so I told him, yes, we could use a little help. If Barnes objects then he shouldn't be in that job."

With that he turned to the next casualty and forgot about Commander Kenneth Laroche Barnes.

For the next half hour, McGregor methodically worked through a steady series of casualties, including the day's first KIA, a Marine from the 1/28 hit in the neck with a grenade fragment. Despite truly heroic efforts, the corpsmen could not control the bleeding, and he died within minutes of arriving at the aid station. Disheartened, Mike McGregor left it to his corpsmen to evacuate the body.

He was surprised when he saw Kelli Moore sitting in the ambulance while Nicole Ellis sutured a wound on her left arm.

"Nicole," he said, "what's happened to Detective Moore?"

He smiled and Kelli Moore, despite the pain of her wound, smiled back. For just a second, McGregor was transported off the bloody hilltop in Yemen and back to Ann Arbor.

"Got surprised by a kid," said the Captain. "Not even twelve by the look of him. One of my guys wanted to put him in flex-cuffs, but I said no. The he jumped at me and pulled some kind of curved knife. Got me across the arm. Nothing serious, my corpsman put a dressing on, but the

CO insisted I come back here. Didn't want one of his girls bleeding, I guess."

McGregor looked closely at the three-inch laceration. "Captain, this is one of those rare cases in which your commanding officer was actually right. This would have kept bleeding and probably gotten infected. Nicole will have this repaired in just a minute, and you'll be back in the fight."

Kelli Moore thanked the PA and walked to where she had left her pack. She quickly changed into a clean shirt, but left on her blood stained green T-shirt. Without looking back, she jumped into her Humvee. Her driver floored the old vehicle while the Captain replaced her helmet and put a fresh magazine into her Beretta.

As Kelli Moore disappeared into the blowing sand and dust, an M997A2 Humvee ambulance pulled into the aid station's parking area. The rear door opened, and Lieutenant Jim Russell hopped out carrying a large medical bag. Ellis and McGregor both knew and respected Russell, and started to walk towards the ambulance to greet him. They were surprised, however, when a second passenger appeared at the door—Commander Kenneth Laroche Barnes, carrying a large field pack, wearing full body armor with helmet and mirrored fragment resistant sunglasses.

Nicole Ellis said under her breath, "Here's trouble."

Kenneth Barnes, the Regimental Surgeon, was not happy. He was rarely happy. Son of Eddie Barnes, known in the trade as 'The King of Scrap', Barnes came from a family with interests in more than a dozen scrap yards, junk yards, and recycling plants in the Chicago area. Despite their wealth, young Kenny Barnes could never escape his family's connection to the grimy blue collar scrap business.

When his father, a tenth grade drop-out and no fan of higher education, balked at his son's plans for medical school, the Navy came to his rescue with a full scholarship. He enjoyed military life and excelled at officer's school where his instinct for power allowed him to become class leader.

After discovering that he didn't really like patient care, Barnes trained in Occupational Medicine—more a business than a medical specialty—and following his required three years on active duty bought out a small occupational practice. Understanding he was really working for the employers, Barnes Occupational Medicine grew rapidly into a string of ten offices serving Chicago's largest employers—including Barnes Scrap and Iron.

Barnes stayed in the Navy Reserve and succeeded in advancing to the rank of Commander without ever being sent on deployment. Assuming an entire regiment would never be deployed, he took the position as Regimental Surgeon in order to punch an important ticket on the way to his next promotion.

The job was not much of a challenge, though he was not prepared for the pushback from his battalion surgeons. He was convinced that each of them believed him unqualified, preferring to consult each other rather than him. Gonzalez at the 3/28 was typical. A former Marine scout sniper, he made it clear that with no combat experience, Barnes lacked the moral authority his position required. Russell at 2/28, like

Barnes, had no combat experience, but Russell was a nerd, and it surprised Barnes that he was even in the Navy. That and his three years of surgical training followed by emergency medicine left him with an annoying sense of superiority.

McGregor, though, was the worst of the bunch. Another former enlisted man, McGregor had a flashy University job and friends in high places. Worst of all, he had that damn Navy Cross. At every meeting, there it was, and every single person in the room knew it.

Of his many life goals, Kenny Barnes put taking Michael McGregor down a peg very close to the top.

Barnes, a large slab-faced man, strode over to Mike McGregor, put out a big, beefy hand, and shook McGregor's. "I heard you needed help up here." Barnes removed his sunglasses as his close set eyes slowly surveyed the aid station and saw only one patient, a Marine who was having a grain of sand washed from his eye, plus a few more awaiting medevac. "Perhaps I was misinformed."

"Things will pick up again soon," said McGregor.

Barnes gave a dismissive snort. "So you can see the future too."

"I do have some experience with these things, Commander."

"I thought you would be up at the objective with your CO," Barnes replied. "Or would that be too close to the action?"

Nicole Ellis winced at the killing glare which was McGregor's response.

The standoff was interrupted by the roar of heavy vehicles coming over the low ridge and heading towards the bridge. The engineers had arrived.

CHAPTER 35

MAJOR KHALID ISHMAIL sat in his command post four blocks north of the warehouse containing the nuclear warheads and cursed Ali al-Ahmar. Where was he? If he had been here with his company, they could have executed a flanking attack on the wretched Americans. If they could damage their heavy transport it was possible that they would abandon the mission. All he could do now was to delay the advance with snipers, small mines and IEDs.

As he predicted, the Americans expended enormous resources in evacuating and caring for their wounded, and it had slowed their advance. He could see their ambulances shuttle back and forth and could hear their medical evacuation helicopters. One thing he could not have predicted, however, was the enormous strength of the operation. A full battalion of their Marines was methodically grinding up his defenses, and reports showed more of their people deployed along every possible route of escape as well as blocking reinforcements from al-Mukalla.

"Major," one of his men called to him. "The Americans have been sighted near the storage building."

This was inevitable. His orders at this point were simple—continue to blood the Americans, but to also do everything to hasten their departure once they had actually seized the warheads. The longer they had to poke around, the more likely they were to create an even greater disaster for Abdullah Nazer. He felt fairly confident that he could prevent the kind of thorough search such a discovery would require. He was also confident that, with the half-hour warning from Nazer's fleet of small fishing boats, their Iraqi expert and the critical elements of the PAL had escaped to the west ahead of the Americans.

Fortunately, the Americans had done nothing to interfere with the tiny cellular network in Arad, and Major Ishmail was still able to receive reports and issue orders to his men. He felt it unlikely that the Marines would move farther north of the warehouse than they had to in order to secure the area for removal of the warheads. But if they did, his building had a small, well hidden, basement which would allow him to remain undetected.

Seizing his phone, Ishmail made a quick call to one of his sergeants concealed with nine other men just across the Wadi to the west of Arad. "Their heavy vehicles will be coming soon. Hit them as soon as they come within range. They cannot retreat; they must keep coming. Damage the vehicles. The drivers will be easier to replace."

"Yes, Major. We are ready. There is no evidence the Americans know we're here."

"God be with you." The Major ended the call. He knew that in less than an hour the Sergeant and his men would, in all likelihood, be dead.

CHAPTER 36

THE SIX MK-25 trucks, one for each of the weapon containers, made up most of the convoy headed for Arad. Each vehicle was capable of carrying two containers, but for safety, the plan was to load only one in each truck. At the rear of the convoy was a single Mk-36 wrecker, essentially a crane capable of lifting over twenty tons.

In the lead was one of only three armored vehicles assigned to the operation, an LAV-25. This lethal eight-wheeled light armored vehicle carried a turret with a 25 mm chain gun, two machine guns, and four marine infantrymen in the back. Captain Mark Ernst, commanding both the LAV and the convoy, was in the lead and was looking for the unexpected. Ernst, one of the few active-duty Marines involved in Ocean Reach, was there because there were currently no reserve LAV units. He stopped the convoy, dismounted, and walked the hundred meters to Colonel

Mark's command post. There he spoke with the operations officer, Lt Col Jim Evans.

"Okay, Captain, here's the situation," Evans said. We have the warehouse and secure ingress straight down the main road. Deploy just outside the town. The 1/28 will tell you when to move in. At that point Captain Jenkins of the engineers will take command until the convoy is reassembled and ready to depart. Send the wrecker in first, they'll use it to drag one warhead out of the warehouse and into the street, where it will be lifted and ready to load. When ordered, send in the first truck. To avoid turning around, the trucks will leave Arad to the east via the cross street in front of the warehouse. There's enough room for the turn and that route is now secure. The convoy will assemble south of the town on this side of the bridge. Clear?"

"Completely, sir."

"All right, let's get moving."

Ernst nodded and jogged back to the LAV.

The convoy crossed the bridge, but about two hundred yards south of the town began to receive automatic weapons fire from west of the Wadi Dhahwan. Multiple heavy machine gun rounds pounded into the cab and engine of the first truck behind Ernst's LAV.

Ernst responded instantly and pulled his LAV forward, made a left turn, and placed it between the source of fire and the convoy. As the LAV began taking hits, Ernst yelled, "Get some fire on those guns."

Even before he spoke, his gunner was already traversing the turret. In seconds he laid the crosshairs of the recently upgraded electro-optical sight on the nearest gun emplacement, and opened fire with 25 mm high-explosive rounds, obliterating the weapon and its crew. He did the same to the second gun position, but not before one of Ernst's Marine riflemen was killed and one wounded. The remaining two Marines in the passenger compartment scrambled out the rear door and added their fire to that of the LAV.

The engineers in the other trucks, who understood their mission was to retrieve the warheads and not to engage in combat, quickly turned and headed east away from the assault.

The ambush, so carefully planned by Major Ishmail and his sergeant, ended a minute later when two circling AH-1Z Viper gunships dispatched the remaining Yemenis with two Hellfire missiles.

Despite the quick reaction, two Marines were dead and one of the trucks had a smashed windshield and engine damage. The LAV had also taken several hits to the engine compartment and was leaking fuel. Ernst ordered his slightly-wounded gunner to secure the LAV while Ernst himself transferred to one of the trucks. His plan, after obtaining permission from Colonel Mark, was to retrieve the LAV with the wrecker once the warheads had been loaded and were enroute to the beach. The damaged truck was to be abandoned.

The three wounded were treated at the aid station where Mike McGregor looked up periodically from his work to glance at CDR Kenny Barnes, who was occupying himself watching the village through binoculars.

CHAPTER 37

SEPTEMBER 13, 2017 0915Z (0515 EDT, 1215 AST)
The White House Situation Room

DESPITE THE EARLY hour, the Situation Room
was packed. Brendan Wallace, wearing jeans and a
starched white shirt, was leaning on his elbows and studying a monitor carrying a live feed from a Predator drone
launched earlier from *Essex* which was now circling high
over Arad.

He'd already received multiple updates from Admiral
Tucker. He had also taken a call from the Saudi Ambassador
who expressed concern about 'rumors' of a U.S. operation
in Yemen. This, Wallace knew, would be a delicate call, as
he had no idea how high in the Saudi hierarchy the nuclear
conspiracy went, or its purpose. He had finally told the
Ambassador a vague story about a potential security threat,
and that a formal announcement would be forthcoming,
hopefully within hours. A call from the Russian Ambassador
was fobbed off onto Sonny Baker. "Bastard wants to know
if this is about their wandering nukes. They probably had

no idea they were in Yemen until their satellites picked up our operation. Give him the brushoff, Sonny. He'll find out what we're up to when those warheads and their Cyrillic markings appear on the six o'clock news."

While Baker and the President were dealing with the Russians, Karen Hiller had taken a call from the White House liaison with the National Security Agency. The NSA had just intercepted and translated a call from Abdullah Nazer to a reporter at Al Jazeera describing an unprovoked American invasion of his small nation.

"Probably trying to build regional support," said Wallace. "That will fall apart once we display those warheads."

"You may be right Mr. President," replied Baker, "but he should know that. The fact that he's speaking up worries me. Could he have something up his sleeve? Could he have moved some of those nukes?"

"Damn it Sonny," Karen Hiller exploded. "Didn't you tell us, just a few hours ago, those weapons were in Arad?"

"He did," interrupted the President. "In fairness, though, Sonny gave no guarantee all six were there. Unfortunately, in the grotesque math of nuclear weapons there is a much bigger difference between zero and one than there is between one and six. In a few hours we'll know."

Everyone at the table nodded in agreement, but no one spoke.

CHAPTER 38

IT HAD TAKEN some time, but the big Mk-36 wrecker was finally in place outside the warehouse. Inside, Marines from the 1/28 had cleared away a large pile of junk piled around the warhead cases—pipe, block and tackle, cargo netting, and assorted rope and cables. The engineers had attached a heavy steel cable to the lift points welded to the first of the massive warhead boxes and, using the crane on the wrecker, had pulled it out into the street.

Lieutenant Colonel Jeremiah Walsh was about to radio for the first truck to be brought forward when he heard a muffled blast followed by the clatter of collapsing masonry walls. The air was suddenly filled with a choking dust. "What the hell?"

First Sergeant Al Johanssen, who had assumed the role of Battalion Sergeant Major when his predecessor had fractured his ankle during a training run, sprinted out the warehouse door and was confronted by an opaque cloud of dust and sand.

As it cleared, he could see that a building about half-way down the street had collapsed, blocking the route the engineers planned to use to move the warheads out of Arad. He knew that two Marines from the MP Company had been standing guard in second floor windows, and were probably now buried in the rubble.

Over the next few minutes, Johanssen watched as four Yemenis emerged from hidden basements and took the injured Marines' rescuers under fire. It then took twenty minutes for the MPs guarding the street and a squad from E Company to hunt them down and kill all four in a running firefight. Meanwhile, more Marines and several corpsmen were digging out their buried comrades. Both survived, thanks to their body armor, but both had multiple fractures. In addition, four more Marines had been wounded, two seriously, in the battle with Ishmail's men.

Jeremiah Walsh was receiving continuous updates on the action, though at times it was easier to just look out the warehouse door, the gunfire was that close. He turned to his senior corpsman and ordered, "Get on the radio and see if we can get a medevac helo to land in that courtyard out back. We have good access , it's secure, and moving the wounded back to the aid station will be tough now that we have to move the warheads in and out on the same road."

The blood-splattered petty officer spent about five minutes in discussion with the medical regulating officer aboard the *Essex*. This officer coordinated the movement of casualties, attempting to utilize resources most efficiently. "No can do, sir," was the response. "First, the Air Boss won't send his helos north of the wadi if he can avoid it, not while there's active combat."

"For Christ's sake," Walsh slammed his fist onto his small portable desk. "They do combat medevac, as long as there isn't any combat?"

"Wouldn't make any difference, sir. Medical regulating wants them triaged by the battalion surgeon. Said the ORs are already full on *Essex* and *Iwo Jima,* and there isn't a surgical team on *Ashland."*

"Very well. We'll have to carry them by stretcher to the south end of town. Have the BAS send their ambulances to pick them up there. The main road is now totally committed to moving the warheads, and considering what just happened, I don't want our ambulances driving down side streets next to buildings that might blow up."

Changing focus, "First Sergeant Johanssen, keep an eye on those engineers. Keep this thing moving, I want us out of this shithole as soon as possible."

"Aye, aye, sir," said Johanssen who headed for the small gaggle of engineers working outside the warehouse.

As the engineers tried to figure out what to do, Marines from A Company carefully searched the houses looking for more hidden explosives. In one house they came across several Yemenis emerging from another hidden basement. The engagement lasted only a few seconds, but produced two more wounded.

Meanwhile, the engineers had found they could back their trucks down the main street where the wrecker had successfully extracted the first warhead from the warehouse.

Because of the damaged truck, one vehicle would have to carry two of the warheads. They decided it might as well be the first, so another massive steel box was lifted onto the truck's bed. It rolled out of town, past buildings meticulously searched—and heavily occupied.

Seeing the potential for delays, Jeremiah Walsh made a quick decision and called Colonel Aaron Mark. "Sir, loading the objective—" he was not about to say 'warheads', even over encrypted radio—"is going to be slower than estimated. Request some vehicles be sent up from the beach to escort our trucks individually so they can be embarked as they arrive."

Mark rarely second guessed his subordinates. "Can do. No sign of opposition so far along the south road. One Humvee per item? It's all we can spare."

" "Perfect, sir."

"I'll make it happen. Falcon, out."

About thirty-five minutes later, Mark saw a long dust cloud moving like a tan snake up the road towards his position. In a few minutes, a half dozen hard-back Humvees arrived, each carrying three Marines, one of them a gunner in the small ring turret manning an M-240G machine gun. Two of them formed up with the first warhead truck and began to move back towards the beach. The others parked just below the crest of the low ridge, about a hundred meters before the bridge.

Colonel Mark was just beginning to relax when his intelligence officer, Major Ashley Greene, hopped out of her vehicle where she was monitoring as many drone and radio feeds as she could handle, and jogged over to her commanding officer.

"Excuse me, Colonel. Something you should have a look at."

Peering into the window of her Humvee, he watched her replay a thirty second video clip, obviously downloaded from the operation's Predator drone.

"The drone has returned to *Iwo Jima* for fuel, but on the way back it picked up this." She pointed to a moving dust cloud much like the column of Humvees that had just come up from the beach.

"Where is this exactly?" he asked.

Greene brought up a map on her computer and showed him the location. "Looks like they know we have people holding the road just to the west of us. They appear to be heading down a single lane dirt path that leads to this bridge across a deep wadi. Once across that bridge they can head south and intersect the road to our current location behind the blocking force."

"How large is that force, Major?"

Ashley Greene, a Qeshm veteran and highly skilled at interpretation of reconnaissance imaging, had already anticipated the question. "I did a little image enhancement. The first unit is something like a Humvee. We know Nazer's forces acquired a number of old French P4s; that's probably it. The second unit is a small armored vehicle, almost certainly one of their BTR-60 variants. Behind them are two trucks. Being at the back, there is so much dust, I can't even guess what they are. Best estimate is four men in the P4 and up to a dozen in each truck. The BTR can carry troops, but it's absolutely miserable in this climate and traveling on a rough road. Best guess is that column has thirty to thirty-five troops. They should arrive at that bridge in about half an hour."

Colonel Mark considered this for a moment. Then he turned to his operations officer. "Jim, what air assets do we have that can hit them before they reach that bridge?"

"Uh Colonel, you may recall that Washington has instructed us not to engage the Yemenis with air assets unless they have attacked us first or present a direct threat to the mission."

"And you don't think a column of Yemeni infantry with an armored vehicle on my flank presents a threat?"

"My judgment, sir is that Admiral Tucker's operations staff would probably say they aren't, not yet anyway. There may be a way we can handle this problem ourselves."

"Go ahead."

"We could get our engineers up there in fifteen minutes. It's a small bridge, and they can blow it almost immediately. The topo map shows the sides of the wadi are steep in that area—no way vehicles can cross without that bridge."

"Let's do it. You there," Mark shouted at two Marines from the engineering unit waiting by a truck about fifty meters away. They trotted over to him. "How are you guys fixed for explosives?"

"Got almost hundred kilos of C-4 in the truck. Didn't take much to blow the door on that warehouse. We're just waiting to see if there is any other demolition work," explained a staff sergeant who looked much too old for his rank.

"As a matter of fact, there is. I'll get you an escort while my ops and intelligence officers explain what we need."

"Aye, aye sir." The staff sergeant snapped a salute and motioned for a young corporal to join him.

To his radio operator he said, "Get me that MP Major." In a moment Mark was given the radio handset. "I have a mission for you," he said and quickly explained what he needed.

Major Jim Griggs had about forty of his Marines deployed along the south side of the town providing security for the warhead trucks as they departed. "We're on it Colonel, Raven actual out." To his company gunnery sergeant he added, "Get me everyone left from first platoon plus five Marines from second and have them loaded into a truck and a Humvee in three minutes." He gave him the names and walked over to Kelli Moore, who was double checking the security of the buildings along the south edge of town.

"Captain, I'm taking what's left of first platoon plus the five men left in second for an urgent mission. You're in charge here."

"You're taking the men from my platoon?" Moore asked. "What's going on Major?"

"We're heading west to cover the engineers who are blowing a bridge in advance of a Yemeni column. If we don't get there first, it could get very ugly, and I just don't need any women in a force on force action."

"This is bullshit! Sir."

"Watch yourself, Captain. Look, I know you think I'm a sexist, and frankly I don't care. It's bad enough having to worry about you and your girls clearing buildings. This could be an infantry fight, and I'm just not sure you're up to it. Now shut up and keep this area secure. With luck we'll be back in less than an hour."

Kelli Moore did not say another word to her commanding officer. She walked over to her platoon sergeant—Brenda Leach, an eight-year veteran with two tours in Afghanistan, and explained the situation. Leach nodded, took a sip from her canteen and spit, vigorously.

CHAPTER 39

ALI AL-AHMAR REWRAPPED the scarf around his face. Even with the windows closed, the choking dust filled his vehicle. His company was way behind schedule, and he was now traveling much too fast for this single lane, unpaved road headed for Arad. He had four American Mk-23 trucks, the same as the American forces now looting their warheads, but his weren't well maintained. First, one of the trucks wouldn't start, so he packed his troops into the remaining three, and left behind his supply and intelligence officers.

About an hour into the road march another truck hit a large rock and had damaged its transmission. He ordered it abandoned, packed the troops into the remaining vehicles, and moved out. He was now only a few minutes west of the critical bridge across a deep, but unnamed wadi. Once past the bridge, he could travel at speed across the desert to attack the Americans.

Assuming his remaining, woefully overpacked, trucks survived.

The four-vehicle convoy traveled with more than twice the force Colonel Mark's intelligence officer had estimated. Each truck now had twenty-five infantrymen sweltering in the back and four in the cab. The BTR carried another fourteen miserable men in the back in addition to its crew of three. Finally, al-Ahmar's Range Rover carried the four company officers, plus a driver. A total force of eighty.

As they crested a small hill about four hundred meters before the bridge, he saw vehicles approaching from the east. Just as the thick dust had obscured his own convoy, al-Ahmar couldn't gauge the enemy's strength. If they charged across the bridge, his company could be destroyed if there was a superior force behind that dust cloud. He quickly ordered his vehicles to back up a hundred meters so they couldn't be seen from the bridge. He had his men dismount, except for the crew of the BTR which he moved to the front of the convoy. He took personal charge of one platoon, twenty-five men, and gave detailed orders to his second in command.

Al-Ahmar and his men moved quickly away to the north.

CHAPTER 40

THE SMALL CONVOY—ONE truck and a Humvee—approached the bridge from the east. Major Jim Griggs, with eighteen MPs and two engineers, stopped about a hundred meters short, stepped out, and looked past the bridge with binoculars. A vague cloud of dust was barely visible just beyond a small hill. He waited a few minutes and, seeing nothing more, decided to go ahead.

"All right men. Dismount."

The MP's set up a defensive position east of the bridge. The Humvee pulled forward to within twenty meters of the bridge, where the engineers began to unload C-4 and several types of detonators. The senior of the engineers, who did demolition work as a civilian, looked the structure over then came back to join Griggs.

"This isn't complicated, Major. If we blow the support on this end, the whole thing will just drop into the wadi."

"Get at it then. We expect company in a few minutes."

The two engineers quickly packed explosives on and around the steel supports and inserted two detonators. Griggs meanwhile focused on the road leading west from the bridge, where he'd seen the little dust cloud. Based on what Colonel Mark had told him, the enemy column should be kicking up a big cloud that should be easily visible by now. He was tempted to walk across the bridge and have a look when the staff sergeant told him they were about to blow the bridge. Once the bridge was down, he reasoned, the enemy's location would no longer be an issue.

The engineers backed away from the bridge, unspooling their fuses. Griggs signaled to his men to fall back towards the truck. His driver was turning the Humvee around. Griggs took a few steps towards his vehicle when he heard a loud 'whoosh'.

He turned just as an RPG-7 blew off the front of his truck, killing the driver and disabling the vehicle in less than a second. This was followed immediately by the staccato of more than a dozen AK-47's.

The sound was coming from about fifty meters north of the bridge where there was a low rise and a scattering of boulders. Dammit! The Yemeni soldiers had somehow flanked them!

Griggs signaled his men to move towards the wadi where they fell to the ground and began to return fire. The engineers lit the fuse and added to the defensive fire. The Marines were still exposed, but they were better marksmen with more fire discipline. Each side was taking casualties about equally when the BTR-60 pulled over the hill and opened fire with its 12.3 mm heavy machine gun. Three Marines were killed immediately.

Griggs was running out of options. He was about to order his survivors to jump into the wadi in hopes a few might escape when the bridge blew.

The engineers had used a small charge, but Griggs and his men were only thirty meters away and in the open. Only one Marine was wounded, but everyone was stunned, their ears rang, and their lungs ached.

Within seconds of the blast, the Yemenis came out of the rocks and rushed Griggs' position. It was over in less than a minute.

Griggs' Marines had already lost eight men, with five seriously wounded. He was in an exposed position under attack by a platoon-sized force and was taking fire from the rear. There was no choice. Griggs rose to his knees and raised his hands. At least he had the satisfaction of accomplishing his mission.

And no women had been lost on his watch!

One of the Yemenis, presumably their leader, shouted at the Marines, "On your feet. Hands in the air."

Seven men rose, three of them with minor wounds. The more seriously wounded remained on the ground.

The Yemeni, caked in dust, sauntered over to him. "You Americans think you can invade anyone, any time," he said in passable English. "You destroy our homes, spit on our customs, and then go back to America as if nothing had happened. Times are changing, my friends. They are changing right here. Today. Turn around and walk to the wadi."

Griggs glanced at the wounded, still lying on the ground; two of them moaning.

"Don't worry about them," the Yemeni officer ordered.

Griggs and his men, five MPs and the engineer corporal, stood in a ragged line about six feet from the edge of the wadi. He had a bad feeling about what would happen next.

"Burn in Hell!" screamed the Yemeni as he opened fire.

Engineer Ryan Smith, on the left end of the line, didn't wait for what came next. He took a step forward and leaped into the wadi, just as the shooting started.

It was almost ten feet to the bottom, but a mound of soft sand cushioned his landing. In a second he was up and running, ignoring the bodies of his fellow Marines hitting the sand beside him.

Smith held his company record in the three mile run, but he was damned well going to break that record today.

Al-Ahmar thought at first he had hit the American, but when he looked down into the wadi, he saw his enemy running hard and rounding a turn that protected him from fire. He pointed at two of his men. "You and you. After him. Cut his heart out. Do not return unless you are covered in his blood."

Both men jumped into the wadi and took off after Smith.

There was a shot behind him. Al-Ahmar spun around. One of the wounded engineers on the ground behind him had managed to draw his Beretta, and while everyone was mesmerized by the executions, he shot Sergeant Karman in the groin. Al-Ahmar dispatched the staff sergeant and the other wounded Marines with long bursts from his AK-47.

But then he had to watch Karman bleed out—the damned American had apparently hit the femoral artery.

He hated when that happened. It was bad for morale.

Smith had his ears tuned like never before. When he first started running, there were two sets of footfalls echoing behind him. Then one slowly dropped away. But the other one was steadily drawing closer. If that Yemeni was even slightly better conditioned, he would soon get close enough for a good shot.

Smith had dropped his rifle when he surrendered, but still had his Beretta strapped to his right thigh. He rounded a turn and he saw a long straight section of the wadi stretch out ahead of him. Just what he was looking for. He tucked himself against the wall and waited. In less than ten seconds the Yemeni—a short, thin young man—rounded the turn and took two long strides before he realized there was no one ahead of him. He stopped short.

Before he could figure it out, Smith shot him twice in the back.

Smith listened for a moment, but the second man had either given up or was far enough behind that it didn't matter. He took a long drink from his canteen, lifted the Yemeni's canteen, and started to lope along the wadi while looking for a safe place to climb out.

Ali al-Ahmar heard the shots and knew that either his men would soon be back with the American's heart, or they would never be back. In the meantime, he had moved his dead, six of them, into a covered position where American drones could not see them. The American bodies, on the other hand, were neatly lined up near the end of the bridge they had destroyed. With four wounded, the Captain worked his way back up the wadi to the point where they had crossed not long before, and then back to his vehicles. He needed to contact both Major Ishmail and his Uncle. The plan had to be revised.

CHAPTER 41

THE USS *ASHLAND*, LSD-48, was cruising at barely six knots on the smooth expanse of the Arabian Sea. By this time her LCACs had delivered five of the six warhead transport boxes and the sixth was inbound. Each had been lifted by Ashland's heavy crane onto the after deck where a strange looking contraption had been constructed to open them.

Captain Eric Lutz, who began his career as a Navy salvage diver and was later commissioned, had been whisked from his billet as senior engineer at the Norfolk Naval Shipyard to design and construct equipment to rapidly open the Russian shipping containers without damaging the warheads.

What he came up with was a modification of a high-pressure waterjet system used for cutting steel at the shipyard's massive machine shop. Water at 80,000 pounds per square inch, and mixed with an abrasive could cut through steel with more precision and less damaging heat than any cutting tool. In this case, the thickness and the high strength of the steel in question required a larger nozzle, higher pressure, and two nozzles spraying liquid nitrogen to prevent heat build-up.

Mounted on the expansive afterdeck of the *Ashland* and surrounded by four-centimeter thick polycarbonate to protect the crew and engineers from high-velocity bits of steel and abrasive, the device, nicknamed the 'octopus' because of its many hoses and cables, was intended to cut off the end of the steel box so the warhead could be extracted. Included in the design was a live video feed which would go both to the White House and to Admiral Tucker on *Essex*.

When the first LCAC had pulled alongside with it two warhead containers, there were a lot of people holding their breath until the crane operator skillfully plucked the heavy steel box from the bed of the truck and lifted it directly into the protective enclosure of the octopus. The second container was placed on the deck just aft of the enclosure, and the engineers got to work. It took some tinkering, but they quickly got the cutter working.

During this time Captain Lutz patiently responded to a stream of questions from Karen Hiller and Sonny Baker.

Eight minutes after it arrived, the massive end of the container landed on the protective steel plate welded to the deck with a satisfying 'clang.' The warhead was carefully extracted and, using a smaller crane, was lifted out of the protective enclosure and placed on one of six dollies specifically built to receive it.

Rick Suarez, accompanied by Air Force and Navy nuclear weapons experts, went into action. After taking readings with several types of radiation detectors and removing one of the warhead's small baseplates, Suarez spoke into his encrypted communications link. "Looks like the real thing," his broad grin carried live to the White House situation room where the President quietly said, "One down, five to go."

The second container was opened easily and its warhead quickly confirmed as genuine. The third, fourth, and fifth followed at twenty minute intervals as the LCAC crews, crane operators, and engineers fell into a rhythm. By time the LCAC with the sixth container pulled alongside, there were five cut and empty containers on the aft deck, five warheads safely secured below, four trucks returned to the vehicle deck, and all the engineers back aboard, except for the two dispatched with the MPs—whose whereabouts were unknown.

Up on deck, Lutz directed the opening of the last of the massive steel boxes. As he looked at the deck he realized he had not made specific plans on how to remove the stack of cut ends, each weighing more than five hundred kilos, from the deck. Even as his team prepared box number six for cutting, he began to work on this new, though relatively insignificant, problem.

The spray of water under immense pressure plus the cloud of condensation from the liquid nitrogen blanketed the container during the cutting process. Only when they felt the vibration and heard the clang of metal on metal did everyone know the last box was open. The octopus had done its job, and the engineers began to power down the various pumps and motors that drove the device.

Captain Lutz entered the enclosure, and using a small flashlight peered into the open end of the stainless steel box.

CHAPTER 42

"Empty? Are you sure?" Karen Hiller shouted. "Just a moment," said Rick Suarez, "I'll have a look myself."

They watched him enter the enclosure on the situation room's monitors. He emerged seconds later. "There is no warhead."

"Jesus Christ," the President exclaimed. "Now what the hell do we do?"

Sonny Baker was trying to think of options in a hurry. "Mr. President, I suggest we have the Marines use the radiation detectors they have with them to conduct a quick search of Arad."

The Chairman of the Joint Chiefs tented his fingers and looked thoughtfully at Baker for a moment. "Keep in mind that we began pulling our people out of Arad as soon as the warhead containers were clear. We don't have the forces on site to perform an aggressive search, especially with the limited radiation instruments issued to the Marines."

Too much was happening too fast. Baker had to pull it together. "Good point Ted. There may be wisdom in getting out now and dealing with number six later. There are already demonstrations in Cairo, Amman, and Dubai protesting another American invasion of an Arab country."

"Just leave a nuclear warhead?" the President said. "Is that your advice? I want to be clear on this?"

"Not leave, Mr. President. We can begin immediate measures to locate it, but right now we have no evidence to work with. It seems unlikely to me that Nazer would hide a warhead in Arad. He could have just as easily unloaded it before they left Mukalla. It could be anywhere. Before anything else, we need information."

"So what do we tell the American people?" Karen Hiller asked. "The good news is that we retrieved five loose warheads. Bad news is that one got away?"

"We can hold off on an announcement until we know more," replied Baker.

"No, no, no." The President leaned forward and glared at his National Security Advisor. "There have already been news leaks about our going in to retrieve WMDs. We can't say nothing. How would we explain the invasion of Yemen or whatever this guy Nazer calls his little empire? Have you seen those satphone videos of Marines in Arad? Just how do we explain that?"

Sonny Baker shrank from the President's attack, but he was rallying his thoughts. He was about to respond when the telephone next to the President rang. Brendan Wallace waved off an aide who reached for it and answered himself. After listening for a moment he announced, "Abdullah Nazer is calling."

CHAPTER 43

ABDULLAH NAZER SAT in his office and peered out across the calm waters to the south. The American ships were too far away to be seen, but he looked anyway. He had been surprised that the White House operator had immediately transferred him to the Situation Room, but perhaps he should not have been. The Americans were nothing, if not efficient. What was totally unexpected was the President's voice on the line.

Nazer gathered his thoughts.

"Mr. President, we have a mutual problem," he began. Nazer spoke excellent English having attended a British school in Aden for ten years. This surprised the President as well as his Arabic translator who had rushed into the Situation Room.

"Agreed," replied Brendan Wallace. "But before I respond to that, how should I address you? Your status is not entirely clear to us."

"Mr. Nazer will suffice for the moment. The institutions of our small nation are still evolving and selection of titles is low on what you Americans would call my to-do list."

"Very well then, Mr. Nazer. To be candid, I don't think we have the same problem. My problem is that you have, or more precisely had, six stolen nuclear warheads. What is your problem, aside from the fact you no longer have them?"

So Wallace had decided to get directly to the point and was doing it aggressively. Had the President's advisors argued for this approach, or was Wallace winging it?

"My problem is that you have invaded my country and killed my citizens." Nazer said.

"And your forces have killed and wounded our Marines."

"Only in self-defense, Mr. President. But let us dispense with this political back and forth. You have succeeded in illegally seizing my property, items for which I paid quite dearly. I understand they will not be returned; I am not that foolish. What I want from you, Mr. President is to get out. Immediately! You have one hour."

"As you are no doubt aware, Mr. Nazer, we are starting to withdraw our people even as we speak."

"Not fast enough, Mr. President, not nearly fast enough."

"And here, I suppose, is where we get to the 'or else'."

"As you are no doubt aware," Nazer said, "one of the shipping containers is empty. That warhead was removed the day it arrived and now resides in a location on the East coast of the United States. In a major city, indeed a city critical to your economy. As you also know, the specialist fabricating the permissive action links for us succeeded in eluding your Marines. He has kept our associates guarding the sixth weapon updated on his progress and, under his guidance, they are constructing a PAL on site. It is, I regret to say, not yet ready for use, but it will be surprisingly soon."

He paused, but there were no sounds on the other end of the line. The Americans were at least competent enough to disguise their panic.

To encourage your immediate departure," he said, "I have just sent a photograph to the email account of your Karen Hiller. If there are Americans in this country in one hour they will surrender themselves to me immediately. There will be no ships in our waters and no over flight by aircraft or your drones. Violate my terms, and I will release this photograph along with the city where it was taken to every major news outlet in the world. No bluff, Mr. President. No negotiation. Consider the reaction of your citizens to this news before you make any decisions."

Abdullah Nazer then had the great pleasure of hanging up on the President of the United States.

CHAPTER 44

BRENDAN WALLACE RAISED his eyebrows. "Well, now we know what he has up his sleeve. Karen let's have a look at that photograph."

His Chief of Staff tapped on a computer, and in seconds a photograph appeared on the large flat screen, which a minute before had shown the empty warhead container. The photograph showed a warhead, identical to the ones unloaded on the *Ashland*, sitting on a wooden pallet in what looked like a garage or loading dock. It was accompanied by three men in black head scarves, one of whom was holding a copy of what everyone recognized as today's *New York Times*.

"It has to be a fake, Mr. President," said Hiller.

"I agree, sir," added Sonny Baker. "No way could they have shipped that warhead to the U.S. so quickly."

The President slapped the table. "Probably, probably! Yes, it probably is a fake, but we don't really know that it was ever in Mukalla, do we? It might have been shipped here directly. Your SEAL team—" the President looked directly at Ted Lennox—"told us there were probably six warheads on the docks. Probably. Not certainly. Do I tell the American people that there is probably not a live thermonuclear weapon hidden in an East Coast city? General, what do you recommend?"

The Chairman sat even straighter in his chair, glanced for a moment at the photograph on the screen and replied, "Mr. President, at the moment we are already well into withdrawal of our people. I'll have to check with Admiral Tucker to be sure, but using helicopters and landing craft we should have everyone out within an hour. My recommendation is to proceed with the retrograde, and then begin planning for location of the warhead."

"So he has us by the balls right now and for the moment we should just give him what he wants?"

"More or less, yes sir."

"Sonny?"

"Not much choice, Mr. President. He undoubtedly has a lot more photographs he can send to the news outlets that will confirm this is a real warhead. We should, of course, do a close analysis of this photograph, but people who think there's a nuke down the street will not be satisfied with some technical analysis of a digital photograph."

"I wouldn't put too much stock in our ability to prove anything one way or another about this photograph," CIA Director Clarkson added. "It's been awhile since I did photo analysis, but this looks like a digital photograph of a print. We won't be able to analyze the original pixels. For now we need to be happy we have five warheads, suck it up, and give him what he wants, which in the big picture isn't much."

"Yet," replied the President tartly.

"Yes, sir. In the meantime we can get a NEST operation underway, quietly, of course—New York and D.C. being the obvious places to start."

Brendan Wallace looked at his Chief of Staff who nodded, her expression mixing anger and frustration. "Okay then, Ted, make it happen. No screw ups, no miscommunications. This is a direct Presidential order, everyone out one hour. Sonny, coordinate a NEST response with Homeland Security. We need results. And soon."

CHAPTER 45

THE FLAG BRIDGE of the USS *Essex* was abuzz with activity when the call from the Chairman was transferred to Admiral Nathan Tucker. Tucker waved a hand for quiet and the entire space fell silent.

When he put down put down the handset a minute later, every eye was on him.

"We all know that one of the warheads is missing," he began. "Abdullah Nazer has called the President and informed him that it has been shipped to an East coast city in the United States. He says they are fabricating a PAL and that in the meantime he is going to release a photograph of the warhead as well as revealing the city where it's located unless all U.S. forces are out of his country by," he looked at his watch, "1900. So by direct order of the President we will comply with this demand. There is no room for error. We don't know for sure if that nuke is in the U.S., but we damn well know he has one."

Tucker turned first to his operations officer. "I need a plan in five minutes." To his Communications Chief, "Get me Colonel Mark."

The flag bridge exploded into controlled chaos.

Three minutes later Tucker had explained the situation to his Ground Combat Commander. "That's about it. What's your situation up there?"

"Admiral, the SEALS, as you probably know, were pulled out by helicopter, which also picked up our people at the north end of town on the way back. My blocking force deployed west of the town is on its way down towards the beach. They reported no contact. The 1/28 is pulling out of Arad and heading south. We have a small force to cover the bridge, my command element, plus some wounded I had planned to send out by helo. My big concern is a group of Marines I dispatched to take out a small bridge to the north-west. We got a short radio call that they were under attack, then nothing. I had planned to send a platoon from the 1/28 up there, but not with the timetable you just laid out. They could have been ambushed and all KIA. On the other hand there may be some wounded, or they may have disengaged and are on the run. I do not want to leave people behind."

Tucker took a deep breath. This was the nightmare of command, orders versus the agony of troops left behind. "Can't be helped, Colonel. Presidential direct order. I'll talk to my ops officer about a pass by the Predator to see what we can find out. Give me the coordinates." Mark did so. "Anything else?"

"No Admiral."

"Colonel, your Marines did a superb job. Not your fault

one of the weapons was missing. I'm sorry there were so many wounded. They were obviously more prepared than anyone expected."

"Yes sir. Our expectations were for a flank attack along the coast to prevent our loading the warheads, not for a delaying action in Arad apparently designed just to create a lot of casualties. But you know the old saying, 'No plan survives first contact with the enemy'."

"Von Moltke, wasn't it? I think they covered that at the academy."

"Right, sir. They covered it at Michigan too."

CHAPTER 46

THE GROUP OF officers surrounding Colonel Aaron Mark sensed that something had changed. Mark was outwardly calm, but those who knew him could tell this was just on the outside. His staff officers were chattering on multiple radios and tapping on computer keyboards. Mark briefly explained the circumstances.

"Bottom line is the command group and the rest of the 1/28 will mount up and proceed as fast as possible to the beach, where we will embark on LCACs. The wounded will be picked up by helicopter along with the medical personnel." He glanced around and picked Captain Kelli Moore out of the small cluster of MPs. "Captain Moore, you and your MPs will provide security."

Surprised that the Colonel even knew who she was, Moore said, "Aye, sir," even though she had a lot of unanswered questions.

"To be on the safe side", Mark went on, "we're going to blow one of the center spans on this bridge to prevent whatever forces are left in Arad from pursuing. Looks like there aren't any of our engineers still here. Captain Singh, can you and the Sergeant Major handle that?"

"Certainly Colonel." The speech was British upper class, but the speaker—who was wearing British desert camouflage—was a tall swarthy man wearing a turban, a broad black moustache, and short beard. His left hand was bandaged with blood oozing through the dressing. His Sergeant Major, even taller, with sandy hair and ruddy face, wore a green beret. The gathered officers all looked at the improbable pair.

"Looks like most of you haven't met our representatives from the Royal Marines," said Aaron Mark with a smile. "Captain Singh is a Sikh, a people with a very long and proud warrior tradition. Since the operation that discovered the missing warheads was British in origin, we naturally welcomed British representatives. They were kind enough to send two of their best." Mark did not mention that Admiral Tucker had opposed including any British involvement, but the White House had overruled him.

Mark wondered why the Sergeant Major had not boarded the trucks with the rest of the 1/28, to which they were attached, when he had ordered only the wounded from that unit to remain. Seeing the two together, however, he could see the senior NCO was devoted to his officer and would remain with him under any circumstances.

"Keep in mind," Mark went on, "that we have twenty-one Marines—two engineers and nineteen MPs—currently missing. They were sent about ten kilometers northwest of here to blow a small bridge. An hour ago we heard they were under fire, and there's been no contact since. I asked the Admiral for a Predator sweep of that area, but haven't heard anything. Keep an eye out right up until the moment you board those helos."

Mark surveyed the officers once again. He knew the sailors and Marines on the ridge would be boarding helicopters in about twenty minutes and would be back to the ships before him. Nonetheless, someone should be formally in command, even for less than an hour.

Jim Evans, his operations officer, spoke softly, "Colonel, if you're thinking about leaving someone in command here, remember that new Qeshm Rule."

Mark looked at Ken Barnes, his Regimental Surgeon. Logically, he should leave him in charge—he was senior and the majority of people in the helo group were either wounded or medical personnel. But he didn't trust him. Barnes was a careerist with no interest in the Marine Corps, except as another ticket to be punched on his way to the top. Barnes face was a mask. The Colonel surveyed the other officers for a moment.

This had been a bad day for the 1/28 and their wounded—and for their medical personnel. They deserved the best leadership he could give them. Captain Singh? That young MP Captain? No, the new Presidential policy that put staff officers in line for command was a valid order.

He walked over to McGregor. "Commander, you're in charge here until you get back to the ship. Okay, let's saddle up. Commander Barnes, you're with me."

As they walked to the Colonel's Humvee Evans said, "I hope Commander Barnes is not politically connected. He looks positively homicidal."

Mark only grunted.

Within a few minutes, Mark and his command element, five trucks and half dozen Humvees of the 1/28, along with a few stragglers from the 2/28, headed over the ridge and south towards the sea.

Unable to squelch the sense of being once again left on his own, McGregor ordered the remaining vehicles moved to the south slope of the ridge and lined up for movement. One of the Marines with a minor leg wound asked, "Why move the vehicles? We're out of here in a few minutes and will be leaving them behind?"

"Do you see any helicopters?"

"Um ... no sir."

"Then until they get here, we will assume they aren't coming and act accordingly. First Sergeant Johanssen, take charge of organizing those vehicles. Be sure Sergeant Leach is able to destroy her comm gear, but not until I give the order. Until we're on those helos we're going to need that equipment. And if we have any snipers have them put eyes on that village. If they see anyone pointing a weapon our way, take them out."

"Aye, aye sir." Johanssen was scribbling furiously in a small notebook. "Just to let you know, the comm gear has self-destruct capability so that's covered. Colonel Mark had all the other remaining radios disabled before his group left. One of these trucks came up with the weapons company 1/28, and there are a couple of M-25 rifles in the back along with a shitload of ammo. I'll find some Marines who can handle them. Anything else, Commander?"

"That should do it." He shielded his eyes and studied the center of the long span. "Looks like our British friends are about to take down the bridge."

Sure enough, seconds later McGregor heard, "Fire in the hole!" in the Sergeant Major's Scots accent. Everyone got behind a vehicle or on the ground. About thirty seconds later there was a sharp 'crack,' followed by the sound of groaning, tearing metal as a six-meter section of bridge fell into the wadi.

McGregor inspected the fallen span with a small pair of binoculars. "Nicely done." After a moment, he surveyed the desert to the northwest, expecting nothing, but wanting to make an effort to at least look for survivors from the missing Marines. To his surprise, he saw a scant column of dust and possibly—he couldn't be sure—some movement.

"Captain Moore," he called. "Take a look at this."

She walked over and looked at what he had been watching.

"Could that be one of your MPs?" he asked.

"Let's find out. Sergeant Leach, take a couple of people and check out that dust cloud to the northwest." The dust was now just visible without binoculars and there was obvious movement. The sergeant sped off in a Humvee and returned in a few minutes with an exhausted, sand-covered Corporal Smith. Two corpsman carried the young engineer to one of the ambulances where Nicole Ellis started an IV and began to rehydrate him.

As she rolled up his right sleeve, Ellis pointed to a tear near the shoulder. "Is that what I think it is?"

"If you're thinking it's a bullet hole, yeah," replied McGregor. "What the hell happened up there?"

After a few minutes, the young Marine felt revived enough to relate what had happened at the bridge and the fate of his fellow Marines.

"You mean he just lined them up and shot them in the back?" said Kelli Moore.

"That's exactly what happened. I was last in line." He took a few deep breaths and a large swallow from a canteen. "When the shooting started I jumped into the wadi and took off. They sent a couple of guys after me, but I ambushed one and the other couldn't keep up."

"Good job Corporal. That was an amazing escape." Kelli Moore's hands were clenched into fists. "But I would give anything to get that asshole into my sights. Do you know where they went?"

"No idea. I saw a little dust in the direction of the bridge when I finally climbed out of the wadi, but that's all I know."

"Sergeant Leach, see if you can bring up that Predator on your computer," McGregor ordered. Griggs did not want to risk his command vehicle by taking it to the bridge so he left it with Sgt. Leech—along with all its communications and intelligence gear. Leach scrolled through the menus, tried several options which turned out to be incorrect, then brought up an image that showed a much larger area than the Predator would show.

"That must be a satellite image," she said. "Yep, and the time on it was about twenty minutes ago. Let me see if I can find that Predator."

"Just a moment." McGregor moved the trackball and asked, "Can I enlarge this?"

"Sure, just right click."

After McGregor worked with the image for a moment she added, "Ah...that's the ocean, sir."

"Yeah, right." McGregor then moved the image back across their position, but when he tried to look to the west, the image ended. "Looks like that satellite pass didn't cover the area we're interested in. Sergeant, if you can bring up the Predator data, let us know."

"Message for you Commander," Johanssen called out. "Two helos just launched from *Iwo Jima* with ETA 10 minutes. They're taking us back to *Essex*."

"Glad to hear it. I don't like being the last ones up here. Makes me nervous"

CHAPTER 47

HACKSAW ONE AND Two were a flight of CH-53s traveling northeast at 1,500 feet. As *Iwo Jima* was already moving away from the landing area to the southwest, they were approaching their target from further west than on their previous missions. Their flight plan was to cross the beach just east of the tiny town of Qishn and head straight to the ridge south of Arad, collect the remaining sailors and Marines, and then head for *Essex* before the 1600Z time limit set by the President. It was going to be close. LCDR Nick 'Greek' Andropolis, in command of Hacksaw One, was relaxed. The operation was nearly over, and while the Marines had suffered substantial casualties, there had been no loss or damage to the group's aircraft.

At the same time, Sergeant Ali Hamidi was seated in the gunner's seat of an old Soviet era ZU-23-2 twin barrel 23 mm. antiaircraft gun positioned there mainly to intercept vehicles, not aircraft. Though antiquated by modern standards due to its simple optical sights, the twin 23 mm auto cannons could be lethal to low-flying aircraft, especially helicopters.

Hamidi was part of a small force concealed in Qishn and intended to blunt any American movement to the West towards Mukalla, or at least to delay then. The antiaircraft gun was mounted on the bed of a truck, concealed in the shadows of a wall under camouflage netting and had escaped detection by the American Predator drone. When his crew told him two helicopters were approaching, Hamidi had pulled the camouflage off his weapon and prepared his men for action. The gun was poorly positioned to engage aircraft approaching from the sea, but it did have a clear field of fire to the east.

As Hamidi began to train the twin barrels skyward, Hacksaw One crossed the beach about two-hundred meters to the east of Qishn followed closely by Hacksaw Two in echelon.

Ali Hamidi gripped the trigger as he aimed his weapon just ahead of the lead aircraft. He opened fire and walked the line of tracers back. He could see the small explosions of the 23 mm rounds along with pieces of the aircraft being torn away.

By the time 'Greek' Andropolis made the call, "Break Right," his aircraft had already been hit nine times, his co-pilot was mortally wounded, and his transmission heavily damaged. Before he could try to auto-rotate, he was hit by shrapnel and released the controls.

Hacksaw One cartwheeled into the ground and exploded in a huge fireball.

At the same time Hacksaw Two broke right, which was exactly the correct call. The pilot, a Lt (jg) not long out of helicopter training, made as sharp a turn as he dared and was almost clear of Hamidi's field of fire when two rounds exploded in the controls just ahead of him. This was quickly followed by failure of multiple systems, but he at least was able to auto-rotate, and they began a sickening descent towards the surf.

After what seemed like an eternity, the big machine hit the surf right side down. The co-pilot and rear gunner were killed by the impact, but the pilot, crew chief, and one of the gunners managed to get clear of the aircraft before it sank in about ten feet of water. The three men helped each other, once they were sure there were no other survivors, into the surf and on to the beach, where they fell onto the coarse sand.

The pilot, Pete 'Pistol' Wagner had heard the rumors already circulating about the loss of the Marines at the bridge. There would be no surrender on this mission. He drew his Beretta from its shoulder holster and indicated to his men to do the same. As Ali Hamidi and five soldiers, all armed with AK-47 assault rifles approached, yelling at them in Arabic, they all opened fire.

Wagner's men were capable marksmen, and three Yemenis were hit before they could return fire. Pistols, however, were no match for automatic rifles, and the three men were gunned down in seconds.

CHAPTER 48

REPORTS COMING IN to the flag bridge showed Operation Ocean Reach winding down. The last vehicles had driven straight onto waiting LCACs, which were now heading for *Essex*. The nuclear weapons were secure on *Ashland*, which was moving east under escort until it came within full air cover of the *Lincoln* strike group, after which it would turn south for Diego Garcia, the Indian Ocean air base where the weapons would be inspected and decisions made as to their disposition. Initially, Admiral Tucker had assumed they would be shipped back to the United States, but there were now second thoughts about allowing nuclear weapons that might have been tampered with into the country. "Above my pay grade," was all Tucker had to say when he heard the change in plans.

Essex and her escorts were preparing to head east towards Singapore where the Marine reservists, mission now complete, would be offloaded and flown back to the U.S. Similar plans were in place for *Iwo Jima*, with her destination being back in the Med.

His operations officer interrupted, "It's the Air Boss, Admiral. I think you'll want to hear this."

The Admiral took the sound-powered telephone. "Tucker."

"Air Boss here Admiral. Hacksaw, a flight of two CH-53s headed up to the Arad area to retrieve our remaining people, may be in trouble. We heard a call to 'Break Right', several explosions and then nothing from Hacksaw One. Hacksaw Two had a garbled transmission, but we believe we can pick out the words 'triple A' and 'auto-rotating', but that's about it. Cannot make contact with either now."

"Wait one." To his intelligence officer he asked, "John, where's that Predator?"

"It gave us coverage of Colonel Mark's convoy loading onto the LCACs. It just went feet wet and is heading for the deck."

"Send it along the beach and over fly this little town of—" He took a quick look at the map to refresh his memory—"Qishn."

"Aye aye, sir. What are we looking for?"

"Two CH-53s. We lost comm with them in that area."

It took twelve long minutes for the slow moving drone to reach Qishn. It took only seconds for its high resolution camera to confirm what had happened. About a hundred meters off shore, the rotor blades and engines of Hacksaw Two were plainly visible in the surf as were the three dead Americans in green flight suits lying on the beach. There were also two dead Yemeni soldiers. Not far away was the charred wreckage of Hacksaw One while the ZU-23, now uncovered, was also visible.

"Jesus," said someone in the back, echoing the sentiments of everyone on the bridge.

Nathan Tucker could not afford the luxury of anger or frustration. To the Air Boss he said, "Predator confirms those aircraft are down. How quickly can we get two more helos up to Arad to extract our people?"

The Air Boss took a quick breath, looked at his status board, and replied, "One of our 53s has a hydraulic casualty, but we can launch the remaining two in about fifteen minutes. Shall I lay on that mission Admiral? There is that Presidential order."

"I know my orders, Commander. Get those aircraft ready to go. I'll contact the White House." Tucker then turned to his communications officer. "Get the Situation Room back on the secure satellite link."

CHAPTER 49

SEPTEMBER 13, 2017 1555Z (1155 EDT)
White House Situation Room

KAREN HILLER HAD Admiral Tucker's call on speaker. The President was listening, but having just given Tucker an order to terminate the operation within an hour, a return call from the Admiral so quickly probably meant some kind of problem. Brendan Wallace wanted his top aide, not himself, to be on record for this conversation.

"Yes, Admiral?" Karen Hiller's tone was curt, sounding more like an annoyed parent than the President's Chief of Staff. Tucker picked up on this immediately.

"Ms. Hiller, we were well on our way to completing withdrawal of our people within the allotted hour when the two helicopters dispatched to pick up the remaining personnel were shot down."

"Shot down?" Hiller said. "Why the hell did they do that?"

"Unknown, Ma'am. There was no warning or explanation. They were engaged by an antiaircraft position just after crossing the coast."

"Was this a position we knew about? Why didn't our helicopters just avoid it?"

"The position was camouflaged and outside the area that received the closest reconnaissance scrutiny. Being an old weapon system and looking at its placement, we suspect it was there to block westward movement along the coastal highway rather than to serve an antiaircraft function."

"Well, I guess they got lucky, didn't they Admiral?"

Brendan Wallace whispered, "That's enough, Karen."

"What's the status of the crews and of the troops they were going to evacuate?" she asked.

"A Predator sweep showed both birds down with very low probability of survivors. Our people south of Arad are still there. The purpose of my call is to request permission to launch a second mission to get them out. The helicopters will be ready to go in about ten minutes and can have them back aboard thirty to forty minutes after that. Considering Nazer's forces are the reason we still have people there, it seems reasonable we should be able to go get them."

The President pursed his lips and thought for a moment, then he gave a slight shake of his head to Hiller.

"Not happening Admiral. Reasonable has no meaning to nuclear terrorists. We agreed to his terms, and we're going to have to abide by them, as horrible as the consequences may be to us. Remember, breaking those terms may be worse."

"Most of the people on that ridge are wounded and medical personnel. Are you suggesting we leave them to be captured or killed by this lunatic?"

"Look Admiral, let me be clear. Neither the President nor I want any of our people, particularly our wounded, to be taken prisoner. Nonetheless, that's the position your ill-navigated helicopters have put us in. They can surrender, and we will do everything humanly possible to negotiate their release once this crisis is over. You may not send another aircraft. Am I clear?"

"Crystal clear, Ma'am."

The President signaled to the communications officer to terminate the connection, and all they heard was static.

Commandant of the Marine Corps Daniel Forrest was the first to speak. "I cannot believe that we are sailing away while dozens of our wounded and medical personnel are left to the mercies of this terrorist. What if they don't surrender and end up getting massacred? Or worse, what if they do surrender and end up getting massacred? Mr. President, I can see no good outcome here."

Karen Hiller was about to tear into the general when the President raised a calming hand. "General, I totally understand how you feel and, frankly, I agree with you. This is a hellish situation. As President, though, I don't have the luxury of only thinking about the people still in Yemen. I have to consider the people back here in the U.S. At best, a public announcement by Nazer that he has placed a nuclear weapon in one of our major East Coast cities would result in panic, probably large numbers of injuries and deaths, as well as economic chaos. At worst, we have to consider the possibility he actually has deployed a nuclear weapon on U.S. soil. Consider that for a moment."

Forrest was silent for a few seconds. "Understood, Mr. President."

Brendan Wallace leaned forward slightly and spoke

directly to Forrest. "One thing we do not need right now is a leak. There is, as of right now, a complete blackout on this information. None of us likes the situation, but for the moment it we will have to live with it...and keep quiet about it." Wallace turned his attention to the Chairman of the Joint Chiefs. "Ted, do whatever is necessary to disable any satellite communication those people in Yemen might have. We do not want them making calls for help to every ship or aircraft in CENTCOM."

"Or to DC, for that matter," added Karen Hiller.

General Dan Forrest looked at Hiller with contempt, his hard eyes boring into her. Even the master of Washington hardball politics squirmed slightly under the relentless gaze.

"I'll see that it's done, Mr. President." Lennox was speaking to Brendan Wallace, but he was looking at Daniel Forrest.

"And Ted, have your people work up a plan to retrieve our people if—and only if—we recover that sixth warhead or at least confirm it's not in U.S. territory.

"Right, Mr. President." Even Lennox knew this was eyewash. Those sailors and Marines were not coming home.

CHAPTER 50

"CO CALLING FOR you Commander," yelled Sergeant Leach.

Mike McGregor walked over to the Humvee, "Colonel Mark?"

"No sir, Admiral Tucker."

"The operational commander, why would he be calling me?"

But McGregor already knew it had to be some kind of bad news. Admirals did not contact junior officers without a very good reason. He took the handset and paused a moment. "Eagle one-two here."

"This is Junction," the Admiral began. "Ops tells me that you are the Battalion Surgeon for the 1/28, and that Colonel Mark left you in command. Am I correct?"

"That's right, sir."

"I'll assume the Colonel knew what he was doing. To put it bluntly, we have a problem. The aircraft dispatched to extract you and your people were shot down along the coast west of your position. Looks like it was done by a small detachment and they likely present no immediate threat to your position. I understand you have damaged the bridge to your north so vehicles from the objective are also no threat. Is that correct?"

"Yes sir," replied McGregor. "Our Royal Marines just took down a six-meter span."

"Good. Our second problem is we've gotten orders that no U.S. forces may enter or over fly Yemen east of Mukalla as of 1600 today. This isn't just us, it applies to all of CENTCOM. Do you understand what I'm saying?"

He did. They were being hung out to dry. He wanted to scream at the Admiral to ignore the fucking orders and come get his people out. But what would be the point? "Understood sir."

"Are you up to this Commander? I need to know right now."

"Uh, yes sir. I've been here before."

Tucker paused for what seemed like a long time. "All right, these are my orders."

McGregor signaled to Sgt. Leach to don a pair of headphones and to take notes.

"First," the Admiral began, "all U.S personnel now in Yemen east of 48.5 degrees east longitude are designated the 584 Composite Unit, the land equivalent of Task Force 58.4. You, Lieutenant Commander McGregor, are designated commanding officer. Your reporting senior is NAVCENT. You may appoint subordinate officers. Movement is at your discretion. Rules of engagement are that the safety of your command takes precedence. This is not a combat mission. You may, however, use deadly force to defend your command from an imminent threat. Surrender is authorized if you feel it's the only option. Is that clear?"

McGregor was numb, but he was recognized what was happening. "Clear sir. May I ask when you think you could send forces to get us out of here? Should we be planning for air or sea evacuation?"

"Unknown, son. Our orders are to clear the area, so all I can tell you is that help will not be coming from Task Force 58. Again, I'm sorry."

McGregor took a deep breath before answering. "Understood, sir. I should let you know that one survivor, one of the engineers, has reached us from the party sent to destroy a small bridge to the northwest of the objective. They were taken under fire by a superior force and after taking heavy casualties they tried to surrender. They were lined up and shot in the back by a Yemeni officer. The survivor escaped through a wadi. He says there is a company-sized force somewhere to our west."

Tucker considered this. McGregor hoped that, once Tucker knew the consequences of surrender, he might rethink the rescue option.

"Thank you for that information, Commander. I'll pass it along. And let me repeat surrender is *authorized*." After a moment he asked, "Do you have any capacity to resist a hostile force?"

"Sure...Hell, yes." McGregor immediately wondered why he said that.

"Very well. All I can add, then, is that the hopes and prayers of every man and woman in this task force are with you. Junction out."

"Thank you Admiral. One more question." McGregor paused for a second. "Sir?" He no longer heard the background hiss of the satellite system and received no reply. He looked at Brenda Leach who made a quick adjustment.

"We've lost the satellite uplink. I think they must have cut us off," she said.

"Can they disable our system remotely?"

"I don't think so. But they can terminate our access at the satellite. I think that's what just happened."

"I guess there's no contacting NAVCENT, or anyone else for that matter. I suppose that's the point." McGregor found that the shock was wearing off and was being replaced by a healthy, satisfying fury. "The bastards don't want us calling for help that nobody can give. The fact that we're trapped in this rat hole is going to be their little secret."

"Uh...you realize that works both ways? No comm, no more orders. You can do whatever the hell you want."

McGregor nodded. "You know, in the end they might wish they hadn't turned off the phone. How about the intel systems. Can we still access them?"

"Maybe, it's a different satellite." She tapped on the keyboard. "Looks like we can still download satellite reconnaissance."

"Good. Anything recent?"

In a moment she brought up an image whose legend indicated a satellite pass twenty-two minutes before. It was a fairly broad area, but they could see Arad, their own position—and most important, about thirty kilometers to the west and a bit north, a small column of vehicles, which appeared to be headed south. McGregor zoomed in and winced when he saw that one of them was a BTR-60. "We can't be here when that thing arrives," he said. "Get everyone together."

In a minute all the personnel on the ridge were gathered into a loose formation. McGregor surveyed the 584 Composite Unit. His 'command' consisted of thirty-six men and women; two medical officers—himself included—a physician assistant, four corpsmen, thirteen wounded Marines, the two Royal Marines—one of them wounded—First Sergeant Johanssen, Corporal Smith, and twelve MPs–interestingly, all of them female. A result, he supposed, of the late Major Griggs wanting to save his women from the rigors of combat. Ironically, they were now left behind on this hilltop in Yemen with a medical officer in command.

McGregor described their situation. He stopped periodically to let remarks like, "This is bullshit," and "No fucking way" settle down.

"It is bullshit, but we're stuck with it. We have to deal with this situation one step at a time. First step is chain of command. Captain Moore you're my executive officer." The MPs all nodded in approval, while Kelli Moore, herself, wore an expression he could not interpret. "Captain Singh is operations."

The Royal Marine snapped a boot pounding salute. "Yes suh!"

"Finally, First Sergeant Johanssen is the unit First Sergeant. No offense to you Sergeant Major"—He nodded at the big Scotsman—"but I think you'll be more valuable with the Captain."

"I believe I will, sir."

McGregor went on. "Right now there is a small convoy to our west, probably the same guys who murdered our people at that bridge. They have a BTR-60, which is armored and mounts a heavy machine gun. We have nothing to deal with it out in the open, so we need to move to a better position. First Sergeant, get us saddled up and ready to move in five minutes. Captain Moore, a word."

Kelli Moore strode over to Mike McGregor looking as if she didn't know where to begin. "I can't believe this. The Admiral is leaving us behind—with no goddamned explanation. He leaves a doctor in charge, and your first order is to prepare to engage a BTR-60. I don't know if I've lost my mind, the Admiral has lost his, or you've lost yours."

"Technically, my first order was to make you XO." McGregor tried to smile, but could not quite manage it. Despite the desperate circumstances, he still wanted to convince the Captain that he deserved this command, or perhaps to convince himself. "I suppose he put me in charge because Colonel Mark made the choice for him. And I don't think I've lost my mind quite yet. You and the Admiral, hard to say."

"Dammit, this is not a joke."

"No, Captain, it isn't." McGregor's pale grey eyes fixed hers. "And as crazy as it all sounds, this is the situation, and we have to deal with it. There is, in fact, a BTR-60 out there, and we may have to deal with it too. Now my question is, what do we have that can disable an armored vehicle?"

"I'm not sure," she answered after a moment. "Let's check the truck that came up with the weapons company. One of my people mentioned they had a Carl Gustav, probably brought by those Brits. Maybe we still have it."

"Isn't that one of those Swedish rocket launchers?"

"Technically a recoilless rifle, but definitely Swedish." A recoilless rifle is a type of tube artillery in which some of the gasses were exhausted to the rear, greatly reducing recoil and allowing some versions to be man portable.

They walked towards the small group of vehicles, each of which seemed to have plenty of water, fuel, and ammunition. Ocean Reach had consumed resources at a slower rate than expected—except, of course, for people.

When Kelli Moore saw Sergeant Major Campbell in the back of the truck, she grabbed a handhold and pulled herself in. "Sergeant Major, is that Carl Gustav in here somewhere?"

"Aye Captain", said Campbell, sounding for all the world like Scottie in the old *Star Trek* series. "Over here."

He opened a case and pulled out something that looked a lot like the AT-4 used by US forces, only larger and heavier. While the AT-4 was a single-use launcher, the Carl Gustav could be reloaded and had a wide variety of projectiles. "Most of our projectiles were in one of the Humvees that left with the 1/28. All we have here is one anti-structure munition, an area defense round—basically a big shotgun shell—and a few illumination rounds."

"Will that anti-structure round take out a BTR-60?" asked Kelli Moore.

"Their armor is very light except on the turret. Probably. Why, will we have to?" The Sergeant Major's question was matter of fact.

"We might," said Mike McGregor. "Sergeant Major, keep that thing ready to go. XO, you're with me. We need to get moving."

As they walked away from the truck, McGregor heard his new XO whisper to Sgt Leach, "Up until a few months ago, this would have been impossible. Now he's not just in command, he's acting like Patton."

Within ten minutes of McGregor's addressing his people, the 584 Composite Unit was loaded into seven vehicles, four Humvees, two field ambulances, and the truck. Kelli Moore, in the lead vehicle, put her arm out the window and waved forward. With only one working radio, they were communicating as they did in the cavalry days, with hand signals.

As the little convoy snaked its way south over the rough, hard-packed sand, the MP in the turret of the rear vehicle rode facing backward, her eyes fixed on the road behind them looking for the pursuing Yemenis. Periodically she put a pair of binoculars to her eyes, but they offered little help. The bouncing of the Humvee's non-existent suspension combined with the fading daylight and the thick dust kicked up by the vehicles in front of her offered little opportunity to see anything more than a hundred meters behind. Even her goggles and headscarf offered only limited protection from the dense cloud. But she peered as best she could into the tan haze, all the time praying she would see nothing more than sand.

Having no advance scouts or overhead Predator surveillance, they proceeded slowly and carefully. Periodically Captain Moore signaled a stop when the convoy passed near a hill or rock formation that offered a better view to the rear or if she sensed a potential ambush location. During one of these forays up a small hillside, she thought about her family. Her Dad and her brother, Bill, would be in their upscale suburban office right now while Mom was probably at a meeting of one of her boards, or maybe she was on the golf course. Did they wonder where she was? Would they believe it? Would they care?

About an hour into their journey, Moore climbed a rock pile on top of a small ridgeline and peered through binoculars after the dust had settled. She walked back to McGregor's Humvee. "Dust barely visible to the north and slightly west. My guess is they're heading towards the position we just left."

"A reasonable assumption," McGregor said. "We have a decent start on them. More would have been better, of course."

Kelli Moore was getting tired of the doctor's cryptic remarks. "May I ask what it is we're going to do with our head start? Or where it is we're going for that matter?"

"You remember that very sharp, high ridgeline running east/west not far south of here?" He pointed to the place he was referring to on the electronic map that sat between him and his driver. Looking down the road, the ridge was just visible beyond a gentle rise.

"Yeah, we drove through the road cut on the way up to Arad."

"That ridge will make a perfect defensive position. If we can hold that road cut, or block it somehow, it will be extremely difficult to cross, even on foot. We still have to take out the BTR, of course."

"So your grand plan is for a few MPs and a bunch of wounded to take on an enemy force large enough to have overwhelmed Griggs and his detachment?"

McGregor nodded. "What the hell else can we do? We'll have the advantage of a prepared position, and most of the wounded can handle a weapon. Besides, Griggs was an idiot. He probably walked into an ambush. The satellite photos did not show a force so big that we can't handle it."

Moore bristled at the remark about her dead commanding officer, even though she had thought exactly the same thing, especially after speaking with Corporal Smith. "Okay. And after that?"

"After that we get the hell out of here. Now let's get moving. We have a lot to do."

Back in her Humvee, Kelli Moore began to think about her talk with McGregor. She had rarely talked to Griggs that way, even though he was a sexist pretty boy who spent most of his time in the gym. And he was an incompetent to boot. But he was her commanding officer. But then so was McGregor. Was it that he wasn't a Marine, but just a medical officer pushed into command by their bizarre circumstances? Those two Royal Marines didn't hesitate to take his orders, and they were clearly hard professionals. Did they know something she didn't?

"What is it about our new CO that gets under my skin?"

She must have said that out loud, because her driver, Lance Corporal Sarah Fletcher, said, "It's pretty obvious Captain. I think you like him." The two MPs in the rear seats smiled and nodded in agreement.

CHAPTER 51

ABDULLAH NAZER HAD recovered from the flood of rage which had overtaken him after he learned of the American seizure of his warheads, and the havoc created in Arad. There was one positive—he felt his talk with the American President had cowed the man, an obvious weakling. The construction of a fake warhead from photographs of the originals emailed to his operatives in New York had worked even better than he had expected. By now there would be a NEST operation underway. They would quickly detect the tiny grains of radioactive materials his people had scattered around New York and Washington. An expanded search would turn up similar deceptions in Boston, Norfolk, and Atlanta. It would not take long for the public to become aware of the search.

He was considering his options when he received the call from his nephew. The young man described in detail his ambush of the Marines at the bridge. For a moment he was irritated that the hot-headed Ali al-Ahmar had shot his prisoners—such men could be valuable hostages. On reflection, however, he realized such an action would further convince Washington of their resolve.

"Well done, nephew. They will see the bodies with their satellites and will know they are dealing with men who will stop at nothing to achieve their aims."

"Thank you uncle. I have called to ask for instructions. Major Ishmail has informed me that the Americans have withdrawn. My original intent was to reinforce him at Arad, but the bridge has been damaged, and we cannot access Arad with our vehicles. What are your orders?"

"It is possible that not all the Americans have gone." Abdullah Nazer spoke slowly and with emphasis. "Their President agreed to no overflight or entrance into our waters as of two hours ago. Two large transport helicopters were heading north and were shot down when they crossed the beach at Qishn. Major Ishmail saw the last American vehicles leaving from south of the bridge only an hour ago. I think those helicopters were intended to pick them up and that they planned to abandon some of their vehicles to meet the deadline I set. They may be on that road even as we speak."

"The wind here has been strong, and the sand prevents us from seeing very far. We are just a few kilometers west of the Arad bridge right now. Shall we pursue them?"

"Yes. Those Americans have no place to go. If they reach the ocean, there will be no ships to come for them. If they take the coast road, they will encounter our forces in either direction. I want you to find them, take a few prisoners and treat the rest as you treated the others. The Americans were as easily manipulated over a small number of prisoners as a large one, but a few would be easier to secure, and displaying dozens of corpses on satellite television would convince the U.S. President that he was deadly serious.

"An order I will carry out with zeal. We will slaughter their arrogant Marines. Perhaps even better, some of their women soldiers would be with them."

CHAPTER 52

THE VEHICLES OF the 584 were parked in a loose semicircle about two hundred meters south of the cut through the high ridge which ran like a jagged tan ribbon across the desert of western Yemen. There was a slight whistle as the hot northwest wind resonated through the rocks. To the east, barely visible in the illumination of a full moon, was the semi-circular defect in the ridge referred to on the maps as 'Simpson's Notch'. Below the notch were strewn boulders, some so large they could be picked out from the road in daylight, even a kilometer away. There was also the tail section of a large aircraft.

McGregor had been approached by Corporal Smith shortly after they arrived. The young Marine pointed to the road cut. "See the split in the rock on the right side? Looks like that fissure extends down twenty or thirty feet. If we can get some C-4 down near the bottom, we can blast loose a good-size piece of rock and block the road."

"Good thinking Corporal," McGregor said. "Do we have enough C-4?"

"We brought fifty kilos in that Humvee." He pointed to the one Kelli Moore had been using. "And I just checked to see what's left. We have about thirty, plus some fuses and detonators."

"It's the best idea I've heard so far. See if Sergeant Major Campbell can give you a hand. He seems to know his way around explosives. And you better get moving. If those guys you met at the bridge are on their way, they'll be here soon."

Smith's face turned somber. "Sir, if that bastard who shot our people shows up, I want to be the one who cuts his throat."

"I think you've got a lot of competition for that honor Corporal."

Smith nodded and jogged away to find the Sergeant Major.

McGregor watched for a moment as Captain Singh began to lay out firing positions, and tried to team the least wounded Marines with those who, though less mobile, could still fire a weapon. McGregor knew that at least six of the wounded were in no shape to fight, and that there would be more casualties. He decided to station Lieutenants Ellis and Russell—along with the seriously wounded—at the ambulances to run the aid station. Neither had much experience with weapons and had never seen combat. His corpsmen, on the other hand, were mostly experienced, and he would need them pulling triggers if they were to have any chance to survive.

He approached his Humvee where Sergeant Leach and Captain Moore were trying to raise any U.S. unit on the HF radio, without success.

"Nobody in range right now," said McGregor. "I think we'll do better once we reach the coast."

"Why's that Commander?" Kelly Moore asked.

He ignored her question and led her away from the Humvee.

"I have an assignment for you. We need to defend that notch." He pointed toward the defect in the ridgeline. "Take your MPs down there and set up the best defensive position you can. I'll need Sergeant Leach with me, but you can take one of the corpsmen. Take the two Humvees with the M240s. There are a few more machine guns in the truck, and you can take one of them, plus as much ammo as you need. We have a ton. There are some pop-up illumination flares in there too; they might be useful."

Captain Moore's bright green eyes were wide and fixed directly on McGregor. "So you're just like Griggs after all," she said. "Send the girls away where they won't get hurt. You need us Commander, we are as close as you're going to get to a cohesive fighting unit. And we're a lot tougher than you think."

"Believe me, I am not coddling you," he replied. "Now that we have a way to block the road, that notch is their obvious alternative. Captain Singh is worried they're going to mount a small diversionary attack down the road, or even over the ridge and then hit us hard through that notch. Or rather, hit you—hard. If they get behind us in the dark, they can attack from any direction and we're all dead. Kelli," he put his hand on her shoulder which surprised them both, "if they do that, you and those girls are all that will stand between us and disaster."

"Right. I see. What are your orders?"

He considered that for a moment. He thought about a number of contingencies, but realized the Moore knew a lot more about those kind of details than he did. "Hold until relieved."

"They only say that in the movies, Doc." She managed a quick smile, threw her rifle sling over her shoulder, and was about to go when she added, "I guess that saying is right; if you need a job done, send a man. If you need it done right, send a woman." Kelli Moore waved to her driver and shouted, "Get that vehicle over here! We have a mission."

About ten minutes later, Corporal Smith and Sergeant Major Campbell walked up. Smith looked at his watch. "We had to use a long fuse. Going to blow in five minutes. Suggest we get everyone down or behind the vehicles."

They did and everyone waited.

At four minutes and change, there was the sharp thunderclap of the explosion followed immediately by the rumbling and crashing of rock as a piece of the wall nearly three meters thick and eight meters high crashed onto the road. Instead of falling as a single huge monolith, however, it shattered into hundreds of boulders ranging from the size of watermelons to small cars.

As the dust cleared, the Sergeant Major said, "If they have explosives of their own, some cables or chains, and a BTR-60 they'll be able to clear that road well enough to get vehicles through with about six hours of hard work."

"Which is why we need to stop them here," said McGregor. "If we leave, they will clear that obstruction and be back on our tails. Did you see them while you were working, by the way?"

"Aye, sir," replied the Sergeant Major. "Headlights obscured by dust coming our way. Best guess is they reach the ridge in half an hour." He took a moment and appraised the situation further. "That road cut is fairly wide, and if they come through there, they'll have the high ground."

"Captain Singh and the First Sergeant are working on that. Can you get into a position to take out that BTR-60?"

Campbell nodded. "Can do sir. We just have to hope they wait to organize themselves. If I was them, I would storm that breach as soon as I arrived. Hitting us before we can prepare a defense will be more of an advantage than full darkness."

"Probably true," McGregor said. "But I suspect they'd like us to surrender, and hope we don't know what happened up at the bridge. Their pals in Arad probably gave them an idea of our strength and that we have two ambulances so we probably have wounded. I'm betting they try some mind games first."

"You could be right, Commander. It sounds like you have some experience in this part of the world."

"More than I really care to remember, Sergeant Major."

"Understood sir. I'd best get moving. I'll take that Carl Gustav with me and see what mischief I can stir up." Campbell walked to the truck where he had the weapon already loaded. He put on a rucksack and picked up both the big anti-armor weapon and his rifle. Despite the heavy load, he moved west at a brisk pace. He turned to McGregor and added, "I'll flash a red lens three times when I return. Try not to shoot me. And Commander, when all this is over I'd like you to visit my family up in Inveraray. We'll round out your education as a Scotsman."

"Be my pleasure, Sergeant Major."

The big man strode across the road and into the barren desert. McGregor was impressed that these two Brits were acting like they were actually going to get out of here. For his part, he wasn't quite so sure.

"Corporal Smith. Over here."

The young Corporal trotted over. "Sir?"

"Very good work on the road. I think that's going to give us a good chance to put together a position that will be hard to crack."

"Thank you, sir."

"Now I have an even more important assignment for you. I think we'll get out of here, but in case we don't it's vital that the people back home know exactly what happened to us. The ambush and the murder of the Marines you were with at the bridge and how we were left on our own when the task force bugged out."

"What do you need from me?"

"Corporal Smith, you look like a survivor. And you're in damn fine condition if you could run all the way back from that ambush. I have written in this notebook—" He pulled a small green note pad from his breast pocket,—"the names of all the personnel currently with the 584 as well as what I know about the circumstances. Add whatever you know about the ambush and whatever names you know of the Marines killed. Take some MREs and as much water as you can carry. Move at night. I want you to head east into Oman. The Omanis are generally friendly, and there are British troops there. Avoid contact with the enemy if at all possible. Do whatever it takes to get this information back home. Make as many copies as you can before turning it in to the chain of command. If they sit on it, and we haven't been heard from, then go public."

"With respect, sir, I would really prefer to stay and fight. I'm a Marine."

"And a damn good one. I don't think one man is going to make a difference in this fight, but you could be the only hope for our families to know what really happened here. We owe that much to our people. We're counting on you to be sure it happens."

Smith saluted. "I'll get ready and start right away. I'll do my best."

"I'll see you back in Ann Arbor, Corporal."

It was a little shocking how easily he was sending people out on missions from which they might never return. The MPs, Campbell, and now Corporal Smith. His thoughts, as they often did, turned to Danielle. Was it better that he had to endure the pain of her death, than her enduring his?

He was brought back to reality when First Sergeant Johanssen walked up and announced, "Looks like the party has started. I put a couple of scouts up in the road cut, and they just reported a small column led by a BTR-60 has pulled up about a hundred meters north of the rock pile. I thought about having them fire a few shots, but decided against it. We know they're here, so I pulled them back."

McGregor nodded. "Kick-off."

CHAPTER 53

IN THE DWINDLING rays of sunset, Ali al-Ahmar saw the rubble blocking the road when his column stopped to look for signs of the Americans.

"What do you think, Sergeant?" he asked his driver. "Is that intended to slow us down while they escape, or are they waiting for us on the other side?"

His driver thought for a moment. "We would stand and fight, no question. Without their drones and helicopters, the Americans won't have the stomach for battle. All we will see is a cloud of dust heading towards the coast."

"Perhaps. The Americans we encountered at the bridge fought hard, but they were ill-prepared and poorly positioned. Even if they are here, I doubt they will put up much of a fight. Let's go have a look." Captain al-Ahmar picked up his radio handset and gave orders to his company, now consisting of seventy-six men. Major Ishmail had been able to send him four men, all he could spare.

They had parked about a hundred meters from the roadblock with the BTR-60 in front in a position to take under fire anyone coming through the gap. Five men were dispatched to scout ahead. As they crawled among the rocks, al-Ahmar could tell they saw something up ahead.

"The Americans are there, sir," reported his sergeant. "Their vehicles are parked a few hundred meters ahead, just west of the road."

One of the privates climbed on top of a large boulder for a better look. He shouldered his AK-47, but before he could fire, the back of his head blossomed red, and he was thrown backward.

Four hundred meters away Al Johanssen, lying on top of one of the ambulances, turned from the night vision scope of his M-25 sniper rifle and said to Mike McGregor, "They know we're here now."

"Yeah, welcome to the party. Bastards."

"Get those men back. Right now," al-Ahmar shouted. In a moment, he was walking towards the rocks holding a bullhorn. "Americans, listen to me. I am Captain Ali al-Ahmar, and I am telling you that fighting us is suicide. We have superior numbers and are fighting on our own soil. We will soon be reinforced while you have no hope of rescue. Surrender now, and we will take you to Mukalla where you will be held as prisoners until our leader and your President can negotiate your release. You have five minutes to send your commander bearing a white flag to the top of those rocks. After that, you will all surely die. American women: your presence here is an affront to my soldiers. I cannot protect you from them. Surrender. Now."

SHORT SEASON

Before the whining sound had even registered, al-Ahmar dropped prone to the ground. And it was just beginning to register when the rocket shell tore through the armor of his BTR-60 and exploded inside.

CHAPTER 54

MIKE McGREGOR WONDERED if Captain Moore's people had heard the threat from their position just over a kilometer away. He hoped they did; they needed to know what they were dealing with. As he surveyed the tired, sweaty faces around him he could see a gamut of emotions. Some were obviously fearful—and rightly so. Some were angry. Many looked determined, but everyone was clearly waiting for him to make a decision. It seemed incredible that only a few hours before they were part of a powerful landing force that could have swept these bastards away with little effort, but not now. Now they were outnumbered, outgunned, and manning their fighting positions with corpsmen and wounded Marines. Despite all this, they were his people. HIS people.

Johanssen broke the silence. "Orders, sir?"

McGregor stood quietly for a moment. Al Johanssen understood that he was struggling with some kind of inner dialogue. Finally, he spoke, slowly and clearly. "We are going to kill every fucking one of them, and then we are going home."

The effect on the Marines and sailors gathered around him was electrifying. Everyone scattered, and now committed to battle, resumed their preparations. Ammunition boxes were broken open, rounds distributed, and magazines loaded. McGregor was grateful that the truck from the weapons company with all their extra ammunition was the one they left behind. Probably a screw-up, but a lucky one for the 584.

CHAPTER 55

WHILE THE OTHER participants from the meeting in the Situation Room were now writing memos and reading reports in their White House offices, Commandant of the Marine Corps Daniel Forrest was back at the Pentagon. The thought of leaving sailors and Marines behind on his watch was repugnant to every fiber of his being. Nonetheless, he'd been given orders directly from the President. He was not about to disobey them.

But he intended to take whatever action was available to him.

He began by calling Isaac Keen at MARCENT. He was not surprised to find Keen at his desk on MacDill AFB Florida.

Keen had been monitoring Ocean Reach and had just taken an angry call from Colonel Aaron Mark, who had reported aboard *Essex* only to discover his MPs, doctors, and wounded had been left on a hilltop in Yemen. Mark and Admiral Tucker had what Keen described as a 'difficult conversation', which Tucker had then kicked up the CENTCOM chain of command, a move which had finally ended with MARCENT.

Keen was in an awkward position. Technically, he reported to Central Command, four star Army General Robert Cunningham, but the Commandant was the Commandant, and to every Marine he was the top of the food chain. "Sir," he began, "Colonel Mark is as unhappy as you are, and I'm not happy either. The idea of leaving people behind on our watch is something no Marine wants to live with. But I don't know what either you or I can do."

"Look, Ike, I know we're in a bind, at least for the moment. Just get the word out to our people to keep their eyes and ears open. I want to hear about any communications from that unit, and I mean anything. We can't restore their satellite uplink; that order went straight from the White House Chief of Staff to NMCC. But have your intel staff examine satellite data from the area—I want to know exactly where our people are. And see if NAVCENT can keep something available to pull them out in case the White House has a change of heart."

"Can do, sir. I'll keep you informed."

"And Ike," the Commandant went on, "you have good connections with the Omanis; see what assets they have near the border. If we can establish contact, maybe we can direct our people to a rendezvous with Omani forces."

Keen thought for a moment . "I'll look into that. Getting another nation involved though . . . Hold on. Wait one"

After a few minutes MARCENT was back on the secure line. "My intel staff just brought me a satellite photo, infrared, taken about halfway between Arad and the coast forty minutes ago. It looks like our people are deployed in a defensive position on the south side of a long ridge. We can identify the Humvees pretty well, particularly the ambulances. On the north side, there's a gaggle of about seventy-five with four vehicles, presumably some of Nazer's men. One of the vehicles looks like an old Soviet BTR-60. It has a big heat plume coming from the back. Do our people have some kind of anti-armor weapon?"

"I don't really know how well armed they are," Forrest said. "Given how they're deployed and that they have somehow disabled an armored vehicle, they're obviously not thinking about surrender. Even with the BTR out of the picture, though, they're outnumbered more than two to one. God help them. Dammit Ike, our people are going to go out fighting, and so will I. We have to find a way help them!"

"It may already be too late."

"Let's not count them out yet, Ike. Keep me informed."

CHAPTER 56

MCGREGOR AND FIRST Sergeant Johanssen were sitting on rocks about two-hundred meters from the road cut, which they could see fairly easily in the moonlight. McGregor wished his people all had night vision, and while everyone's helmet had the small attachment for NVGs, none were available at Twentynine Palms. The old mantra of supply, "We ran out." Assuming the operation would conclude before dark, no effort was made to find the devices elsewhere. In all the 584, only the wounded LAV driver, who was active duty, had them, plus Singh and Campbell.

So far, there had been three minor forays into the rocks. Each time four or five men, using the deep moon shadows for cover, had advanced far enough to have a clear field of fire and had emptied one magazine each in the general direction of their positions. Captain Singh, who had taken over the sniper position from Johanssen, had killed two and wounded one. Despite his wounded hand, his marksmanship with the night scope was superb.

A shattered bullet had hit one of the Marines, already suffering from a shrapnel wound to the leg, in the left shoulder. One of the fragments had also hit HM2 Courtney Kales in the left cheek, a mirror image of McGregor's own facial wound. McGregor had applied a quick dressing, not wanting to take the time to close the wound with sutures. The big dressing made the wound look worse than it was.

"I'm sorry, that's going to leave a scar," he said. "They can do a nice scar revision later, though."

"I don't think so, sir. I think yours is kind of distinguished. I'll live with whatever I get."

"One might be distinguished, but two is just tacky. Be sure to keep your head down."

She nodded and headed back to her fighting position, loaded down with her rifle, magazines, two canteens, body armor, and aid bag.

Half an hour later and still waiting, McGregor and Johanssen were munching MRE crackers, the modern equivalent of hardtack, when McGregor heard a faint scratching. He looked down and saw a jerboa, a small desert rodent that looked like the kangaroo rats of the American southwest. The jerboa became part of military history as the symbol for the British 7th Armoured Division, the 'Desert Rats.' McGregor grinned, broke off a small piece of cracker and dropped it on the sand. The little creature snatched it and scurried away. "At least he'll be alive tomorrow."

Before Johanssen could respond, Sergeant Leach, who had been checking their perimeter to the rear, pointed south. "Look Commander."

He turned just in time to see three pale red flashes. After five seconds, the signal was repeated. And then again until they heard footsteps.

"Sergeant Major Campbell, I presume?"

"Aye. Back from the other side."

"We heard the results of your work," Johanssen said. "Glad to see you made it back."

"Piece of cake. There's a spot about three clicks west of here where the top of the ridge isn't quite so steep. I was able to get over then haul this beast—" He held out the Carl-Gustav—"into a decent firing position about a hundred meters north of the BTR. They have the north side of the ridge guarded pretty well, but no patrols out to their rear. Bloody amazing! The round penetrated into the engine compartment, no problem. Killed one, wounded another of the buggers as a bonus. Had to make a bit of a detour before heading back."

"We heard a lot of small arms fire," McGregor said.

"Aye, they were spraying rounds all over the place. Then they sent a couple of lads after me. I used the same trick as young Corporal Smith—got into a little wadi and let one of them go by, then dispatched him with this." He held up a wicked looking weapon that McGregor recognized as the legendary Sykes-Fairbairn fighting knife. "The other one got lost in the dark. So what have I missed?"

"Not much. You probably heard them emptying mags

from their AKs from up in the rocks. Captain Singh took out a few with the M-25. We took two wounded."

"I count five of them KIA and one wounded. And their major weapon system is out of action. With the engine out, they can't even traverse the damn machine gun. I call that progress."

CHAPTER 57

CAPTAIN KELLI MOORE heard the distant automatic weapons fire from her position south of the notch. She ached to know more about what was happening back at their main position, but without a functional radio, she could not keep sending people back just to get a report. About twenty minutes earlier, Sergeant Leach had come down in the Humvee to let her know about the Sergeant Major's successful engagement with the BTR. They discussed the fact that the Yemeni action was so far fairly trivial and aimed at keeping them all on edge. They agreed something bigger had to be coming.

Moore surveyed her preparations once again. She had two of the M240G machine guns well dug in and a third in one of the Humvees as a mobile firing platform, which could move to add fire wherever it was needed. Each weapon had eighteen 200 round ammo cans, 3600 rounds

per gun—substantial ammo load by any standard. Each of
the automatic weapons was manned by two of her MPs.

There were two additional fighting positions, each with
two MPs armed with M-4 5.56 mm rifles and 420 rounds
each. They had scrounged a few hand grenades, and Moore
had three illumination flares. She shared a position in the
center with Kim Stoller, their corpsman. Stoller, a nursing
student at Michigan, had no deployment experience, but
she had thrown herself into digging as secure a position as
possible and had even incorporated a few pieces of heavy
sheet metal from the aircraft which had apparently been
responsible for creating the gap they were now preparing
to defend. At the moment, each team was also preparing
a fighting position to fall back to, if necessary. Everything
that could be done was being done. All that was left was
the waiting.

CHAPTER 58

THE BATTLE HAD begun. About two dozen of al-Ahmar's men had moved into the rocks and opened up with a heavy stream of fire in the general direction of McGregor's positions. A steady, but disciplined, return fire from their two M-240G machine guns and the M-4 rifles began to take its toll on the attackers. Captain Singh, still manning the sniper rifle, was making a mark as well.

After half an hour of trading fire at a range of about a hundred meters, ten of the Yemenis mounted a frontal assault, delivering fierce fire from their Ak-47s as well as throwing grenades. The well prepared positions and M-240 machine guns gave the defenders a decisive advantage.

The rest of the assault force, however, ran down the road and once clear of the rocks moved west into the open desert. Their plan was immediately apparent. While McGregor and his troops were occupied with a direct assault, at least a dozen Yemenis would get past them into the desert and conduct a flanking attack. They would be in a position to attack from almost any direction.

McGregor looked to First Sergeant Johanssen, with whom he was sharing a fighting position.

"We need to go after them," Johanssen said. "We can't let them run around back there all night. Most of our guys are wounded and not too mobile. I'm on this."

Johanssen ran quickly to Sergeant Major Campbell who grabbed the Carl-Gustav, and the two men headed back towards the rear.

McGregor decided he had to help deal with this critical threat. His people were already taking the frontal attack apart. In a minute he found Johanssen, Campbell, Captain Singh, and HM2 Brad Greene. "I'm joining your little grouse hunt."

"Unwise, Commander," replied Captain Singh as he loaded few fresh rounds into the magazine of the sniper rifle.

"Probably, but here I am."

"Very well then, here's the plan."

Johanssen gave a quick outline of what he had in mind. The group spread out and began to advance. Sergeant Major Campbell pointed the Carl-Gustav skyward and fired. There was an orange flash from the exhaust and they could see the round as it started on its upward trajectory. After a few seconds it burst into a brilliant flare that illuminated the desert like a small sun.

About a hundred meters to the south, they could see seven men advancing in a widely-spaced skirmish line. Singh, already in a sitting position, fired two quick shots.

One man went down immediately, and the man to his right staggered, obviously hit, but kept moving forward. At this point the Yemenis opened fire as did McGregor—also seated—Campbell, and Greene. After about thirty seconds, during which well over a hundred rounds were fired by both sides, all the Yemenis were down.

During the firefight McGregor felt what seemed like a hard slap on the side of his right thigh. The pain had now progressed to an aching, burning sensation. Looking down, the waning light of the flare revealed a six inch furrow, about a quarter of an inch deep on the outside of his leg, halfway between the hip and knee. It was just starting to bleed. The aching became more intense, and it took concentrated mental effort to pull a battle dressing off his body armor, open it, and wrap it around his leg.

He tried to stand, which he was able to do, but the throbbing became even worse. It occurred to him that his wound was no worse than those suffered by most of their other wounded. Were all of them hurting this much and still fighting? Hoping to get a better dressing and something for pain, McGregor looked for HM2 Greene, who was not far behind him, applying a battle dressing to First Sergeant Johanssen's left arm.

"First one hit me right in the chest, knocked me down," Johanssen said, "but the plate in my body armor stopped it. As soon as I got back up, one of them hit me in the arm."

"Through and through wound Doc," Greene said, "but I think the arm is fractured."

McGregor felt for a pulse. "Circulation's okay." He scratched Johanssen's fingertips. "Can you feel that?"

"Yeah, but it's really starting to ache." Johanssen looked down at the dressing on McGregor's leg. "Jesus, Doc. They got you too?"

"Just a divot. We need to get back to the ambulance and let Russell take a look at your arm." They began to walk back, slowly. As they walked, he realized the seven men they'd just killed did not account for everyone they saw break out from the road cut.

They all began to move faster when they heard fire coming from near the vehicles.

As they approached the ambulances, they saw several dead Yemenis on the ground, and three more advancing very close to the wounded. Behind one of the ambulances, they saw Lieutenants Russell and Ellis, under fire. HM2 Kales had pulled back from her fighting position to help, and one Marine with multiple dressings was firing an M-4 while lying on a litter. To McGregor's surprise, his friend Jim Russell was standing totally exposed and firing at the Yemenis with his pistol.

As they got closer, it was difficult to tell exactly what was happening. People were running back and forth; weapons were being fired in several directions, and there were frantic shouts in English and in Arabic. Finally, as they arrived at the small aid station, things seemed to have settled down. There were now four dead Yemenis on the ground, one only a few meters away. Still that didn't account for ...

McGregor was about to ask Russell for a report when they heard a high pitched cry.

McGregor and Campbell rushed around to the far side of ambulance where they saw Nicole Ellis. A Yemeni soldier was behind her with one arm around her neck and the other holding a knife to her throat. "Back," he screamed. "I will kill her."

McGregor took a step forward, raising his hands, but this apparently alarmed the man. He pulled the knife away from her neck and stabbed the young PA in the side of the leg. She gasped, but did not scream. Then she surprised everyone. "Will somebody just shoot this asshole?"

For a few seconds they all stood frozen. Then Captain Randeep Singh, standing behind and to the left of McGregor, considered the tactical situation. He held the Mark-25 sniper rifle in his wounded left hand. There was no way to raise the weapon, get his right hand to the trigger, get the long barrel on target, and fire before the young woman's throat was cut. His right hand, however, rested on the butt of the WW2 era Browning automatic pistol his grandfather had carried up Monte Casino. In a move he had attempted only at the range, but never in combat, the Royal Marine drew, cocked the hammer, and in one continuous motion drew, raised the weapon, and fired.

The shot exploded, and the Yemeni crumpled to the ground. McGregor stepped forward to see a bullet hole below his right eye and Nicole Ellis bent forward gripping her right leg.

"Let's take a look at that leg." Jim Russell helped her to a litter and began to cut away the leg of her camouflage pants.

Singh, holstering the pistol, came up behind the Sergeant Major and gave a satisfied smile. Campbell said, "A little low sir. You were aiming for his eye weren't you?" They headed back to their positions.

As Russell cleaned and dressed their PA's wound, he reported on their other casualties.

"They hit us pretty hard, Mike. Lot of grenades. We have three KIA, two of the wounded from the 1/28 plus one of their platoon corpsmen, Andre Watson."

Damn. Watson, a tall, impossibly thin, African American was less than a year way from becoming his family's first college graduate.

"Three gunshot wounds, all extremities. One pretty bad, probable amputation. Six with grenade shrapnel, only one looks really bad, going to cost someone an eye."

"Plus First Sergeant Johanssen took a bullet in the arm," McGregor said. "Greene thinks the humerus is fractured. Take a look at it when you have a chance. Circulation and nerves seem all right to me, though."

"And then there's Nicole's stab wound. Not too deep though. I am worried we have so little for pain control, and we're about out of antibiotics. And what happened to your leg?"

"Grazed by a bullet. Should be okay until I can get more definitive care. To be honest, we'll either be out of here very soon or it isn't going to matter. Use up whatever we've got. We won't need it later."

Russell just nodded and went back to work.

With all the wounded being given what care was available, McGregor took a short break. He sat on the hood of his Humvee and sipped a cup of MRE coffee he'd heated with the little propane stove he brought with him everywhere. He was talking with the two Royal Marines about whether to send someone to the ridge top to recon the Yemeni positions when the battle began at Simpson's Notch. Fierce barrages of automatic weapons fire were almost continuous. Tracers were visible in the dark. Two times they spotted pop-up illumination flares, but the terrain did not permit them to see any of the action.

"We need to know if they're going to hit us again," McGregor said. "If all their remaining troops are hitting Captain Moore, we need to get some help over there. But we have so many wounded, we can't spare anyone until we know for sure if they're playing us or if they really are committed to the attack on the notch. Sergeant Major, I know I'm asking you for more than anyone else, but I need you to recon their position."

"Certainly, Commander. As long as I don't have to haul that bloody Carl-Gustav, should be no problem." He picked up his ruck and his weapon, and he headed off.

"Don't feel you're abusing us Commander," Captain Singh said. "We've done field exercises tougher than this. After all, you do know what RM stands for don't you?"

McGregor look at him expectantly.

"The Real Marines," which he delivered with an exaggerated Cambridge accent.

McGregor had to laugh. "Just don't let my First Sergeant hear you say that."

CHAPTER 59

MCGREGOR LAY ON the hood of his Humvee, trying to keep his leg elevated. About ten minutes after Campbell left, two quick shots rang out, then silence.

Five minutes after that, Campbell was back.

"Nobody's left alive north of those rocks," he said. "They had two lads with a radio watching their rear, but it looks like the rest of them went off to hit us through that notch. Their vehicles are there, nothing useful in any of them. If we had more mobile people, I'd say hit them from the rear on foot. As it is, probably best to just head over in the vehicles."

"Agreed," replied McGregor. "Let's take one ambulance with HM2 Greene and Lt Russell. Two Humvees. You and Captain Singh in one. Try to find a couple people who can still pull a trigger. Sergeant Leach and I will take the other."

In five minutes they were on their way. It took only a few minutes more to travel the distance to the notch. There was a haze of cordite smoke hanging in the still air, which stung McGregor's eyes and assaulted his nostrils. The sun was beginning to glow on the eastern horizon, and that, combined with the moon, allowed for fair visibility.

Unfortunately.

Both of Captain Moore's Humvees were riddled with bullet holes. Between the Marines and the notch lay dozens of dead Yemenis, with even more mingled among the U.S. positions. The ground was littered with thousands of shell casings—several fighting positions were filled almost ankle deep with them. Only two of the Marines were moving.

"Dear God," McGregor said. "Is everyone else dead?"

He had his people spread out and look for wounded. He, too, began to limp from position to position. The first two Marines he found were dead. The third was Kelli Moore. She was on her back, no body armor, a curved dagger protruding from her left chest. She was barely breathing, but she was breathing. Her neck veins were distended and her face dusky blue.

Tension pneumothorax.

Jim Russell immediately saw what McGregor saw. He produced a large needle from his medical bag and said, "Mike, I've got this."

"The hell you do. Give me that."

Russell gently pushed him away. "Mike, trust me. I'm on this. Check the others."

He produced a large pair of shears and cut up the side of the Captain's camouflage and t-shirts and exposed the knife.

She had a tattoo—an elaborate Celtic design—on her

left side just below her green sports bra—its symmetry was shattered by the knife blade protruding from the center.

Russell felt for Moore's upper ribs and inserted the needle just above one of them. There was a prominent hiss as the air that had collected around her lung began to escape, allowing the lung to expand. He then gently pulled the knife from her chest and covered the wound with a dressing that would prevent more air from entering.

How many times had McGregor told people Russell was the smartest guy in the regiment? He had to trust him on this. McGregor glanced at a blood-soaked Yemeni officer with a K-bar knife protruding from under his chin. He turned back and noted the empty sheath on Kelli Moore's belt. So she'd given as good as she got.

What would the late Major Griggs say about that?

Not far away, McGregor found a corporal he didn't recognize still holding a dressing against the fatal chest wound of a second Lieutenant. The Lieutenant's eyes were already getting cloudy. He gently pulled the corporal's hand away from the wound. "She needed a surgeon. You did all you could."

Seeing the young corporal was still bleeding from several untreated shrapnel wounds he got her up and helped her back to the ambulance, where Brad Greene began to dress her wounds. As he turned to find more wounded, he added, "Don't worry about your Lieutenant, we'll get her in a few minutes. Everyone's going home."

About ten meters from the dead Lieutenant, he found HM3 Kim Stoller lying in her fighting position. He noted the Captain's bars on her body armor and understood that she was wearing Kelli Moore's. Stoller was conscious, but seemed disoriented. He saw battle dressings on both legs and her right arm. Nonetheless her pulse was strong.

He shook her and forced her to look at him. "Stoller, what the hell happened here?"

The young corpsman slowly focused, then grasped his hand and sat up. He then saw that she had been lying on a burned and shredded flak jacket. So the shrapnel wounds had come from a grenade, which had damaged her body armor. And Moore had given hers to her corpsman.

The corpsman took a deep breath. "It was...they started out up there. Up in those rocks. They must have had a lot of ammunition since they just emptied magazines from their AK's for a while. We put out a lot of fire too. After about twenty minutes, they just...charged. It was like squad rushes, a couple of dozen rushing forward about twenty meters and then going to the ground to provide cover fire for the next group. We chewed them up, but they kept coming." Her voice was strengthening. "When they got within fifty meters, the ones still alive just charged straight at us. I had been moving around trying to treat the wounded and contribute to the fight as best I could, but we were getting hit faster than I could work. Then I got hit by the grenade. I was knocked out for I don't know how long. When I came to, I hurt all over and was wearing Captain Moore's kevlar. Is she okay?"

"Knife wound in the chest. Russell's putting in a chest tube right now. I think she'll be all right."

"And the guy that gave it to her?"

"Knife wound to the neck. He's not all right."

"Knife wound, that fits. They fired so many rounds they ran out, and finally so did we. I saw a couple of our girls fixing bayonets."

What Kim Stoller had failed to see was the final act of the drama. Six Marines lay dead, four wounded plus herself. All the Yemenis were dead or dying, save one. Captain Ali al-Ahmar was in a rage unlike anything he had ever known. The bodies of his men littered the ground all around him. Killed not only by Americans, but by American women. Had they done this just to humiliate him? Was their arrogance and pride so great? Revenge was all he had left. Not far ahead of him he saw one American still on her feet, moving about looking for . . . what? Ammunition probably; she was out, and so was he. He would kill this one close up.

Ali al-Ahmar gripped the ivory handle of his dagger and withdrew the curved eight inch blade. He crept forward, silently—she had not seen him yet. At the last moment, he burst out of the darkness and took hold of her throat. Captain's bars. Their officer! His revenge was even sweeter now.

The foolish captain grabbed at the arm holding her throat. That was when al-Ahmar thrust his dagger into the side of her chest.

She gasped in pain. He pulled her close, close enough to feel her warm breath on his arm, feel her curves pressing up against him. So sensuous, so enticing. Perhaps afterwards. He smiled, savoring his victory, about to thrust the blade even deeper.

He did not really feel the blade pierce the floor of his mouth, slice through his tongue, and traverse his left eye.

His immediate reaction was utter disbelief, that he, Captain Ali al-Ahmar, was being killed by this woman.

Then she twisted the blade, and he felt no more.

It took them half an hour to regroup and take stock. In total, six MPs were KIA. Six more, including HM3 Stoller were wounded. They would survive, but most required urgent surgery.

As far as McGregor could see, none of the enemy had survived. The 'girls' had held the notch. What would Griggs say now?

The wounded were evacuated first, and then the truck sent to retrieve the bodies. Back at the road, the medical personnel gave emergency care, but McGregor ordered everyone loaded into the remaining vehicles as soon as possible. The two shot up Humvees were abandoned.

As soon as the sun was high enough for driving, the 584 Composite Unit headed south.

CHAPTER 60

SEPTEMBER 14, 2017 0450Z (0750 AST)
USS *Bataan* (LHD 5), Gulf of Aden

T HE USS *BATAAN* was cruising west through the Arabian Sea on its way to the Red Sea and the Suez Canal. Accompanying the big amphibious ship were two fleet auxiliaries, the USNS *Lewis & Clark*—a stores and ammunition ship—and the USNS *Pecos*—a replenishment oiler. Escorting the three larger vessels were two Arleigh Burke Class destroyers, the *Nitze* and the *Spruance*. The ships were deployed in a loose formation making fifteen knots in the gentle swells.

On the bridge, her skipper, Captain Joseph Castelli, looked out across the flight deck at the placid green sea ahead. *Bataan* had just participated in a highly success-ful amphibious raid against a secret Iranian Quds base on Chabahar Bay. Located on the Gulf of Oman, the base was well situated for small boat attacks on shipping headed for the Persian Gulf. It was now smoldering rubble, and almost three hundred of their garrison were dead or wounded.

Following the raid, *Bataan* had disembarked the 26th Marine Expeditionary Unit in Dubai, part of the U.S. plan to shore up the defenses of the western gulf states. She had taken aboard a battalion of the 7th Marines and was now heading for home, along with other ships which had seen heavy service and were in need of overhauls. *Bataan's* serviceable aircraft had been transferred to other ships or to shore installations, while those aboard were destined for major repairs.

Castelli had good reason to be satisfied with the results of his mission, but his greatest satisfaction was the result of a decision made thousands of miles away. Several months after departing Norfolk, the Flag Officer Selection Board results were published in an all-Navy message. Captain Joseph Castelli was selected for advancement to Rear Admiral (lower half). All that remained was announcement of the date.

In recognition of Castelli's selection, the Task Force commander, Admiral Mark Garrett, had helicoptered to Bahrain for an early flight home and had turned over command of the small group to Castelli. It was not unusual for the senior captain to also command a small group of ships, especially when the only mission was a peaceful cruise home. Nonetheless, Joe Castelli loved to look out at the ships around him and to think of them as his own Task Force.

Everything was coming together.

"Navigator," Castelli said, "what's our closest approach to the coast of Yemen? I don't want to get caught up in this White House mess." Castelli knew there had been some kind of very secret operation in eastern Yemen that resulted in an order direct from NMCC to stay clear of Yemeni waters and air space. He had also received a personal communication from MARCENT to report any contact with something called the 584 Composite Unit, whatever that might be. He had asked for clarification, but had received none.

"Eighty kilometers, Captain."

Castelli would have been just as happy bypassing the entire area and taking the long route around Africa. That was a lot of fuel, though, and while he had considerable discretion as to routing his small group, he didn't have that much.

Castelli's thoughts were interrupted by one of the petty officers who held out a sound-powered telephone. "For you, Captain. Communications Officer."

Curious, Castelli took the handset. "What?"

"Sir, we just received a call on the NATO aircraft emergency frequency. Low power, and not easy to hear. They identified themselves as the 584 Composite Unit and requested secure communication on a frequency compatible with their SINCGARS HF unit. We did that, and their commanding officer has asked to speak with you personally. Asked for you by name, sir."

Who the hell were these people, and how did their CO know his name? His instinct was to ignore it, but there was that directive from MARCENT. "Okay, put him on."

After a few clicks Castelli heard the hum and distinctive sound of the frequency hopping FM SINCGARS radio. "This is *Bataan*."

"This is the 584 Composite Unit. We are twenty-six sailors and Marines, twenty-three of us are wounded, some critically. We were left behind when Operation Ocean

Reach shut down. You remember what that's like, don't you Captain? Being wounded and left behind?"

Joe Castelli nearly dropped the handset. He had put that day out of his mind. His leg had healed, he had been promoted to Commander, and his career had moved on. Participation in that mission had helped put him on the fast track, but the details were best locked away in some back room of his psyche.

"Who the hell is this?" But he already knew the answer.

"Lieutenant Commander Michael McGregor, sir. And we need your help. Sailors and Marines are dying right here on the beach. It's up to you, Captain."

"McGregor? What the hell—."

"That's Lieutenant Commander McGregor. Sir."

Castelli took a deep breath. Was this really possible, McGregor an officer? "Well, Lieutenant Commander, you may not know about the orders involving entry into Yemeni territorial waters."

"Actually, I do. I also know neither you nor I would be here had Colonel Ahrens been thinking like that. Captain, this is entirely up to you. It's a shitty position to be in, I get that."

"And what part of a direct order from the National Military Command Center do you not get, Commander?"

"Captain, what do you think your father would do right now?"

God damn it, did everyone in the Navy know his father? But angry as he was, he had to admit, it was a good question. What would Dad do?

He thought back to the day at Quantico when the elder Castelli had told him, "It's the Marines, Joe. They place a high value on 'no man left behind.' It isn't just eyewash; they really mean it, and I admire them for it."

Joe Castelli took several deep breaths and looked out the bridge window towards Yemen. He had never disobeyed a direct order in his life. And he had a career. He was doing exactly what he had always wanted to, and if he went in and got McGregor, he would be throwing it all away.

Son of a bitch.

"Give me your position." He wrote down the answer and handed it to his navigator. "Wait one."

"Navigator, how long to a location from which we can launch LCACs with less than a thirty minute run to the Oman-Yemen border?"

"LCACs sir?"

"You heard me. Well?"

"At flank speed, just over two hours, assuming we leave the auxiliaries behind."

Castelli turned to his operations officer, CDR Charlie Anderson. "Get the XO and Lieutenant Colonel Burke. Meet me in the Flag Officer's sea cabin in two minutes."

Anderson, puzzled, picked up the sound powered telephone and called the XO, currently one level below on what would normally have been Castelli's bridge.

"Here's the thing," Castelli said. "You all know that some kind of big regimental-size amphibious raid just took place in eastern Yemen. Very high security. The whole thing was shut down yesterday quite rapidly, with orders directly from NMCC going out to all ships and stations in the CENTCOM AOR to stay clear of Yemen, its airspace, and its territorial waters. There was also an order from the Commandant via MARCENT to report any contact with something called the 584 Composite Unit. The raid was carried out by Task Force 58, so it makes sense that some of their land forces could be designated 584."

Joe Castelli looked at the other officers, and began to see understanding in their faces. They were starting to see what was coming. Good, he wanted them to go into this with their eyes open.

"About five minutes ago," he said, "I received a direct communication from this 584 Composite Unit. They were, in fact, left behind and have succeeded in reaching the beach about eighty kilometers north of here. There are twenty-six sailors and Marines, of which twenty-three are wounded. They want us to pull them out. Given our orders, I want to have them move to the border with Oman where we could get them by LCAC. I need your input. Colonel, it would be your people who would actually have to land and cover their extraction. Let's start with you."

Lieutenant Colonel Isiah Burke was a third generation Marine, an academy grad, and was regarded by many as a good bet to become the first African-American Commandant. "Captain, pulling them out just across the border might not violate orders, technically. But it's still dicey. And to get to the launch point for the LCACs we would probably have to at least a cut a corner of the Yemeni waters. Nevertheless we all know what's right. Sir, I will personally lead this mission and can guarantee that every man and woman in the battalion will volunteer as well. The 1/7 does not leave people behind."

"I had a feeling you would see it that way." It was why he'd led with Burke. "Ops?"

CDR Charlie Anderson, a man of nondescript appearance, but with a sharp incisive mind, was clearly agitated and he spoke rapidly. "Frankly Captain, we have the clearest possible orders directly from NMCC, and have no choice but to obey them in detail. We have no idea why they issued that order or what's at stake here."

Colonel Burke murmured, "Politics."

Anderson slapped the table.

"No, Colonel. You are not going to get this vessel to skate around a direct order then write it off as politics. There may be risks we don't know about, or we might be putting some other operation at risk. Just because we don't know the reasons behind our orders doesn't mean they aren't valid, or that we can just ignore them. Captain, the simple fact is that we can't save everyone."

Burke glared at Anderson, unblinking. "The real risks, Commander, are being assumed by those wounded sailors and Marines you propose to leave on the beach. Your risk will be purely to your career."

"Enough." Castelli raised a hand. "XO, you want to get into this dog fight?"

"Captain," Nick Kelso replied, "I'm here to support you and to carry out your decisions. I think something this big falls squarely on you. Clearly, though, NMCC knows our people are there and the intent of their order seems to be that they want them left there."

"We don't know that." Isiah Burke was now calm, but intense. "Something is obviously going on in Yemen, sure, but we can't assume the intent is to abandon our people. I simply will not accept that."

"Colonel," Kelso said, "NMCC had the means to get them, and they chose not to. That's what we know. What we don't know is why."

"Thanks, Nick." The XO was a recently promoted Captain, and Castelli relied on him heavily. He was not, however, a guy to stick his neck out. "Okay, give me a minute." His senior officers stepped out of the small cabin, leaving the skipper sitting alone.

Castelli leaned back and thought about his father. He allowed his mind to wander for a moment. Two nights before he had watched a movie on his tablet computer, *Casablanca*, one of his favorites. One line seemed particularly relevant, "Of all the gin joints, in all the towns, in all the world, she walks into mine." Now he knew just how Rick had felt.

God damn that McGregor.

CHAPTER 61

SEPTEMBER 14, 2017 0505Z (0805 AST)
On the beach

ACCOMPANIED BY SERGEANT LEACH, Mike McGregor sat by the radio. Leach, one of only three people in McGregor's small command who had not been wounded, asked if she could get out and help with the casualties.

"Now that we're in contact on the SINCGARS, I should be okay. I'll call if I need you. Report to Sergeant Major Campbell—he and Singh are setting up a perimeter, and you're one of the few left who is still fully functional."

She headed towards Campbell, who was digging in one of the surviving M-240 machine guns. McGregor looked at the two ambulances where Russell and Ellis, along with the surviving corpsmen, were doing their best to care for the seriously wounded. McGregor wanted to be with them, but the radio was their lifeline, and he needed to be where he was.

Several times people looked his way. Every face, except perhaps for Singh and Campbell's, showed individuals at the end of their endurance.

Singh strolled over and sat next to McGregor in the shade of the Humvee. "We have a reasonable perimeter set up. Or as good as it can be with so many wounded. They are good lads though. They'll hold up."

"Lasses too, Captain."

He smiled and nodded. "Oh, I'm not about to forget that."

"We have the vehicles arranged so we can bug out to the east if the need arises. They all have enough fuel to reach Oman." He paused, "If it comes to that."

The thought of loading their wounded and making another run for it through the heat and dust of another desert day was almost too much to bear. They were nearly out of pain medication, as well as IV fluids. If they had to make a run for Oman, they would lose people on the way. "I'm hoping it won't come to that. Do you really think we can just pack them up and head for the border?"

"Yes sir, I do. One thing you must learn if you're to lead people in battle is to expect extraordinary things from them."

CHAPTER 62

"CHENG, HOW'S THE plant?"

His chief engineer, a salty former Warrant Officer replied, "We just finished swapping out that feed pump. Second boiler should be coming online in about ten minutes."

"Good work. We may need flank speed very soon. Make it happen."

"Sir? Flank speed? May I ask . . . "

Castelli was already gone. He walked down several levels to the intelligence spaces. He decided that circumstances required him to be open and direct with his intel staff.

"May I have your attention please."

The quiet chatter around the darkened space dropped off.

"There are wounded American sailors and Marines on the beach about eighty kilometers from here." He pointed towards a large map display and handed the position McGregor had given to his senior intel officer. "As you know, we have direct orders forbidding us to go get them. In five minutes I need to know what Yemeni forces are in a position to threaten them as well as what opposition they might face if they move east towards Oman. My hope is that they can reach Oman where we can pick them up by LCAC."

The petty officers operating the large computer terminals began to pull up satellite images and hi-res maps. Several of his intelligence officers asked rapid fire questions. While he waited, Castelli considered putting through a call to MARCENT, who had ordered them to report contact with the 584. He decided against it. Neither MARCENT nor the Commandant was about to condone his bending orders, even a little. This was on him.

In less than five minutes his intel chief—in Castelli's opinion the best in the business—said, "Sir, this is on the fly, but we do have a ton of satellite data, including a real-time feed. Someone other than us is obviously very interested in that stretch of desert. Heading east towards Oman there's nothing for about eighty clicks, but then there's trouble. Looks like two companies of infantry at the small city of Al Ghaydah, one at the airport and the second at the east edge of town. Each has a BTR-60. It would be a long, hard trip to get around them, and that's assuming those Yemenis just stay where they are. Can our people deal with that kind of force?"

"Doubt it. There's only twenty-six of them and twenty-three are wounded."

"Jesus. That would fit with what we saw to the north. There were something like seventy-five dead, presumably Yemenis, scattered on the south side of this ridgeline—"

He pointed at the computer map display —"and a damaged BTR on the north side. Our people have already been through a hell of a battle."

Castelli only nodded. After a moment, he asked, "Threats to the west?"

"About fifty kilometers by road there's a small unit, more than a platoon but less than a company, at Sayhut. Looks like they're moving from prepared positions and getting ready for a road march. They have two vehicles scouting the road to their east, so presumably they're heading that way. It will be hours before they're a threat, though. The only immediate threat is a group of three vehicles, two old P4's and a truck mounting a ZU-23. That thing could be devastating against unarmored vehicles."

"How far?"

The officer brought up the live satellite feed. "Quick estimate, maybe forty minutes unless something slows them down."

"So our people can't go east, can't go west, and that doesn't really matter because in less than an hour they will be shredded by that ZU-23. Is that about right?"

"Sorry sir, but yes, that's right."

"Good work."

Without another word, Castelli left the intel space and headed back to the flag bridge. When he arrived he told the young radioman to get him back in touch with the 584.

CHAPTER 63

MIKE MCGREGOR SURVEYED the remnants of his command. Almost everyone was wounded or tending the wounded. In most cases wounded were caring for each other. Kelli Moore was now conscious and lying in the back of an ambulance with a chest tube connected to a Rube Goldberg contraption Russell had patched together out of tubes and bottles to help keep her lung expanded. Moore, and everyone else, was looking at him.

"Spoke with someone in a position to help us. Waiting to see if he will." McGregor knew very well this was a longshot. Castelli was under the same orders as Admiral Tucker. Sure Castelli owed him for Syria, but how much? This would be a career breaker. Still, he knew there were men who had done more—and with less at stake.

The SINGHARS squawked and McGregor hopped back into the Humvee and put on the headphones.

"McGregor, you are still an insubordinate son of a bitch."

It was Castelli. "So does that mean you're coming for us?"

"I'm working on that, but there's something you need to deal with right now. I have a real time satellite feed showing a couple of small vehicles plus a truck with a ZU-23 heading your way from the west. My intel people tell me they will be at your position in just over thirty minutes unless you can slow them down. Got any ideas?"

McGregor sighed loudly. That weapon could tear them apart from a mile away, and he had nothing that could hit back at that range. "I'll put my best people on it, Captain. Does this mean that you can get us if we buy a little time?"

"Yeah, maybe. Like I said, I'm working on it. Baatan out."

Mike McGregor stepped out of his vehicle. "Captain Singh! Sergeant Major Campbell!"

The Royal Marines appeared in a matter of seconds and both saluted as crisply as they would have on the parade ground. "Problem, sir?" asked Singh.

McGregor described the problem and the two men nodded. Singh pulled a folded map from his pocket and studied it for about thirty seconds. "On the way, Commander," said Singh, who had a clean new dressing on his wounded hand. He and Campbell pulled a few small boxes from the back of their truck, jumped into one of the surviving Humvees and sped off to the west.

McGregor walked over to Kelli Moore. "Breathing better?"

"Much. But I can...hardly believe how much...this damn knife wound hurts."

"I know what you mean. This thing on my leg is throbbing like the world's worst toothache." He looked down and saw blood was again oozing through the dressing. "I hope they have enough pain meds on the ship. We're down to our last few doses, and those are going to the worst cases like the First Sergeant. He's going to need some serious surgery. And soon."

Moore turned her head to face McGregor more directly. "Doc, how'd you... pull this off?"

"Well," he said, "nothing all that dramatic. Earlier this year I saw an article in the *Navy Times* about the new LANTFLEET commanding officers. Someone I knew from way back was listed as CO of *Bataan*. Then, a few months ago, he showed up again in message traffic as being selected for Rear Admiral."

"I'm guessing this guy was involved... with your Navy Cross?"

"What do you know about that?"

"Don't look so surprised... your Lieutenant Ellis told me."

"Let's just say we were in a similar situation quite a few years ago. When I looked at the satellite photos yesterday, I saw a small group of ships south of Oman heading west. One was obviously an LHD, and the angle was such I could make out a 'five' on the island. *Bataan* is LHD 5, so I thought he might be inclined to help. Assuming we could get this far."

"How did you make contact?... Our satellite uplink... is shut down."

"We can thank the late Major Griggs for providing an alternative. He really has that Humvee of his tricked out with everything, including ground to air communication."

"We call it the Batmobile."

341

"I thought a ship that operates aircraft and has SAR capability would monitor all the emergency frequencies. I made contact on the NATO aircraft emergency frequency, but just barely. Then we were able to get a better HF connection on the SINCGARS. That's about it."

"And he just agreed...to violate a direct order...from the White House?"

"Not yet. He's talking about pulling us out through Oman."

Don't know...if we can manage that. But then...I never really thought...we'd make it this far."

"Yeah, I figured that. But you were right about one thing."

"What's that?"

"You are a lot tougher than I thought."

CHAPTER 64

IT HAD BEEN about fifteen minutes since McGregor dispatched the Royal Marines to deal with the ZU-23 and he was curious. He climbed on top of one of the ambulances—not a simple task with his leg wound—and took a look through his binoculars. He saw a rapidly-moving spot on the road which he hoped was the Humvee.

In a few minutes, Singh and Campbell reported in. "Progress Commander. We used the last two kilos of C-4 on a small bridge across a wadi about five kilometers west of here. They can go north around it, but if they want that bloody ZU-23 with them, it will take at least an hour, probably longer. Does your friend have any air support or naval gunfire?"

"I'll ask."

In a few minutes he was back on the HF link to Castelli. He explained their situation.

Castelli was silent for a full minute then told McGregor, "Wait one."

CHAPTER 65

CAPTAIN JOE CASTELLI reflected for a moment on the fact that he had never been forced to make a genuinely difficult decision. He'd climbed through the ranks by being cautious, competent, and diligent while aggressively following orders. Until today. The safe option, Oman, was off the table. He would either violate a direct order, or obey it and proceed with his mission.

Son of a bitch.

He walked over to CDR Charlie Anderson and, while looking north through the big bridge window, said, "You're right Charlie, we can't save everyone. But we can save them."

Castelli looked around the flag bridge to be sure everyone he needed was present. "Ladies and Gentlemen, there are wounded American sailors and Marines on the beach about eighty kilometers north of here. I intend to violate a direct order from NMCC and go get them, there's no time for any other option. Anyone who feels they cannot participate in this action may leave the bridge right now, and the ship's log will reflect your non-participation."

CDR Charlie Anderson and one Lieutenant (junior grade), walked briskly from the bridge. Everyone else remained at their stations.

"Thank you," Castelli said. "Officer of the Deck, you are now the operations officer. Have two LCACs ready to go in half an hour. We'll need at least a platoon of Marines to provide security on the beach."

At this, Isiah Burke smiled and nodded, then rushed off the bridge.

"Air Boss, get our Predator armed, fueled, and launched. Head for these coordinates." He handed him McGregor's location. "Time is critical. XO, task *Nitze* to remain with our auxiliaries, who should reduce speed to ten knots. *Spruance* will stay with us." He picked up a handset and called the bridge one level down. "New course three five five. Flank speed as soon as we have steam. Officer of the Deck, I don't know exactly what we're getting into, so sound general quarters, and signal Spruance to do the same. If we're going to do this, we're going to do it right."

He picked up the radio handset and made contact on the SINCGARS. "McGregor, expect an LCAC pickup in about an hour and a half, maybe sooner. Have your people in vehicles and ready to go. I'll see what I can do about that ZU-23."

"Thanks, Captain," McGregor said.

"Don't thank me yet."

The Predator, being much easier to fuel and arm than a traditional aircraft, was in the air in less than fifteen minutes.

Flying at top speed, it reached McGregor's position in just under half an hour.

In the air operations center of Bataan, Lt Jeremy Franko, the senior UAV operator, was in direct communication with his skipper. "Captain, I just overflew the position you gave me and can confirm there are five vehicles—two Humvees, two ambulances, and a truck. I could see some wounded on stretchers. Now heading west."

A minute later, Franko signaled again. "Captain, I now see three vehicles heading east. Two small vehicles I can't identify and a truck carrying a multibarrel antiaircraft gun, probably a ZU-23. They're less than three kilometers from our people."

"Is that thing a threat to the drone?"

"Doubtful skipper. I'm high enough and between them and the sun, so they can't see me."

"Good. Take it out."

"Ah, Captain, the Air Force still technically controls all weapons launches from our UAVs. We normally have to check with Nellis before going weapons free."

"Franko, we're already violating a direct order from NMCC, and you're worried about protocol? Pull the damned trigger. Now."

"Aye Captain. Wait one . . . Weapon away."

Sixty kilometers to the north, a Hellfire missile dropped from beneath one of the Predator's wings and accelerated. In a matter of seconds, the ZU-23, as well as the truck, was reduced to smoldering scrap metal. The two P4s, fifty meters in front and behind the truck, made wide 180-degree turns, and headed west at maximum speed.

"Target destroyed. Looks like the other two vehicles are bugging out. Orders, Captain?"

"Good work Franko, head back east and cover the landing of our LCACs. Once they're underway, bring it home."

McGregor and the Royal Marines heard the explosion and saw the distant column of smoke. Sergeant Leach, now back on the radio, walked over and reported what had happened.

Relaxed for the first time in more than twenty-four hours, McGregor looked in on each of his people. He gave instructions to begin loading the seriously wounded into the ambulances and to stage their vehicles on the beach. Feeling he had done all he could do, McGregor began scanning the ocean. Soon he spotted two enormous LCACs approaching on the horizon. In a few minutes, the roar of their big turbine-driven fans was audible even from several kilometers out.

McGregor turned and was surprised to see Sgt. Leach looking into the mirror of a Humvee, combing her mop of short blond hair. Jim Russell was shaving, and one of the corpsmen was using a gauze pad to wash dried blood from Kelli Moore's face. Inspired by his people, Mike McGregor looked at himself and decided the least he could do was make some effort to look more presentable. He removed his blood stained desert camouflage shirt and donned a clean one from his old ALICE pack, which was still stowed in the ambulance. As he transferred his rank insignia, the LCACs approached the beach, slowed, and pushed far enough up onto the sand to unload two LAV 25s, which then headed out from their position to provide security, one east and one west. Two Humvees landed, and a Lieutenant Colonel walked over to McGregor. He surveyed the battered remnants of the 584 and shook his head.

McGregor saluted. "Mike McGregor, commanding the 584. Or what's left of it."

The lieutenant colonel returned the salute, then shook McGregor's hand. "Lieutenant Colonel Isiah Burke. It's a pleasure to meet you. My people will help get your wounded loaded and ready to go." He scanned the carefully prepared defensive positions along the 584's tiny perimeter. "We'll take care of securing those automatic weapons as well. Would you mind telling me what the hell happened here?"

McGregor gave him a sanitized version of Operation Ocean Reach, and how they came to be where they were, and in the condition they were in. "Colonel, I don't really know what happened that led the White House to leave us behind, but I know you're taking a big chance by coming here to get us. All I can say is that everyone here —" He swept his hand towards his small command —"is very grateful you did."

"Doc, years ago I had a CO who gave me the best advice I ever received. He told me that so-called hard decisions are rarely hard, that the right answer is usually obvious. The hard part is being willing to accept the consequences. Once you get past that, life as a Marine gets a lot easier."

"Who was that officer?" asked McGregor, who had a feeling he might know the answer.

"Major Henry Ahrens. Unfortunately, I lost touch with him."

"Recently retired," said McGregor.

"You knew him then?"

"We crossed paths in Iraq. I'm happy to say he took his own advice."

Wary of the fast approaching Yemeni column, which the Predator detected only about thirty minutes away, Burke's Marines quickly loaded the 584 then embarked their own LAV's. Ten minutes later, both LCACs were roaring across the smooth green waters and were recovered by *Bataan* a half hour after that.

As the LCACs were unloaded, Castelli watched from the upper level of the well deck. As his medical department triaged one bloody casualty after another, he knew he'd made the right decision. When McGregor, his leg still oozing blood, began to supervise loading the KIA—all stacked in the back of the truck—into body bags, Castelli could no longer bear to watch.

After speaking with his XO about coordinating evacuation of the most serious cases, Joe Castelli went to his cabin to write his report. And probably end his career.

CHAPTER 66

KAREN HILLER AND Sonny Baker sat silently with a few senior staff. Everyone was glad the President was out of the White House on his way to a prayer breakfast. He had been informed of the rescue in Yemen, but for the moment, he was leaving the fallout to his staff.

Baker read and re-read the brief message:

FROM: USS BATAAN (LHD 5)
TO: CENTCOM
VIA: NAVCENT
INFO: MARCENT
SUBJ: EVACUATION OF 584 COMPOSITE UNIT
ENCL: (1) List of Personnel Recovered

    1. At 0945 local time (0645Z) USS Bataan recovered by LCAC the 584 Composite Unit, LCDR Michael McGregor commanding, Location approximately twenty-five kilometers east of Qishn, Yemen.

2. Thirty-five personnel recovered include twenty-three wounded and nine KIA. One member is currently reported MIA. Encl. (1) lists personnel by name, rank, and SSN.

3. Bataan's medical department and embarked fleet surgical team assisted by Battalion Surgeons from the embarked Marine detachment are treating casualties as expeditiously as possible. Medical evacuation of at least twelve of the wounded will be required. Request CENTCOM medical regulating team arrange for same.

4. Bataan is holding current position pending orders.

J CASTELLI

HILLER CRUMPLED THE paper and hurled it at the screens. "Is there no one left who can follow a God damned order? And how the hell did they even contact the *Bataan*—I thought we cut off their satellite link?"

"We did," Baker said. "I understand they used the NATO air emergency frequency. I guess they were smarter than we gave them credit for."

"Smart? He was ordered to surrender. Wait until the President has him court martialed, then we'll see how smart he is."

"So we leave a bunch of our wounded behind, and they decide not to surrender to a psychopath and manage to get out despite us? Then we court martial their CO? Yeah, that's going to play well in Congress."

Sonny Baker knew that Karen Hiller was a mirthless political animal who probably would want to court martial this Lieutenant Commander. But he also knew Brendan Wallace would never even consider it. Yes, he would order people to be placed at risk if the national interest was at stake, but he would not punish them for finding a way to survive.

Or if he did, Sonny's resignation would be on his desk ten minutes later.

But now wasn't the time to fight this out. "Karen, have you thought that maybe we can get some information from this 584 unit that will help us find the missing warhead? They were the last of our people in Yemen. Let's have the intel officers on Bataan debrief them and find out if they saw anything unusual."

"I thought we agreed to keep a lid on that missing warhead. And besides, what the hell could they know?"

"It's not like they're in a position to tell anyone. Besides, by time they get back, this will have probably gone public. Everybody on Ashland must know by now, and so does the command staff on *Essex.* A leak is inevitable. Unless we find the missing nuke, and soon, that's going to get out too. Who knows, maybe one of these people saw a truck or a helicopter. Nothing to lose."

Karen Hiller looked intently at Baker, her chin resting on her hand. "Oh, go ahead then, Sonny. See if you can salvage something from this mess."

There were a few raised eyebrows at Hiller giving in, but no one doubted that if anything went wrong she would exact a heavy political price.

Hiller suddenly stood to leave. Her staff, caught off guard, all shot out of their chairs. "And Sonny, I do not want that bastard Forrest writing up a bunch of Medal of Honor citations. He has been working the back channels, trying to undermine us, and we do not need any more publicity than absolutely necessary." She turned towards the door, but added on her way out, "I told the President not to nominate him. He has no political sense at all."

As Karen Hiller burst out of the Situation Room, less than two miles away Daniel Forrest was smiling broadly as he made a flurry of encrypted telephone calls. The list was long, but the first was to Colonel Aaron Mark aboard *Essex*.

CHAPTER 67

INSTRUCTIONS FROM SONNY Baker's National Security Council worked their way quickly through the chain of command.

In less than an hour, Castelli's staff interviewed everyone from the 584 not currently on the operating table. It was quickly evident, however, that none of the sailors or Marines had seen anything that could be interpreted as the warhead being moved. Disappointed, they decided to get everyone together as a group and see if a different dynamic might bring out something that hinted where the sixth warhead had been concealed—if, indeed, it was ever in Arad.

The intel staff, led by Commander Ray Hansen—who had been briefed by his counterparts on *Essex* and *Iwo Jima*—gathered the survivors in any condition to talk in a small conference room and went through the entire operation—again.

"So nothing visible on the roads heading to or from Arad during your approach?"

McGregor, exhausted and in a lot of pain, had already answered this question several times. "Nothing I could see. Didn't they have Predators up? Wouldn't our intel people have seen more than I could see?"

"Look Commander, work with us here. A nuclear weapon is missing and we need to cover every possibility."

"Guys, I just didn't see anything that wasn't ours going into or out of Arad. I was busy most of the time with casualties."

They next spent time with Singh and Campbell, who were trained in intelligence gathering and gave answers that were detailed and precise. McGregor could tell both had gone through intel debriefs many times in the past.

"The one thing I found unusual," Singh said, "was the number of tiny—and well concealed—cell towers through-out the town. The briefing materials said nothing about a local cell network. No doubt, that's how they coordinated their defense."

"You're right; the intel guys on *Iwo Jima* told us the decision was made not to do much electronic surveillance before the op."

"Wouldn't have mattered," said Singh. "The smart thing would have been to activate it only after we landed. It does suggest much more preparation that we expected. Clearly, Arad was more than just a transit point. It sounds like the kind of place I might have hidden away my back-up nuke."

"That's a good thought, Captain. But it doesn't tell us where to look. I just don't see us going back there to poke around—not with the kind of defensive muscle they showed us yesterday."

"Any other thoughts," asked Hansen?

Both Royal Marines shook their heads and answered in unison, "No, sir."

Hansen took off his glasses and rubbed his eyes. "Okay, let's run with this approach. Did anyone else see something that seemed wrong or out of place. Didn't have to be related to the nuke, just different than you expected."

This got more results.

McGregor described the unusual efforts to create casualties, but not necessarily deaths. "We saw way more leg wounds than we expected. Even after we had the warheads, they kept up with the IEDs and attacks from those hidden basements. It was like they just wanted us out of there and to make staying as expensive as possible. Maybe the last nuke was hidden somewhere north of the warehouse and they didn't want us snooping around up there."

"That's a good point and the intel staff thought about that—especially with that one hour ultimatum—but the tech guys tell us that a nuke outside that warehouse compound should have at least given a blip on one of the neutron detector passes."

"Unless it was very well shielded," added Singh.

"In that case, we still have no idea where to look."

Hansen went on, and despite a handful of good ideas and observations, nothing worth pursuing came up. He turned to Sgt. Leach. "Sergeant," he said, "you spent time in most of the areas our people occupied. Anything seem unusual?"

"There was one odd thing. Well, maybe not odd, but ... "

"Don't hold back," Hansen said.

"Well, there was a bunch of junk the engineers had cleared away and piled along the walls of that warehouse—pulleys, pipes, cargo nets, things like that. I think everyone assumed the Yemenis had used them to move those big steel boxes. But one of the engineers told me that gear couldn't even budge those things, that they weighed over ten thousand pounds."

So are you thinking they—the warhead? You think they used it to move the missing warhead! Could they? How much do those things weigh?"

One of the junior intel officers picked up a handset and spoke for a minute. Everyone sat in silence while they waited. After two painful minutes he said, "Task Force 58 says they weigh in at about three hundred kilograms. Did they have gear capable of lifting that much?"

"I think so," Sergeant Major Campbell said. "You could use those pipes to rig a tripod capable of lifting that much, and their pulleys and cargo nets would handle it too. But where would they have moved it?"

"Well, there were at least three shovels in that pile of junk," Sergeant Leach said.

"Really?" Hansen said.

CHAPTER 68

HARVEY LYON HAD just briefed the President on the discovery of radioactive particles in both New York and the District. "Looks like Nazer is pulling the same trick as he pulled in Europe. Divert scarce resources and try to create a public panic."

"Exactly," said Brendan Wallace. "But what does that tell us? Is he using this to conceal the real nuke or just distract us and keep us from looking elsewhere?"

"Too soon to tell, Mr. President," Sonny Baker said.

"Dammit, we're behind the curve. Nazer keeps us jumping to his tune while we accomplish nothing. And what about that call you got last night from that bastard? " The President pointed at Sonny Baker. "I give a simple order and the next day some skipper blows up a bunch of Yemeni vehicles and beaches a landing craft. Is that thing under control?"

"The skipper and his XO have been relieved and are being flown back to Norfolk. SURFLANT will deal with them.

Most of the people he pulled out were wounded and are getting care on *Baatan* or have been flown to military hospitals. The two Royal Marines were also flown off." Sonny Baker desperately wanted to move the discussion along and away from what was already being called "The *Baatan* Mutiny."

"There were Brits in that group? Who the hell authorized that?"

"Uh, you did sir. You may recall that Admiral Tucker wanted to exclude the British, but that you overruled him."

"Right, right. Well, hopefully we can count on them to keep this all to themselves. Sonny, see if those two could be posted somewhere remote for a while?"

Baker, who was not concerned about the Royal Marines, replied, "Of course, sir." Hoping to move on he looked to Alex Clarkson.

"Alex, anything from CIA?"

"Not much. There was a conversation one of my ops people had with the intel chief on *Baatan*."

Baker groaned, silently he hoped, at the continued mention of *Baatan*. "And?"

"Well, one of the people they took aboard described seeing shovels and materials like pipe and cargo nets in the warehouse where the warheads were stored. They think they might have dragged one nuke out back and buried it."

"So they just buried it in the back yard. Like a buried treasure. For God's sake Alex, is that the best they could come up with?" Karen Hiller's temper was beginning to flare and the meeting was less than five minutes old.

"It's not solid, I agree. But it's at least plausible."

"Alex, you are absolutely not going to overfly that site and you're sure as hell not going to put anyone on the ground. A little remote surveillance and that's it. We can't afford to waste high level assets on this crap. Are you hearing me?"

"Minimal assets and nothing remotely in or over Arad unless it's in orbit. Got it."

"Have you been working anything more promising?"

"We're working our Saudi contacts, but not much so far. We're trying to screen aircraft that leave Mukalla after they land, though a lot of flights go into places like Sudan and Somalia where our assets are pretty thin. The Navy is still using helicopters to screen ships leaving Mukalla and other ports in eastern Yemen, but assets are way less than potential targets."

"So the short answer is no. Unless someone has something useful to add this meeting is over. We need action, and I mean now. We will meet every twelve hours until we get it."

CHAPTER 69

THE OFFICE ASSIGNED to Project Doorstop was cramped, chilled from the excessive air conditioning required to cool the hardware, and smelled of stale coffee and yesterday's pizza. There, the three junior analysts reviewed every source of satellite imaging capable of showing the warehouse in Arad and specifically the attached, small, walled courtyard—overhead and off axis, real-time video and archived stills, daytime images and night-time infrared.

Bill Goetz, the senior of the three, was considering the wisdom of asking for more help when Kelsey Finch, the aggressive and most junior image analyst on the team, said, "I think we have something here. It's from one of the old KH-11s and came in about two hours ago."

"Show me."

"Here's the courtyard. There's a shadow in the middle consistent with a low mound, approximately one by two meters."

"Like a pile of dirt next to a hole?"

"Yeah. And there are objects next to it that could be a couple of the pipes the Navy reported. What do you think?"

Skeptical, Goetz looked closely at the high definition screen and said, "That's pretty lean evidence, Kelsey. A little mound of sand and a few pieces of pipe. If you're right though, they probably dug the damn thing up. But if they did, where the hell is it now?"

"Well, the bridge to the south is still down so it sure didn't go that way. Only option is north. There isn't much traffic on that road now so we may be able to locate it. We have authority to retask that new bird if we get a good lead. I think this is it!"

"Not so fast," said Goetz, "you know what it costs to retask one of those intel birds? If we're wrong, they probably won't give us another chance."

"Yeah, but if that nuke gets away because you were too cautious we'll probably end up tracking drug mules—or something even worse." Kelsey Finch was positive this was the lead they had been looking for and she was not about to let it slip away.

"Okay, how about this? If I'm wrong I'll fix you up with Lydia Karpenko, we run together three days a week."

Goetz, suddenly interested, replied, "Isn't she the Russian translator with the big..."

"Yeah, she's the one. Well? There's no time to waste here Bill."

"You're on," said Goetz who was already dialing their contact engineer at the NRO, the National Reconnaissance Office, which actually operates the intelligence satellites. After providing exact coordinates to NRO, Goetz sat back in his chair. "In twenty minutes we'll have a pass which should image the entire highway north from Arad to the Saudi border. We can watch in real-time. When is Andy due in?"

"Any time. He's supposed to relieve me, but no way I'm leaving." She took several big gulps of an energy drink and typed furiously on her keyboard.

When real-time video began streaming in twenty minutes later all three analysts were fixated on their monitors. Each looked at slightly different angles and contrast, but the information was essentially the same.

As empty highway rolled past, each became more and more pessimistic, though Bill Goetz' potential disappointment was tempered by the thought of an evening with the buxom translator. But then there it was. A truck led by a smaller vehicle, probably a large SUV, about an hour south of the Saudi border. They were obviously traveling together and the combination was highly suspicious. Goetz grabbed his secure line and dialed a number he had been provided at the National Military Command Center. The NMCC watch officer made several quick calls, the first of which was to Sonny Baker.

CHAPTER 70

SEPTEMBER 17, 2017 1845Z (1445 EDT)
Office of the Commander Naval Surface
Forces Atlantic, Norfolk VA

CAPTAIN JOE CASTELLI finished his interview with the Chief of Staff for COMNAVSURFLANT in less than fifteen minutes. Once they'd landed in Diego Garcia, he and his executive officer had been flown on a circuitous route, which ultimately led them back to their home port of Norfolk. There, his XO received orders to report to the Naval Station at Jacksonville for unspecified duty. Castelli had been sent to see the boss.

The Chief of Staff had been surprisingly friendly. He'd ordered coffee and spent a few minutes reviewing Castelli's written report. Then he got down to business.

"Captain," he said, "I'm pleased to tell you that your request for retirement has been approved, effective day after tomorrow."

"But I didn't ... "

"Of course you did. By the way, would you mind re-signing your request? Just a formality. Paperwork."

Ah. So they'd decided to offer him a quiet retirement in lieu of a nasty investigation that would end with a huge political flap and possibly jail time for him. SURFLANT was giving him the best deal he could, and Castelli would be stupid and ungrateful to decline. He stepped over to the desk and scrawled a signature. That his retirement could be processed in a few days was unusual, but when properly motivated, the Navy Personnel Command was capable of moving at light speed.

The Chief of Staff handed Castelli a stack of papers, which covered everything from retirement pay to health insurance. "We have you scheduled for retirement briefings and a physical tomorrow, then you're done."

"Thank you." At least the Chief of Staff was slightly junior to Castelli, so he was spared the indignity of calling him 'sir.' He turned to leave.

"Castelli," the Chief of Staff said.

He stopped and turned.

"Off the record, I want you to know this was not my recommendation. Admiral Piotrowski was apparently pleased one of his skippers had the balls to do what you did. And some very senior people seem to agree with him. When they saw the video from your medical department of the casualties being triaged, and the bodies unloaded, the brass understood your motivation. And frankly, the fact that those people you pulled out provided some intel on the possible location of that last warhead didn't hurt either."

Intel? Castelli resisted the urge to ask.

Apparently he didn't have to. "Your intel staff was ordered to keep a tight hold on the debrief of those survivors. Apparently that included even you."

"Above our pay grades."

"No doubt. But whatever it was, it may have given the Admiral just enough leverage to get you this retirement. Even so, you must have known how it would end."

"I did. From the moment I heard McGregor's voice on the radio, I knew exactly how it would end. Please thank the Admiral for his consideration. And can you tell me what's happening to my XO? He's a good man and does not deserve to go down with me."

"He's been sent to a staff job at Jacksonville. This won't help his career, but it won't end it, either."

Castelli doubted that. There was an old saying that dominated Navy thinking. *Things went wrong and you were there.* Nonetheless, the Admiral was again doing the best he could. "What about Colonel Burke?"

"Commandant seems to have given him top cover. Isaac Keen down at MARCENT either agreed with him or had his arm twisted. Last I heard, Burke is walking away clean. Might catch up with him if he ever gets to flag rank, but for the moment the Corps is looking after its own."

Castelli nodded and again turned to leave.

"Captain, just a moment. A Marine Corps messenger is waiting for you in my outer office. Came down from DC this morning. Said he has an envelope for you to be delivered personally." He picked up his phone and directed his yeoman to find the Marine.

On the way out Joe Castelli was handed a plain envelope

with, 'Captain Joseph Castelli, USN –eyes only' written on it. Inside there was a single sheet of stationery labeled Headquarters Marine Corps, with a handwritten note.

"Captain, circumstances preclude any formal recognition of your service.

Nonetheless I want to thank you personally for your courage and your sacrifice.

I will not forget it."

It was signed "Daniel Forrest."

He couldn't help but smile. This was unexpected, but perhaps it should not have been. The Marines really took this stuff seriously.

Joe Castelli left the Chief of Staff's office and, as he exited the nondescript building, was for once not surprised to see his father waiting for him. The elder Castelli walked briskly over to his son and gave him an unexpected hug and a handshake.

"Welcome home, Joe," he said.

"They retired me, Dad. Kicked me out."

"I know." Joe Castelli had finally stopped being surprised at his father's connections. "And I couldn't be prouder."

"I'll never have another command."

"That's the paradox, Joe. By going after our people you guaranteed you would never have another command. But if you sailed on and left them behind, you would have proved you were unworthy of another command. The name Joe Castelli would have been forever linked with desertion of dozens of wounded sailors and Marines. You would have been an embarrassment, buried in some back office and forgotten. Better this way."

Slowly, Joe nodded.

"Now, let's stop at your condo, get you out of that uniform, and go get a few drinks. You still like martinis don't you? I have dinner reservations later at Maxwells, and we can talk a bit about the next phase of your life. I have a feeling some very good things are about to happen."

They walked towards Vince Castelli's car and chatted amiably about nothing at all.

CHAPTER 71

PRESIDENT BRENDAN WALLACE sat at the head of the table, leaning forward on his hands, as he moved his gaze from one senior advisor to the next. "I've got some interesting news for you."

The deadpan monotone set everyone in the room on edge.

After a long pause, he went on. "Sonny tells me we may have found the missing nuke. That until a few hours ago it was right where we found the others."

"Mr. President," said Baker—who wanted to point out the warhead was buried too deep to be picked up on radiation detectors.

Wallace ignored him. "Now I hear we have nothing close enough to intercept the damn thing before it reaches the Saudi border. That's assuming it really is the warhead."

Wendy Hiller jumped in. "We have to assume it is, or put another way there's no upside to thinking it isn't. What else would they have buried in their back yard?"

"All right then," resumed Wallace, "do we tell the Saudis? I think it's safe to assume that if they get their hands on it, they will probably keep it."

Sonny Baker nodded in agreement. "And we certainly can't take it away from them."

"Not with us using their bases and burning their oil we can't," the President said. "Sonny, assuming they get hold of the PAL encoder, can they deliver that warhead?"

"We know they have a bunch of old Chinese Dongfeng intermediate range missiles. That system can easily lift this warhead and can hit most targets in the Middle East, and all targets in Iran. They could also convert it to a simple gravity bomb. Their F-15s could deliver it, particularly now that we have degraded Iranian air defense to almost nothing. As for Israel, they would have a much tougher time penetrating their air defense. I doubt they would target Israel, though. Their second strike capability would annihilate the Saudis."

"So the short answer is yes," said Wallace. "That leaves us with one question. Do we tell the Saudis or not?"

Alex Clarkson, who had gotten a heads up from his analysts and had just arrived by helicopter, spoke first. "Given the volume of truck traffic as you get further north of the border, I cannot give assurances that we won't lose track of it."

"You followed that car with the PAL plans all the way down to Arad," Karen Hiller said.

"Yes," Clarkson replied, "but we had time to prepare a lot of surveillance assets. Also, we're dealing here with a very generic truck that could easily get lost in traffic once it crosses the border."

"I agree, Mr. President." Sonny Baker leaned forward and looked directly at Wallace. "It's just too risky. If we lose track of that warhead we may never see it again until it goes off somewhere. Besides, I don't think the Saudis would use the damn thing."

Wallace did not consult with anyone else. This was on him. "Okay, Sonny, call the Saudi Defense Minister. Let's hope we can wrap this thing up today. Feel free to interrupt my breakfast meeting with ... "

"The Small Business Administration," injected Hiller. As she followed the President out of the Situation Room, Sonny Baker waited for one of his aides to place the call.

CHAPTER 72

"**I** RECEIVED AN INTERESTING call from the Saudi Defense Minister. Seems they have a new nuke—at least that wasn't a surprise. Are you ready for the surprise?"

"His ministry invited Muhammad Nazer in for a chat. Apparently one of the Yemenis transporting the warhead implicated him. He quickly gave up the whole scheme. Seems the plan was to use the nukes on the Iranians and eliminate the Shia threat. They hoped we would be blamed and then forced to evacuate the Middle East, leaving the Saudis as the dominant power. Apparently the King was not entirely pleased—but not all that displeased either. They've cut a deal with Abdullah Nazer for a PAL and in return will beef up their military aid and press ahead with their pipeline. The Saudis seem pretty happy with the outcome. Too bad I'm not."

"With this much Saudi backing there's not much we can do about Nazer—at least not right now," Sonny Baker said.

"Agreed," replied Wallace. "But get him a back channel message that we are keeping a very close eye on him, and that U.S. policy could change very suddenly if he steps out of line."

"So what do we tell Congress and the press about the operation?" asked the Chief of Staff.

"Announcing that six nuclear warheads were on the lam will create a lot of public excitement, not to mention questions about their original source, even if the administration gets the credit for going after them," Baker said.

"Could be an opportunity to make Putin look bad," replied General Ted Lennox.

"It would create a shit storm, no doubt about that," said Brendan Wallace. "On the whole, though, we may be better off letting Vladimir owe us one. We can get word back to the Kremlin that we have their warheads—send them photos, serial numbers—but will keep the lid on it."

Sonny Baker saw a plan coming together. "Just say we seized a cache of WMD accumulated by an insurgent group based in Arad. We can be vague about the nature of the weapons—ongoing operation or something like that—and blame it on al Qaeda in the Arabian Peninsula or those ISIL fanatics; whoever fits best. There may be some leaks, too, many people know, but we can just stick with the WMD scenario. Besides, who is going to believe another terrorist nuke story?"

There were general nods of agreement.

"I'll take care of dealing with Nazer," Sonny said. "Karen, can you work up something with the communications office?"

"Of course." Her tone was agreeable enough, but the look she gave Baker was sharp and penetrating. "What about the Commandant? He's still pissed off about our leaving those Marines behind. He could be a wild card in maintaining our cover."

"Karen, I don't think you're the right one to be dealing with Dan Forrest, and Ted —" The President looked at the Chairman of the Joint Chiefs—"I don't mean to override your authority, but this is better handled from the White House end."

Lennox nodded. The Chairman would apparently just as soon avoid revisiting the abandonment of wounded Marines and Navy personnel in order to maintain political cover, even if it seemed essential at the time.

"Sonny, you get along with him pretty well. See if you can get him on board?"

"I will, Mr. President."

The meeting went on to smaller and smaller matters. Finally, the President stood and said, "I'll leave the rest of you to finish up." He abruptly left the room, Karen Hiller close behind.

CHAPTER 73

SEPTEMBER 25, 2017 1515Z (0815 PDT)
Marine Corps Air Ground Combat
Center, Twentynine Palms

LIEUTENANTS JIM RUSSELL and Nicole Ellis were
having breakfast with McGregor in the officer's area of
the mess hall—now known as the dining facility or DFAC,
in the world of military acronyms. The sticky grits, over-
cooked eggs, and stale coffee were heaven.

McGregor was no longer in command.

After transferring a dozen of the most seriously
wounded along with the KIA to Oman for an Air Force
flight to the huge military hospital at Landstuhl, *Bataan*
had been diverted with one destroyer to the base at Diego
Garcia. There, orders came through disestablishing the 584
Composite Unit and returning its personnel to their original commands—for most, the 28th Marine Regiment or
the MP Company. They were directed to proceed back to
Twentynine Palms, where the regiment had left an administrative group to demobilize the command as it arrived.

Ironically, they were the first ones back, most of the 28th being still aboard *Essex*, *Iwo Jima*, and *Ashland*.

At Diego Garcia, Captain Joe Castelli and his XO were relieved, and a Captain flown down from Bahrain to take command. As he departed *Bataan* by boat, the entire crew, in dress whites, manned the rails and rendered a sharp hand salute. One in which McGregor and the members of the 584 who could still stand were happy to join.

The administrative personnel, not privy to most of the details of Ocean Reach, had received orders to retain all personnel at Twentynine Palms for security reasons. The night before, First Sergeant Johanssen had arrived after a sixteen-hour flight from Germany, a long metal rod now in his left arm. Even he could not get answers or cooperation.

Nicole Ellis said, "It was great seeing the First Sergeant, but I'm getting really sick of this place. I need to get out of here and back home. Any idea when that's going to happen?"

McGregor was about to answer with a wisecrack when a deep voice behind him said, "What's your hurry Lieutenant? Tired of the desert so soon?"

They all stood to greet Colonel Aaron Mark.

"Seriously, there's a big security blackout on this operation, which I'm sure you can understand better than most. We may be here another week or two. And, by the way, McGregor, well done back there. I'm proud of you all."

"Appreciated, sir. But we lost a lot of good people along the way. And some of our wounded will probably never return to duty."

"The price of battle, Doc. And you're right; I just heard

First Sergeant Johanssen will probably be submitting his retirement papers. They don't think that arm will recover one-hundred percent."

Damn. He and Johanssen had a long and close relationship. "What about Captain Moore? Have you heard anything about her? They don't tell me shit...Sir."

"I did hear that she's doing fine. Sounds like you did a great job, Jim. They watched her for a few days in Germany then flew her back to Balboa. Should be discharged any day."

McGregor smiled.

"What about those Royal Marines of yours?" Mark asked. "I've heard nothing about them."

"They were flown up to Oman along with the wounded," McGregor said. "I never heard anything else. To be honest, we probably wouldn't have made it without those guys."

"I met them when they came aboard Essex," Mark said. "They seemed like serious characters. I forwarded your award recommendations on to the Commandant General of the Royal Marines, but I doubt there'll be much action on them from our end, sorry to say. And probably not for our own people either."

"Why is that, Colonel?"

"You were an independent unit at the time of the action with no chain of command to endorse your recommendations—at least nobody below NAVCENT, and he isn't touching this hot potato. He was the one who disestablished the 584 and returned everyone to their original commands. Then he made sure everyone involved got out of the CENTCOM AOR as soon as possible."

"Well, that sucks ... Uh, Colonel"

"There may not be much you can do. White House orders have been ignored, with good reason, but still ... "

"Not your problem, sir. Or theirs."

"Commander, my advice is to let this one lie. You brought your people back against incredible odds, and believe me, plenty of people know that. You'll be home soon. Really, let it go."

CHAPTER 74

September 27, 2017
Muscat, Oman (Reuters)

"A DETACHMENT OF BRITISH Royal Marines based in Oman encountered a U.S. Marine along the border with Yemen. Corporal Ryan Smith of Green Bay, Wisconsin had apparently become separated from his unit during the recent American operation which seized a cache of unspecified WMDs from a cell of the jihadist group al-Qaeda in the Arabian Peninsula operating out of the small town of Arad."

"According to Sergeant Major William Campbell, who was leading the patrol, Smith was fatigued and dehydrated from his overland journey, but otherwise in excellent condition. Smith was flown to the American air base in Qatar for a medical examination and transportation home."

CHAPTER 75

SERGEI AND ANATOLY Grishkov were knee deep in the cool waters of the River Earn, casting large flies upstream in search of the elusive Atlantic salmon. Just downstream with his own pole was Sir Roger Pearson, not long retired from MI-6 and now running the fishing lodge that was used as both a safe house and a facility for debriefing agents returned from the field. Piotr Kulakov, another experienced fisherman, was just upstream.

Both Grishkovs were rapidly adapting to their status as former naval officers, former Russian citizens, and fugitives from the SVR and the FSB. Both understood there would be no return to Russia or to any place with Russian influence. Putin wanted all of them dead, of that there was no doubt.

Each man had been entirely straightforward with the intelligence and technical specialists sent in to debrief them. The senior Grishkov, known to MI-6 as Stella, had naturally been the richer source of information, including the technical data which had allowed for a detailed examination of the captured warheads. Initially, the debriefers regarded Anatoly Grishkov as simply a bit of baggage brought along by Stella. They were thus surprised at the breadth of his technical expertise as well as his insight into a broad range of Russian naval topics.

Kulakov, it turned out had been deeply involved in the Stella operation. He had traveled all over Russia, gathering information for his boss, Admiral Grishkov, which he was now divulging to the British.

Once the debriefing was complete, each man, by then hopefully fluent in English, would be provided with an impenetrable cover and sent to live somewhere safe. They would be paid a reasonable pension, better than that provided by the Russian Navy, and set up in a comfortable household. They would, of course, be subject to appropriate surveillance and would make themselves available to the Security Services as needed.

The elder Grishkov looked downstream towards his nephew, who was looking very much the sportsman in a tweed cap and jacket and was handling the long fly rod as if he had been using one all his life. "Have you given any thought to what you would like to do once we are finished here?"

"I believe I would like to become an English gentleman."

They both laughed.

CHAPTER 76

IT WAS A cool, sunny October morning. A light wind blew bright red and yellow maple leaves across the paved area behind the reserve center used for outdoor formations. The reservists from the 1/28 and the MP Company were standing at attention, as were members of the command staff of the 28th Marine Regiment—including a stone-face Commander Kenneth Barnes. Most important, all surviving members of the 584 Composite Unit, including the Royal Marines, were assembled at the front of the formation. Several were leaning on crutches, two were in wheelchairs.

Commandant Daniel Forrest, accompanied by the Sergeant Major of the Marine Corps, exited the rear of the building and marched to the front of the formation, where the Commandant returned the crisp salute of Colonel Aaron Mark.

"All sailors and Marines are assembled as ordered, sir," said Mark. He then executed a left face and strode to take up a position at the left of the formation.

Two Marines from the Commandant's staff appeared, one carrying a stack of red folders and the other carrying oblong red boxes. The Sergeant Major bellowed, "Attention to orders."

Daniel Forrest stepped forward and handed the first folder to the Sergeant Major, who read the Purple Heart citation for the first member of the 584 Composite Unit wounded in action during Operation Reach. The Commandant had, after several long discussions with Sonny Baker and then with his headquarters staff, agreed to fast track awards for the 584. Karen Hiller hadn't liked it, but Sonny Baker made it clear everyone needed a quick resolution. In truth, President Wallace secretly supported Forrest's effort. He just couldn't take any active role in a situation involving a violation of his personal orders.

Forrest finished awarding the Purple Hearts and proceeded to award Captain Randeep Singh, with the concurrence of the Commandant General, the Silver Star and the Purple Heart. Sergeant Major Campbell received the Silver Star as well.

Kelli Moore watched with pleasure as her corpsman, HM3 Kim Stoller, received the Navy Cross, the second highest award for bravery in combat. It had been Moore's recommendation backed by the testimony of the other MPs that Stoller had repeatedly exposed herself to enemy fire to treat the wounded, resupply ammunition, and—despite minimal combat training—personally kill at least five of the Yemenis. Moore was also pleased that LCDR Mike McGregor was awarded the Navy Cross, his second. Having finally wormed the story of his first award out of First Sergeant Johanssen, she had a deeper understanding of what McGregor was really made of.

Finally, the Commandant ordered, "Captain Kelli Moore front and center."

She stepped to the front of the assembled sailors and Marines and saluted the Commandant. He smiled warmly as he pinned her Purple Heart to the left breast pocket of her utility uniform. She was about to salute and return to the formation when Daniel Forrest was handed a second box.

The Sergeant Major of the Marine Corps opened a folder and read:

"The President, on Behalf of Congress, is pleased to present the Medal of Honor to Captain Kelli Bridget Moore, United States Marine Corps Reserve, for services set forth in the following:"

CITATION:

FOR CONSPICUOUS GALLANTRY AND INTREPIDITY AT THE RISK OF HER LIFE AND BEYOND THE CALL OF DUTY WHILE SERVING WITH THE 584 COMPOSITE UNIT, OPERATION OCEAN REACH. ON THE NIGHT OF SEPTEMBER 13-14, 2017 CAPTAIN MOORE WAS TASKED WITH DEFENDING A GEOGRAPHICAL LOCATION KNOWN AS SIMPSON'S NOTCH. DURING AN ATTACK BY A GREATLY SUPERIOR ENEMY FORCE CAPTAIN MOORE REPEATEDLY RALLIED HER MARINES TO DEFEND AGAINST AND TO COUNTERATTACK THE ENEMY. IN DOING SO SHE CONTINUALLY EXPOSED HERSELF TO ENEMY FIRE AND PERSONALLY ENGAGED THE ENEMY, KILLING AT LEAST SIX WITH SMALL ARMS FIRE. SHE SKILLFULLY MOVED HER MARINES TO ALTERNATE POSITIONS MAKING MAXIMUM USE OF TERRAIN AND THE FIRE OF AUTOMATIC WEAPONS

TO INFLICT HEAVY LOSSES ON THEIR ATTACKERS, ULTIMATELY DEFEATING THEM IN DETAIL. WHEN HER CORPSMAN WAS SERIOUSLY WOUNDED BY GRENADE FRAGMENTS, CAPTAIN MOORE, WITHOUT HESITATION, PROVIDED FIRST AID WHILE UNDER CONTINUOUS ENEMY FIRE AND THEN GAVE THE WOUNDED SAILOR HER OWN BODY ARMOR. IN A FINAL ACT OF BRAVERY SHE ENGAGED THE ENEMY COMMANDER, KILLING HIM IN HAND-TO-HAND COMBAT AND WHILE DOING SO SUSTAINED A CRITICAL CHEST WOUND. CAPTAIN MOORE'S LEADERSHIP, COURAGE, AND EXTRAORDINARY DEVOTION TO DUTY PREVENTED AN ENEMY BREAKTHROUGH INTO THE REAR OF HER COMMAND THUS TURNING THE TIDE OF BATTLE. HER ACTIONS REFLECT GREAT CREDIT UPON HERSELF AND UPHELD THE HIGHEST TRADITIONS OF THE UNITED STATES MARINE CORPS AND THE NAVAL SERVICE.

THE COMMANDANT ORDERED "About face," and Kelli turned to look at the beaming faces of her fellow reservists. The Medal of Honor is not pinned to the uniform like other medals. It is hung around the neck, suspended from a pale blue ribbon with small white stars. Daniel Forrest draped it around her neck. Like many recipients before her, she found it to be heavier than she had expected.

Forrest stepped around to face her and came to attention. "Captain, I am honored that the President has permitted me to award this medal."

Kelli Moore, now quite numb, was just able to deliver a proper salute, which the Commandant returned, before she resumed her place in formation.

The Commandant turned to face the formation and glanced at his Sergeant Major who ordered, "Dismissed." There were no speeches. The citations had said all there was to say. As the formation broke up, there were some smiles and some tears. Some congratulations and some who simply drifted away.

First Sergeant Johanssen, wearing his second Purple Heart, found Mike McGregor. "Great about the Captain and the Medal of Honor. You must have had to work hard to get that through."

"I didn't do a thing. I was interviewed by a Colonel from his staff who said he had never seen General Forrest so focused on anything as taking care of the 584."

"He's a good man. I'm happy to see he remembered you too. I think you're the only guy still in uniform wearing two of those Navy Crosses. Just remember, though, I won't be around to help with number three. Retirement takes effect in a month."

McGregor said nothing; he simply looked at his friend with what was often called a 'thousand-yard stare.'

CHAPTER 77

FOR THE FIRST time in years, Michigan was not only leading Ohio State in their annual showdown, but was leading by a lot—three touchdowns by late in the third quarter. It was a beautiful day for football, brisk and sunny.

Mike McGregor and Al Johanssen had arrived early for tailgating with friends. After a few beers and brats, they were headed to their usual seats when Johanssen said, "Guess who I saw a few days ago? I was waiting for an x-ray when in walks your friend Detective Moore."

This caught McGregor's attention. "How is she doing?"

"Very well, her first day back at work was four days ago. She seems more relaxed than she used to be. She asked about you."

"Really? What did she ask?"

"Just wondered how you were doing. Very casual. We talked a few minutes and then I went in for my x-ray. She was gone when I was done."

McGregor just nodded.

The game was going better than anyone had predicted, with the new freshman already putting up two touchdowns on long runs, plus another on a punt return.

"Joe, is it okay now to say that kid is a future superstar?"

"Yeah Doc I have to say you're right about that. Over fourteen hundred yards and only a freshman. You do have to admit, though, you were wrong about one thing."

"And what was that?"

"It wasn't a short season after all."

EPILOGUE
December 5, 2017 1450Z
Aboard the Carlisle to Glasgow train

THE STYLISH COUPLE in the first class coach gazed out at the Scottish countryside speeding by. The trees were largely bare, and the fields lay fallow, but the rolling landscape had a stark beauty nonetheless. The man, in his forties, wore a tan tweed suit—nicely tailored—and fashionable tortoise shell glasses. He and his companion, a young redhead in a grey Italian wool suit, could have been traveling to Glasgow on business.

The couple went by Johann and Lena Weser. Johann, a wealthy investor, had emigrated, so their story went, from Zittau to the Isle of Man to take advantage of the Isle's banking laws. Johann had opened several investment accounts, and had slowly begun to increase what was already a substantial fortune.

They had taken the ferry from their home in Douglas to Heysham on the west coast of England; a rough crossing on the stormy Irish Sea. There they caught a train that would ultimately take them to Glasgow. Not wanting to remain on the remote island forever, their plan was to explore potential homes outside Glasgow. In addition to real estate shopping, however, the couple had a second purpose for being on this particular train. For this reason, they had selected a day and time in which travel was usually light and were sitting alone in a cluster of four seats, two and two across a small table.

Their reverie was interrupted when a portly man in rough outdoor clothing sat down across from them. He looked as if he had hiked some distance to the train station. Actually, he hadn't. He had taken a series of trains that ended in Carlisle earlier that day. He had taken his lunch in a local restaurant, where he then changed out of his perfectly-tailored blue suit and into the clothes he was now wearing. The suit was neatly folded in his carry-on bag.

Maxim Korshkin smiled and extended his hand to Johann. "Alexi, my old friend, I cannot say how pleased I am to see you."

"And I you, Janos." This he said very softly. "After all we have been through, I am gratified to see you survived the whole thing. I was worried."

Lena said very quietly, "This man is Janos? I thought he was Czech?"

"My cover, young Anna—I'm sorry, Lena. There is no Janos, just a figment of my imagination. I have passed for years as a minor player while Janos handled the big—and dangerous—deals. In this case, the mythical Janos also allowed me to slip critical information to the British security services. None of us really wanted that Saudi lunatic to actually use those things."

"Well done, my friend, but you had nothing to worry about. Before shipping them I deactivated the detonating circuits. Impossible to detect."

Korshkin chuckled. "I suspected you might do something like that. Well, the Americans now have five of them and my contacts tell me the Saudis have the other. This chapter is closed."

Johann leaned even further forward. "I'm curious, how did you manage to convince everyone that Janos was in Prague?"

"I have a couple of rough young men there who deal with logistics, but they have no idea who I am. Everything was done with disposable mobile phones. I have retired, though. This last deal—your deal my friend—has provided me with everything I need. I have told the lads in Prague they are now Janos and may do whatever they wish. I'm certain they will be caught or more likely killed in short order—both are total idiots. Then Janos will disappear from the stage forever."

"Very clever. But you went through a lot of effort to contact us through our new identities. I'm sure it wasn't to tell us about your retirement."

"No, no," said Korshkin. "You brother—" He looked at Lena —"contacted me and asked that I pass on some information to you. The contact was very secure, I assure you, and I took extraordinary precautions in coming here. First he wanted me to pass along a way to contact him in an emergency." He handed Johann a small mobile phone. "It's a burn phone, use it only once. Second, he wanted to let you know that, with the recovery of the warheads, that the SVR and the FSB have greatly reduced their efforts to find you. I would not take a holiday in Moscow or hang about near a Russian embassy, but on the whole he believes you're in the clear."

The couple was both obviously relieved. Life as fugitives had taken a toll.

"What of Boris?" asked Lena. "Do you know anything about him?"

"We met very briefly. He lives somewhere in London, though I don't know where. He has a bushy moustache and told me he has had some silicone injections in his face. He said you would not recognize him. I later spotted him one evening, purely by accident, at a club near Leicester Square. I was able to recognize him from his new identity photos. Seems he is something of a playboy."

Johann smiled. "That would be Boris. Well, at least he can afford it."

They chatted a few more minutes, then an announcement came that the train was approaching Glasgow.

Maxim Korshkin said, "I have a flat in Glasgow, ownership totally disguised. Please join me for dinner. I am an excellent cook, and the place is swept often for listening devices. I wish to hear more about exactly how you managed this extraordinary coup. And to spend some time getting to know your lovely wife."

"Yes," said Johann. "Yes, that would be splendid. And can you get some of that Scottish beer? I've grown rather fond of it."

SHORT SEASON

MIKE MCGREGOR SWIRLED the excellent bourbon in his glass while he tried to understand just what he was feeling. Four days earlier, he had been working the evening shift in the ER, his bullet wound healed enough to permit a regular work schedule. His mind, too, had healed, and he found comfort in his work and in the routine daily of life. On this evening he was examining a grad student who had fractured his thumb playing basketball when he saw a familiar face. Detective Kelli Moore, escorting a bleeding man in handcuffs, was trying to get her suspect past the front desk and into an exam room.

McGregor excused himself and brought the pair into a room, annoying the front desk staff in the process. "Detective Moore, are you beating up the suspects again?"

"Never laid a hand on him, Doc." She said this with a gentle humor. "He tried to jump out a closed window, head first."

McGregor spotted Nicole Ellis in the hallway. "Nicole, see what you can do about this scalp laceration."

Ellis stepped in, and was surprised to see Kelli Moore. "Captain Moore, I didn't know you were back to work."

"It's Detective, and yes, I started back just before Thanksgiving. A bit stiff, but doing pretty well. That cut you fixed on my arm is healing okay too, though the scar is still kind of red."

"It's only been three months; scars mature. Give it 'till next summer."

"I'm just pulling your chain. I appreciate all you did for me. You too, Doc." She grinned, just a little.

She had indeed lightened up a bit. "Actually, that was Russell's work."

"Right, I remember you said he was the smartest guy in the regiment. Lucky for me."

Okay, how did he navigate a potentially new relationship after all that had happened to both of them? Being direct was always good. If you got rejected, at least it was over quickly. "Say Detective, as long as we're back to our old lives, how about having a few drinks on Saturday?"

"Love to. Where and when?"

Ah. He might have wanted to prepare an answer to that before he asked it. "Um…How about Gratzi on Main Street? Seven thirty?"

Sitting at the bar, waiting for Kelli Moore, McGregor realized he was scared. Well, why not? Life was back to normal, but everything had changed. What had been a flirtation between him and Moore now promised to become something different.

Or did it? Moore, always a complicated woman, was somehow different than she used to be, more laid back, less cynical. Or was it he who was different? He began to think this date was coming way too soon when he saw her come in the door.

It was a frigid December evening, and Kelli Moore slipped out of a long overcoat. Underneath she was wearing a black dress, very short, with red high heels which really called attention to her long legs. The sleeves were just long enough to cover the scar on her left shoulder, but short enough to show off her strong arms. A red belt and a necklace of big, red cinnabar beads completed the outfit. She was instantly the center of attention for every man in the restaurant.

She looked around for a moment, spotted McGregor at the bar, and flashed him an electric smile that sucked all the oxygen from the room.

She strode across the bar and sat down next to McGregor. She put her hand on the back of his neck, pulled him close, and kissed him—hard. Then, as if nothing had happened, she asked, "What are you drinking, Doc?"

For the first time in more than two years, Danielle was no longer on his mind.